The Space Between the Divine and the Unholy

Michelle Morningstar

ISBN: 978-0-578-39834-1

Published by: Unquiet Tomb Press

First Edition: March 2022

Cover design and logo by: Michelle Morningstar

Cover photo by: Jon Towner

www.michellemorningstar.com

I dedicate this book to all my friends.
The idea was to create something I could share with
each of you; to give a part of myself to you. Thank you
all for the support and encouragement, not with just this
book, but all my creative endeavors—no matter how
strange they may have been.

The dreamy Victorian town of Port Townsend, WA.

In memory of
Peter Thomas Ratajczyk (Peter Steele)
1962 – 2010 †

Slugcult rise!

Special thanks to Judy Aguiar for devoting her time
and talent to editing this story.

Special thanks to Jason L. Armstrong for making
me think and challenging my logic.

Special thanks to Aric H. Burton for
encouragement, proofreading, and stellar ways to
execute ideas to make them even better.

I.
II.
III.
IV.
VI.
VII.
VIII.
IX.
X.
XI.

CANTICLE ONE

"If you don't get caught, you deserve everything you steal."
—Daniel Nayeri

"You're going to be some of the very first people to see a newly discovered annex in the catacombs. It's fortunate that I was able to arrange for you both to accompany me—not an easy task this time, but being Director has its perks." Fiona smiled giddily. "So, what do you think?"

Drucilla walked over to a freshly bored-out hole in the wall of *Capuchin Monastery Catacombs* (recently been turned tourist-attraction) and poked her head into the entryway to get a look at the interior of the dilapidated crypt. The atmosphere was dark and somber, which was fitting on such an uncommonly cool and dreary summer day in Palermo. The tomb had a musty scent of a dry, dusty old library and cold crumbly stones. The dirt had obviously not settled, because she could feel the irritation in her sinuses.

"Apparently, the maintenance staff found a small hole and noticed it was open on the other side. They broke the wall down just a few days ago. I wonder what secrets it holds. Isn't it exciting?" Fiona exclaimed.

"I mean, sure, I guess, there's a whole lot of dead people in there, so that's cool," Drucilla responded morbidly as she squinted to get a better view at the mummified remains that lined the dimly lit annex. She glanced up at the temporarily rigged lighting as it offered a bit more visibility into the corridor.

Drake stood beside his sister and briefly looked into the opening but was clearly disinterested. He shrugged, put his headphones back on, and walked away to the other end of the hall. Drucilla watched him pull a book out of his backpack, opened it to his bookmark, and casually leaned against a structural column. He stood below a wall of mummified hanging corpses behind wire cages.

I wonder if they hung them there to keep the tourists out, or maybe to keep the mummies in? she mused to herself and chuckled inwardly. "I'm gonna go check it out," Drucilla announced as she glanced at Fiona and back into the crypt. She dropped her backpack to her feet.

"I wish you wouldn't. I'm not really supposed to let you back there. At least not until we've confirmed that it's safe," Fiona advised.

Drucilla looked around the gallery. There was no one there with her other than her mother and brother. She held up one hand and shrugged as if to suggest, *who would know? There's no one here.* "Mom, the museum's closed to the public for the UCLA archaeology crew to check out the room, right?"

Fiona exhaled and rubbed her temple as she peered at her headstrong teenager. She wanted her children to have this experience, but at the same time, she hoped they would respect at least some boundaries.

"Then why did we waste our last high school summer vacation and come all the way to backwater Italy if we're not supposed to see this?" Drucilla groaned and held Fiona's stare as if to demand her mother bend to her will.

"Fine! Fine. Five minutes, be quick about it; the rest of the team will be arriving shortly. Don't go too far inside and watch the ground. It's not stable, and you could break your ankle," Fiona relented.

Drucilla turned away from her and rolled her eyes. She unzipped her pack, pulled out a flashlight, and turned it on. She grasped onto a cool, rigid broken stone protruding from the wall opening with her other hand to steady herself. She stepped over jagged pieces of rubble and slowly headed inside. She looked up to the ceiling and to the left and right of the crypt. Thick heavy webs and dehydrated foliage lined the wall opening at one point, but clearly, nothing alive had occupied this space in centuries. She noticed the addled corpses resting in the open chambers that resembled bookcases lining the crypt walls. She slowly and curiously walked by them, examining their tattered burial clothing and offerings left by loved ones. Some of the bodies were covered head to toe; others were open with exposed skulls and displaced bones.

The lighting wasn't bright enough to illuminate to the end, and it degraded the further she ventured inside; it was getting harder to see. The ground had become progressively rockier and challenging to traverse. She gingerly stepped around cracks and divots in the flooring as she attempted to keep her balance. She glanced around the crypt, fascinated by the fact that no one had set foot in the place for at least a few hundred years. New discoveries and exploration were her favorite thing about archaeology.

Drucilla heard her mother's voice yell something unintelligible. She looked back to the light and figured she was calling to her to come back. As she turned away, her foot slammed up against a small solid object. She turned her flashlight to the floor. A rotted, wooden box that fell apart upon impact lay at her feet. Wooden splinters and a rosary lay strewn across the broken stone floor with crudely faceted red beads glinting in the dim light.

It's a Catholic catacomb. I'm sure there were thousands of rosaries buried with these mummies. She picked up the rosary and held it up to the light of her flashlight. It was made of delicate, red crystal beads; at least, she thought they were crystal. Between every tenth bead was a silver ball of scrolling filigree. The end of the rosary was an amulet. It looked like a lion or some creature with swords behind its head, not a cross like you might expect. The image was exceptionally worn, so she couldn't be sure. It looked like the type of ornate rosary that an aristocrat might own.

With a good cleaning, this would make a pretty cool accessory. She quickly looked around to see from where it may have fallen or whom the apparent owner might have been. None of the corpses stood out as remarkably different from one another. "Mine now," she said. She slipped the rosary into her pocket. No one knew it was there, so no one would know it was missing. She wasn't a religious person, but this was something unique and curious.

"What was back there? Did you see anything that was interesting to you?" Fiona asked, pressing Drucilla for information as she grabbed Drucilla's wrist to help her over the rocky debris.

"No, not really. 'Just a lot of corpses." Drucilla climbed back out of the broken-down wall. She stuck her hand into her pocket and fidgeted with the newly acquired rosary.

"The museum already had their crew retrieve quite a few objects; some still attached to the bodies that were found lying on the floor when they opened the crypt. They're in the next room if you'd like to take a look," Fiona offered, knowing her daughter's fascination with the macabre.

Drucilla nodded and grinned.

They walked back to the make-shift lab room, which was just another museum annex, a short distance from the newly excavated crypt. After entering the lab, Drucilla dropped her backpack on a table, opened it, and pulled out her sketchbook and pen. She laid it next to her on the table. She loved the dreary structure of the catacombs and had intended to sketch the interior columns and alcoves. She looked around at the ceiling of the make-shift lab. The light and shadows played against the arches that crisscrossed down the hall with the occasional pendulum light that swung leisurely. The ceiling was crumbled in places, which gave it a beautifully neglected appeal.

One of Fiona's coworkers entered the lab from the other end of the room. She set down her laptop case and backpack and waved to them.

"Oh, it's Caroline, give me two minutes," Fiona said to Drucilla.

Drucilla nodded.

Drucilla reached for her sketchbook, opened it up, and began to draw two-point perspectives. As she sketched, her thoughts drifted to her newly acquired treasure in her pocket. She wondered who owned it or what kind of life it had before she found it. *Who was the jewelry artist, and what was the inspiration for something so Avant-Garde?* Drucilla shoved her hand into her pocket and wove her fingers through the string of beads.

"Drucilla, Drake, come here," Fiona beckoned from the other end of the lab. Fiona's voice snapped Drucilla out of her daydream. Drucilla looked up, nodded, and put down her sketchbook and pen. She walked over to her mother and a woman she had not yet met. Drake sauntered over slowly behind her, placing a bookmark back into his book.

"Guys, this is Caroline Dixon. She's the funerary archaeologist. She studies the treatment and commemoration of the dead and their burial contents," Fiona said. She introduced her teammate to her children.

"Drucilla. Drake," Caroline said. She extended her hand out to shake theirs.

"It's their last summer before high school graduation. I thought they would enjoy seeing the catacombs," Fiona commented.

"Twins?" she asked, taking notice of their similarities in appearance.

Drucilla nodded at Caroline. Drake glanced at Drucilla.

"Fascinating. So, do you both plan on becoming archaeologists like your mother?" Caroline asked.

"Definitely not," Drake responded with absolute assurance.

"Maybe," Drucilla shrugged unsurely. Drucilla didn't know what she wanted to do at this point in her life. She loved art, but archaeology was an interest, as well.

"Come see what we've recovered," Caroline said. She waved for everyone to follow her to the artifacts.

Drucilla walked over with her mother and inspected various artifacts that spread out across three long, white tables. Drake seemed disinterested as he opened his book, put his headphones back on, and sat on a stool next to one of the tables. However, Drucilla was eager to place her hands on the fabrics and trinkets, some still resting on the dry, fragile bones from where they were first placed centuries ago. Near one set of remains was a metallic bowl. She reached for it and carefully picked it up. It was about ten inches in diameter and had strange, crooked symbols etched around the outside. She turned it around in her hands, intrigued by the markings. The symbols were crudely engraved by something hot. They looked like scorch marks instead of chiseled markings. It wasn't a foreign language, at least not one she had ever seen before. They looked a lot like strange runes. She had seen glyphs before, but not like this.

"Dru, don't pick that up," Fiona said sternly, managing to look up for a moment.

"I was just trying to get a better look. What language is this?" Drucilla held the bowl out to her.

She glanced at it for a moment, then back to Drucilla. "They're probably just old Italian symbols. Please put it down. I can't have you here if you're going to disrupt the artifacts; you need to be careful. Maybe you and Drake should go and explore? We won't be here much longer," Fiona said, devoid of patience.

"Drake. Drake! Are you listening to me?" Fiona beckoned as she attempted to get Drake's attention. He sat in the corner, seemingly in his own world. He was always reading something political and egg heady. However, this trip *The Prince* by Niccolò Machiavelli consumed him.

"What?" he snapped. He looked up and slid his headphones to the side.

"Drake, maybe you and Dru should go check out the rest of the museum? You'll have it to yourselves," Fiona suggested.

"Mom, honestly, I'm kind of tired," Drucilla said, cutting her off, "I think I'm gonna just go to the hotel and lay down for a bit. I'm getting a headache," Drucilla said. She rubbed the back of her head. "I think it's from sleeping on the plane."

Drake glanced at Drucilla and then back at his book.

"There should be ibuprofen in my backpack," she pointed to the chair behind her and went back to her cataloging.

Drucilla walked over to and opened Fiona's backpack. She shoved her hand inside and started rummaging. She felt more than one bottle and wondered what she was holding. She pulled her hand out while holding three different bottles: *Hydromorphone*, *Lorazepam*, and *Zolpidem*.

"I don't see it in here," Drucilla said. She held the three bottles and eyed her mother with suspicion.

Fiona sighed heavily, walked over to her backpack, and fumbled through her things. Drucilla stepped back.

"What are these for?" Drucilla asked, still holding the prescriptions in her hand.

Fiona pulled out a bottle of ibuprofen and offered an exchange of medication bottles. "I'm uh…I'm not sleeping well," Fiona responded. She quickly shoved the bottles back into her pack.

"Ooookay—" Drucilla was unconvinced as she side-eyed her mother. "Drake! Are you staying here or coming with me?"

Drake lifted his eyes and slid his headphone to the side. "And watch you sleep? Are you five?" he groaned. "No, I'm gonna stay here," he moved his headphones into place and returned to his book.

Drucilla sighed to herself as she walked back to the desk to pick up her sketchbook and backpack. She opened her pack to drop her sketchbook and pen inside, but the pen missed its destination, fell to the floor, and rolled under the desk.

"Damn!" Drucilla got down on her hands and knees under the table to search for the pen. The pen was nowhere to be seen. Unexpectedly she noticed out of the corner of her eye, a few feet behind the table, her pen tightly wedged between the shelving and the stone wall.

How did it get in there? Drucilla crawled a couple more feet to grab the pen. She reached out and pulled at it to dislodge it from the shelving. She freed her pen and slid out from under the table, unzipped up her backpack, and dropped the pen inside.

"All right, I'm outta here." Drucilla pulled the straps of her backpack up onto her shoulders, and then she kicked Drake's ankle as she passed him on her way out of the room. Drake glared at her and put his hand up as if threatening to backhand her.

"Do it!"

"Guys, knock it off," Fiona shouted.

Drucilla gritted her teeth, turned away, and shoved the door open with both hands, her rosary dangling outside her coat pocket. Drake glanced at it with suspicion and watched her as she walked out the door.

CANTICLE TWO

"Oh my God! Where did you get that? It's so cool!" Katia looked excited as she grabbed the rosary hanging from Drucilla's wrist and rolled the beads between her fingers.

"When we were in Italy with mom last summer," Drucilla replied.

"You didn't tell me about this!" Katia looked at it in amazement.

"I forgot about it until yesterday. and well, that's because Mom doesn't know I have it. I found it," Drucilla said under her breath.

"Dude! Did you steal this from the catacombs?" Katia said, wide-eyed.

"Shh, come on!"

"You you illegally stole an artifact?!" Katia exclaimed as she dropped her jaw.

"Katia, shut up! You're gonna get me in trouble!"

Katia started laughing in disbelief, "Oh, my God, do you know how much shit you're going to be in?"

"None if you keep your mouth shut!" Drucilla snapped at her, slamming her locker closed and hiking her backpack onto her shoulder.

"Well, we just caught Bengtsson's attention," Katia moaned, looking past Drucilla's shoulder at the physical science teacher standing in the doorway of his classroom with his back against the door. His eyes intensely fixed on Drucilla's wrist from across the hall. He was a moderately intimidating man with his albinism and exceptionally tall stature with gangling arms and gaunt facial features. A wavy platinum-blond lock hung over his left eye.

Drucilla cautiously turned around as she pulled the sleeve of her sweater down over her wrist. She held the amulet in the palm of her closed hand.

Katia and Drucilla continued to chat as they walked down the hallway to their first-period class; Drucilla attempted not to draw attention to herself. As Drucilla passed Mr. Bengtsson, he purposely leaned toward her so she would bump into him, and she did. Drucilla quickly pulled away from him as he grabbed her wrist with the rosary and held it up. The amulet dropped from her palm and fell against her forearm. He looked down at it momentarily as if he recognized what it was. He squinted as he ran his finger over the raised carving of the amulet. Drucilla snatched her wrist back and glanced suspiciously at him. Bengtsson's grin slowly grew across his face.

"Watch your step," he said. A bright red blaze flashed across his eyes, like a mirror catching the light as he smiled down at her. He slowly turned away and walked back into his classroom.

Drucilla gasped and darted her head around, looking for Katia, who was a few feet ahead of her. Katia stopped and noticed that Drucilla was not standing next to her. Instead, she was in front of the door of the science class.

"What?" Katia said, noticing the look of panic in Drucilla's eyes.

Drucilla seemed distraught from the encounter as she briskly walked to catch up to Katia.

"' You ok?" Katia asked.

"Yeah. Yeah, I'm uh, good," Drucilla replied with a moderate level of confusion in her tone.

"Second bell, ladies, you're late," Ms. Paulson said, standing in front of her classroom door.

Drucilla and Katia made their way into the classroom and to their desks. Since the sixth grade, Katia was Drucilla's best friend when Katia first moved to Los Angeles. She was cute, bubbly with long red curly hair, always dressed in black. Katia was also a bit of a weirdo like Drucilla and fascinated with the LA deathrock scene from the '80s. She opened her biology textbook with "I love Rozz" in multi-colored ink on the binding, and the lyrics to *Ashes* by Christian Death scribbled on the cover: *"Soul of my soul, do you feel me? Touch the beating, heart of my heart."*

"Are you going to Belynn's party tonight?" Katia asked.

"No. Why the Hell would I do that?" Drucilla scoffed.

"Because Drake is going, and I figured you'd go, too."

"I don't go everywhere Drake goes," Drucilla sneered. "Honestly, he's pissing me off right now, and I don't want to be around him."

"I want to go, and as my best friend, you are legally required to go with me."

"Katia, I know you've got this massive chick boner for my brother, like everyone else in this school, but, he's a dick, and Belynn is a useless oxygen thief. 'Both can go to Hell."

"Please?" Katia batted her eyes at Drucilla.

"No, I have a huge art project I need to work on this weekend. If I'm going to get my painting of Adrian in the Superintendent's High School Art Show, I need to finish it like yesterday."

"Please? It's the last major party of our senior year'" Katia continued to coax Drucilla.

"I can't. I want to get into the Conservatory of Fine Arts program next year at UCLA."

"I'll never ask for another thing as long as I live."

"See, now you're just flat out lying to me," Drucilla snarled and opened her biology textbook.

Belynn walked in fashionably late to class.

Speak of the devil, and she appears, Drucilla thought.

"Miss Averly, you're late. Please take a seat," Ms. Paulson said.

Belynn held her nose in the air as high as possible as she walked past Drucilla. She stopped to look down at her. "Hi Morticia, little early for Halloween, are we?" She laughed at Drucilla; some of her classmates giggled, as well.

Drucilla usually dressed in black clothing. With her black hair and cornflower blue eyes, it made her look extra witchy. Drucilla looked up at her slowly and wrinkled her nose. She began to sniff the air. "Is…is that you? That smell? Ugh!" Drucilla pinched her nose. "Christ, you're supposed to bathe occasionally, not just cover it with perfume," Drucilla started mock gagging. "Does anyone else smell cat food?"

The class erupted in giggles, and Belynn's smug smile turned to fury. "Fuck you, Dru," Belynn said. She flipped her off and stormed off to her desk.

"Ladies, that's enough! Do you want detention?" Ms. Paulson yelled at them.

Drucilla slumped down in her seat. She looked over at Belynn, glaring back at her and whispering something to her friend while pointing at Drucilla.

Katia looked at Drucilla. Drucilla shook her head slowly.

After school, Katia and Drucilla hopped in the back of Drake's car and made their way home.

"Are you guys going to Belynn's tonight?" Drake asked.

"No," Drucilla answered unenthusiastically.

"Ignore her. She's going with me. She owes me!" Katia looked at Drucilla, then pointedly looked at Drucilla's wrist.

"Oh, oh, that's messed up, Katia. We're going to have to discuss loyalty," Drucilla said, annoyed.

"What are you guys talking about now?" Drake asked.

"Yes, what are we talking about, Katia?" Drucilla stared at her with intent.

Feeling backed into a corner, Katia blurted out, "I let her cheat on a bio quiz. I let her copy my answers."

"Hahaha, what?" Drake laughed in disbelief. "I thought you were getting an *A* in bio?"

"Yeah, um, I didn't study for this quiz. I was busy doing uh, girl shit," Drucilla responded.

"Ok, whatever," Drake shook his head.

Drucilla glared at Katia. Katia shrugged at Drucilla.

"I'm going to go after ten if you guys want a ride," Drake said.

Drucilla looked at Katia. "Fine, you win."

Katia threw up the horns with her index and pinky fingers extended.

They pulled into Drake and Drucilla's driveway and got out of the car. Katia and Drucilla made their way to the backyard, through the gate, and up to the backdoor.

"Oh, can I stay over?" Katia asked.

"Yeah, of course," Drucilla answered.

Drucilla opened the double glass-paned door and entered the large, bright yellow craftsman home through the sunporch. Katia and Drucilla kicked off their shoes and dropped their backpacks. They ran through the kitchen, headed for the refrigerator, and started poking around for snacks.

"You're lucky your mom is never home." Katia hopped up to the breakfast bar kitchen island and rested her chin in her hands.

"If you say so," Drucilla shrugged. "Damn, we only have diet soda."

Katia nodded to Drucilla and opened her palms. Drucilla tossed her a can, taking one for herself, as well.

"So, where is she this time?" Katia tapped her nails on the top of the can before opening it.

"Peru, I think? I don't know. She's been on that Nazca project for the past twenty years. She does like teaching or something a couple of times a year for new dirt diggers," Drucilla headed out of the kitchen to her bedroom.

"Still, that's pretty cool," Katia said, popping open the can and taking a sip. She jumped down off the stool and followed Drucilla.

Drucilla's house was essentially a museum of random artifacts; some on the walls, some in curio cabinets, some priceless, and some just plain interesting. Everything from Viking horseshoes from the 11th to mid-13th century to ancient Egyptian papyrus scrolls. The house might look like you'd think an archaeologist's house would look. Everything was old, brown, and relatively dull unless you liked old museums. It had that smell of a musty library that no matter how many candles you burned, you couldn't get rid of the antiquated scent.

Ten o'clock rolled around, and Katia struggled to find something to wear, even with making full use of Drucilla's closet. Drucilla was sitting with her legs propped up on a small couch in her bedroom. She had her sketchbook on her lap and had just completed a sketch of a horrific, decrepit banshee. She tapped an old brass tipped pen with a worn wooden barrel against the spiral on her sketchbook, examining her work. The tapping caught Katia's attention.

"I thought you were super religious about felt-tip. You're using calligraphy pens now?" Katia asked.

Drucilla turned her head to the side and examined the pen. "It's the craziest thing. I dropped my pen in the museum's lab when we were in Italy. I crawled under the table and found it wedged against the wall. I could have sworn it was my sketch pen when I saw it. It wasn't until I got to the hotel and pulled it out of my pocket that I had mistakenly picked up this old thing." Drucilla rolled the pen between her fingers.

"So why are you using it?"

Drucilla held up the pen, "Dude, I've made about twenty-five sketches with his pen since I came back. It's never run out of ink. It still writes perfectly. This thing is amazing. I don't even know where to put the ink in when it runs out!"

Katia turned her attention back to Drucilla's closet. "You know, you don't own nearly enough short skirts." Katia abruptly changed the subject and flipped through Drucilla's clothes like it was her personal clothing boutique.

"Check the bottom drawer of my dresser," Drucilla said, turning her attention back to her artwork.

"Ooh!" Katia stopped what she was doing and sat on the floor in front of the dresser. She greedily opened the drawer and fumbled through the folded skirts. "So, why are you so mad at your brother?" She asked, not looking up.

"He's up to some sketchy shit."

Katia stopped and looked at Drucilla, "Like what?"

Drucilla put her sketch pad down on her leg and turned to face her, "You know how he's been dressing differently this year and has a new car and stuff?"

"Yeah, because your dad died, and you guys got a huge inheritance?"

"We what?" Drucilla sat upright.

"Drake told Killian that your non-existent dad—that you've never met—died while you were in Italy, and you and he got a huge inheritance. I mean, I don't know why I had to hear it from my brother and why you didn't tell me yourself?"

"Killian told you that?"

"Hey, just because you have a crappy relationship with your brother doesn't mean we all do." Katia turned her attention back to the drawer.

Drucilla sat silently and watched her. She had no idea what Katia was saying. It was time she talked with Drake.

✝✝✝

They arrived at Belynn's house at about 11 pm. There seemed to be about a hundred cars parked up and down the street. Drucilla was surprised that the cops hadn't broken it up. However, considering this was Brentwood, many celebrities lived on this street. The police were probably used to these kinds of massive gatherings. *Holy shit! Is that a valet? God, she's nauseating.* They climbed out of Drake's car and headed towards the house. It was a typical rich girl, teenage house party—lots of music, lots of kegs, and a lot of kids on the sprawling front lawn. Katia ran up ahead to see if she recognized anyone. Drake and Drucilla hung back.

"Hey dickface," she started with him.

"Dickface?" he curled his lip.

Drucilla stopped walking. "What's going on with you, dude? Are you selling drugs or something?"

"Yes, Dru, that's exactly what I'm doing. You caught me. Can I interest you in some Oxy? Maybe some coke?"

"Drake!"

He sighed deeply, clearly annoyed with her. "Dru, I don't have time for this—"

"Make time!"

He stared at her and crossed his arms.

Drucilla glared at him. "Katia told me that we received an inheritance from our dead dad. We don't have a dad, and we've never had one. You need to tell me what's going on. Now!"

Drake reached into his pocket and pulled out some sort of old gold coin. He rolled it around between his fingers and looked up at Drucilla. "Not yet. We'll talk about this another time."

"At least tell me where you got the car and the other crazy shit you have. Look, if you're involved in something…I don't know, illegal, I won't tell Mom. I just want to know if you're ok."

Drake scoffed at the implication and shook his head. "Dru, you have no idea what's going on, and I intend to keep it that way. For your sake," Drake responded. He walked away from her.

"What the fuck is that supposed to mean?" she shouted after him.

"It means—don't worry about it. It doesn't concern you," Drake shouted back as he put some distance between them.

Drucilla gnashed her teeth and walked towards the house behind him. She entered through the side gate into the backyard and made her way to the pool house. *I hate high school parties! They're so unbelievably contrived and boring. 'Just a bunch of tragically dense girls trying to outdo each other with dresses and labels that didn't even matter at the end of the day. It was all for the same purpose: who could hook up with whom. They're all idiots!* Drucilla leaned against the wall inside the pool house, watching people play beer pong, and other idiots throw each other in the pool. The music was loud, and even though the room was full of drunks, it was still quieter than it was outside.

"Hey, girl!" A handsome young man said. He leaned up against the wall next to Drucilla.

"Hey Adrian…" she said casually.

"Addams uh, Cold Chill," he said, reading the label on Drucilla's bottle. "When did you start drinking beer?"

She put the bottle to her lips, turned it straight up, and looked at him out of the corner of her eye.

He watched and laughed.

"There's never any hot guys here," he whined while scanning the room. "Where is your wombmate?"

"He's off somewhere, being a douche. Probably trying to convince some brain-dead teenage girl to touch his junk."

"God, he's cute. Do you know how unfathomably attractive your brother is?"

"Well yeah, he looks like me," she laughed.

"…and Katia?" Adrian inquired.

"She heard that some rock band was here, somewhere. So, she's off stalking them."

"Oh really?" His interest was piqued.

"Pshhh, I don't know," Drucilla shook her head and took another drink. "So, how is life after high school?"

"Eh, not much different. I still work for my homophobic dad until I can move to Seattle,"

"Oh yeah? What's up there?"

"It isn't LA," he laughed. "Oh, did I tell you about the guy I hooked up with at *The Iron Fist?*"

"You know, you need to stop hanging out at those clubs. You're gonna get hurt, or worse," she warned, taking another drink of her beer.

"Blah, blah, blah—"

"I'm gonna go find Katia and get out of here. 'You need a ride home?" Drucilla asked.

"No, I'm going to see if there's any decent take-out before I head out," Adrian grinned at Drucilla.

Drucilla pulled her bag over her shoulder, put her arm around Adrian's neck, and kissed his cheek. "Love you!" she said. She headed out to the patio.

"' Love you too, honey!"

As soon as Drucilla left the pool house, Katia rushed up to her. "Oh, my God! You are not going to believe who's here!" Katia bounced excitedly.

"I'm sure I couldn't care less, but, go ahead and tell me," Drucilla said unenthusiastically. *God damn, I'm bitter.*

"Dru!"

Drucilla heard a voice call to her from the other side of the pool. *Christ, it's Belynn. I thought I was going to avoid her tonight.*

"What are you doing here? No one invited you to my party," Belynn yelled almost incoherently. She attempted to make her way towards Drucilla, wobbling in a pair of obnoxiously tall high-heeled, thigh-high boots. Everyone stopped what they were doing to watch the spectacle.

Drucilla said nothing.

"I said leave!" Belynn slurred.

"Belynn, it's cool. It's a party. Can't we just chill?" said one of Drucilla's classmates to defuse the situation.

"No, Zack. I will not relax. This bitch thinks she's better than me." Belynn looked Drucilla up and down, sizing her up.

"I really don't. I just don't care about you. Like, at all. I think that's what pisses you off most," Drucilla seemed unfazed by Belynn's attempt at intimidation.

Belynn stopped a couple of feet away from her. "Do you really think I care about what you think?"

"Well—" Drucilla took a sip of her beer. "I think you can't possibly fathom what it's like not to be adored by everyone, and when someone doesn't fall to your feet and start kissing your boots, you get insecure. You're a typical spoiled brat."

Enraged, Belynn took a step back and, with a quick swing, kicked Drucilla right in the face. She hit the ground on her side with a thud. Drucilla's wrist with the rosary smashed against the cement; she felt one of the beads crush under her wrist.

"How do you like these boots now, bitch!" Belynn yelled.

The still gathering crowd gasped and got quiet. Drucilla felt a cut on her lip, and the metallic taste of blood began to fill her mouth. She raised her wrist and noticed the bead that had broken. There was a small drop of blood dangling from the glass shard. As soon as she saw it, a small neon blue lightning bolt shot across her wrist and disappeared. Drucilla blinked rapidly and thought it to be strange. Drucilla slowly looked past her wrist to Belynn's face.

"Whadya do? Break your tacky little bracelet?" Belynn taunted and laughed again.

"Why do you have to be such a bitch, Belynn!" Katia yelled as she knelt and grasped Drucilla's hand to help her to her feet.

A dark cloud of mist started forming between Drucilla and Belynn. All Drucilla could make out was a tall, wispy figure of a woman. It looked like a banshee with long, wild hair, and a flowing gown was taking shape between them. Katia looked at the figure in shock, then back to Drucilla. The banshee wailed and thrust her hand deep into Belynn's chest and then forcefully withdrew it, ripping out her still-beating heart. Blood poured from the ventricles and the gaping wound in Belynn's chest. Belynn's eyes widened and fixed on Drucilla. They watched in horror as Belynn's eyes turned to a dead, white, overcast as she attempted to gasp for air. Katia released Drucilla's hand and got up to help Belynn. Katia suddenly noticed that no one else was there. Belynn was standing rigid, gasping for air, and grabbing onto her chest. There was no monster, no blood, just Belynn struggling to breathe. Katia wondered if she imagined it; maybe she had too much to drink.

"I think Belynn's having a heart attack!" One of their classmates yelled.

Belynn fell forward to the ground, onto her chest. Drucilla could hear the cracking of exposed ribs breaking under the dead weight of her lifeless body. The banshee turned to look at Drucilla as it dropped the bloody organ. It hit the ground with a splat in front of her feet like an offering. The banshee dissipated into nothing

The patio erupted in the terrified screams of a multitude of drunk teenagers that echoed throughout the property. Some people fled as fast as their feet would take them out of the yard, others gathered around Belynn and tried to revive her, but it was too late. Stunned, Drucilla looked at Katia, who stood motionless in complete terror.

Drucilla got to her feet and reached for Katia's hand. "We need to go!"

Katia recoiled and took a step back. "What did you do, Dru?"

"What?"

"What did you do?!" Katia screamed, crying with her hands covering her mouth.

"I didn't—" Drucilla stammered.

Katia looked down at Drucilla's bag. Her sketchbook had fallen out, the page open to a sketch she had made earlier of a banshee. It bore a striking resemblance to the apparition that had just appeared. Katia looked back at Drucilla, turned, and ran away. Drucilla, still in shock, bent down to pick up her bag and stuffed her sketchbook back into it. She stood back up and saw Drake on the other side of the pool. He stood there calmly, with his hands in his pockets, just watching her.

"Let's go!" Drake yelled and motioned for her to come to him. She tossed her bag over her shoulder and followed him out of the property's back gate to the alleyway. She looked back over her shoulder and saw Belynn's lifeless body, face down, and her heart about three feet away from her. There was a lot of blood, and it was starting to pour into the pool. The blood mixed with the chlorinated water and gave the water an eerie brownish-red tinge as the pool light diffused throughout the water.

Drake closed the gate as the twins made their way down the alley. He didn't say anything for some time. Drucilla could tell that he was trying to find the right words to say. She didn't say anything either. She was still trying to figure out what had happened.

Finally, Drake broke the silence. "Are you ok?"

"No, I'm not fucking ok!"

He nodded. They got to his car and climbed in, neither of them saying a word. They drove out of the neighborhood. People gathered around on corners and tried to figure out what had happened. Others were crying outside of their cars. The fire department and paramedics finally arrived as the trucks sped past them with lights flashing wildly. Everything seemed to be happening in slow motion. Every second seemed like hours. Drucilla hunched over in the car seat, trying to bury her head in her knees. She began to cry uncontrollably.

Drake headed north to the greasy-spoon diner about ten minutes away in Westwood. When they arrived, they pulled into the parking lot and got out of the car. Neither of them said a word. After they got inside, the waitress seated them near a window and filled their cups with coffee. Drucilla just stared out the window and tried to make sense of what happened.

Drake fidgeted with the paper coaster under his coffee cup. "You want to know what's going on? I mean, with me, Dru?"

Drucilla looked silently at him.

"You and I took something from Italy," he said, matter-of-factly.

Drucilla looked away from him and stared out the window. "Did I do this, Drake? Was this me?" she asked, not wanting to know the answer.

Drake didn't speak.

Drucilla looked back at him. He nodded slowly. Her eyes welled up with tears again, and she couldn't stop it.

"Can I get ya'll anything to eat?" the waitress asked.

"Dru, you should really eat something if you don't want to wake up with a hangover," Drake suggested.

Drucilla didn't look up.

"Bring her some toast, please?" he asked the waitress.

"Sure, I'll be right back."

"Dru, we need to talk about this," he started again.

"Oh, now you want to talk!" Drucilla sobbed.

He reached across the table to her hand and pulled her sleeve back to expose her wrist. Drucilla briefly looked down at the rosary on her wrist and quickly looked away, crying.

"How did you know about it," Drucilla sniffled, looking down at her wrist again.

"I noticed it when you left the lab." Drake twisted the beads between his fingers and ran his finger over the link with the missing bead. "It was hanging out of your pocket." Drake released Drucilla's wrist and reached into his pocket. He pulled his hand out and slapped an old worn coin in front of himself. Drake slid the coin across the table toward Drucilla. The coin had a depiction of some sort of creature. It was not quite like a dragon, but it seemed to represent something with horns. The other side of the coin was embellished with symbols that she didn't recognize.

"Why are you showing this to me?" Drucilla sniffled.

"Because I found this," he responded flatly. "What I'm about to tell you is real. I'm not bullshitting you. Ok?"

She nodded slowly, wiping the tears from her stinging cheeks.

"This coin belongs to Lucifer—" he started. "I found it when we were leaving the catacombs. I thought it could be an artifact that someone misplaced or lost during cataloging, but it didn't appear anywhere in the logbooks when I checked. So, I figured I'd hang on to it for the time being." Drake leaned in closer to her and put his hand on the coin, pulling it towards him. "Lucifer visited me that evening." Drake picked up the coin and shoved it back into the front pocket of his pants. He put his hands on the table and intertwined his fingers as he glanced out the window.

Drucilla didn't say a word. She had stopped crying and was just studying the expression on his face. Her brother was a complete asshole at times, but, she knew when Drake was lying to her, this wasn't one of those times. The waitress returned with the toast and a small dish of assorted jams. She smiled at Drucilla and walked away.

"What are you talking about? Lucifer? As in the devil? Are you sure? Drucilla asked in a hushed voice to keep the waitress from hearing. After this evening's events, this wasn't that hard to believe.

"Lucifer... He doesn't look like I thought he would. He's a bit taller than me, probably six-foot-three, give or take an inch. His skin is—" Drake made a motion with his hand as if he's touched something disagreeable. "His skin is translucent, almost opalescent with a blueish hue. You can sort of see the veins and muscle fibers through his flesh. He has no hair, no eyebrows, completely hairless; he's bald. His eyes…his eyes look like what snakes have. They're yellow with these slits for pupils. But, aside from that, he's a pretty handsome dude. He has very chiseled features, and he's just a guy. Someone you would probably find attractive, I guess is the best way to put it."

Drucilla didn't move. She couldn't move. She just stared at him.

Drake leaned back in the booth and crossed his arms. She glanced at his wrist. It was the first time she noticed an extremely expensive-looking platinum watch on his wrist with tons of diamonds.

"We made a deal," Drake said, crossing his arms.

"What are you talking about? What kind of deal?"

"The coin was his. Theoretically, when a demon loses a relic, it has to be given back freely. They can't just take it. Lucifer offered me a life of power and wealth in exchange for the coin."

"Woah, woah, back up. You're serious, aren't you?"

Drake held her stare for a moment to allow her to process what he had explained.

Drucilla's saddened face changed to confusion. She folded her arms and leaned back in her seat. "If you made a deal, why do you still have it?"

"I didn't trust him. I didn't think he would keep his word, so I told him he could have the coin back when I die."

"So, you get to have anything you want for like the next eighty years or something?"

"Fifteen. Fifteen years."

"Fifteen? So, you're going to die when you're thirty-two?" Drucilla asked.

"Something like that…Yes," he replied, unconcerned.

"I swear, Drake, if you're fucking with me right now—"

"Dru, I have no reason to lie to you about this. You know things have been off. You've asked me on multiple occasions about what's going on with me, and I never answered you. The money, the car, doesn't this make sense to you now?"

"Are you telling me you've essentially sold your life for money? Are you an idiot?"

"No, there's more to it than that, but, that's for another time." Drake glanced out the window again like he was waiting for something. "Dru, I'm going to go away for a while."

"What do you mean going away?"

"I will be leaving soon." Drake looked at her briefly, then back out the window.

"When will you be back?"

"I won't. I'm sorry." Drake pulled his wallet out and started fumbling around. He pulled out a card and slid it over to her. "You can reach me here if you need me. I'll do what I can to help you."

"Drake, I don't understand what's going on. Why are you leaving?"

"I can't tell you right now, but you will know in time." Drake pulled out his phone, sent a message, and put the phone back in his pocket. He reached into his other pocket, pulled out his keys, and handed them to her. "Here. Take my car. Go home and get some rest."

"This is all very weird. I don't understand what's happening," Drucilla said, panicking.

A tall, middle-aged gentleman entered the restaurant in a black suit with long slick white hair held back in a neat ponytail and approached their table.

"Mr. Blackwood, are you ready to leave?" the man asked.

"Yes, Leviathan," Drake said. He slid out of the booth, walked over to Drucilla, and kissed her forehead. "Everything is going to be ok. You will be safe. I promise you this," Drake assured her as he looked directly into her eyes. "Please, don't worry."

Drucilla reached out and grabbed Drake's hand. "You saw it, right? I mean, with Belynn?" Drucilla asked, hoping for confirmation.

He held her stare for a moment as he ran his finger over the edge of the coin in his pocket. He didn't offer confirmation or denial. Drake turned and walked away with the mysterious man. They left the diner walked out to a long black car waiting outside the diner. The driver opened the door for Drake and his mysterious companion. Drake didn't look back at Drucilla. He and the gentleman climbed inside the vehicle. The driver pulled the car away from the curb, and they disappeared down the dark street.

Rudolf Meyers:
Todten-Dantz
Ergäntzet
und herausgegeben
Durch
Conrad Meyern
Maalern in
Zürich
Im Jahr
1650.

CANTICLE THREE

"Fear doesn't shut you down; it wakes you up"
—Veronica Roth

Katia refused to answer Drucilla's calls. Drucilla hadn't been in school since the incident at Belynn's party. It had been a week, and Drucilla decided to go to school; she didn't want to get behind on her schoolwork. She entered through the back hallway entrance. She hoped that she wouldn't be noticed as she briskly walked to her first class; she didn't have the energy to interact with anyone.

"Hey, you're back," Adelia said. She recognized Drucilla from the back. Drucilla turned around to face her friend.

"Hey, Del. Yeah, I took some time away."

"You were there when Belynn died, right? I mean when she had the heart attack. How scary! Now, I'm glad I didn't go."

"Heart attack?" Drucilla asked.

"Yeah. The rumor was that someone had put something in Belynn's drink, which caused her heart to stop. Is that true? Everybody is talking about it," Adelia asked.

Drucilla squinted and darted her eyes around the hallway, trying to make sense of what she had just heard. She didn't understand why no one told the truth about the banshee. "I really don't know. 'Sorry." Drucilla walked away. At this point, she was starting to question her sanity. Regardless, it seemed that heart failure was the official story.

Drucilla walked down the hallway, past Belynn's locker, on her way to first period. She stopped to see Belynn's locker plastered with photos, flowers, cards, stuffed animals, and other various paraphernalia. There were photos and posters of her plastered all over the hallway.

"Of course, the school is making a huge deal about her death," Drucilla mumbled to herself.

She looked around to see random girls still crying in the hall, primarily for attention. *Belynn was a bitch to everyone but her own little clique. She would undoubtedly get a four-page spread in the yearbook. That's what happens when beautiful people die; basically, canonized for all intents and purposes.*

Drucilla walked into her classroom and sat at her desk. Her classmates gasped then became silent as she took her seat. Drucilla could feel their stares burrowing into her.

"Um, okay—" Drucilla said to herself.

Katia was at the other end of the room. She wouldn't even look at her. Drucilla stared at Katia, hoping to get her attention. Finally, Katia gave a slight glance and then quickly turned away.

"Drucilla, welcome back," Mr. Yoshida said. "I hope you're feeling better?"

"Yeah, I'm okay," she said softly, opening her political science book.

Mr. Yoshida started talking about their mock presidential campaigns in which Drake was doing very well, but his vacant seat was a haunting reminder that he was not returning. Drucilla couldn't concentrate on what he was saying. Her mind was all over the place. She knew she probably shouldn't have come, but Drucilla was three months from graduation, and she didn't have much choice. She had planned to start college in the fall at UCLA, but now she didn't know what she wanted. *Maybe I could go to Seattle with Adrian.* She began to think about Drake again and where he was. Their mother didn't know that he was gone, and she wouldn't be back home for another month. Drucilla didn't know what she was going to tell her mother when she came back.

The final bell rang, and Drucilla headed out the backend of the hallway onto the back lawn, the opposite direction from where she lived. She wasn't going home just yet. Her mind was racing as she struggled to sort out her feelings.

She briskly walked across the parking lot towards the adjacent street. She noticed a man and a woman out of the corner of her eye. Both with albinism, leaning against a compact SUV. She remembered that Bengtsson had albinism. The woman had long wavy hair, and the man had short wavy hair, both unusually tall, much like Mr. Bengtsson. *Maybe this was a family trait? Perhaps these people are related to him? Brother and sister, maybe?* Drucilla glanced at them a couple of times as she walked past but didn't say a word. They looked at each other as if to silently communicate and then back at Drucilla. Drucilla bit her lip nervously, pulled out her phone, and checked for missed calls as she kept walking. She didn't want to appear paranoid or alarmed by their presence, even though Drucilla was quite concerned about why they were watching her so closely. She kept walking for what seemed like hours. The sun was setting, and she realized that she was somewhere in Westwood Village, but she didn't care.

Drucilla kept playing Belynn's death over and over in her head. She started fidgeting with the beads on her wrist, trying to put together how she managed to manifest a sketch into an actual being that attacked Belynn. She wanted it to attack her. Then suddenly, it hit her. Drucilla imagined that a banshee would come and rip her heart out, and it happened. *Did these beads grant wishes? Were these all wishes?* Her mind began to run wild with the possibilities of wishing beads. Drucilla's stomach squeezed, and she realized that she was hungry. As luck would have it, she was outside of the same greasy-spoon diner where she and Drake had been the night Belynn died.

She entered the diner; she took a seat near the window. Drucilla opened up her bag and took out her biology book. A bubbly, blonde waitress bounced over to Drucilla with a pen and notepad.

"Hiya! How are you doin'? What can I get for ya?" she asked, clearly on amphetamines.

"Can I get a grilled cheese?" Drucilla handed her the menu that she had not opened.

The waitress smiled at her and bounded off. Drucilla glanced at the end of the diner just as the entrance to the restaurant opened. The man and woman from the school's parking lot entered the restaurant and took a seat at the opposite end of where Drucilla was sitting. Drucilla's forehead creased, and her eyes narrowed as she observed them climb into a corner booth. They both turned to look at her and then back to each other. The waitress showed up with menus, but they waved her off. As Drucilla got a better look at them, she noticed a strange symbol they both wore around their necks. The emblem was a ten-pointed star, like a decagram but interlaced like vines. Now that Drucilla was thinking about it, Mr. Bengtsson wore the same one. *Maybe they're part of some weird religious cult. I know Bengtsson is some sort of fundie. God, I hope they aren't on a bizarre mission to convert the school.*

Drucilla turned her attention back to her biology book.

After about an hour of failing to focus, she finally put her book away. She kept getting distracted by the beads around her wrist. Drucilla started thinking about her next wish. She took off the rosary and arranged the necklace in a neat but loose coil. She picked up a coffee mug and thought to herself: *I want Katia to call me right now.* She held the beads still raised the cup a few inches above the beads. WHACK. Nothing. The beads didn't break.

She raised the mug and tried to crush them again. WHACK. *What the Hell?* she thought. She tried to recall how it happened last time. *Maybe I have to be angry? I mean, I am angry,* she thought. *No, that's not it. Why isn't this working?*

Her concentration was abruptly interrupted by her phone. It vibrated within her bag with an audible hum. She fumbled through her bag furiously, trying to get it out. She hoped it was Katia calling. She glanced at the phone screen. It wasn't Katia; it was her mother.

"Hey, Mom."

"Drucilla! Are you kids behaving?" she asked, unusually chipper.

"Um, I guess?"

"I tried calling your brother. He didn't answer. Is he with you?" Fiona asked.

"No? I'm in Westwood Village."

"Alone? What are you doing there?"

"I have a big test to study for, and I wanted to get out of the house." Drucilla cringed at the lie.

"Dru, have your brother call me, okay? It's important."

"Okay, what's so important?"

There was dead silence on the other end of the line.

"Mom?" Drucilla asked, concerned.

"Dru, I'll be home in a few days; we'll talk then, okay?" Fiona replied.

"Is everything okay?" Drucilla asked with a bit of aggression in her voice. She couldn't handle another blow.

"Oh no, everything is great. Better than great, actually. We'll talk in a few days, okay?' Fiona said, calming Drucilla.

"Okay…"

"Don't stay up too late, and good luck on your test!"

"Okay, bye." Drucilla tucked her phone back into her bag and saw her sketch of the flowing banshee. Looking at it brought up the grim reminder that she potentially murdered someone. She hadn't sketched anything in a few days. She didn't feel up to it.

Out of the corner of her eye, she noticed that the strange couple was still staring at her.

Annoyed and tired, Drucilla groaned and realized that she needed to figure out a way home. She pulled her phone back out of her bag to call Adrian. The call went to voicemail. Frustrated, Drucilla continued to scroll through her phone. She saw Katia's number. Drucilla paused for a moment before scrolling past it. Then she remembered that she had Drake's number. She pulled out the business card for some lawyer and punched in the number scribbled on the back.

The phone started ringing. "C'mon, Drake pick-up," she said. She swung her feet back and forth under the table. A pre-recorded greeting started with instructions to leave a message.

"Damn it!" she whispered to herself. She put the phone face down on the table.

I need to get home, even if I have to walk back. Drucilla stood up, pulled her bag over her shoulder, and headed for the door. The strange couple was still staring at her. She was irritated and in no mood to deal with this couple's creepy attitude. Drucilla had to walk past them to get out. She walked about two steps past them and stopped. She turned to them and looked at them in anger.

"What's your deal?" Drucilla yelled at them, making a big shrugging gesture.

Neither of them said a word. They stared at her in silence. His red eyes flashed for a moment.

Drucilla inhaled sharply, and her body tensed. *That's what Bengtsson's eyes did.* She quickly turned away and pushed open the door. She caught a sticker on the inside of the door with a number for a Taxi service on her way out. She pulled out her phone and punched in the number as she headed for the parking lot.

It was a warm enough evening that she didn't need her jacket. The street was tranquil, but it was a Monday night, so she didn't expect much action from the bars around there. Drucilla paced around the diner's parking lot, waiting for the taxi to arrive. She didn't know how long Katia would avoid her, but she was becoming increasingly irate the longer she ignored her. Drucilla threw her head back and looked up at the stars. She couldn't see many of them in the city. The light choked the sky with a dull, dark, bluish-orange hue. Drucilla exhaled as she dropped her chin back down. She was suddenly eyeball-to-eyeball with one of the cultists. The woman stood behind him. Startled, Drucilla gasped and took a step back. The man tightly grabbed her wrist with the rosary and held it up. He looked at the beads wrapped around her wrist and then past her wrist to Drucilla's terrified eyes.

Let me go, you weird-ass cultist!" she screamed. Drucilla struggled to get away from him. She tried to pry his fingers off her wrist, but he was far too strong.

"Gadreel. *Ne prodas. Quod stella reprobi*," the woman spoke, clearly in Latin.

Drucilla's eyes widened. She didn't speak Latin, but she understood some words, "The Fallen Star" being the only thing she could make out.

"*Et nolite timere. Quod stella reprobi*," Gadreel seethed back at her.

The woman gasped as if she heard something she wasn't expecting.

"Nor his brothers," he said in English with a thick, almost Italian accent.

"What do you want from me!" Drucilla hollered, still trying to pull herself away from him.

His grasp was tight but effortless. He held on to Drucilla as if he was holding a feather. His strength was unfathomable.

The woman pushed Gadreel to the side as he continued to hold Drucilla against her will. She grabbed

Drucilla's face with one hand and held her steady she looked into Drucilla's eyes.

"*Que videt,* Armaros?" Gadreel asked the woman.

Armaros, how do I know that name?

"She is not Divine," Armaros said, clearly so Drucilla would understand.

Armaros slid her hand behind her long coat and pulled out what appeared to be a long ceremonial jambiya knife from behind her waist. The gilded hilt glinted in the streetlight.

"*Sacrifice est ad eam,*" the woman said.

Everyone was caught off guard by a loud car pulled up to the corner, a car full of drunk people yelling and being obnoxious. Distracted by the commotion, the man loosened his grip, and Drucilla was able to rip her hand away from his grasp. Armaros lunged to grab her, but Drucilla managed to dodge her. Drucilla scrambled to get her footing and ran full speed across the street to a gated cemetery. Drucilla grabbed onto the handles of the gate and pulled as hard as she could. The entrance was locked. She looked up and realized the wrought iron gate was too tall to climb over. She heard them behind her, closing in. She ran along the side of the fence, desperate to find another opening. She couldn't breathe; tears were streaming down her face. Drucilla was terrified.

As luck would have it, she found what she was looking for, a missing bar in-between the wrought iron bars that were just wide enough for her petite frame to squeeze, though. Drucilla slipped through the bars and looked back. Gadreel and Armaros were too large to fit through the opening. She turned and ran down a winding path among the monuments and headstones, deeper into the cemetery. Drucilla darted behind a gravestone and peeked around the side to see two distant figures unfurl wings from their backs and launch themselves over the twelve-foot fence. Drucilla's jaw dropped as she gasped at the sight. *What are these people?* She couldn't believe what she was witnessing. The only thing she knew was that she had to get far away.

Terrified, she took off running again to put more distance between them. She didn't know where she was going, but she hoped for another exit, somewhere with many people. She could hear them searching and speaking to each other in Latin. The only thing she could make out from their chatter was *sanguis angeli*, something about the blood of an angel.

What does that mean? Why do they want angel blood? Her mind raced as fast as she did. Drucilla found a row of mausoleums and hoped she could hide inside one of them or hopefully confuse them within the small marble structures. While running, she looked back again to see if they were still following her. She turned around and accidentally tripped over a broken sprinkler head and swiftly fell to the ground. She scrambled to get to her feet, knowing that this was costing her precious time.

Drucilla felt a sudden powerful and tangible presence behind her. She knew she wasn't alone. Two translucent clawed hands gripped Drucilla's shoulders from behind her. A calming but oddly trusting voice whispered in her ear.

"Break the bead on the ground and summon the dead," the voice instructed.

"What?" Drucilla asked, stunned. She couldn't move; she was gasping for air.

"Smash the bead against the ground. Do it now!" The presence demanded.

"*Ibi*!" Armaros said. She finally spotted Drucilla. They ran over towards Drucilla as their eyes began to emit a red glow. Armaros readied her blade.

Drucilla didn't know why; maybe she was at a lack of options, but she did what the voice told her to do. She pulled the rosary tightly around her knuckles, squeezed her eyes shut, knelt, and punched the ground beneath her as hard as she could. Drucilla felt the bead crush under the knuckle of her middle finger. Her mind flooded with thoughts of ghouls and corpses pulling them down underground to their deaths. As she opened her eyes, a tiny, bright blue spark jumped from her fist, shot up her wrist, and disappeared into her arm.

Like a wish had been granted, the ground heaved beneath their feet and caught the couple off guard.

"Gadreel!" the woman yelled. Gadreel looked around frantically at the disturbance happening around them.

Something was coming, something big. A rumbling coming from beneath Gadreel and Armaros intensified and grew louder as the headstones began to shimmy.

Panicking, Drucilla quickly crawled next to a small tree and wrapped her arms around it.

The ground exploded in random places from beneath them. Decayed, oozing, spindly arms violently thrust out from under their feet, reaching upward they grasped tightly to their legs. One arm, then another arm, then another, all were bursting through the pristine, emerald-green lawn. More and more decomposed hands gripped them and dragged them down into the ground. Gadreel and Armaros shrieked in terror as they tried to free themselves, but for every rotted hand they tore away, two would take its place. The dead hands pulled them further and further under the grass. Gadreel and Armaros' screams mixed with the moans and wails as the dead drew their prey deeper underground. The sound of Drucilla's screams soon drowned out their own. Gadreel and Armaros' screams became increasingly muffled until the ground engulfed them. The shaking stopped, and the ground calmed. All was silent as a single headstone fell over.

Breathless and trembling, Drucilla pulled herself up and stood in shock at the settled earth. She blinked rapidly in disbelief. She remembered the voice that told her to break the bead. Drucilla desperately looked around to see if anyone was still there.

"Hello, are you still here? Who are you?" she shouted out.

There was nothing but dead silence. The presence was gone, along with cultists.

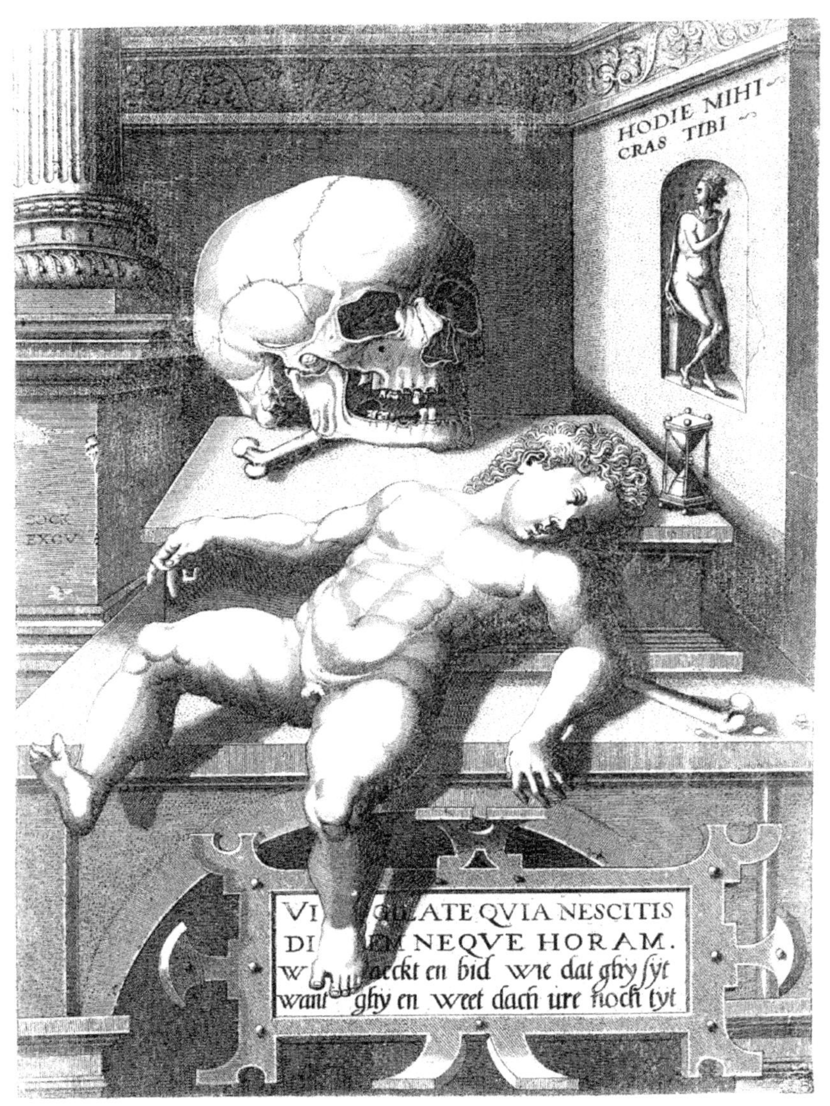

HODIE MIHI
CRAS TIBI
VIGILATE QVIA NESCITIS
DIEM NEQVE HORAM.
Waeckt en bid wie dat ghy syt
want ghy en weet doch ure noch tyt
COCK
EXCV.

CANTICLE FOUR

"God sends meat, and the devil sends cooks." —Thomas
Deloney

The long black car pulled into the driveway entrance.
The headlights illuminated a large iron gate decorated
with intricate wrought iron artwork. Large, round door
pulls were set on the front as if a giant could use them to
pull open the gates. The gates terminated into thick,
heavy, pointed finials on the tops. The driver rolled down
the window and punched a series of numbers into the
keypad. With a loud clink, the gates slowly creaked
open. The moonlight illuminated the grounds and the
house, bathing it in a dim grey glow. The drive was lined
with mournful willow trees with branches so low that
they scratched grooves into the earth below as they
slowly swayed back and forth. The driveway was
severely neglected and needed repair, causing the drive
up to the front of the house to be quite rough. The car
crept up to the grand stone staircase that led to the front
door. Drake stepped out onto the pebble driveway and
looked up at the house; Leviathan followed. The house
emitted an eerie glow from the windows as if someone
was using low-wattage bulbs throughout the house. A
hulking figure with long white hair motioned to the door
to guide Drake up the stairs.

Drake greeted him cordially, "Good evening, Oriens."

Oriens simply nodded as Drake and Leviathan entered the dark foyer together. The surroundings momentarily struck Drake. Oak furnishings and priceless paintings adorned the halls of the mansion. Gas sconce lighting flickered inside its glass housing as Drake walked down the hallway. Drake entered the parlor to his right with Leviathan. The room was opulent and adorned in deep burgundy hues and textiles. The antique carpet was loomed by hand over a century ago, true to its era, judging by the mansion age. Lucifer sat in a deep, tall-backed chair in front of an unlit fireplace, waiting for Drake's arrival.

Upon seeing Drake enter the room, Lucifer stood up to greet him.

"Right on time," Lucifer grinned, "Please, take a seat."

Drake took a seat in the chair facing Lucifer. Lucifer straightened his suit and sat back down. He leaned in toward Drake. The fireplace burst into a blaze, crackling and popping, then settled into a slow, easy burn.

Drake sat in silence for a moment before he spoke. "I want to change the terms of the deal," Drake blurted.

Lucifer cocked his head to the side as if he didn't think he heard him quite right, "Come again?"

"Things have changed. There's an issue, and I need to change the terms."

"What kind of issue?" Lucifer inquired.

"My sister needs my protection, but I can't protect her if I go with you."

Lucifer stood up and walked over to the bar. He popped the stopper out of a lead crystal decanter and poured himself a drink. He motioned to Drake with the decanter in his hand, offering him a drink, as well. Drake shook his head and slid back into his chair. "Why do I care if your sister requires protection? She was not part of our deal, and you specifically requested that she should never be involved in any of our dealings. So why now?" Lucifer said. He sipped his drink.

"She…" Drake paused and thought before he spoke. "I think she's in trouble. I think Drucilla is in over her head. I don't know; I mean, I don't think she's safe. Something doesn't feel right."

"Please, continue," Lucifer said.

"She has um, she has a thing," Drake said, looking at his hand and making a motion around his wrist, looking confused. "I think it's dangerous."

"What kind of thing?" Lucifer asked, becoming increasingly curious, leaning against a heavy mahogany desk.

"It's like, a really old, I dunno, rosary type thing, I think. Drucilla found it in the catacombs about a year ago."

Leviathan inhaled sharply.

Lucifer and Leviathan exchanged concerned looks. Lucifer shook his head at Leviathan to reassure him.

"That does not matter; it will not matter," Lucifer reassured in a low voice. He paced for a moment.

"How can you be certain?" Leviathan quietly said to him.

Lucifer ran his hand over his bald head. "Well," he looked at Leviathan, "It appears that player two has joined the game," Lucifer mumbled as he slammed the heavy-cut, crystal highball glass down on the desk with a hard thud. He covered his mouth with his right hand as if he was in deep thought.

"I tell you what, Drake. I am willing to concede considering this new information," Lucifer stated. "If I find your terms acceptable, what is it that you require—exactly?"

"What do you mean if you find my terms acceptable?" Drake snapped, darting up from his chair and standing in front of Lucifer. "I want my sister protected. By you. That's my deal. Take it or leave it."

Lucifer, stunned at the audacity, clenched his jaw, sneered, and stared angrily at Drake, his snake-eyes illuminating like a cobra ready to strike. Lucifer got within inches of Drake's face. "Do not take my generosity for granted. I can blink you out of existence like that," Lucifer snapped his fingers.

"Is that right?" Drake retorted, getting in Lucifer's face, and not backing down. "Because from what I understand, you really have no other choice. If you want control of your Cabal again, you'll do as I ask," he asserted emphatically.

Lucifer crushed the crystal highball in his hand to sand and dust, locking eyes with Drake.

Drake stood his ground, unflinching. The stand-off stretched on for a moment. Abruptly, Lucifer's stern looks faded into a slight smile. It was as if he realized, he had an edge.

"Fine! Fine. I will see that she is protected, but I cannot promise she will remain that way after your time in this realm has ended," Lucifer warned.

"I want you to protect her: personally. That's my demand," Drake said firmly.

Lucifer threw his head back and roared in laughter. "You must be joking?"

"Do I look like I'm joking?" Drake said, stone-faced.

"What do you want me to do, Drake? Ensure she arrives at school on time? Or do you want me to make sure she eats her vegetables?" Lucifer chuckled to himself.

"I watched my sister summon a wraith type of thing and murder a classmate in cold blood in front of a hundred people, because of that thing she's wearing. I am not joking," Drake snarled.

Lucifer's smile faded, and Leviathan looked stunned.

"What exactly does your sister know of this rosary?" Lucifer asked.

"She doesn't know anything, as far as I know. But I expect that to change quickly now that she knows it can manifest whatever devious thoughts and ideas she cooks up in her brain," Drake responded.

"Interesting," Lucifer contemplated."However, if you want me to protect her, I have an alternate demand."

"Bullshit! No deal," Drake said with annoyance as he sat back down in the chair, waiting for Lucifer's next move.

"Fine," Lucifer sat in the chair, facing Drake. "We can sit here, in this room for the next fifteen years. I have the time, do you?"

Drake scowled.

Lucifer pulled out a nail file and shaped his claws into a more nuanced point.

Drake got out of his chair and walked over to the bar, pulled the stopper out of the crystal decanter, and took a long swig from the bottle. He turned to Lucifer.

"What is it?" He groaned reluctantly, not looking at Lucifer. He wiped his mouth with the back of his sleeve.

"Oh, you are ready to negotiate. Good," Lucifer slipped the nail file back into his breast pocket. "I have decided that it is time I take a sabbatical. After all, I have not had a break in well, never."

Drake hopped backward to sit on top of the mahogany desk. He crossed his ankles and took another swig from the decanter.

"Okay?" Drake shrugged, clearly starting to feel the effects of the whiskey.

"In fifteen years, you take my seat in Hell," Lucifer said calmly.

Drake coughed violently, "What? Are you serious?"

"You will be one of the Seven Kings of Hell: The King of Pride and Vanity," Lucifer proffered. "Quite a prestigious offer, if I do say so myself."

Drake thought it over in his head for a moment. If he were going to die anyway, this would be the ideal outcome.

"So, say I accept your offer. What about the rest of our deal?" Drake queried.

"You mean your mother?"

"Yeah, is she…?"

"Yes, yes, of course, your mother is fine. She is completely cured, as far as anyone knows. There is no trace of the disease in her body," Lucifer confirmed.

Drake nodded.

"Do we have a deal?" Lucifer challenged.

"I'll run your Cabal and take your place in Hell in exchange for my mother's life and your protection of my sister," Drake reaffirmed.

Lucifer once again extended his hand, and Drake accepted it.

Quis est homo qui vi-
vet et non videbit
MORTEM.
PS. 88.
Hagæ-Comitis
ex Officina H. hondius
1642.

CANTICLE FIVE

"You see, insanity runs in my family. It practically gallops."
—Joseph Kesselring

Drucilla came home from school and drove her brother's car up to the front of her house. She noticed her mother's car in the driveway. She took a deep breath. She had no idea what she would tell her mother about Drake. Drucilla ran through multiple freak-out scenarios in her head; everything from grief and panic to anger and blame. She didn't know how this was going to go down. Regardless, she needed to put on her big girl pants and get through it. Drucilla stepped out of the car and headed up the driveway. As usual, she entered the house through the back door; Drucilla's mother must have just arrived. There were multiple suitcases in the sunroom, and Fiona was standing in the kitchen sorting through the mountain of mail that accumulated while she was away.

Drucilla kicked off her shoes and dropped her bag on the bench by the door.

Fiona looked up and smiled. "Hi baby," she said. She held out her arms to hug her.

Drucilla hadn't hugged her mother in two months. She'd barely seen her that year at all.

"How are you holding up?" Fiona asked.

Drucilla paused for a moment, because she had no idea how to answer that question. She was caught off guard by it. *Should I tell her the truth and burst into tears about how abandoned I felt and how it was because of my own doing? Should I lie and act like everything was manageable?* But then there was the problem of Drake. Drucilla couldn't think of an acceptable or believable lie.

Drucilla looked at Fiona and tried to hold back the tears welling up in her eyes. She had no control over it.

Fiona squeezed her tighter and rocked her.

"I know. It's been so long. You being here all by yourself this month. I was shocked when Drake told me he was joining the military and had to leave immediately," she started.

Drucilla blinked rapidly in disbelief. She pushed back from her mother and stared at her face.

Fiona smiled at Drucilla and wiped her tears off her cheeks with her thumbs.

"It's going to be ok! He promised me he was going to go to college in two years. I can't believe he had to go to boot camp the day after he signed up. Is it always that fast?" Fiona asked.

"I, I don't know," Drucilla replied.

"Well, he was pretty adamant about going," Fiona exhaled deeply. "I couldn't exactly say no. You know how he gets when he has his mind set on something."

Drucilla nodded, confused.

"Whose car is that?" Fiona asked, pointing to Drake's car on the street.

"Uh, it's Drake's. He's letting me drive it while he's, um, away. I guess," Drucilla said. *I mean, it wasn't exactly a lie.*

"Did he get that with his sign-on bonus?" Fiona asked before shrugging. "Wow, that's fast. The military moves a lot quicker than they did when I was your age," she stared at the car through the window for a moment. "They gave him enough money to buy a new BMW?" Fiona raised her eyebrow at Drucilla.

Drucilla shrugged.

☩☩☩

Drucilla and her mother decided to have dinner at Fiona's favorite Greek restaurant in Sunset Park. They've been going there for as long as Drucilla could remember. The owner's sister used to work with Fiona at UCLA years ago in the archeology department, so they treated the Blackwoods quite well. The restaurant was a small, hole-in-the-wall place, but it was homey and never busy.

"Mmmm," Fiona groaned happily as she slightly bounced in her seat and stuffed kalamata olives in her mouth. Fiona and Drucilla were both passionate about them. Drucilla supposed that's where she inherited it.

"I swear you only come here for the olives," Drucilla mused.

"And the Dolmas," Fiona added.

"Mom, what is it that you needed to tell Drake that you couldn't tell me on the phone?" Drucilla prodded.

Fiona stopped her happy chewing and locked eyes with Drucilla. Her smile faded. She picked up the napkin off her lap and patted her mouth. She slid her hand across the table to Drucilla. Drucilla offered her hand, and Fiona squeezed it. Fiona rubbed her thumb over Drucilla's knuckles; she examined Drucilla's hand and slightly smiled at her.

"I don't want you to get upset because everything is fine, ok?" she warned.

Drucilla drew her hand back slowly and suspiciously. She crossed her arms. Drucilla knew this was going to upset her. Fiona always said, "Don't get upset," when she was about to deliver upsetting news. Drucilla narrowed her eyes in anticipation.

"About six months ago, I started getting these horrible headaches," she started. "I tried everything to control them but, they started to affect the vision in my left eye. I saw the doctor about it and had some tests done. They found that I had a rather large growth behind my left eye, wrapping around my optic nerve."

"Figures he would know. Drake is always the first to know everything. Why don't you ever tell me anything? Why is it always Drake?" Drucilla asked, becoming increasingly upset.

"I didn't mean for Drake to find out either," Fiona explained, ignoring the implied accusation of favoritism. "However, I didn't realize he was home, and he heard me scheduling my radiation appointments on the phone. I had to tell him, but I made him promise not to tell you until I could. He only did what I asked. I decided to get the treatments in Peru while I trained my assistants to pick up the slack in the event of..." Fiona paused and tried to think of the best way to explain the inevitable. "Well, in case I'm not there anymore."

Drucilla stared at her and nodded slowly and angrily as Fiona explained herself. "But I'm fine!" Fiona said, shrugging and smiling.

"How is this fine, Mom?" Drucilla asked.

"I don't know how it happened but, I had another scan done last week, and there was no trace of the tumor. It vanished. I haven't had a headache, and I feel great. The radiation was so effective that it shrunk the tumor completely. That is what I think, anyway," Fiona said. She smiled and threw another olive in her mouth.

A cold chill ran up Drucilla's spine to the back of her head. Drucilla knew what was happening behind the scenes, and it terrified her.

"Dru? Are you ok?" Fiona asked, concerned by Drucilla's sudden look of fear.

"Fine, I'm fine," Drucilla exhaled, shaking off the panic.

"I think that's awesome, Mom," Drucilla said and gave her mother a fake smile. Drucilla took a bite out of her gyro.

There was a long period of silence between them. Drucilla glanced up at her mother. Fiona focused on her food. Drucilla felt that Fiona didn't want to talk about it anymore, so Drucilla didn't press the issue.

"Are you looking forward to college?" Fiona asked, breaking the silence and trying to change the subject to a less tense matter. Fiona loved talking to her children about going to college ever since elementary school. Fiona was always involved in planning for their future.

"Yeah, I guess," Drucilla responded.

"Did you find out if you get to room with Katia?" Fiona asked, taking a bite out of one of her Dolmas.

Katia. I didn't even think about that. Drucilla didn't think Katia was ever going to talk to her. Drucilla was sure Katia had put in a request to live with someone else, if not attend another college altogether.

"Dru?" Fiona asked, trying to snap Drucilla out of her concentration.

"Oh! Um, I don't know. We get to request it, but I won't know until I get there," Drucilla said, not looking up from her plate at her mother.

"You know you can stay at home."

"I know but, you aren't home much anyway. Living on campus will probably make me less lonely. Especially with Drake being gone."

"Well, it's just four years, and then you can decide where you want to live after you graduate. Did you decide on your minor yet?"

"Yeah, I didn't I tell you? Fine art," Drucilla responded.

"What?" Fiona was taken aback by her response. Fiona was sure that Drucilla wanted to be an artist. "You mean majoring."

"No," Drucilla responded, pushing a small chunk of tomato to the edge of her plate with a fork. She looked up at her mother and smiled briefly. "I want to be an archaeologist, like you."

Fiona blinked her eyes rapidly.

"Is that ok? Are you upset?"

"I...I just didn't know you had that much of an interest in it.".

"Well yeah, Mom. I mean, you take us all over the place, of course, I'm interested. I love it, and I think this is what I want to do."

Fiona's face lit up in excitement and pride.

"Drake never had much interest in archaeology. He's very politically minded, you know. I think he just wants to make the world a better place," Fiona remarked.

Drucilla shrugged.

"I know he'll run for office one day. I think he'd make a wonderful leader."

Drucilla rolled the beads around on her wrist while Fiona talked about how impressed she was with Drake, his maxed-out GPA, and his college prospects. Drucilla felt a bit left out. Then again, Drucilla always felt that Drake was favored.

"I'm so proud of you, Dru," Fiona said.

Drucilla perked up at that last part. Fiona leaned back in her chair and smiled.

"Do you know how you and Drake came into this world? Did I ever tell you the story?" Fiona asked.

"Yeah, lots, but go ahead," Drucilla mumbled.

"I was visited by an angel when I was exploring the Sistine Chapel. He identified himself as the Arch Angel Raphael. Even though I wasn't a believer, I needed to believe in something. I suppose that's why I went there. I was thirty-five and had never been married. I mean, I had a few prospects, but they would never work out. I guess I just couldn't be in one place long enough to make anything work," Fiona explained.

Drucilla stared blankly. She's heard this story before, but this is the first time she realized that Fiona was telling the truth. Fiona wasn't a "Woo-woo" type of person. Drucilla didn't give her credit for that before. She always figured her mother just loved to tell the feel-good kind of stories. After the events from the past few days. Drucilla needed some answers.

"I always thought I'd have to choose between my job and a family. The reason Raphael visited me was to tell me that I could have both and that I didn't need to be married to have children," Fiona explained.

"Mom, what did the angel look like?"

Fiona's eyes lit up. This is the first time that Drucilla asked her for details about the seraphim.

"Oh, it was so long ago. Very lightly complected, very light hair. I don't think he got much sun,"

"Tall? Thin?" Drucilla pressed, becoming increasingly concerned.

Fiona shrugged. "Honestly, I don't remember that much detail. But yes, I believe he was tall and lean. Why do you ask?"

"I don't know. I don't think you ever described his appearance before."

Fiona thought to herself for a moment, then shrugged. "Coincidently, after meeting with the Seraphim…."

"How did you know he was a Seraphim?"

"Well honey, he told me he was the Arch Angel Raphael."

"Yeah, but how did you know he wasn't just some weirdo?"

"I thought that at first. It wasn't until everything I had agonized over suddenly lifted. What else but a divine presence could intervene and change my life so profoundly? You're here because of that divine intervention."

Drucilla's eyes narrowed. She started to wonder who her biological donor really was. *No, that's crazy. This is crazy.* She argued with herself inside her head.

"Anyway, I was offered a handsome grant for consulting work at a dig site in India. I realized with what I was being paid; I had enough money for IVF, which is how you and Drake came to be. I chose your DNA donor from a catalog of men who had the characteristics and attributes that I felt were most important. I wanted my children to be smart, empathetic, creative, and ethnic. So, I chose an Egyptian donor," Fiona said.

"Does he know about us?" Drucilla asked.

"He does. We'll contact each other every year or two. He loves to get updates about you and your brother," Fiona answered.

"What's he like? You never really told us anything about him. Nothing in detail anyway," Drucilla remarked. The thought that she could be divine started to take up residence in her head. *No, I couldn't be.* She remembered the incident in the graveyard with the winged beings. *Those weird angel-type cultists said I wasn't. But how would they know? Should I tell my mom what happened?* Drucilla's eyes started to dart around; she was confused more than ever. Her intrusive thoughts competed with the story her mother was trying to relay.

"Drucilla, are you ok? You look lost."

"No. No, I'm ok, just…thinking." Drucilla didn't want to panic her mother.

"The only thing I really know about him was that he was a pediatric doctor and surgeon in Cairo and had three children of his own. He was a donor because his sister-in-law could not have children with his brother. He decided to assist other prospective mothers in the same position. Your heritage gives you kids the most beautiful complexions and features," Fiona smiled as she admired her daughter.

"Except Drake has dark, nearly black eyes, and mine are blue like yours. And why does Drake get to be tall, and I'm stuck being tiny? I mean, we're supposed to be twins," Drucilla lamented.

"You do look alike. Not identical but, you can tell you're from the same gene pool," Fiona joked. "You know, I had Drake's IQ tested when he was eleven and again when he was fifteen. He was off the charts. The first test put him at 179; the second put him at 200. So, if we averaged those scores, he was a genius by any measure," Fiona said proudly.

"I'm smooth-brained one of the family," Drucilla scoffed.

"Drucilla, you are a fantastic artist, and you're always so quick to pick up anything new. You're an excellent problem solver. You've got a temper, which I'm sure you get from your grandfather, but you're brilliant. He has the analytical genes; you have the creative ones," Fiona reassures.

"Yeah, but Drake, the golden child, he's the one that's going to be president one day. I know Drake had been taking a bunch of college prep courses like civics, political science, and US government before he fucked-off to the military," Drucilla moaned.

Fiona shot Drucilla an unamused look at her profanity.

Later that evening, after Fiona had gone to bed, Drucilla sat outside on the patio in the warm evening spring air. Drucilla had her phone in her hand and the business card with Drake's number. She tried redialing, but it again went straight to the answering service.

Drucilla hung up and called it again. Again: answering service. Drucilla groaned and hung up. She shook her head and curled up into a fetal position on the chaise and thought, *why bother giving me your number if you're just going to ignore me?*

"Ugh, damn it," she said. She redialed the number one more time. This time she waited for the prerecorded message to finish.

"Drake. It's Dru. I don't know why I can't ever get a hold of you, but I need to talk to you. I need to know what's going on. I know you probably won't or can't tell me, but Mom is home, and she told me that you knew about the tumor, and now it's gone. Damn it, what's happening? Does this have anything to do with—you know—him?" Drucilla said nervously. "I'm confused, I'm scared, and I need you to talk to me. Please!" She pressed the disconnect button.

CANTICLE SIX

"Egypt is full of dreams, mysteries, memories." —Janet
Erskine Stuart

It was Drucilla's first year out of college and at her first dig site in Egypt. Her mother accompanied her, and Fiona was very excited to be working with her daughter on the same team. They were staying just outside of Luxor. Everything was going as planned until Fiona got a call that her mother had a bad fall and was injured. Fiona had to leave the dig site, fly back to the states, and help her mother convalesce.

"Honey, are you sure you'll be all right?" Fiona asked. She dashed around the temporary quarters picking up random things and stuffing them into her tote bag.

"Mom, it's fine. Go back and take care of Grandma. We're good," Drucilla reassured her.

"I feel so guilty leaving you here," she said, searching her phone for her boarding pass.

"It's not a big deal. I mean, it's going to take a couple of days to open up KV-20 anyway, so there's really no point in you worrying about it."

"Oh, I really wanted to be here with you when they break into the tomb," Fiona said, holding Drucilla's face.

Drucilla rolled her eyes.

"Mom, you're going to miss your train."

"I know," she said, hiking up her backpack onto her shoulder. She grabbed her rollaway suitcase and picked up her tote bag. "I'll call you when I get to Grandma's, okay? Don't hesitate to call me on anything, ok? I mean it. Anything—call," she said. Fiona pushed the door handle with her fingertips. Drucilla grabbed the door handle from her and opened the door.

"Oh, and Drucilla, remember not to…."

"Not to leave the quarters after dark. Don't answer the door for anyone. I got it. I'm not fifteen anymore," Drucilla groaned.

Fiona stuck her bottom lip out in a pout as if she would cry, "I'm so proud of you!"

"Mom, just go!"

"Bye. 'Love you!" Fiona yelled, heading down the alleyway to the waiting car.

"' Love you, too!" Drucilla called after her while shaking her head in amusement.

The team was staying in temporary quarters at a hotel in Luxor near Al' Asasif. They were working with the Supreme Council of Antiquities of Egypt in opening tombs and cataloging artifacts in the Valley of the Kings. They had only been there for a week before Fiona got the call about Grandma. This dig was Drucilla's first out of college. Drucilla was there to help out with cataloging, not the most glamorous job. Unfortunately, Drucilla wasn't on the team that got to open the sarcophagi and dig around in the burial chambers.

It was around 6 p.m., and Drucilla figured she should venture out for food before it got too dark. There was a lot of looting and robbing around the area, so it was best to return home before sunset. Drucilla stepped out of the hotel, put in her earbuds, and started her music app. It was a warm evening. The area where she was staying was quite lush for being a desert. Across the street were acres of barley. You could find anything from carob to olives, apples to pomegranates down the road. Drucilla headed down the street and into a small grocery shop around the corner. After entering the grocery, Drucilla noticed a middle-aged woman behind the counter, tending the shop. Drucilla went to the cooler and grabbed a bottle of water. As Drucilla placed the bottle on the counter, her rosary clattered against the countertop. The woman at the counter stared at it for a moment then looked at Drucilla. She said something in Arabic, but Drucilla couldn't understand it.

"I'm sorry, I don't speak Arabic," Drucilla said and mimed that she didn't understand her.

"Your beads, they're quite old," The woman said in English.

"Oh! Yeah, they are," Drucilla said. She pulled her wallet out of her backpack.

The woman stared at the rosary again; intensely. "Where did you get them?" the woman asked abruptly.

"I found it in an antique shop in Italy…in Palermo," Drucilla lied.

She looked at Drucilla suspiciously. "Twenty-five *LE*," she said.

Drucilla placed the money on the counter and grabbed the water bottle.

"That's a good find. You should have it appraised. 'Could be worth a fortune," the woman commented.

Drucilla turned away and began to leave.

"Are you a student with the archaeologists?" The woman asked, pointing to Drucilla's UCLA backpack.

Drucilla glanced at her backpack and back to the woman. "No. I mean, I was. I graduated. I'm working now. My team is working on excavating and cataloging the tombs," Drucilla said. She opened the shop door.

"Those tombs shouldn't be disturbed!"

Here we go, Drucilla thought. "I agree with you. But the S.C.A. of Egypt gave us the grant to come out here and work with them."

"They have no right, either. They don't speak for all of us," the woman said, visibly annoyed.

"Um, thank you, have a good day," Drucilla said and got out of the store as quickly as possible.

A few restaurants were at the end of the street, so Drucilla figured she would check them out. She got the nagging feeling that someone was watching her. Drucilla looked around and noticed an attractive, well-dressed gentleman with perfectly styled reddish hair across the street looking at a magazine at the newspaper stand. He casually leaned against the wall and flipped through the pages of *Vogue Arabia.* He almost seemed out of place.

Drucilla paused to watch him. She squinted her eyes; he didn't look at her. Drucilla turned her attention to the sidewalk ahead of her and continued on her way to find dinner.

Drucilla stopped at a place called *Ankh* on the west side of the Nile. It was an upscale resort-style restaurant. They appeared to cater to tourists with Americanized accents and decor. Drucilla took a seat at a small table outside on the patio. She set her backpack down on the chair next to her. She pulled out her phone and checked her emails. Out of the corner of her eye, she caught that same attractive, redhead gentleman a couple of tables down at her right. He looked like a model. *Maybe he's doing a photo shoot, or maybe he's on vacation.* From the way he was dressed, he seemed wealthy. Drucilla stared at him for a moment, hoping he would look at her. She was strangely fascinated by him. He set his book down momentarily to take a sip of coffee and looked at Drucilla as he set his cup back down. They locked eyes for a moment. He smiled, Drucilla didn't smile back, and he went back to reading his book. There was something about him that she couldn't quite pinpoint, but she felt strangely attracted—more so, connected to him. She couldn't understand it. *Screw it, whatever. I'm gonna talk to him.*

Drucilla picked up her backpack and pulled it over her shoulder. She walked over to his table and waited for him to look up at her. He slowly looked up from his book, and Drucilla took off her sunglasses.

"Hi," she said nervously.

"Good evening." He smiled.

"Um, I'm sorry for interrupting, but do we know each other?" *Hey, dudes have used that line on me before...What do I have to lose? I suck at flirting.*

"I do not believe so," he said, standing up. "I am Lou," he extended his hand to Drucilla.

"I'm Drucilla," she said. She shook his hand, maintaining eye contact. She noticed how his gestures and mannerisms were articulate and proper, almost like royalty.

"Please, take a seat," he offered.

Drucilla looked around the patio and out over onto the Nile.

"Are you from here or on vacation?" Drucilla was attempting to make small talk. She put her elbows on the table and rested her head on her left hand. Her rosary tapped her elbow. He looked at it for a moment, then back to her and grinned. Drucilla noticed what he was looking at her rosary. She quickly shoved her hands under the table. He stared at her for a moment, like he was reading her mind. She curiously leaned her head to the side, wondering what was going through his head.

Finally, he clasped his hands on the table and leaned forward.

"How is the dig going?" he asked out of nowhere.

Taken aback by his question, Drucilla's wondered why he would ask something like that. Drucilla figured he must have seen her backpack and thought she was a student.

"Uh, we're currently working on opening KV 20. It should be a couple more days before we've broken through to the burial chamber. I'm sorry, but how did you know I was an archaeologist?"

He smiled at her for a moment before leaning back into the chair.

"I know your brother."

Drucilla blinked wildly.

"I'm sorry, what did you say?"

"Yes, Drake Blackwood is your brother, is he not?"

Drucilla didn't say anything for a moment; she just stared at him in disbelief. A myriad of thoughts rushed through Drucilla's head. *Have I met him before? Does he work with Drake? Where is the connection?*

"How do you know my brother?"

"Drucilla," he said. He leaned forward and stared into Drucilla's eyes. "I am Lucifer."

Startled, Drucilla gasped and jumped out of her chair. She stood behind the chair, grasped onto the back, and dug in her nails. She stared at him in wide-eyed terror.

Lucifer's glamor faded into a translucent-skinned being with amber snake-eyes and sharp chiseled facial features. He crossed his arms with his long, clawed nails resting on his biceps. Strangely, Lucifer's natural, demonic appearance was more beautiful than his human one.

"Please, return to your seat. People are starting to stare," he said in a quiet, smooth voice. He changed his glamor back to the human façade.

"No!" Drucilla said. She shook her head furiously.

"Drucilla, I am not going to hurt you. I did not come here to hurt you. I came to talk to you. Trust me. You will want to hear what I have to say. Can you please calm down so we can have a chat?"

Drucilla looked around and noticed that people were indeed starting to stare and whisper. Drucilla took a breath and tried to calm herself. She reluctantly sat and scooted the chair back up to the table.

"Did Drake send you here?" Drucilla whispered nervously.

"No. Drake did not. I am here of my own volition. I am here because you need my help."

"Your help? Why would I need your help? Did something happen, or were you planning on stalking me until I got myself into a situation where I needed your help?"

"Or until you found my presence attractive enough that you would come to me on your own."

"Oh, so you made yourself into a fishing lure. Got it."

"Drucilla, there is talk in our dominion of your relics. My brothers, and others who are unholy, recently discovered that they are here on Earth. They do not know where or who has them, but it is only a matter of time before they locate them and, in turn, you."

Drucilla started looking around nervously.

"Drucilla, I do not know how or why you have those relics, but I know nothing happens by chance. You are supposed to have them. I have known for years that they have been in your possession. You have certainly been able to appropriate some interesting pieces through your, shall we call it purloined inventory, would you say?"

"I don't know what you're talking about," Drucilla said, breaking eye contact and looking away.

"I am not asking for confirmation about things I already know."

"So what? Are you going to narc me out or something?"

"Why would I do that? I want to offer my protection as I have with your brother."

"I'm not interested in making any deals with you, Lucifer," Drucilla stood up to leave the table.

"Then do not. You can accept my help, deal free."

"I'm fine. I got it." Drucilla turned and started to walk away

"Drucilla, let me offer you a piece of information, no strings attached. They cannot take the relics from you. The relics are useless unless you offer them freely. Think of it as a feature of the enchantment. Do not give them to anyone, even if you think you can trust them. The Unholy can be very effective with glamours and disguises."

Drucilla stopped for a moment and turned to study Lucifer's face. She couldn't tell whether he was lying to her or not. However, she had no good reason to trust him.

If what he is saying isn't true, why didn't he take the rosary? If it were true, it would make sense why he couldn't. Drucilla slowly stepped backward away from Lucifer. She turned and walked off the patio.

"Goodnight, Drucilla!" Lucifer shouted after her.

Drucilla stepped out of the restaurant and gauged how long it would take for her to get back to the hotel. The hotel was about two miles away. *If I walked quickly, I might be able to get there before dark,* she calculated. Her mind played the exchange she had with Lucifer repeatedly in her head. She's now on Lucifer's radar. He knows where she is and the relic she carries. Drucilla stopped in her tracks. *He said, "those relics" explicitly referring to more than one. Do I have more? And who exactly are the Unholy?* Now she was perplexed. Drucilla wrapped her hand over the rosary on her wrist.

Fifteen minutes into her journey, she realized that she was, in fact, not going to make it to the hotel before sundown. Drucilla was still about a mile away and could hear the thump-thump-thump of bass coming from a club on the corner. A line was starting to form to get in; it looked like a lively place.

"Dru?" Drucilla heard her name called out behind her. Drucilla turned around to see who it was in the group of people.

"Yes?" Drucilla replied, looking around.

"Dru. I thought it was you!"

"Oh hey, Kevin," Drucilla said.

Dressed in black pants and a short-sleeved black button-up shirt, Kevin's short, thinning blonde hair was gelled and messy on the top of his head. *Bit of an out-of-style look, but these geeks don't get out much.*

"We tried calling you to see if you wanted to come out with us tonight. I left you a message on your room door," Kevin explained.

"Yeah, my phone has been acting up since I got here. I get the alerts late. Sorry about that." *I also don't really want to hang out with my supervisor.*

"No problem. Do you want to come and hang with us?"

"I'm not dressed for it, but thanks anyway," Drucilla waved as she walked back towards the hotel.

He waved back, and Drucilla continued down the road. Drucilla was debating on whether she should go hang out with them. She didn't know them, but it would give her an opportunity for some human interaction for the remainder of her time in this town. She was going to be here another month. After getting to her hotel without incident, Drucilla decided to change her clothes and meet up with them.

✝✝✝

Drucilla arrived at the club about an hour later. It was warm, so she wore a short, dark-red slip dress and left her rosary on her wrist. Drucilla glanced around the club looking for her team.

"Hey, Dru! Glad you decided to join us," Kevin yelled. He caught Drucilla upon entry.

"Yeah, well, I didn't have much going on tonight."

"Not sure if you've formally met, but this is Tina, Tom, and Valerie," Kevin yelled over the loud music, introducing the folks at the table.

Drucilla shook everybody's hand. "Everyone, this is Drucilla. This is Fiona's daughter. You will probably be seeing more of her since Fiona had to attend to a family emergency."

Drucilla looked around the table and noticed that Tina was an older woman, a little younger than Drucilla's mother, and worked on the actual dig site.

"Drucilla, yes, I believe I will be working with you next week?" Valerie yelled.

"Yeah, I think so," Drucilla shouted back.

"Shots? Kevin called out to Drucilla over the loud electronica music as she arrived at their table.

"Yeah, cool," Drucilla responded while nodding and sitting down.

No one was talking to each other. It was loud, and everyone was just taking in the surroundings. Kevin returned with a bottle of *Dula Stag*, five-shot glasses, and an extra dirty martini.

"Hey, you like lots of olives in your martinis, too!" Drucilla yelled, noticing his choice of drink.

"This isn't for me; it's for you. From that guy up there," Kevin pointed to a man Drucilla couldn't see from the swirling bright red and yellow lights in the room. "I think you have a fan," he grinned.

Drucilla squinted her eyes. She was desperate to see to whom Kevin was referring at the bar. Unfortunately, visibility was lacking from the lights and the smoke in the air.

Drucilla and her group took a few shots each around the table. After about four shots or so, Drucilla finally decided that she had enough courage to find out the identity of her secret admirer. She picked up her martini and quickly walked over to the bar. Upon seeing the gentleman, she exhaled and rolled her eyes. She placed the glass down on the bar in front of herself. "You just can't stop stalking me, can you?" Drucilla asked Lucifer.

"I am allowed to go out and enjoy the world; besides, you did not say goodbye. I was worried that I had scared you off," Lucifer admitted.

"I'm not scared. I don't know if I trust you," she said suspiciously. Drucilla pulled the bar chair out, climbed onto it, and sat next to him.

"Fair enough. Do you not want to sit with your friends?"

"I don't even know 'em," Drucilla said and sipped her drink. "'Just people I work with. Honestly, you're the only person, other than my mom, whom I've said more than five words to in the past week that I've been here. We just met a few hours ago." Drucilla took another sip of her drink.

An attractive Egyptian woman with long black hair dressed in gold walked past Lucifer and flirted with her eyes. He smiled at her as she walked past him. Another woman in red did the same, except this one dragged her fingertips across his forearm as she walked by.

"Does that happen a lot?" Drucilla asked.

"Constantly," Lucifer responded, watching the women walk past.

Drucilla shrugged. "I mean, I get it. Your appearance is, uh, exceptional by human standards."

Lucifer, a reasonably attractive fellow in his human glamour, appeared to be about thirty-five years old and emitted a seductive scent of bergamot, bourbon, and smoke. An effective lure for human women, no doubt.

"Is that a compliment?" Lucifer smiled.

Drucilla shrugged again and finished off the rest of her martini.

Lucifer seemed amused by Drucilla's awkwardness.

"So, tell me, who are *The Unholy*, and why are they after my rosary?" Drucilla asked pointedly.

Lucifer took a drink out of his highball glass and set it down in front of him. "I do not need to ask if you are a religious person. I know you are not, so we can cut out the seven stages of grief and get right to the acceptance part."

"The 'acceptance part'?"

At this point, she felt the world getting fuzzy and unstable. *Apparently, four shots of whiskey and a martini are my limit.*

"I think I need to get some rest," Drucilla slurred to Lucifer as she slid down off the stool.

Lucifer reached over and grabbed Drucilla's arm to stabilize her. "Let me call you a cab," Lucifer said and pulled out his phone.

Drucilla nodded. Another beautiful Egyptian woman walked by and smiled at him. "Well, I can guess what you're going to be doing tonight," Drucilla said. She watched the woman walk past.

Lucifer stepped off the bar chair and held Drucilla by the arm as she walked through the dance floor to the front entrance. Drucilla and Lucifer exited the doors and stood outside. The night air made Drucilla feel a little less fuzzy, but now she was exhausted. Lucifer stood by her side as the taxi came to pick her up.

"Thanks, man," Drucilla said grinning as he opened the door for her.

"Goodnight, Drucilla." He held her arm as she slid into the taxi's backseat.

The taxi pulled away from the club and headed towards the hotel at the edge of the *Al' Asasif Necropolis*. The road that led to the hotel narrowed to a point where it became pedestrian-only several hundred feet from the hotel itself. The driver got Drucilla as close as possible and then let her out in front of one of the narrow, alley-like streets. Drucilla thanked the driver and stepped out of the taxi. There was no way that she would make it the rest of the way to the hotel in her ridiculously high-heeled stilettos. She loosened the straps and slid them off before making her way down the alley. Drucilla was starting to sober up a bit. *Never go to bed drunk unless you want a wicked hangover.*

Drucilla's room was one of several that had direct access to the pedestrian street. Fiona had explicitly asked for that because she felt the convenience was necessary for the odd hours the team sometimes worked. Drucilla dropped her shoes and fished her keycard out of her purse.

Suddenly, Drucilla heard a heavily accented woman's voice yell, "There! There she is!" Drucilla quickly turned and saw the woman from the shop earlier, with two large men headed right in her direction.

"What the fu—" Drucilla gasped.

Drucilla dropped her purse and bolted down the alleyway as fast as possible. The two men were on her heels and the woman was running to catch up, "Bring me that bracelet!" she commanded them.

Drucilla turned and looked over her shoulder; they were right behind her. Drucilla turned left down another alley and ran as fast as her legs would take her. The passage soon gave way to an open desert with nothing but sand stretching out in front of her. The moon was full and, fortunately, illuminated the entire area. Drucilla fled into the desert. The sandy terrain slowed her a little, but she tried to stay on the rockier parts. The ruins of the necropolis were directly in front of her. Drucilla decided to make her way there, hoping she could find a place to hide within the ruins. Her feet were tender from running barefoot, but she made it into an area with maze-like, high rock walls and quickly ducked into an alcove.

Drucilla opened her throat as wide as possible to exhale and inhale deeply without making much noise. The men were walking around slowly, searching for her; they made no effort to be quiet about it. Drucilla heard the woman's voice mumbling something in Arabic. They were coming closer, and Drucilla knew she needed to get moving again. Drucilla dashed straight ahead to a ruined row of burial chambers. She ducked into one of the doorways and hid inside one of the chambers.

Drucilla stood in darkness, silently waiting until she thought it was safe to leave. After a few moments had passed, she poked her head out and didn't see anything moving. Slowly and cautiously, she made her way back through the ruins towards the ruins' entrance. Without warning, Drucilla felt a hand close around her neck. They had been hiding among the stone walls. One of the men grabbed Drucilla and slammed her against a stone wall. Drucilla struggled to pull his hand off her neck, but he held her forcefully steady.

"Her bracelet! Take it from her! I don't care what you do with her," the woman ordered.

The other man reached for Drucilla's wrist, but another hand closed around it first. Drucilla looked aside, and Lucifer had stepped out of the shadows. He grasped her wrist with the rosary and slammed it against the stones, breaking a bead. Drucilla saw the familiar spark of lightning shoot up her arm. The ground started violently shaking all around them. Obelisks and stone hedges crumbled and fell over as the sands shifted and ancient, dry bones found their way to the surface, clawing and grabbing at the woman and the two men. The woman struggled and kicked a skeletal arm, shattering the bones and breaking free from its grasp. The woman screamed and ran away towards the open desert. The two men were not so quick nor so lucky. They wailed and thrashed as more and more skeletal arms dragged them down into the churning sands. As Drucilla watched them disappear beneath the desert, she couldn't help but think of the winged creatures back in California and the similarly gruesome end they had met in the cemetery.

Lucifer shot Drucilla a pointed look, and they both turned in the direction that the woman had fled. Lucifer and Drucilla ran after her. Drucilla stopped short of catching her and reached her arm towards her, silently willing her to halt. A large, billowing cloud formed in front of the woman. The smoke coalesced and whirled faster and faster until a humanoid form burst from the dark, smoky clouds. The form grew monstrously more enormous and towered over the woman. The mysterious being growled as it loomed over her with its long horns and glowing eyes. The horned beast slowly reached out to her to grab her. The woman screamed as she dropped to her knees. She frantically clawed at her chest. Hyperventilating, she let out a final gasp and fell forward onto her face. Her body lay lifeless.

The mysterious beast turned to look at Drucilla and Lucifer with fiery eyes. It seemed to study and regard Lucifer for a moment. With a loud, low growl, it finally dispersed in a plume of smoke.

Lucifer and Drucilla stood shoulder-to-shoulder and looked at the woman's body. Drucilla looked back at Lucifer with amazement. "A Jinn! How did I manage to summon a Jinn?"

"You did not summon a Jinn. That is an Ifrit, and he is the guardian of the necropolis," Lucifer said with certainty.

"But I thought that I…" Drucilla mimed the motion of reaching her hand out to stop the woman.

"No, that was not of your own doing. It was just fortunate timing and an amusing coincidence," Lucifer smirked.

"Why didn't it attack us?" Drucilla asked, looking at the place where the Ifrit dissipated.

"I can only assume that we did not appear to be a threat," Lucifer shrugged.

"He looked like he recognized you."

"He recognized what I am—an Unholy," Lucifer said.

"Ok, ok, I really need you to explain this whole *Unholy* thing," Drucilla demanded.

Lucifer and Drucilla walked through the desert back toward Drucilla's hotel.

"Ah, not so intoxicated now?" Lucifer asked.

Drucilla glanced over to him, unamused at his attempt at snark.

"That would require that you understand the true history of the universe," Lucifer said.

"I've got time…"

"Very well," Lucifer said. He straightened out the sleeves on his jacket. "There are three factions in the universe: The Divine, The Unholy, and The Cataclysms. Let's start with The Divine. Ophanim are the oldest Divine race of celestial beings. They belong to the highest cosmic order known as Thrones. Thrones are so ancient that they exceed the comprehension of time. As far as anyone knows, they've always existed. To humans, they appear as a whirlwind composed of interconnected, eye-covered rings of burning blue fire with four wings. They reside in the cosmos, where material elements begin to take shape. They maintained the cosmic harmony of life in the universe. There are ten known Thrones in existence, and each Throne is the representation, embodiment, or master of an aspect of life and existence of all beings, celestial or terrestrial."

"I've seen those before in old Catholic engravings and woodcut art," Drucilla interjected.

"Possibly." Lucifer nodded. "Gaia is the Throne of Life and Fertility. Calliope is the ruler of Death. Nova embodies Arcane Knowledge, and Time belongs to Kairos Fatia. Then there are the Material Elements: wood, metal, and stone, which are a part of Gathos' realm, and the Environmental Elements: wind, water, fire is Aurora's domain. Furthermore, Min is the Throne of Spirit and Morality, Astronomy is the realm in which Urania rules, and Cybele rules the Animalia kingdom."

"Finally, there is the mightiest Throne of all: Thoth. He is the creator of universal knowledge," Lucifer explained.

"So, Thrones made humans?"

"I am getting to that," Lucifer said. "With the Thrones being the masters of these fundamental constituents, they required assistance to bring each of their contributions to fruition. They created a lesser race of Divine celestial beings known as Seraphim, or Angels, as they are now commonly known. The purpose of the Seraphim is to carry out the necessary duties in the making of the grand experiment of life. There is a hierarchy in the Divine realm. Ophanim, which are the highest order of Thrones. Then, Seraphim, that could be Virtues or Seraphs."

"How do you fit into this? Are you a Seraphim?"

Lucifer shot Drucilla a cold stare as if he was offended by the question. He promptly ignored her inquiry.

"Now, to your question. The Nephilim were the first human hybrid. The Nephilim were half Seraphim. To make the Nephilim hardier to sustain existence on earth, they needed four essential elements: oxygen, carbon, hydrogen, and nitrogen. This new hybrid was nearly perfect, except they were obstinate and physically overpowering with an unlimited lifespan. Their vast intellect allowed them to evolve faster than the experiment allowed for, which caused them to revolt, become unhinged, and be unresponsive towards their makers. The Thrones, struggling to control them, decided to end the experiment and the Nephilim altogether."

"Wow, so no more Nephilim," Drucilla surmised.

"Trial and error, as you humans say. The new experiment was what is now known as Human Beings," Lucifer continued, motioning to Drucilla.

"Humans, made from the same four elements as the Nephilim with the Seraphim aspect removed, and cosmic essence added in its place," Lucifer said.

"What's 'Cosmic Essence'?"

"Cosmic Essence is you; your soul, I suppose would be the best interpretation. It is what makes you unique. It is what drives you to learn, grow and evolve. Unlike their predecessors, humans are unique as they never stop evolving," Lucifer explained.

"I get it," Drucilla responded.

"Humans were considerably more docile and responsive than the Nephilim. To prevent them from revolting and to control their rapid procreation abilities, they would also become physically and mentally weaker as they aged and eventually die after a brief period—roughly a century per human life. This experiment was so successful, beyond the highest expectation of the Thrones, that the Thrones reproduced these human-type beings on multiple planets around multiple stars in multiple galaxies. However, not every Throne agreed to populating the blossoming new universe with so many humans. Their concern was that they might try and take over the Thrones with their sheer numbers. This notion caused a rift between the Thrones and even some of the Seraphim."

"So, you were one of the Seraphim who took issue with how the universe was created, right?" Drucilla asked.

"I am no Seraphim," Lucifer spat.

"Oooookay. Sorry," Drucilla groaned.

The sun began to creep up ever so slightly towards the horizon as the sky changed from navy blue to deep orange. They continued to walk from the desert back onto the street.

"The dedication that some of the Thrones had to humans had caused the Seraphim to become obsolete and created tension in the Celestial Empyrean. Some of the Thrones decided that they no longer needed the assistance of the Seraphim, tossed them aside, and subsequently ignored them in favor of the humans. Other Thrones refused to follow this new universal order and decided to create their sovereign order, claiming the first planet Eorthe, which you call Earth, as their property. This action enraged other Thrones and Seraphim. A war broke out over Eorthe. The war eventually ended with three Thrones along with myself and seven of my brothers being cast out of the Celestial Empyrean to the Infernal Sphere beneath Eorthe. My brothers and I are known as the Seven Kings or the Kings of Hell. All inhabitants of The Infernal Sphere are *The Unholy*," Lucifer said.

"I don't understand. Why are the *Unholy* considered wrong? This seems like a blatant miscommunication. Maybe if you all talked about it, you could have resolved your differences. 'Just saying," Drucilla commented as she timidly glanced at Lucifer.

Lucifer gave Drucilla s slight smirk; he found her naïveté endearing.

"In addition to the Divine and Unholy factions is a third faction of Seraphs known as the Cataclysms. Seraph of Death, Harbinger of Misery, Champion of Scourge, and Patron Saint of Calamities. The purpose of the Seraphs is to serve as executioners or exterminators of so-called failed experiments. They act as a service to both the Divine and the Unholy regarding human beings of the universe. The Seraph Azrael leads the Cataclysms. Azrael and his assemblage are autonomous and exist outside of the hierarchy. They are bound to neither the Divine nor the Unholy," Lucifer said.

"Is the war still going on?" Drucilla asked. She stepped up to the entrance of her hotel room.

"It's at a stalemate. The Thrones disappeared from existence and have been missing from the dominions for eons. Currently, the Seraphim are in command of the Celestial Empyrean and still rule to this day; while we rule the Infernal Sphere," Lucifer responded.

"So why do the Unholy want my rosary?" Drucilla asked.

"That is a little more complicated. Let us just say that whoever controls the relics could potentially shift control of Eorthe to another faction. Your rosary contains more power than you will ever know," Lucifer said.

"I'm beginning to see that," Drucilla responded. She ran her fingers over the beads.

"Your time on Earth is short, Drucilla. That is by design. I will leave you with one warning: Never let the relics out of your possession, Not for your mother nor a close friend. When you die, a new heir will be chosen."

Drucilla looked to her door, and as luck would have it, her keycard was still in the door lock slot. She turned the door handle and then turned back to Lucifer.

"Lucifer, you keep saying relics. I don't—" Drucilla stopped mid-sentence when she realized Lucifer was no longer behind her. "…have any other relics."

Drucilla looked around. Lucifer had vanished.

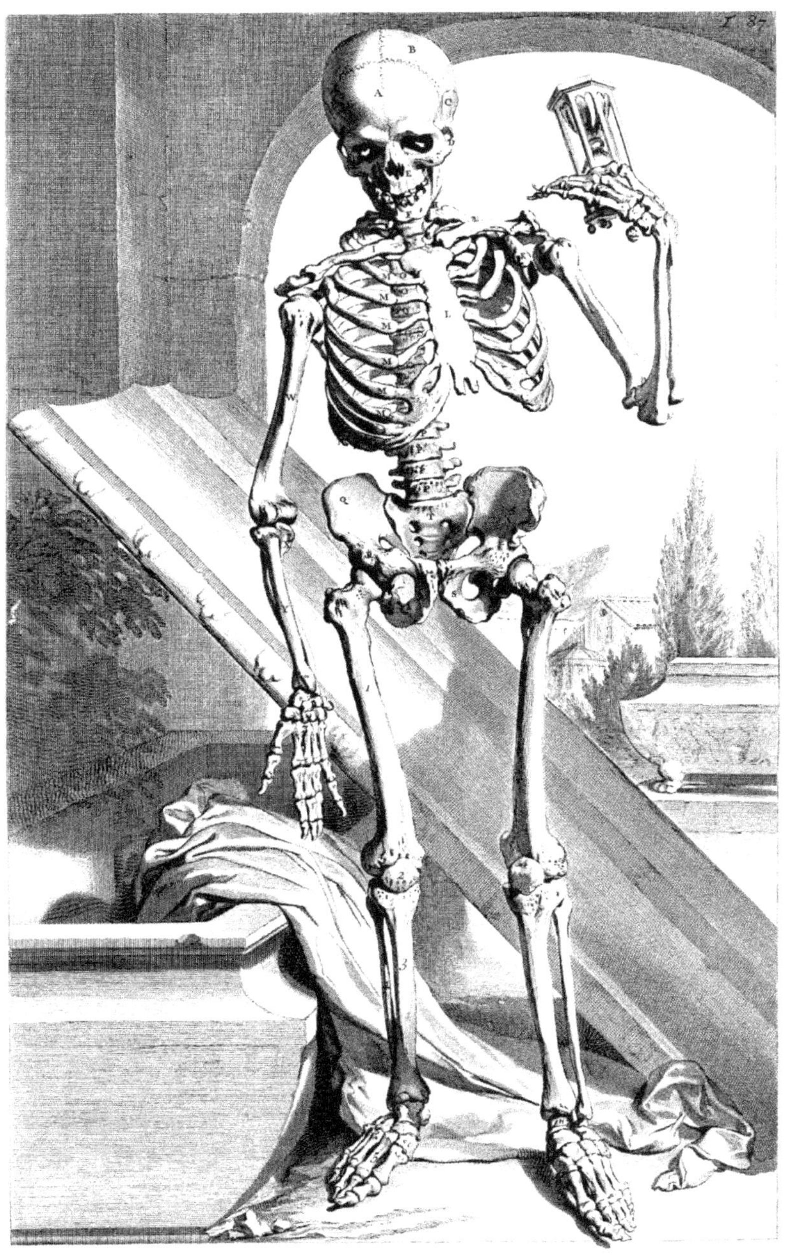

CANTICLE SEVEN

As Drucilla entered the warmth of Adrian's mother's house on that bitter cold winter day, she noticed that the wake was small and intimate. Roughly twenty people spread out between the living room and dining room. Drucilla attributed that to the weather; she didn't think anyone wanted to venture out on a day like this. It didn't usually snow in southern California, but the occasional freeze happens. Adrian's mother's house was a large two-story colonial house with modern appliances and contemporary décor, something out of those modern home and gardening magazines. Relatives and family friends from three generations filled the living and dining room. The air was heavy, with emotion only outweighed by the distinct scent of pastries and cold cuts.

Drucilla scanned the room and saw a few classmates from high school. No one she was particularly close with, but good friends of Adrian. There was an easel set up near the buffet table. It was taken from Adrian's senior photos. His bright smile, barely overshadowed by his light amber eyes and smooth mocha complexion, made him look particularly angelic. Adrian was a beautiful man. Drucilla never really respected that before because she had seen him nearly every day when she was growing up. Adrian was funny, courageous, and no matter what, he'd never let any tragedy or bad experience shape his life. Everything would just roll right off his back; he'd beam his megawatt smile and move onward. Adrian was someone Drucilla always wanted to be but never had the nerve.

Drucilla remembered when he snuck a concoction of mostly gin and ginger soda to her graduation in a thirty-ounce tumbler. She was hammered by the time she had to walk on stage and get her diploma. Drucilla remembered tripping down the stairs. *Mom was so pissed off.* Drucilla giggled to herself as she reminisced about it.

"Drucilla!" Arms extended to her as Adrian's mother pulled her into her chest and hugged her. She was dressed in black lace and a fancy mourning hat complete with beaded embellishments and a small lace veil. Mrs. Parker's eyes were puffy and red. Drucilla squeezed Adrian's mother tightly. Drucilla noticed that she always had the best hats. Drucilla was sure half the reason she went to church on Sunday mornings was to show off her newest crown.

"I'm so glad you could come," Mrs. Parker said. She tried to force a smile.

"I'm sorry I didn't make it to the funeral, I…."

"Don't you worry about it," Mrs. Parker said, cutting her off, "This is where he would want you to be anyway."

Drucilla hated funerals. She always tried to dodge them when and where she could. She felt like she was slightly betraying Adrian because of all people, Drucilla should have been at the funeral, but Adrian knew how Drucilla was always absorbed in her own world since Drake left. She was sure he would have understood.

"No, Mr. Parker?" Drucilla asked.

"I think he's at the funeral home, dealing with some details," Mrs. Parker nodded. *Clearly, she's covering for him.* Drucilla suspected.

"How have you been? I haven't seen you in a couple of years," Mrs. Parker asked.

"I'm ok. I just got back from Greece last month. It was an experience, to say the least. I was in Denmark last year for a few weeks uncovering boat graves. You know, Viking burials? Egypt and India before that. These past four years since I graduated UCLA have been quite an adventure," Drucilla replied while inwardly thinking: *I learned that angels and demons are real, that humans are an experiment, and that I can raise the dead with a rosary. Oh, and I also made friends with the devil!*

"That's fascinating; you'll have to tell me more about it one of these days." Mrs. Parker smiled and then looked over Drucilla's shoulder at the newly arrived guests.

"I need to speak with you when I get a moment; it's important," Mrs. Parker said, "Give me ten minutes?"

"Sure, of course," Drucilla politely acquiesced.

"Oh, and there's some lavender buttercream cake in the kitchen. It was Adrian's favorite. He told me it was yours, too. 'Help yourself," She smiled, patting Drucilla's cheek softly before walking away.

Drucilla walked through the living room and into the kitchen. There was a rudimentary lavender cake set out on the dinette. The color wasn't as bright as when Adrian would make one, and the embellishments were elementary at best. Adrian was a fantastic pastry chef. Everyone else's attempts just seemed mechanical and heartless.

The kitchen door swung open, and to Drucilla's surprise, Katia was standing in the doorway. She was taken aback by seeing Drucilla. They were both friends with Adrian, so it made sense for her to be there.

"Hi," Drucilla said nervously.

"Hey," Katia nodded back stiffly.

They stood in the middle of the kitchen, awkwardly silent, just looking at each other. It had been years since they said even a single word to each other. Drucilla looked at Katia's hands and noticed a wedding ring on her third left finger with an enormous diamond in the center.

"Are you here with your husband?"

Katia broke her concentration and looked at her hand. "Oh yeah. Todd is here with me."

"Well, congratulations. That's awesome." *Of course, his name is Todd.*

"We were married last summer. We eloped. We didn't have a big wedding or anything, so we didn't invite anyone…" she said nervously, as her eyes darted around the kitchen, trying to look at everything but Drucilla.

Drucilla nodded.

"Well, what about you, Dru? Are you here with someone?"

"Uh, no. There isn't someone, unfortunately. I mean, there was for a bit, but uh, not anymore."

"I see. That's too bad. I'm sorry," Katia said. She looked down for a moment before looking back up to Drucilla.

Drucilla shrugged. Drucilla and Katia seemed to be fumbling their way through the awkward conversation as well as could be expected.

"So, how's the archaeology thing going? 'You work with your mom now?"

"I did. I'm taking a break, trying to figure things out. I don't know if I want to continue with archaeology anymore. I resigned a couple of weeks ago. I'm going to move up to Washington State soon, so …yeah."

"Oh? What's up there?"

"Mom is selling the house in LA. She's moving to Florida with Grandma. Grandma is selling her house in Washington, and I'm going to buy Grandma's house and live up there for a bit. I'm thinking of opening an art gallery. You know, until I figure out what I want to do next."

"That's really great, Dru. I'm glad things are going well. You always were a stellar artist."

"Well, it won't be my work that is being shown—just a place for local artists. Well, I may show my work. I don't know," Drucilla paused for a moment. "So, I heard you ended up going to UC Berkley. What did you study?"

"I received a degree in bioengineering. I'm doing cellular and genetic engineering for a company called *Varstadt* in San Francisco."

"Like gene editing and modifying; stuff like that?"

"Yeah, kinda, I mean something like that," Katia nodded and looked at the ground. She glanced back up at Drucilla. "Hey! I see City Councilman Drake on the news a lot. I hear he's going to run for Governor?"

"I guess. I don't know. We don't have much contact these days."

"He left for the military pretty suddenly after high school, didn't he?"

"He did. He went into the military for two years. Then he shuffled off to Harvard. He got his Doctorate in Poli Sci and is City Councilman now, and I uh…." Drucilla scrunched her nose and shook her head like she was trying to shake something out of her mind, "Yeah…I don't really want to talk about Drake, if that's ok?"

Katia nodded and rocked on her heels. "So, Killian and Sierra. That's wild, right?" Katia asked, trying to keep the conversation rolling.

"Yeah, your brother and my cousin, we could potentially be in-laws soon."

"Well, um, I'm going to get back to Todd. It was good to see you," Katia said.

"Yeah, good to see you too."

As soon as Katia left the kitchen, Mrs. Parker beckoned to Drucilla from the back stairs in the kitchen that led to the second floor.

"Dru! Dru!" she whispered loudly.

Drucilla turned around, and Mrs. Parker motioned for Drucilla to follow her. They headed up the stairs to Adrian's bedroom. It looked the same. Lavender netting was draped over the windows and bed, interlaced with fairy lights and big, bold silver stars, colorful masks, and framed pop-art prints. Everything was flashy and colorful. Oddly, it looked as if he hadn't lived in the room for a few years. You could tell from the out-of-date home decor magazines stacked neatly on his nightstand, which wasn't all that odd, but the lack of anything current was a giveaway.

Mrs. Parker shuffled through the high-piled pink fur rug and sat on Adrian's bed.

She held a shiny black box and fought back her tears. Drucilla sat beside her. Mrs. Parker looked up at Drucilla and slowly handed the box to her. Drucilla accepted the box and studied her face.

"Is this Adrian?"

Mrs. Parker nodded slowly.

"I want you to take him," she said, placing her hand over Drucilla's hand.

"Are you sure?"

"Please, take him. He loved you so much. I feel he would be at peace with you, and his soul could finally rest."

Drucilla looked down at the box for a moment. She understood, but she was a little angry that she understood. Drucilla knew this was about Adrian's father. She nodded and hugged Mrs. Parker. She released Drucilla and started to cry. They sat together for a few moments, and then Mrs. Parker patted her face dry with her handkerchief. She inhaled deeply, looked around the room, and then stood up, straightening her hat.

"Do you mind if I stay here for a moment? I'd like to take a little time…it's just so surreal. Would it be ok with you?"

"Honey, you stay as long as you need, and if there's something of his you want to take with you, please feel free," she said and then added in a shaky voice, "This room is going to be gutted and most of his things given away. Mr. Parker is going to make this his new office." Mrs. Parker looked around the room, clearly upset that her son was about to be erased. She then gingerly ambled to the door and quietly left the room.

Drucilla waited until Mrs. Parker was away a few moments and then looked around the room. She turned her attention back to the urn and noticed it had a lid. Drucilla slid her hand over the glossy black box. She curiously shoved her thumbnail under the lip and attempted to pry it up. It didn't budge. Drucilla pulled out her keys and tried to force the key under the edge. With a crack and a pop, the box lid started to separate.

"Oh my God! Girl, are you really trying to look in the box?" Drucilla heard Adrian's surprised voice behind her.

"Shit!" Drucilla yelled, startled. She fumbled and dropped his urn to the floor.

"Girl, you are morbid! I cannot believe you were going to do that!" Adrian shouted. "Wait, you can hear me?" Adrian asked, surprised.

Drucilla turned around very slowly. She wasn't sure whether she wanted to see his face. Reluctantly, Drucilla looked up to the voice.

"Adrian," she said, looking at his face. He looked exactly as Drucilla remembered him—flawless. She started to tear up.

"No, no, don't do that shit. I've seen enough of that bullshit this week," Adrian waved a finger in her face.

Drucilla quickly wiped away the tear that was forming under her eye.

"Yeah, I can see you. I don't know why, but I see you," Drucilla sniffled and gave a shaky smile. "Can anyone else see you?"

Drucilla picked up the urn, studied it curiously, and then looked back at Adrian.

"Honestly, I think it's just you. I mean, I've been hanging around here for four days now, and no one can see me or hear me. I think Mama can sense that I'm here, or maybe she just wants to think I'm here."

Drucilla stared at him in disbelief.

"I see Katia is here…," Adrian said, changing the subject.

"Adrian, what happened to you?" Drucilla said, cutting him off, ignoring his question.

"Oh, you didn't hear?"

Drucilla shook her head.

"Well, it was an accident; let's just get that out of the way. My Sir and I were doing a little experimentation with, uh, asphyxiation." He made air quotes around *asphyxiation.* "I don't remember much, but I blacked out. The next thing I remember is the morgue, and then I'm here in the house with my parents. My dad was yelling at Mama about how she needed to be quiet about their degenerate, homo kid and just tell everyone that I drowned in the bathtub. You know, gotta keep the ol' Deacon's image maintained. Did you know that asshole isn't even here?" Adrian said, disgusted. "That son-of-a-bitch didn't even allow my funeral to be held in the church! They had it at the funeral home."

"Yeah, I didn't see him," Drucilla said quietly, "Your mom said…."

"Let me guess; Mama made up some shit about why he isn't here?" Adrian said, angrily cutting Drucilla off. "Pssh. He is probably shopping or getting a *handy j* from Miss Sylvia in the church closet. Whatever," He scowled and crossed his arms.

"Eww…" Drucilla laughed, sniffling.

"I am not kidding. Ol' Deacon gets up to all kinds of perverted stuff. He doesn't think we know, but everybody knows," Adrian winked and nodded.

"Why does your mom stay?"

"Where's she gonna go? She can't divorce him. That would be scandalous in the church," Adrian said, rolling his eyes. "Church folks are different from normal folks; everything that happens to church folks is everybody's business."

They sat in silence for a moment.

"Do you want to come home with me?"

"As far as I know, I go where that box goes," he pointed to the urn in Drucilla's hands.

"She gave me your ashes."

He paused and looked at Drucilla and nodded. "I heard," Adrian said, unsurprised.

Drucilla looked at him empathically.

Adrian scoffed, "I am not surprised. Ol' Deacon doesn't even want a crumb of my dead gay ass in the house, does he?"

"I don't know how to answer that."

"It's fine; I don't wanna be here anyway," he shrugged and waved it off.

Drucilla walked over to his vanity table and picked up his red-framed ridiculously bougie sunglasses. She put them on and looked at herself in the mirror.

"Can I have these?" Drucilla said, admiring herself, turning her head from side to side.

"I suppose. It's not like I have a use for them," Adrian said, leaning against the wall next to Drucilla.

"I think that he would love for you to have those," Mrs. Parker said, poking her head back into Adrian's room.

Drucilla took the glasses off and folded them up as Mrs. Parker walked back into the room. She leaned her head to the side and looked at Drucilla lovingly.

"Don't be embarrassed. I've been talking to him too," Mrs. Parker smiled. "I like to think he's popping in from time to time to see how we're doing."

Drucilla gave her a weak smile.

"I just wish Mr. Parker was here to see how much love Adrian has in this house." Mrs. Parker rubbed her hands together.

"Don't worry, Mama. I'm sure he's getting his own love right about now," Adrian said, knowing she couldn't hear him. He walked over to his dresser grabbed the end of it with his legs straddling the corner. He tightened the grip on it and started wildly humping it. "Oh, Ms. Sylvia! Oh! Oh! Yes! Ms. Sylvia," he started flailing his head and arm like he was on a mechanical bull.

Drucilla burst out laughing but quickly held her stomach and promptly changed it into a coughing fit without missing a beat.

"Oh honey, are you all right?" Mrs. Parker rushed to her side, patting her back.

"I'm fine; throat is a little dry. Dehydrated, I think." Drucilla coughed.

"Let's get you some water," Mrs. Parker said. She took Drucilla's hand. Drucilla grabbed the urn as they left the room.

Drucilla looked over her shoulder and mouthed the word *asshole* at Adrian.

Adrian bit his bottom lip, scrunched up his nose, and continued to thrust his hips against the dresser forcefully.

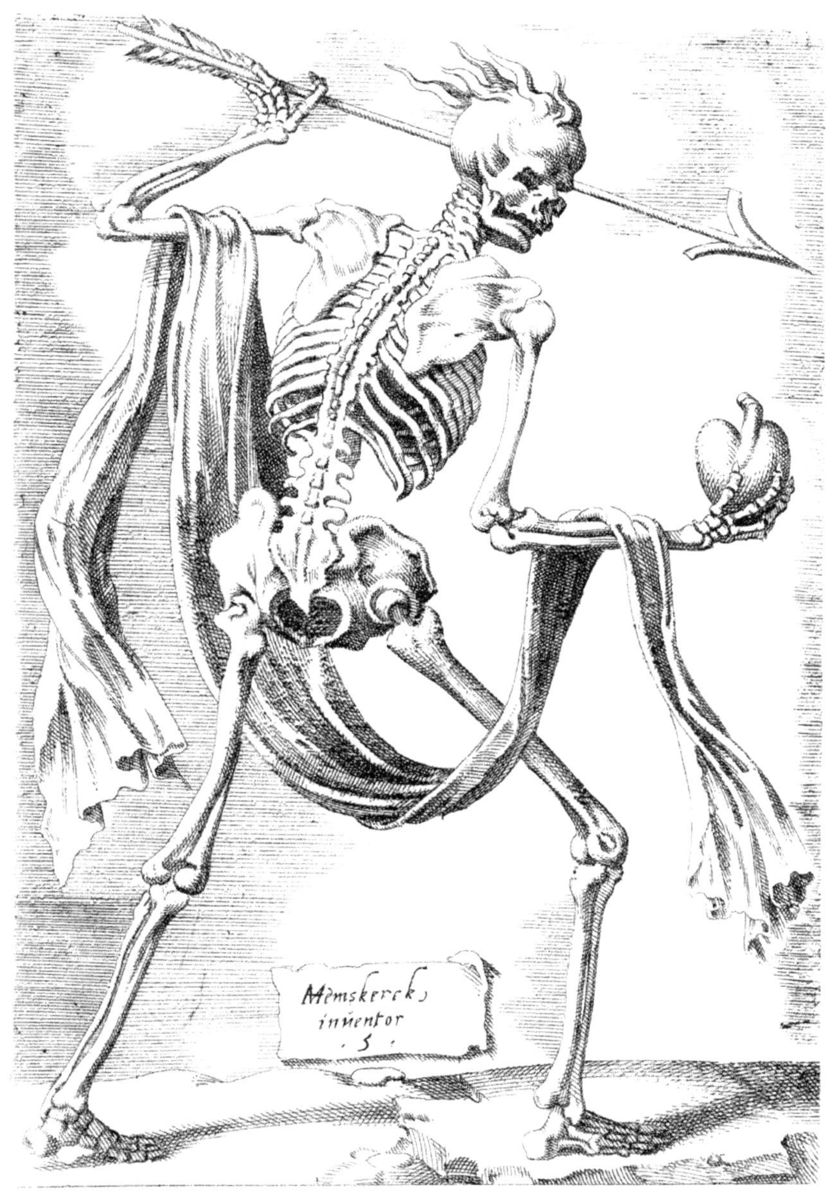

Hemskerck,
inuentor
. S .

CANTICLE EIGHT

"It will have blood, they say: blood will have blood."
—Macbeth

Drucilla sat at a large mahogany table in a room full of people dressed in business attire. To her right was her brother. He slowly turned his head to face her. He nodded and then turned his attention to the rest of the room. Everything seemed to move in slow motion. Drake sat in an oversized elaborately carved chair like a King's throne. Drucilla sat in a similar chair. They were the only two people at the table who sat in these elaborate thrones. It's as if they were a king and queen at court, but they were dressed in modern attire instead of medieval clothing. Drake slowly interlaced his fingers together, looked around the room, and leaned forward. Drucilla turned her head to the left to look out of a large cathedral window. The trees were made of silver, and the sky above was red. As Drucilla stared through the window, the sky began to glow brighter and brighter until bright white light shot through the windows in giant rays, filling the room. The light scared her. She turned to look at Drake wide-eyed. His eyes widened in fear at the increasing light.

Bzzzt bzzt bzzt

Drucilla awoke startled by the buzzing of her phone rattling on the coffee table.

What the hell was that about? She shook her head, trying to shake off her dream.

Drucilla, irritated, snatched her phone to see who dared to awaken the slumbering beast. She let out a heavy sigh. Groggy-eyed, she pressed the answer button. "Mom?" she said, rubbing her face and yawning.

"Oh, were you asleep?" Fiona asked.

"Yes," Drucilla responded, clearly annoyed. "Is everything ok?"

"Everything is fine over here, honey. The weather is wonderful, and Grandma is going out for walks on the beach every day!"

"Great, that's great, Mom," Drucilla said, trying to snap herself out of her haze.

"Are you all moved in?"

Drucilla looked around her newly acquired Victorian house in Port Townsend, Washington. She left Los Angeles a couple of weeks ago to start her new life in a new state and get her gallery off the ground.

Boxes on top of boxes lined the living room wall of her grandmother's former house. The walls were in desperate need of a new coat of paint. It was flakey and discolored in some places. Drucilla thought it was initially supposed to be a light, teal green, but she wasn't sure. She felt the last time it was painted was when her mother was a child. The push-button light switches with tarnished brass plates were dated, and so were the kitchen appliances from 1988. It was Drucilla's house now. She was free to make it her own.

"Moved in? Yeah. Unpacked? Heh, ask me next month."

"Listen, I wanted to tell you that Drake is giving his campaign speech in a few minutes; I didn't think you wanted to miss it."

"Drake—" Drucilla cringed. *You mean the asshole that completely forgot that I exist. The one that never called, never emailed. Hell, I didn't even get a text. The last time I heard from him was two Christmases ago when he decided to send me a Christmas card with his signature clearly printed on the cards. I didn't even get a handwritten signature.*

"Yes, your brother. You can stream it on the KTLA website," she advised sagely, as only someone who had just learned about streaming could do.

"I'm not even sure I have a brother."

"Honey, don't be like that. You know how busy he is. He's doing some pretty big things."

"Yeah, big things. Yay, the golden child," Drucilla mumbled morosely.

"I didn't mean that you weren't…."

"Mom, Mom, it's ok. It doesn't matter. Um, I'll check it out, ok?"

"Drucilla, don't act like this. We're family."

"Tell <u>him</u> that!" Drucilla growled. "I'm not the one that gave everyone the middle finger and walked out!" Drucilla could feel her blood pressure rise.

"Drucilla, you need to calm down!"

"Mom, I'm not going to have this conversation right now!"

"I'm sorry, I woke you. I'll call you later," Fiona said in a calm voice.

Drucilla hung up the phone, pulled out her laptop from her backpack, and placed it on the coffee table in front of her. She navigated to the KTLA website and waited for the live stream to start. She threw a small blanket over her stomach and leaned back on the couch. If she was going to have to watch this, she was going to be comfortable. The stream came to life, and Drake walked confidently onto the stage and stood behind the podium. He looked good. His hair wasn't in its usual disheveled, wanna-be, bad boy style. He was wearing an obnoxiously expensive designer suit and appeared confident and self-assured.

"He's going to attempt to relate to all Californians wearing that?" Drucilla mockingly commented to the live stream. She shook her head and rolled her eyes.

Drake paused for a moment behind the podium and began to address his constituents. "Thank you, California! Thank you for the great privilege of being able to address this convention this evening. Please allow me to skip the vague rhetoric. Let me instead use this valuable opportunity to deal immediately with the questions that should determine this election and that we all know are vital to the people of California."

"We know all too well the struggles and the uncertainty that Californians are facing. Jobs are at an all-time low, and Californians are worried about themselves, their families, and their futures. Our current governor said that he...."

Disgusted, Drucilla leaned over and slammed the lid closed. It was all she could take. She was too angry with him to deal with any of his bullshit rhetoric.

She looked over at the mantle where the shiny, black box that contained Adrian's ashes sat. Drucilla had draped her rosary over the top. She hadn't worn the beads for a while; not since she moved into the house a couple of weeks ago. But today, she picked it up, wrapped it tightly against her wrist, and pulled her sleeve down over it.

"Well, Adrian," Drucilla said, looking at the box. "It's not Seattle, but I hope it's close enough."

The squeezing feeling in the pit of Drucilla's stomach nagged at her and demanded sustenance. She figured that now would be an excellent time to venture out for food. She picked up her phone and placed her earpods in her ears. She grabbed her coat and opened the door to walk out of her house.

"Hey, be careful out there," a voice said behind her.

Drucilla turned around to face the voice. Adrian manifested before her.

"I'll be back before the streetlights turn on, Dad." Drucilla glanced at Adrian.

"Smartass."

Drucilla stepped out and locked her front door with her phone app. It was early evening as she took a walk down to Water Street. Water Street is the central hub of Port Townsend, conveniently located five blocks east of her house. It had only been two weeks since her arrival, and she still hadn't had a chance to walk around and check out things.

After walking several blocks, she arrived on the main strip and stood in front of her newly leased gallery space. She peeked inside one of the windows. Her leased space was on the ground floor, the corner of one of the Victorian buildings. The new space had many windows that let in an abundance of natural light. She wanted this gallery space as soon as she saw it. Fortunately for her, the previous tenants of the location only had a week left on their lease and were not renewing. She jumped on the opportunity. Drucilla noticed the electricians were finally finished hanging all the pendulum and directional lighting. It wouldn't be long now before she could open her gallery to the public. She only had a few pieces to hang for now, but that would soon change. She wanted a space where she could exhibit all the local talents in the area. Her goal was to give them a place to display and sell their art. She thought about selling her own, but she hadn't created anything in years.

Many of the shops on Water Street were closed for the night. Drucilla casually walked down the sidewalk away from her gallery. She spotted an antique furniture store across the street and three businesses down. She walked across the street and stopped in front of the building.

Ford Bradshaw & Co.

The sign was painted in gold, gilded lettering on the protruding wall sign and across the large glass window.

Drucilla opened the door to a pleasant tinkling bell. Upon entering the shop, she noticed it was unique but dark and moody. The main area had a lot of usual antique décor. The shop walls were lined with cherubs, vines, and fillagree. Tall bookshelves, full-length antique mirrors, and a fantastic mahogany dining set graced the floor as you walked in. Drucilla checked the price tag: $8800.00. It was lovely and super spendy.

"Nice, isn't it?" said a large man behind the counter. He was tall, attractive with heterochromatic eyes; one green, one grey. It was apparent he was a powerlifter.

"Yeah, I love it. I don't eighty-eight hundred dollars love it, but it's great," Drucilla said, flinching at the price tag.

"That table is from 1915. It's completely carved by hand, from the rosettes to the clawed feet. It was made by a man named Douglas Foster. This dining set was an anniversary gift for his wife, Mabel. The story goes, it took him about ten months to complete. He hand-selected the wood and had it imported from the Bahamas. She fell in love with a similar dining set when they visited Nassau during their honeymoon. He attempted to duplicate it for her. I think he did a great job."

"Wow, if that isn't love, I don't know what is," Drucilla said in amazement.

"Are you looking for anything particular?"

"I'm just looking to outfit my new place. I moved here last week."

"Oh yeah? Where 'bouts?"

"I bought the pink Victorian on Beecher Street," Drucilla explained.

"Oh! Miriam Blackwood's house!"

"Yeah, you know her?" Drucilla asked, more than a little surprised.

"Yes, I do. Miriam used to walk up and down this street almost daily for years. She had this little chihuahua—"

"Pinky."

"Yeah, Pinky! How do you know her?" he asked with a chuckle.

"I'm her granddaughter."

"Wow, that's awesome. I haven't seen Miriam in over a year. Is she all right?"

"Yeah. She's not great, but she's ok. She doesn't have Pinky anymore; he passed about eight months ago. She's moved to Miami with my mom. Mom is taking care of her now that she's has retired herself."

"Well, that's cool. I'm Dominic, by the way. Dominic Novikov." Dominic came out from behind the counter to shake Drucilla's hand. His hands were large and engulfed Drucilla's hand. He seemed larger now that he was standing next to her.

"Drucilla. You can call me Dru." Drucilla paused a moment. "So, Ford Bradshaw and Co. Who's the Co?

Pretty Boy Floyd? 'You keeping bags of money in the back?"

Dominic's mouth gaped open. "Would you believe you're the only person ever to get that reference?"

"Yeah," Drucilla said. She nodded and grinned. "I would."

Dominic laughed.

"I came down here in search of food. Where's a good place?"

"*Siren's* is across the street. Do you like burgers and beer?"

"Oh yeah."

"I'm about to close here in a sec. Would you like to join me? Miriam and I were good friends. She was also a good friend of my uncle."

Drucilla nodded. She needed to make some new friends here, and this seemed like a good opportunity.

Dominic closed his shop. He and Drucilla crossed the street, made their way up to the pub's second floor, and sat at a table facing the ocean. They dined on thick, greasy cheeseburgers piled high with everything and washed it down with local craft beer.

"So, did you come here alone?" Dominic asked.

Drucilla thought about that question for a moment. She couldn't exactly tell someone that she's only just met that she lived with her best friend who wasn't among the living. "Yeah. I did. I've leased the bottom floor space of this building. I'm opening a gallery in a couple of weeks." Drucilla said, stuffing fries into her mouth.

"Oh really? Are you an artist?"

"Nah, not really anymore," Drucilla said modestly. "I draw a bit, but that's about it. I'm actually an archaeologist. I minored in Fine Art and decided that I wanted to devote more attention to fine art and help out local artists, you know to get recognition and have a place to display their work. My mom is an archaeologist, too. I used to go on digs with her when I was growing up. I thought my mom was the coolest and had the coolest job, but I also realized that it's incredibly lonely, and you don't get to spend much time at home. What about you?" Drucilla took a sip of beer.

"Well, I grew up in Seattle. Moved-in with my girlfriend right out of high school. That lasted all of one year. Like you, I have a fascination with archaeology and artifacts, but also antiques. I bought the place across the street about ten years ago from my uncle. He wanted to retire, so I just took over for him. I've been here ever since."

Drucilla smiled and nodded. Drucilla caught the TV out of the corner of her eye. They were replaying highlights from Drake's campaign speech on cable news. She squinted her eyes to try and hear better as if that would help. Dominic followed Drucilla's gaze to the TV, as well.

"Oh, yeah, that guy. He's been on all the political news channels a lot. Apparently, he's some young badass; he thinks he's the next JFK or something. His speeches are like crack for these political junkies. They think he's amazing. I think he has some good ideas for California. I mean, he seems like a douche, though."

Drucilla snorted beer into her nose, trying not to laugh.

Dominic glanced at her and smiled. He turned his attention back to the TV screen. "Oh hey, he has the same last name as you."

"Yeah, he looks like me too," Drucilla said. She looked at Dominic and winked as she took another drink, seeing if he caught on to the reference.

He looked at Drucilla, looked at the TV, then looked back at Drucilla again, eyes wide. "Wait... " He pointed at the TV, then to Drucilla.

"Twins."

"No shit?" He looked back and forth again. "That's your brother?"

"Unfortunately."

"Hey, I'm sorry about the douche comment."

"Nope. You are absolutely correct. He's a raging, penis-headed douchebag." Drucilla nodded again in agreement.

"No love between you two, I take it."

"Not even a little bit." Drucilla glanced at her phone to see if she had missed any calls, then placed it face down on the table.

"I mean, it's kinda cool. What if Drake becomes president one day?"

Drucilla glowered at him, completely unamused. "Don't you start that crap, too?"

"Well, I bet you don't have a Russian grandmother screeching in your ear with: Why don't you be a doctor like father and brother. Why don't you give great-grandchildren? Why don't you make something of yourself like, brother?" he mocked in a high-pitched, heavily accented Russian voice and miming a hand puppet with his thumb and fingers.

"Oh, yeah? Today, just like twenty minutes before I came down here, my mom literally called me and was mad because I wasn't excited about my brother's speech. Apparently, I should be falling all over him because he's doing 'Pretty big things.' Her words. Whereas I am not!"

"Ouch. Well, truth be told, I was actually considering being a doctor at one time." Dominic absent-mindedly picked at the label on his beer bottle.

"Oh yeah? What happened?"

"I signed up to be an EMT right after I split up with my ex to see if it's even something I could handle. I took the courses and got certified etcetera. Let me tell you, the job of an EMT is the single most fucked-up job you could ever have."

"Oh, now you gotta tell me the horror stories," Drucilla demanded, getting comfortable in her seat with a beer in hand.

Dominic leaned in and put his bottle down in front of him.

"'Got a call one afternoon. A dude killed himself by face-planting into a big container of potassium cyanide."

"Wait, what's potassium cyanide?"

"It's like a harsh chemical used commercially for fumigation, electroplating, and extracting gold and silver from ores. Anyway, his co-worker became sick just by walking into the room. The dude had to be carried out by EMT in hazmat suits. Apparently, he got cremated because the levels of fumes around him were way too high to have him in a casket at the church."

"Oh, gnarly! Ok, I have one…" Drucilla set her bottle down. "When I was in college, a guy tied a tow strap around a pole and the other end around his neck. He drove straight back into a ravine. Decapitation. Girlfriend was in the passenger seat."

"Aww, man!" Dominic laughed and then paused in thought for a moment, "That's nothing. I had a case where a guy was pulled over, out of gas. His buddy was there with a gas can. The gas tank was on the traffic side. A semi came by and hit his buddy. 'Guts for about a mile…Random body parts all over the road. His shoes and ankles were still right next to the car."

"What? No way!" Drucilla said incredulously. "Ok, ok, I have one," Drucilla said, attempting to one-up. "When I was living in LA, my neighbor's uncle who lived with them, did like, a bunch of cocaine and got into the shower. He ended up passing out or going into cardiac arrest probably both; I can't remember. Basically, he fell over and knocked the knob all the way to the hottest setting. He ended up dying but was boiled from the heat of the water. His family was out of town, so he sat under the running shower for two-to-three days before being found."

"Ho-holy shit, dude!" Dominic cringed.

"Ok, my turn," Dominic said, taking a sip of his beer. "I had a customer here whose teenage son committed suicide by tying a rope to the garage door opener. So, when she and her husband came home and pressed the garage door opener, it hung him."

"Oh, my God!" Drucilla exclaimed as she covered her mouth in shock. "Do you know how utterly messed up that is?"

"Dude, she's still super fucked up over it," he said, taking another drink and leaning back in his seat.

Drucilla paused for a long moment before saying, "I had a friend accidentally die from asphyxiation," she said, staring out the window. "My best friend, actually. He died about six months ago. He used to go to these fetish clubs in LA, you know with leather and bondage, etc. I told him to stop doing it. They do all kinds of drugs and stupid stuff at this particular club he frequented. It was kind of known for that. The guy he was playing with accidentally strangled him or something."

Dominic's face fell. "Oh, wow. I'm so sorry, Drucilla."

"I'm fine. My friend's dad is a real piece of human garbage. See, he's a Deacon in a Baptist Church and refused to accept his son was gay. I remember in Jr High when he was in eighth grade; his dad caught him making out with another boy in his treehouse. His dad beat him so hard that he couldn't come to school the next day. Shortly after that, his dad made him go through conversion therapy. Didn't work, obviously.

"Damn, that's really awful," Dominic said. He shook his head empathetically.

"I have his ashes in my house. His dad didn't want them in his house," Drucilla said, looking up at him.

Dominic sat silently, staring at her.

"I just weirded you out, didn't I?" Drucilla said. She buried her face in her hands. "See, this is why I have such a hard time making friends. I say weird shit."

"Clearly, you're new here. I'm the town weirdo," Dominic chuckled. Dominic set his beer down and cocked his head to the side. "Dru, do you believe in God?"

Drucilla thought about it for a minute, hoping he wasn't going to proselytize to her before she answered.

"If you had asked me that question ten years ago, I would have firmly told you, no. But now, today?" Drucilla shook her head. "There's something, but it's not God," she said. She leaned back in her chair. "Wow, I have had entirely too many of these beers, and I really need to head home."

"Do you need me to walk with you, or are you ok to go alone?" Dominic asked like a gentleman.

"You know, normally I'd say no, but would you mind?" Drucilla pleaded.

They walked down the stairs across the street and made their way up Beecher Street to Drucilla's house with only sporadic streetlights lighting their way.

"Dom, why did you ask me if I believe in God? Do you?"

"It's complicated," he responded. "As I alluded, you're not the only one that's weird."

"What does that mean?"

He was silent for a moment as if he was trying to figure out how to say what he wanted to say. "How do you feel about the occult, superstitions, religion in general?"

"Well," Drucilla thought for a moment. "I think there are things out there that steer and even influence us to do certain things for some unknown celestial reasons. We don't get to know what they are, because they either won't tell us or can't tell us. Either way, there are things that humans can do that they can't, and they need to slip their hands up our backs and move us around like hand puppets. I think they're assholes. Just because we have souls and are mortal, not these grandiose celestial beings, does not mean they're better than we are. If they're so great, why don't they just concern themselves with their own drama and not worry about us peons? You know why they can't? Because they're weak, and they know they're weak. They need us; we don't need them." Drucilla said. She looked expectantly at Dominic before realizing that she had just gone on a tangent.

Dominic froze in his tracks and just stared at her.

"What?" Drucilla said, looking back at him.

"Dru, that's the most honest and relatable description I've ever heard," Dominic said, clearly resonating with her words.

Drucilla shrugged.

"Who are you?" he asked, squinting at Drucilla to examine her more closely. He appeared to be joking but also serious.

"Me? I'm certainly not the one that Lucifer chose. I can tell you that much," Drucilla threw her arms in the air and kept walking.

"Lucifer? What?" Dominic said, clearly confused.

"Ok, maybe I'm just drunk, but I'm going to be really honest with you, Dominic, and if you run from me, that's on you," Drucilla wagged a finger at him.

"Ok, you have my attention."

"For all intents and purposes, I think I'm a witch of some sort. I don't know. I have this weird ability to see spirits. My best friend, Adrian, who died? Yeah, he's a ghost, and he lives with me in my house. With that, we're just scratching the surface."

"Go on," he said, crossing his massive arms. Drucilla couldn't tell whether he believed her or not.

"California's beloved Drake Blackwood is a result of a deal with the devil, and because of his stupid deal, he's abandoned me, and I hate him because he chose power over me," Drucilla suddenly felt dizzy. She had kept this bottled up for so many years; it was like a dam breaking. Everything that she had been holding back was spilling out. Drucilla started tearing up. "My stupid brother gets power and influence, and all I got was a stupid rosary that—" Drucilla stopped and held up her wrist, the amulet from the rosary dangled in the glow of the streetlight.

The look on Dominic's face suggested that Drucilla had said too much. "Rosary," Dominic said, his eyes fixated on the beads and amulet.

Drucilla exhaled and pressed her lips together; she feared she had said too much.

Dominic paused for a moment like he was accessing something in his brain. "Do you mind coming by my shop tomorrow night after closing? I think I have something you need to see," Dominic said abruptly.

"Like what?" Drucilla asked suspiciously.

"I'm not being creepy, I swear. I think I have some information that might interest you. You're totally free to say no. No hard feelings," Dominic said with sincerity. "But that rosary. I've seen it before, and if it's what I think it is, Drucilla, you have something powerful there. Like on a celestial level. I'd also like to get a better look at it if you're ok with that."

"You aren't the first one to tell me that it's powerful. I just don't know what that means."

"You know, for a minute there, I thought you were nuts. But now, after seeing that rosary, I know that you're telling me the truth," Dominic said, reassuring her.

CANTICLE NINE

"What if these objects could speak? What would they tell you about themselves?" —Ari Berk

"Can I hold it?" Dominic asked quietly with a hint of excitement in his voice.

"Uh, yeah, I guess." Drucilla slowly and cautiously extended her hand out and poured the beaded rosary into his giant, upright palm. Dominic slowly pulled the relic towards him.

"Amazing," Dominic said in a low voice.

Drucilla watched him scrutinize the beads and amulet, on guard and ready to snatch it back from him if given the slightest hint that he may run away with it. "Is it what you were expecting?"

Dominic paused, bouncing the pools of beads in his palm. "It's heavier than I imagined." He hastily made his way to his desk and swung the desk lamp over to his hands. He picked up a loupe placed it into his eye socket. He closely inspected the blood-red ruby beads in a better light. "You have to tell me how you acquired this," he said while studying and rolling a single bead between his fingers.

"Well...I found it. Kind of," Drucilla said uneasily.

He pulled the loupe from his eye and looked at Drucilla. "How do you just find something like this?"

Drucilla swallowed hard. "I've never told anyone, but I guess there's really no point in keeping it a secret now. I mean, now that you know it exists," Drucilla said. She rubbed the palms of her hands together hard to alleviate anxiety. She quickly walked over to an antique stool near his desk and seated herself. Dominic continued to examine the rosary.

"Dru, this isn't something that someone just leaves lying around. I hope you understand that…Not something like this."

Drucilla inhaled deeply. "Drake and I went to Palermo, Italy with Mom about fifteen years ago or so. There was an area of the catacombs that was recently discovered. The wall had just been knocked down so we could access the new area. They had the lighting all rigged up and had just started the process of excavating. Mom oversaw the cataloging of the remains and artifacts. I was wandering around alone. You know, just exploring. I accidentally kicked over a rotted box that contained the rosary. No one was there. No one would have known it was missing. I just sort of stuck it in my pocket." Drucilla shrugged. "I didn't think I was doing anything harmful at the time. It's just an old rosary. Nothing special. Nothing important. I mean, people are buried with rosaries every day. You know?"

"Did you ever learn anything in particular about this rosary?" he asked, not quite ready to surrender the relic back to Drucilla.

"I didn't, honestly. I mean—" Drucilla exhaled slowly while she fumbled for the right words to say. "Ok, this is going to sound insane, but remember when I told you I'm like a witch or something? Well, there's more to it than that. I can apparently control the dead with it. You know like, wraiths, zombies, and ghosts. Things like that. I don't know how to explain it. It's all because of this rosary."

"Go on." He gestured for Drucilla to continue. Dominic was apparently unfazed by the development that Drucilla could perform necromancy.

"Well," Drucilla reached out for the rosary, which he handed back. "There have been some incidents. Once when I was around eighteen, I willed a Banshee into manifesting," Drucilla said. *And subsequently ripped the heart out of a classmate,* Drucilla thought the last part in her head.

"Just a couple of years ago, I managed to gain control of a bog witch that was attempting to kill me in Denmark. Like, I actually ordered it to stop attacking. I'll have to tell you the story another time; that was crazy. Then there was this time when some guys tried to steal my rosary in the Valley of the Kings, and I summoned the dead to help me, and an Ifrit popped out, but that may have been unrelated. There are so many other stories," Drucilla explained.

The loupe fell out of Dominic's eye and clattered on the desk as he stood with his mouth hanging open.

"Dominic?" Drucilla waved her hand in front of his face.

He shook off his shock. "That's wild. Is that all you know?" he asked.

"Well, I mean, yeah, it's not like this thing came with an instruction manual."

"Actually, the relic kind of did. That's what I wanted you to see," Dominic said. He hurriedly ran to the corner of his office and opened an old-fashioned secretary with a skeleton key.

"Geez, Dominic, where do you get all this stuff?" Drucilla was amazed at his shop's library of curiosities that probably contained every occult and religious reference book ever written.

"This? This is nothing compared to what I have in my house," he quipped.

Dominic pulled out a worn-out leather journal with lots of small papers shoved within the pages. He vigorously flipped through it. "Here!" he exclaimed. He pulled out a folded slip of old paper and handed it to Drucilla. "I knew I saved this old journal for a reason."

She unfolded antique paper carefully to reveal a rough sketch of the rosary and a bit of Latin writing. "I can't read this," she said as she handed him back the piece of paper.

"You don't read Latin?"

"No. I mean, I know some words, but no. I don't really understand the language."

He grinned at her and said, "Check this out." He placed the paper on the desk and shined the light over it. He pointed to the beads on the drawing with the words written on them.

"*Tenensque lenticulam sanguine—*" Dominic said and looked at Drucilla, hoping she'd recognize some words. "It did say something about *Deus* at the top here at one time, but the writing had rubbed away."

"Ok, I get the blood part, *sanguine*."

He pointed to another couple of words, "*Angelus captum*."

"Ok, I still don't understand."

"Hold up the rosary," he said. He turned the light to Drucilla's hands. "What do you see?"

"Ruby beads," Drucilla said unenthusiastically.

"No, look closer," he said. He handed Drucilla the loupe.

"Ok," Drucilla replied. She placed the loupe in her eye.

"Do you see it now?"

Drucilla continued to examine the beads. "No, I don't, I—" Drucilla responded but stopped. Just before she could finish her sentence, she caught a slight movement inside one of the beads. "Wait, it's moving!"

"*Angelus captum* means captive angel. *Tenensque lenticulam sanguine* means blood vial," Dominic said, hoping she was going to put it together.

"Captive angel's blood. You're telling me this is angel's blood?" Drucilla pulled the loupe from her eye.

"You see, these aren't ordinary beads. They're vessels of Divine blood," Dominic explained.

Drucilla dangled the string of beads to the light again in disbelief. She studied the movement inside as she turned the necklace back and forth—the light played against the crystals' rudimentary facets.

"Look here." He picked up the amulet end. "This isn't 'just a lion. In many cultures, the lion is a symbol of power and knowledge, and to some, it means king. If you look closely—these are wings, and these crisscrossed rings with eyes represent the Ophanim. You can kind of see it because the image is so small. This bird is an Ibis, the Egyptian symbol of Knowledge, and the portrait at the bottom is Apollo, which is another persona. The image is Ophanim Thoth, order of the Thrones."

Drucilla squinted to try to see what he was talking about. She placed the loupe back in her eye socket for a better look.

"On the edge here, on the back, these lines—" Dominic pointed out.

"You mean these cuts and dents?"

"The cuts are too uniform to be natural," he replied. "This looks like Angelic Script."

Drucilla handed the loupe back to him. He placed it back into his eye socket and studied the edge of the crucifix.

"What does it mean?" Drucilla asked eagerly.

Suddenly, as quickly as his excitement started, it faded.

"What?" Drucilla asked, "What does it say?"

"It says a name, possibly the owner of this relic," he said, unsure of himself. He was concerned with what he was reading.

"Ok, who owned it? What's the name?" Drucilla asked eagerly.

"That can't be right," Dominic said quietly. "I'm afraid my knowledge of angelic script is fleeting," he mumbled, confused but nervous.

"I don't understand. What are you seeing?"

Dominic leaned back against his desk, crossed his arms, and looked at Drucilla inquisitively. "What do you know of Hell? I don't mean where the damned are sent, but what do you know of the hierarchy of demons and other inhabitants?" Dominic asked.

Drucilla quickly shook her head as if to shake off poor hearing. "Hell?" she wondered where he was going with this.

"There are seven Kings of Hell," he started and made his way over to his bookshelf. Dominic pulled out an old Demonology book. He flipped through the pages until he found the one he was looking for. "There's Mammon: avarice, Asmodeus: constitution, Leviathan: lechery, Amaymon: malevolence, Hades: wrath, Belphegor: acumen, and Lucifer: pride." Dominic placed the book on the table in front of her. The book was open to images of crudely sketched depictions of demons in various poses.

"I know Hades and Lucifer," she responded gravely.

"There are also Queens, but only three," he continued, "Aurora: Elements such as air, fire, and water; Nova: Arcane knowledge, which is sorcery and magick, and then there is Calliope: Death, necromancy."

Those are the names of Thrones Drucilla thought.

"Where are you going with this?" Drucilla asked. She didn't need another lesson in Throne's lore.

He flipped the page to Calliope's image. It was a drawing of a woman with long black hair, a skull for a crown, a dress made of flayed flesh, and she held a large sword. Her fingers interlaced with the hair on the head of her foe. She pulled his head back as if she were about to slit his throat or stab his neck. Her foe was a muscular man with tight curly hair and four wings in a state of defeat. Behind her was an army of the dead: ghosts, corpses, and specters.

"Here, this," he said. He put his finger on the image of a long rosary around her neck. Drucilla looked at her relic, back at the picture, then at Dominic. "The name on your relic is Calliope," he said.

"Wait, you're telling me this rosary belongs to a Queen of Hell? This is crazy. It's just a drawing. It doesn't mean anything. I mean, why would a queen just leave a relic like this for me to find? Why me?" Drucilla asked, agitated at the notion.

"You're not asking the right question. Not, why me, but rather to what end? She didn't lose her relic. She specifically placed her relic in your path," Dominic responded.

I've been told that before, Drucilla recalled her conversation with Lucifer. "I just don't know why a Queen of Hell would give up her rosary. Clearly, this relic wasn't meant for humans, right?"

"I don't know. Maybe Calliope wanted to see what a human would do with it. Why do we purchase toys for cats? To watch them play with them. I can't speak to her intentions, but it's clear to me that you were meant to carry it. She chose you," Dominic said with chilling certainty.

"Why does everyone keep saying that?" Drucilla asked, becoming irate. She stood up and began to pace the library.

"Who else told you that?" Dominic asked.

"Never mind, it's not important."

"Who else knows that you have the rosary?"

"Drake, my friend Katia," Drucilla replied. "Um, Lucifer," she said under her breath.

"Lucifer?" Dominic asked, surprised. "You—you talk to Lucifer? Did I hear that correctly?" Dominic asked.

"It's a really long story."

"Ok, so Lucifer, the King of Hell, knows you have this, and he didn't try and take it from you?" Dominic asked, surprised and a bit like he didn't believe her.

"Apparently, it goes against Celestial Law or something. The relics must be given freely. I guess it doesn't work if someone takes it." Drucilla hoped she didn't sound like she was clinically insane.

"Celestial law. Of course." Dominic held his finger over his lip, his thumb tucked under his chin as if to be deep in thought. "Drucilla, we have a lot of work ahead of us."

Drucilla smiled to herself. She was elated that she might get some answers to the myriad of questions she had for a large portion of her life.

Me & te fola Mors feparabit, *Ruth 1.*

CANTICLE TEN

*"Corrupted from memory, no longer the power. It's
creeping up slowly, the last fatal hour."* —Ian Curtis

Election Day arrived, and Drucilla was dodging her mother's calls. Drucilla knew she wanted to talk about Drake. Adrian was busy measuring for wallpaper, starting with the longest wall in the living room. Drucilla sat on the couch, updating her website with new photos of artwork to be displayed at the gallery that week. It was a typical Tuesday otherwise.

"That's like the fourth time she's called," Adrian stated impassively.

"I'm busy. Mom can watch the stupid election without me."

Adrian stared at Drucilla for a moment, then looked back at the wall and contemplated.

"Hmm, this wall alone is 30-feet in length and 11-feet high."

Drucilla glanced up at him, then went back to her work.

"This wallpaper is 20.4- inches wide and 32.80-feet in length per roll," Adrian said, figuring out numbers in his head.

"So?" Drucilla said and shrugged.

"So, I think I misjudged. We only bought six rolls," Adrian crossed his arms in annoyance.

"Go order more," Drucilla responded, half-paying attention.

"Girl, I had this shipped from France. It's going to take another eight weeks to get here, and now my entire week is ruined! Everything hinges on this wallpaper!" Adrian pouted angrily.

"Put part of it up. I don't know, pick something else. Stop being so dramatic."

"Shut up, ok?" Adrian was visibly annoyed by Drucilla's lack of caring. "This is my project."

Drucilla rolled her eyes and continued to stare at the screen.

Bzzzt bzzt bzzt

"Oh, just answer it already!" Adrian glided out of the room in a huff.

Drucilla sighed and pressed the answer button on her phone. "Mom..."

"Dru! He's ahead! Isn't that amazing?" Fiona said excitedly, "Are you watching?"

"No, Mom. I'm not. I'm working."

"Drucilla, this is important. You know if this were you, he'd be watching," Fiona attempted to guilt-trip her.

"Heh. No, he wouldn't."

"Why are you acting like this?"

"Mom, he doesn't give a damn about either of us. He never calls. He never emails. Hell, when was the last time you saw him in real life, not on TV?"

"That isn't the point. We support each other in this family," Fiona retorted.

"No, you and I support each other. Drake just does whatever the hell Drake wants. Face it, Mom. We aren't part of his life. He's too busy being a dick!"

"Oh shit. She's gonna blow," Adrian mumbled as he peered at Drucilla from the kitchen, punching his fist into the newly risen dough in a bowl in his arms. Adrian fumbled, and the bowl hit the ground with a loud clang.

"Honey, what was that?" Fiona asked. She heard the crash.

Drucilla shook her head and held her finger to her lips to shush him.

"It's the cat, Mom. I gotta go. He's destroying the house," Drucilla said and pressed the end button and placed her phone face down. Frustrated, Drucilla got up off the couch. She headed to the closet and grabbed her coat. "I gotta run to the gallery really quick. I'm missing files. I grabbed the wrong flash drive. Do you need anything while I'm out?"

Adrian sat on the end of the coffee table, crossed his legs, placed his hand on his face, and thought. "Something tall, intense eyes, muscular, maybe a nice beard."

Drucilla groaned and threw her arms in the air.

"Some nutmeg and heavy cream. Oh, and some of that amazing sourdough culture. None of that stuff in the packet; the real stuff they make over at Casey's. You know, in the jar."

†††

Drucilla rushed to the office of her gallery to search for the flash drive. She shuffled through her top desk drawer but couldn't find it. She was sure she put it there.

"Looking for this?" Lucifer stood behind her, holding up the flash drive between his clawed fingers.

"Thanks." Drucilla walked over to Lucifer, snatched the drive, and walked past him.

Lucifer leaned against one of the foundation beams and crossed his arms. "Do you not want to know why I am here?"

"Nope."

"I thought you might want to know the election's outcome." Lucifer smiled and admired his claws.

"Well, you thought wrong. I'm pretty sure I can find out online, anyway."

"Drucilla, are you still angry with me?" Lucifer asked.

"Just don't, ok?"

"Very well. Are you even going to introduce me to your new friend?"

"Dominic? And why would I do that?"

"Well, we will have to meet eventually," Lucifer said pointedly.

Drucilla sighed heavily as she headed to the front door of the gallery. She stopped and turned back to Lucifer. "Can I ask you something?"

"Of course..."

"Does Drake ever talk about me?"

Lucifer dropped his grin and gave her a stern look, trying to read her face. "No."

Drucilla stared at him for a moment as she tried to read his expression.

"But, in his defense, he is ramping up his new role. He is the new governor of California, after all."

They stood silently, looking at each other for what seemed like forever. The church bell rang in the distance five times, breaking the tension. It was five o'clock.

"I have to run a couple of errands for Adrian. I need to go."

"Drucilla—Drake does not hate you. I know you think he does, but he has bigger things to worry about."

"Great. That was super helpful." Drucilla glared at Lucifer.

Lucifer shrugged and blinked out of existence.

Drucilla's phone started vibrating in her pocket. She pulled it out. Coincidently, it was Dominic. She answered, "What's up?"

"It appears California has a new governor. He won with 92% of the votes. That's insanity. The most any candidate has ever had at any point in history."

"I'm glad I don't live there anymore," Drucilla responded. "Hey, you wouldn't want to come over for dinner Friday, would you?"

"Yeah, I guess I could manage that."

"Come by at seven. I think it's time you met someone," Drucilla said. She smiled to herself.

CANTICLE ELEVEN

"Master of puppets, I'm pulling your strings." —Metallica

Drake and his advisors moved swiftly through the California Senate chamber through a second-floor corridor. The corridor was a large room decorated in red and mahogany furnishings. An electric reproduction of the original gas chandelier hung from the coffered ceiling. A hand-carved dais capped off recessed bays framed by Corinthian columns that supported the gallery above. The massive stone columns were softened by tied-back, dark red curtains that could be drawn closed for privacy. High arched windows ran along the bottom below rectangular pane windows. Behind the rostrum, there were two chairs with red velvet cushions, reserved for the president *pro tempore* of the Senate and the assembly speaker, but they were never used.

Drake and his entourage entered the hallway towards the governor's private office through double doors.

"If you will all excuse me, I have some private business I need to attend," Drake said.

"Sir, you have a press briefing in forty minutes," an advisor reminded.

"I'll be ready," he replied, ushering them out of his space and closing the doors behind them.

Lucifer leaned against the recessed window bay and looked out the window. He turned to Drake and grinned with satisfaction.

"Congratulations, Governor." Lucifer approached Drake, who sat behind his desk, searching for his laptop.

"I believe it is in your top drawer," Lucifer said, gesturing to the desk.

Drake stopped and looked at him puzzled, then opened the desk drawer. He slid the laptop out and opened it.

"So, where have you been?"

Lucifer shrugged as if to indicate he wasn't doing anything in particular.

Drake raised his eyebrow suspiciously at Lucifer. "I have a conference shortly, and I need to look at the talking points. I don't want to go out there unprepared."

"No, of course not. I want to give you some time to adjust to your new surroundings; also, we have an appointment this evening,"

"Tonight? I can't tonight. I have a charity dinner event, uh thing," Drake said, staring at his laptop screen.

"Oh yes, ten thousand dollars a plate, is it?" Lucifer asked. He strolled over to Drake's desk.

"Yeah, something like that."

"Well, they will just have to accept your donation without your attendance." Lucifer reached across the desk and slammed Drake's laptop closed.

Drake stood up and put his finger in Lucifer's face. "Look, you wanted me in this position, and now I need to do my job," Drake growled.

"This is not the job. This is a necessary step to get to your real purpose here. Now, I need you to make up an excuse for why you cannot attend. Do I make myself clear?" Lucifer said. He got within inches of Drake's face.

Drake shoved his laptop off his desk with a loud crash, knocking his lamp to the ground. Papers went flying. The door to his office abruptly swung open.

"Are you all right, Sir?" a guard in a military uniform asked. He scanned the room and saw no one other than Drake.

"Yeah, I'm just a bit uh, tired. I accidentally dropped my laptop," Drake said, straightening his suit and chuckling to break the tension.

"I'll get someone to clean this up for you right away," he said. The guard looked puzzled and closed the door slowly behind him.

Lucifer sat halfway on the edge of the desk with his arms folded and looked at Drake.

"I have to say, out of every one of my subjects, you are the most frustrating," *But also, the most formidable,* Lucifer thought to himself, *and I suppose that it is a double-edged sword.*

Drake sat back down behind his desk and put his face in his hands. "How's my sister?" Drake asked calmly. He looked back up at Lucifer.

"Funny you should ask. I saw her a few weeks ago on Election Day, to be exact. She was not at all happy with your success."

"Yeah, I suppose she's not my biggest fan."

"You will be pleased to know she has made a new friend—a large fellow. Not someone with whom you would want to tangle. He seems to be keeping a watchful eye on her," Lucifer added.

"A boyfriend?"

"More like a guardian, a right-hand man…if you will," Lucifer said, half-joking.

"That doesn't mean you get to renege on our deal. You promised to protect my sister," Drake reminded him.

"And I have been. If Drucilla gets in over her head, I will be there. Believe me; I know everything that is going on in her life, regardless of whether she wants to talk to me or not. I do not think she likes me too well either. Granted, not as much as she hates you, but I do not think I am hitting any high marks with her."

"Well, you're literally the Devil," Drake gestured to Lucifer's appearance.

"She is a tiny angry little thing, is she not?" Lucifer chuckled to himself.

Drake stood up and walked around his desk. He thought for a moment and then picked up his desk phone. He pressed a button and held the black corded receiver up to his ear. "Ms. Ramirez? Listen, I won't be able to make the charity dinner tonight." He looked up at

Lucifer. "I have a family emergency. I apologize for the late notice. Please be sure the proper people who need to know are aware? Thank you." Drake hung up and addressed Lucifer, "Ok? Now what?"

"It is time you met with your new colleagues. Your true purpose," Lucifer said, examining his claws.

"You mean your cabal."

"Cabal, secret society, oligarchs, what have you." Lucifer shrugged. "I am certain they will approve of you."

Drake laughed to himself. "I think you have that backward."

"Have the car drop you off at your residence in an hour," Lucifer replied with a smile.

Drake entered the secret chamber and stood just inside the room near a large oval table. Everyone was dressed in black suits with dark red sashes. Some had multiple medallions, while some only had one or two. There was a sort of hierarchy judging by the woman with the most medallions pinned to her dark red sash. Her place was at the head of the table. She stood and waited for Drake to arrive at his seat. "Everyone, I would like to introduce you to our newest member. This is Drake Blackwood: the newly elected governor of California," the woman declared. As the council nodded in cordial greeting, the woman formally requested of Drake directly, "Please, Mr. Blackwood, have a seat."

The room was dead silent as the cabal watched Drake walk towards a vacant seat at the end of the table. Drake looked up at the dark grey walls and noticed what appeared to be painted portraits of past leaders. The cabal seemed to be at least four hundred years old from what Drake could gather from the style of the paintings and the clothing worn.

Drake took a seat. Lucifer sat in the chair directly behind him against the wall and leaned forward. Drake looked back at Lucifer, who extended his hand and pointed to the leader to draw Drake's attention.

"Mr. Blackwood, I am High Priestess De Luca," she said. She paused for a moment to examine him from across the table. "You're quite young—"

"Yes, I am uh, twenty-nine years old," Drake said, clearing his throat and looking around inquisitively. He was the youngest in the room.

"Impressive resume, as well. Harvard with a political science degree specializing in American government, politics, and international relations, and you were top of your class," The High Priestess told the group. "I see you have also spent two years in the military…."

"Yes, that's right."

Drake turned around and glanced at Lucifer and then turned back. Drake felt like he was being interrogated.

"Drake is our rising star," Lucifer said. He got up from his chair and walked around the table. "I handpicked him, specifically for our little family. He is bright, ambitious, brilliant, and adapts quickly. He is one of the better subjects I have had throughout the centuries."

"Lord Lucifer, as always, you have our utmost faith and confidence." The High Priestess respectfully nodded to Lucifer and then turned her attention to Drake. "Mr. Blackwood, we have a small task for you. A project for which we want you to be personally in command." The High Priestess continued her proposal, "We are having a bit of a cooperation issue with one of our business partners. We want you to gain his cooperation…by any means necessary."

An older gentleman to the right of Drake slid a folder in front of him. Drake lifted the cover, glanced at the contents, then closed it again.

"You will find everything you need inside," The High Priestess stated.

Drake leaned back in his chair and laced his fingers together on this lap. "What's in it for me?"

The room erupted into gasps and chatter among the cabal. Lucifer grinned slowly and nodded, clearly satisfied with his response.

"I am sorry…did I hear you correctly?" The High Priestess asked, stunned. "This is for you to prove your worth and viability to the coven, not to make deals. That is not how this works."

"Prove my worth?" Drake asked, moderately insulted by the demand.

The room erupted into chatter again.

The High Priestess looked to Lucifer and back to Drake.

Drake got up and walked around the table. "I was chosen by Lucifer to fulfill a role here within the coven, a role that obviously doesn't exist yet. I wasn't chosen to be a foot soldier. The King of Hell doesn't just groom someone to take orders from a group of aging oligarchs with too much money and not enough ambition to do anything other than watch the world burn by a fire they were too lazy or too incompetent to set themselves."

The room went silent.

"Let's get something straight here. You need me; I don't need you. I don't know who you think I am, but I have no intention of carrying out your menial assignments. If you're looking for an obedient servant to carry out orders, you have the wrong idea about who I am. But if you're looking to lift your coven from this clubhouse and become an actual reputable player, then we may be able to work together. But if this kid's table shit is working for you, stop wasting my fucking time."

The High Priestess seated herself quietly.

Drake–leaned over the table, "What's it gonna be, folks?"

Lucifer beamed with pride and excitement. Drake was performing better than he had anticipated.

CANTICLE TWELVE

✝

Dominic raised his index finger and slowly attempted to prod Adrian, coming closer and closer to his cheek. Adrian slowly leaned back, staying just out of his reach.

"What are you doing?" Adrian asked Dominic and looked over to Drucilla. "I know he's not trying to touch my face!"

"Dominic, maybe try asking Adrian before you touch him," Drucilla suggested, wrinkling her nose.

Dominic dropped his hand and looked at Drucilla. "May I touch him?"

"He can hear and see you. You can ask him."

Dominic was taken aback. "You're right; that was rude." Dominic turned to Adrian. "Forgive me. I'm new to this. It's my first time. Adrian, may I touch you?"

Adrian turned to his side and offered a shoulder to Dominic. "Yes, but be gentle," Adrian was intimidated by Dominic's enormous physique.

Dominic slowly raised his hand again and extended his index finger. He got within half an inch of touching Adrien's biceps.

Adrian started growling and snapping wildly like a wolf. Terrified. Dominic yelled and leaped back, clutching his chest. Adrian burst into laughter. "Your face!" Adrian squealed, clapping and giggling like an insane person.

Drucilla giggled a little.

Dominic looked at them wide-eyed.

"I'm just teasing you. Go ahead, and touch me," Adrian said, grinning.

Hesitantly, Dominic attempted to touch Adrian again. Adrian grinned. Dominic dubiously held eye contact with Adrian. Finally, Dominic pressed his finger against Adrian's skin. "He's cold. I mean, you're cold but solid."

"Well, yeah…I'm dead."

"How does this work? How is this even possible? I don't understand this," Dominic said, pressing Adrian's skin repeatedly. "Why can I touch him? Why doesn't my hand go through him?"

"Settle down there, Cowboy. You keep it up, and we're going to have to take a trip to the bedroom, if you know what I mean," Adrian's eyes flickered as he flirted.

Dominic turned bright red and dropped his hand immediately.

Drucilla started walking around Adrian. "So, this is what I learned," Drucilla said. Drucilla unwrapped the rosary and handed it to Dominic. Dominic looked down at the rosary and took it from her. Adrian faded away.

"Adrian's corporealness is his decision. You know…whether he wants to be solid or ethereal. But his physical presence is short-lived, no pun. He pulls energy from his surroundings. He can exhaust it in a matter of hours. He will dissipate until he can recharge again. I still haven't figured out how some people can see him and others can't. However, Adrian is reactive to a combination of rosary and me. Again, I think. You're holding the rosary, and he's invisible. But he comes back when I put it back on," she explained. Drucilla took the rosary back from Dominic and wrapped it onto her wrist, and Adrian reappeared.

"Where do you go?" Dominic asked Adrian.

Adrian looked at Drucilla.

"He's probably still here, just not corporal. I mean, he can see and hear us, but we can't interact with him," Drucilla said. "Also, he's bound to his ashes. Adrian can travel away from the house as long as I have some of the cremains with me."

"Wow. Clearly, there is a lot I don't know about the relic," Dominic responds.

"When Adrian starts being overly catty with me…" Drucilla unwrapped the rosary again and handed it back to Dominic.

"What do you mean me, being overly catty. Gir…" Adrian lamented as he faded out again.

"Huh…" He stared at the empty space that Adrian had occupied. "So, he's still here in front of us…We just can't see him?"

"Or hear him. He's essentially on mute," Drucilla said. She took the rosary back from Dominic and put it on her wrist.

Adrian became corporeal again.

"Y'all are just rude now," Adrian crossed his arms. "How would you like it if..."

Drucilla took the rosary off again and handed it to Dominic.

They both started chuckling.

Drucilla put the rosary back on her wrist.

"Nuh-uh, you all can make your own dinner. I got better stuff to do than deal with both of you," Adrian complained as he glided out of the room.

"Adrian! We're just kidding!" Drucilla yelled after him.

"Nuh-uh!" he yelled back, gliding to the kitchen.

"He's pissed," Dominic said.

Drucilla looked at Dominic and grinned menacingly as she unwrapped her rosary again.

172

CANTICLE THIRTEEN

"If you're playing with fire, you're playing in Hell." —
Danzig

Drake sat in the Governor's office behind an enormous mahogany desk, with new, heavier lamps. His advisors sat on a long navy-blue pin-tucked chesterfield, quietly chatting amongst themselves as they worked on a speech for another charity event. A large, newly commissioned portrait of Niccolò Machiavelli hung on the wall behind Drake. He typed silently on his laptop.

"I have always wondered what your obsession is with Machiavelli," Lucifer asked. "Ever since you were a teenager. You were far beyond your years. What is it that you find so intriguing about him?"

"Will you all excuse me? I need to make a personal call." Drake said. He looked up at his advisors. Drake didn't need his advisors to think he was insane by speaking to someone who wasn't there.

His advisors nodded and promptly gathered their belongings and exited the office.

Drake inhaled deeply after they left the room and looked over his shoulder at the wall above his head. He then turned his attention back to Lucifer. "He's the most brilliant political philosopher in history. 'It is better to be feared than loved, if you cannot be both.' That quote should resonate with you, Lucifer."

"Touché!" Lucifer laughed.

Drake went back to typing then stopped. "What do you need, Lucifer?" Drake asked pointedly.

"Well…" Lucifer straightened his suit and sat in the chair beside Drake's desk. "I figured you would want to know what your sister and her large friend have been doing."

Drake sat up straight and looked at Lucifer.

"I do not know whether I have mentioned this to you, but you know that your sister is a bit of a thief? A grave robber? She has managed to appropriate many objects here and there from various archeological sites over the years. 'Some quite valuable, others only valuable to, uh… certain collectors."

"Has she been caught by authorities? Does she need legal assistance? Bail? Tell me how much, and I'll cut a check," Drake asked, looking back at his screen.

Lucifer got up and paced around the room, deep in thought. "There are two relics, in particular, that are of the most interest. One, which you well know about, is the rosary of Queen Calliope, which Drucilla wears around her wrist. The rosary contains the sentient blood of a Throne enchanted by Calliope power and cannot just resurrect the dead but control it. She essentially has her own undead army at her fingertips whenever she wants it. Then, there is the most powerful and troubling of the relics: the pen of Queen Nova. This pen writes the greatest symphonies ever written. The greatest novels, treaties, and even works of art were created with this pen."

"What makes the pen so dangerous?"

"The pen is also sentient. It changes appearance, which makes it harder to locate."

"So, it changes appearance and creates amazing works of art. That doesn't sound dangerous."

"That is not the only function of the pen. The pen creates portals between the dimensions. One could simply march an army straight into the Infernal Sphere or into the Celestial Empyrion, and there is nothing that either side could do about it. Also, the pen transforms into a stabbing or piercing weapon," Lucifer said.

Drake nodded, stood up, walked around to the front of his desk, and leaned against it. "You're saying my sister has this pen in her possession, right now?"

"Yes, and apparently, she has caught the attention of my brothers. I do not think I need to explain how catastrophic an outcome would be if she were to relinquish these relics," Lucifer replied gravely.

"I don't think my sister is just going to give them up for the asking. Especially if she knows how powerful they are."

"Your sister is unaware that she is in possession of the pen," Lucifer explained. "That one is the most troubling. Suppose someone were to see it and ask to borrow it. She could give it up freely, and what exactly would stop her from giving it to your mother, her friend, anyone who asked? We can be very persuasive, especially with the right glamour."

Lucifer changed his appearance to look like Fiona and walked over to Drake. Appearing as Fiona, Lucifer sat in the chair in front of him, crossed his arms, and spoke with Fiona's voice and inflection, "She would not know the difference between glamour and the real thing."

Drake blinked a few times at the startling resemblance. "So, tell her not to give up the pen?"

"That is not how the game works, Drake. We are not able to meddle after the game has begun. I cannot explain anything to her. I can validate her suspicions, but I cannot tell her anything beyond confirming what she already knows."

Drake stood silent with his hands in his pockets. He eyed Lucifer with suspicion as he ran his finger over the edge of the coin he carried with him. "But you can protect her from them, can't you? That's part of our pact."

"Yes, to an extent. I have explained that the relics are powerless unless it surrendered willingly; however, protecting her does not have anything to do with explaining that she possesses another Unholy relic."

"To an extent? If her life is in danger because of the pen— "

"Yes, of course, I will step in as part of our deal," Lucifer assures Drake.

"What can we do to head this off?"

"We will need to hide her," Lucifer said, changing back to his usual self.

"How do you suppose we do that?"

"There may be a way. We will essentially have to create a blind spot. It will take the entire coven to do it. I am not powerful enough on my own. We are talking about my brothers, who are kings. There are six others, and I am just one."

CANTICLE FOURTEEN

"Hear me and make all spirits subjects unto me."
—Behemoth

†

Drake and his security team entered a large white dining room. Large crystal chandeliers hung from the ceiling with big, bright crystal swags. The floor-to-ceiling windows were treated in sheer white draperies tied back with emerald-green silk ropes; the floor was a Moroccan pattern in a similar green hue. The dining room held about twenty unoccupied tables, with white linen tablecloths and a bouquet of deep green ferns and calla lilies in tall cut crystal vases. The host seated Drake at a large round table with six chairs in a quiet corner. It was early afternoon.

"My sincerest apologies for running late," The High Priestess said, peering down over Drake as she arrived at the table.

Drake stood up. "Please sit down, Ms. De Luca." Drake took his seat after she did.

"Thank you for meeting with me this afternoon," she said, situating herself.

The conversation halted for a moment as the waiter handed her a menu.

"Oh, no need," she said, waving off the menu. "I'd like the Tuna Tartare with Koshihikari rice and the smoked red beet and oxalis. Mr. Blackwood?" she asked, looking at Drake.

Drake briefly scanned the menu. "The almond-crusted Dover sole would be great." He handed the menu back. Drake watched as the waiter walked away with their order.

High Priestess De Luca placed a napkin on her lap and took a sip of water. "Have you ever been here before?" she asked, attempting to make small talk.

"I have. I believe I've brought a few dates here in the past," Drake clasped his hands and rested his elbows on the table.

"No, Mrs. Blackwood, I take it?" High Priestess De Luca noticed the lack of ring on his third finger.

"Someday. But I don't think you asked me here to talk about my personal life."

"Mr. Blackwood, I think we may have started in a disadvantageous position. I would like to start again. There was a miscommunication, and I would like to rectify our misunderstandings."

"What did you miscommunicate?"

"Mr. Blackwood, allow me to introduce myself formally. My name is Alexandra De Luca of House De Luca. I come from a wealthy Italian family in a small town called Salerno, near Naples in Italy. My family has been involved in this coven for over two centuries. My third great grandfather took part in building this coven when he came to America in 1801. The De Luca name has always led this coven. We have installed many political leaders through the years—everyone from James Polk to Theodore Roosevelt to even you, Mr. Blackwood. I have been the High Priestess of this coven for nearly thirty-five years. You are but the third subject that Lucifer has brought before us. Undoubtedly, you will not be the last," she said. She seemed satisfied with her implication that Drake was just another pawn.

"Are you trying to intimidate me, Ms. De Luca?" Drake seemed almost amused at the idea.

"I want you to understand that your involvement in the coven is contingent on your allegiance and participation. We welcome your insight and your experience. Lucifer would not have brought you to us if he did not feel…." She paused. "We trust Lord Lucifer, unquestionably."

"I see."

"Our coven is deeply rooted in a long-established, time-honored way. Things are done in a particular order by specific members at precise times. We encourage you to ask questions, to understand our ways, and involve yourself wherever you feel your insight and knowledge would be applicable."

"Ms. De Luca, please understand, I am no one's subordinate. Lucifer didn't bring me into the coven to take orders like some lackey. Lucifer is unsatisfied with the way things are being run in the coven."

"Mr. Blackwood, let us not make things more difficult than they need to be. All right? I trust that

Lucifer has a role for you within our coven, but that is for us to decide with Lucifer's guidance," she explained.

The waiter arrived with lunch and placed the plates in front of them. Drake picked up a fork, poked at the sole, and then set it down. He folded his hands and looked at De Luca while she took a bite of her lunch. "Do you know what I think?"

"Please, feel free to speak candidly," she said. De Luca confidently set down her fork and took a sip from her water goblet.

"Niccolò Machiavelli said: 'I'm not interested in preserving the status quo; I want to overthrow it.'"

"That is a very cogent perspective. You clearly understand the purpose of the coven."

"I've learned that just because something always was, doesn't mean it's always the best. I'm not a person who lets tradition or normalcy dictate how I lead. I've learned that if you're passionate about something, you should never let anything stand in the way of greatness," Drake said and paused for a moment. "Right now, Ms. De Luca, you are an obstacle."

De Luca's eyes widened in shock. "I apologize. I don't think I understand what you are implying?" She asked incredulously, clearly offended at Drake's audacity.

Drake glanced up at his security detail and nodded. The three men grabbed De Luca, lifting her from her chair by her arms.

"What's going on here? I am the High Priestess!" she shouted. De Luca struggled to free herself from their grip.

"Early retirement, Ms. De Luca. I'll be sure to inform the coven of your departure." He waved off his security to remove her.

"No! I forbid this!" she shrieked. She desperately kicked and pulled.

The security dragged her through the back door of the dining area; her shouts of protest and anger echoed throughout the restaurant.

"Well played!" Lucifer said, grinning. He leaned back and crossed his legs in the chair beside Drake.

Drake started to eat his lunch.

"Do you know how long I have been trying to rid myself of that woman? My last subject failed, but he was not nearly as ruthless and cunning as you are."

"Are we done?" Drake asked, setting down his fork. He looked at Lucifer sternly.

"Yes, that will suffice," Lucifer said. He peered at Drake inquisitively and felt slightly disrespected himself.

CANTICLE FIFTEEN

"I'll keep it in a hidden place." —Bjork

✝

Dominic and Drucilla ventured to the far end of Drucilla's backyard. They strode across through the dry fallen leaves that crunched beneath their feet. It was a cool mid-autumn evening. One of those evenings where you could feel the rush of cold air descend the mountains into the low-lying areas of the state's northwest corner. They came to a stop at a small structure at the far end of the property. It seemed to be a potting shed that looked somewhat newer from what Dominic could determine.

"Is this what you wanted to show me, your new shed? I mean, it's a nice shed," Dominic shrugged. He shoved his hands deeper into his pockets to keep warm.

Drucilla pressed the combination lock buttons and turned the knob with an audible click. She pushed open the door and hit the light switch on the inside wall. Two small pendulum lights and a couple of swags of fairy lights illuminated the small 10 x 14-foot shed. The tables were lined with terra cotta pots, a few bags of potting soil, a couple of cans of paint, and some gardening hand tools.

"Why do you need a secure lock on your shed? There's not really anything in here." Dominic looked around in case he was missing something.

"It's not what's in here," Drucilla said. She held up her hand and looked around the inside of the shed. "It's what's here." Drucilla stomped twice on the decorative faux-grass rug they were standing on to draw his attention to the floor.

"Something in the floor?" Dominic looked confused.

Drucilla grabbed one end of the carpet and flipped it back to expose a trap door.

"I had this shed built over a subterranean shelter. This shed wasn't here when I bought the house. Drake and I used to play down in this shelter when we visited Grandma. She used to take us during the summer months when we were kids; when Mom was on a dig."

Drucilla pulled the handle up and flipped the trapdoor open, backward onto the floor. The light at the bottom illuminated the cement stairwell. She made her way down the staircase. "C'mon." Drucilla motioned to Dominic as she stepped down further into the shelter.

At the bottom was another door with a lock. Drucilla pressed the combination into that door lock, and it clicked again. The subterranean shelter was small but slightly larger than the shed above by another twenty square feet. The walls and floors were finished, so it didn't smell or feel as damp as expected.

"It's odd that your grandma would have a subterranean shelter here in Washington state, isn't it?"

"I think we've determined that I belong to a weird family," Drucilla said with a smile.

The walls were lined with framed rock-band posters of *The Cure*, *Type O Negative*, *Bauhaus*, and *Siouxsie and the Banshees*. A round clawfoot table with a couple of antique chairs sat on the brown ceramic tile of the floor. A gilded, red Persian rug covered the floor. At the back of the shelter, on the main wall, were floating shelves. There was a myriad of ancient relics displayed, as you'd see in a gallery, complete with backlighting.

"Drucilla. How long have you been collecting?" There was so much to take in that Dominic didn't know where to start.

"Not as long as you'd think."

A set of canopic jars sat on one of the shelves; on another, an exquisitely jeweled human skull. A golden scarab Egyptian pendant and an ancient carved Mayan statue were displayed on another shelf. Below were ancient Paleolithic eggs, a Chinese bronze wine vessel, and a Greek Corinthian bronze helmet. There were also random cases containing beads, currency, jewelry, and weaponry.

"Dru, your collection is like nothing I've ever seen before," Dominic mumbled in amazement. "I mean, I thought I had some cool pieces, but this...." Dominic made an extensive motion to the wall. "This is, Wow."

"Now, you understand why I keep this place locked up like Fort Knox," Drucilla commented.

Dominic turned his attention to the rock-band posters, noticing how out of place they seemed in a room that looked like a museum. "Let me guess; these posters have been here since you were a kid?"

"Yeah, I found them when I was fixing the place up. I had forgotten about them. I decided to put them back up."

"Why are there lipstick prints all over that tall guy on the *Type O Negative* poster?"

"Do you really not know who that is?"

Dominic shrugged.

Drucilla chuckled to herself and pulled a three-foot-wide, intricately carved Japanese chest away from the cubby in the wall, scooted it to the middle of the room, and sat on the floor in front of it. She pulled apart the Karakuri lock and dropped the lid back.

"This is where I keep the real crazy shit."

Dominic sat in the chair directly behind her and looked over her shoulder.

Inside the chest were Indonesian patterned fabrics folded neatly. She pulled them out one at a time and placed the fabrics on the floor. Inside the chest were some carved stone idols, large raw crystals, wooden beads, and other baubles tucked between larger boxes.

"Dru, how did you manage to accumulate this collection?" Dominic asked with a concerned tone.

"From digs mostly. Some from bazaars in India; the fabrics anyway," she said, poking through the box.

"Aren't artifacts supposed to go to a museum or an institute of some sort?"

Drucilla ignored the question. She came across a small leather bag in the box and tossed it to him over her shoulder.

"What's this?" He opened the leather bag and spilled the contents into his hand.

"Athenian Owls, 400 BC or somewhere around there." Drucilla continued digging through the box.

Dominic bolted up and held a coin up to his eye in front of the light.

"I need to start carrying my loupe. These aren't real, are they?"

"Yeah, of course, they are," Drucilla responded, almost insulted at the question,

Dominic emptied the entire contents of the bag; some of the coins fell to the ground from between his fingers. "There's gotta be, what, at least thirty of them?" he said, picking up the ones that fell onto the rug.

"' Should be sixty-one." Drucilla continued to dig through the chest and placed more items on the floor next to her.

"Dru, do you realize these go for about two and a half thousand each?"

"Something like that. I found the coins on a site in Athens during an internship. Oh, here, check out this ax." Drucilla handed Dominic a Viking ax wrapped in lambskin.

"I found that in Mammen, near Viborg in Denmark a few summers ago. One of the last sites I worked. I believe it was used for ceremonies. You can tell it was never used for its intended purposes."

The silver ax was decorated in swirls of interlocking knots. The leather was still bound to the hilt. The blade was still relatively sharp. Dominic ran his hand over the top edge. "Denmark, huh?' he said, fascinated with the artifact in his hand.

"Boat graves, ceremonial ship burials. That kind of thing."

"Dru, are you a smuggler? Are you stealing artifacts?"

"I'm gonna be really honest with you, Dominic. Being a gallery owner isn't very lucrative. Artists usually become famous after they've died, and they usually die poor." Drucilla turned her attention back to the box.

"That doesn't really answer my question." Dominic scrunched his nose and shifted his eyes around the room. He walked over to a waist-high display case. He noticed an old pen sitting on top of the glass. The pen didn't look like part of the display. It looked out of place.

"What's with the pen?"

"What pen?" Drucilla asked, standing up to see what he was looking for.

A handmade wooden pen rested on its side. The pen had a copper tip and copper bands inlaid near the end. There wasn't anything special about it other than the tiny carved symbols on the side and that it was probably a few decades old.

"Oh, that! Yeah, that's a weird story...." Drucilla picked up the pen. "When I was in Palermo, in the catacombs, my sketch pen rolled under a table and somehow wedged itself against a shelf and the wall. I mean it was really in there. I managed to free the pen and dropped it back in my bag. When I pulled the pen out later that evening to work on my sketch, wasn't my pen at all. It was that old chunk of wood. The weird thing is I swear on my life that when I picked it up, it was my sketch pen. It changed shape or something. Believe it or not, it still works after having it for fifteen years and about a hundred sketches later. The ink still flows. Which is a good thing because I have no idea how to refill it if it ever ran out." Drucilla chuckled to herself at how absurd that sounded.

Dominic's eyes shifted from Drucilla to the pen: back and forth. "You found this in Palermo? Was this at the same time you found your rosary?"

"Uh, yeah, that would be the same time. Why?"

"I can't be certain until I investigate further, but you said the pen changed shape, and it never runs out of ink," Dominic repeated.

"Well, I don't know if it actually changed shape. From what I remember, I was dealing with a headache, so I may have imagined it."

"Drucilla, offer me the pen."

Drucilla looked at Dominic suspiciously. "You can pick it up."

"Just humor me, please."

Confused, Drucilla picked up the pen and handed it to Dominic. He took the pen from Drucilla and stuffed it in his pocket.

"What are you doing?"

Dominic maintained eye contact, pulled the pen back out of his pocket, and held it between them. The pen had transformed from a simple lathed wooden pen to a black iron stylus. It appeared to be a thick-handled object with a bulbous tapered tip on the other end. The shape of the object resembled a lit tapered candle with a heavier bottom end. It was about seven inches in length, and the small carved symbols on the handle were more pronounced than the previous incarnation."

"Where's the pen?" Drucilla asked.

"This is it. There's nothing else in my pocket."

"Whaaaat?" Drucilla thought for sure he was pulling her leg. She grinned. "Ok, Dude, you got me. Give me my pen." Drucilla held her out.

"Dru, I'm not kidding," Dominic said. He pulled his pockets out inside out.

"This is a trick."

"Really, after everything you've seen, you think it's a trick. Here, take it." Dominic offered the stylus back to Drucilla. Drucilla took the stylus from his hand and looked at it curiously. She then looked back up at Dominic.

"Right, so if I just shove the pen back in my back pocket and pull it back out, it will look like my old pen?"

"No. It already does."

Drucilla furrowed her brow and looked back down at her hand. The iron stylus changed back old worn wooden barreled pen.

"But it..." she stammered as she looked wide-eyed at Dominic.

Dominic and Drucilla locked eyes in disbelief.

"What is this?" She stared at Dominic and hoped that he would have an answer.

"It's Nova's pen. It has to be." Dominic stated.

"One of the queens?" Drucilla asked.

"Yeah, like Calliope. Like your rosary, it's an Unholy relic. Drucilla, you've had another in your possession the whole time."

Drucilla recalled the time that Lucifer told her that she had relics—plural—in her possession. *This must have been what he meant.* Drucilla always thought it was something more interesting. That's the real reason she transformed the bunker into a vault. At the time, she didn't know what celestial relic she had in her possession. Things were beginning to make more sense to her. She needed Lucifer to confirm.

✝✝✝

They entered Dominic's house and made a dash for the library.

Dominic climbed up the library ladder and pulled out a book with the words *Ancient Demonic Vestiges* inlaid in gold on the cover. He carried the book down the ladder

193

and placed it on the table. Drucilla sat on a swivel stool and watched Dominic open the book and scan the pages and images.

"Here we go," Dominic said. He moved his lips as he scanned the page.

"Well? Do I have Nova's pen?"

"Well, now I'm not entirely sure. It is depicted as a feathered or plumed quill; sometimes, it's a bone with a point dipped in blood for ink. Other times it's a stylus used for etching stone and clay. It's hard to say."

"The stylus part tracks, right?"

"Yeah, but this says nothing about it changing to the wielder. Although I'm sure, that's implicit considering the different depictions. However, it does say that theoretically it transforms into a weapon and can open portals to other universes." Dominic stopped reading and looked up from the book at nothing in particular. He had a confused look on his face. "That can't be right."

"Wait, what?" Drucilla hopped off the table and stood next to Dominic. She pulled the pen out of her pocket to reexamine it.

"What type of weapon?" Drucilla asked. She tried to imagine what that would look like. She glanced down at the image on the left side of the open book. The picture was of a Spartan warrior with a javelin in his hand. She flipped the page, and there was an image of Vlad the Impaler.

Drucilla and Dominic looked at each other in amazement.

Ipse morietur, quia non habuit disci-
plinam, & in multitudine stultitiæ suæ
decipietur.   Proverb. 5.

CANTICLE SIXTEEN

"And don't forget when your elders forget to say their prayers, take them by the legs and throw them down the stairs."
—Siouxsie Sioux

"It is Walpurgisnacht," Lucifer said. He smiled brightly at Drake.

"What's Walpurgisnacht?" Drake asked. They hurriedly made their way up the main stairs from the street to the front doors of an old stone library that now served as a historic site. The current city library had been modernized and moved to another location.

"April 30th is an important night for the coven. Walpurgisnacht is also known as Walpurgis Night or Witches' Night. This night was named after the English Christian missionary Saint Walpurga in 710 AD. This is also celebrated as the first coven meeting hundreds of years ago," Lucifer explained.

Drake and Lucifer made their way inside. They hurriedly walked across the outdated marble hallway to a pair of heavy wooden doors on the opposite end of the entrance. The old library was musty and cold. Upkeep had been minimal to this nearly dilapidated building. They opened the doors and stepped down the long winding stone staircase to a large hallway that terminated in two heavy iron doors.

"The entire room was fortified in iron to ensure protection from supernatural elements," Lucifer explained.

Drake entered the room with a heavy slam behind them and walked briskly and with purpose. Lucifer was close behind him. The twenty coven members stopped their chatter and watched Drake curiously as he moved from the door past his assigned seat and instead took the chair at the head of the table reserved for the High Priestess. Drake sat, placed his elbows on the table, and intertwined his fingers. He silently looked around at each member as they began to whisper and scowl at the audacity of Drake sitting at the head.

"Ms. De Luca has been relieved of her duties as High Priestess effective immediately. She's currently on a plane back to Naples. I think I can speak for all of us when I say we wish her good luck in her future endeavors," Drake announced.

The room erupted into chatter and disbelief.

"This is an outrage!" An older gentleman stood up and pounded his fist on the table.

Drake turned to him and slowly shifted his eyes to the gentleman's face.

"Whom do you think you are? 'Coming in here and taking over like this! The High Priestess and her family have led this coven for centuries!" He shouted.

"So?" Drake said nonchalantly and shrugged.

The older gentleman became even more irate, "So? Is that all you have to say for yourself? I demand that she be reinstated this instant!" he gnashed his teeth.

Drake got up and looked around the room at the other coven members. He walked over to the older gentleman.

"And you are?" Drake asked. Drake crossed his arms, stood over him, and stared intensely at him.

"Lombardi. Stefano Lombardi. I am the High Sorcerer. I am second in command!"

"Neat," Drake smirked. Drake put his finger to his lips, then turned to address the coven.

"I'll tell you what, Mr. Lombardi…." Drake walked around the room; all eyes were upon him. "Oh, excuse me, High Sorcerer." Drake corrected himself. He looked down at Lombardi. "Let's take a vote. If anyone in this room is satisfied with the former leader of the coven, please feel free to gather your things and leave immediately. I'll take your departure as a, Yes." Drake crossed his arms as he looked around the room.

Again, the room broke into a low cacophony of chatter; no one was leaving.

"Cowards!" Mr. Lombardi screamed, "Every one of you! She is your High Priestess! You will respect her!"

The coven watched silently. Mr. Lombardi noticed that no one agreed with him.

"Are you satisfied?" Drake asked, looking down at Mr. Lombardi.

"You! You will never be my High Priest. You vile, disgusting child!" He pointed his finger at Drake.

Drake, devoid of patience, motioned for his security to apprehend Mr. Lombardi.

The security gripped Mr. Lombardi as Lombardi attempted to cast a spell by starting a chant. One of the guards covered his mouth tightly, interrupting it.

Drake walked over to Mr. Lombardi and leaned his head to the side. Mr. Lombardi struggled to break free but could not get out of their grip.

"Dispose of him; I don't care where—I don't care how—Get him out of my coven," Drake demanded, without an ounce of compassion.

Mr. Lombardi's protests were muffled by the security guard's large hand. He kicked and struggled violently as he was hauled out of the room and through the iron doors.

Lucifer leaned against the wall as he chucked silently to himself.

Drake glanced at Lucifer and walked back to his chair. He leaned his arms over the back of the chair. "All of you are witches." Drake looked around the room at each member.

The coven members whispered to each other; some shrugged and nodded.

Drake walked around the table slowly and stopped in front of a particular woman. "Everyone but you," Drake said. He looked down at her suspiciously.

She slowly turned around to meet his stare. Whispers of shock could be heard around the room.

"Ms. Bianchi, is it?"

The woman looked around the room and then back to Drake. She slowly nodded.

"What do you bring to this coven?" Drake folded his arms. He waited for an answer.

Ms. Bianchi sat silent for a moment before she spoke. "I'm a wealthy donor, Mr. Blackwood."

"Newly accumulated wealth from what I understand. Tell me, how exactly does the daughter of a dairy farmer from Wheaton, Minnesota, accumulate such vast wealth? About five-hundred million dollars in money and assets, is that right?"

She slowly nodded, locking eyes with Drake.

"You have no real education. You attended college for a year in journalism then dropped out. You're unmarried, so it isn't from a wealthy spouse—no lottery winnings. If I had to guess, I'd say you are being paid handsomely for bits of information here and there. Does that sound accurate?"

Ms. Bianchi's eyes widened in fear. She started to tremble.

"No, don't worry. I'm not going to kill you," Drake scoffed. "I actually admire that. It's impressive. You've been selling out this coven for ten years, and De Luca had no idea. Even more, reason why she wasn't fit for her position."

Ms. Bianchi sat stunned as the other coven members glared and whispered about her.

"You have exactly ten seconds to leave my chamber," Drake said. He looked directly at Ms. Bianchi.

She scrambled to pick up her bag from under the table, tossed it on her shoulder, and briskly walked to the door.

"Wait!" Drake called to her just as she reached the door. He fixed her in a hard stare.

She stopped but didn't turn around.

"Ms. Bianchi."

She slowly turned and looked at him.

"I trust you will not mention anything that has happened in this room to anyone outside of those doors." Drake slowly moved towards her.

Her eyes began to well up in terror.

"Please, I have a daughter," she whispered.

"For now," Drake responded, unmoved by her statement. "Everywhere you go, everyone, you talk to— we'll know."

She swallowed hard.

"Leave before I start feeling less charitable."

Ms. Bianchi flung the door open and bolted out of the room in tears.

Drake walked to the head of the table, took his seat, and thought for a moment. "I have a demand. It's a great demand, and I will not tolerate refusal. Am I making myself clear?" Drake said, glaring at the faces in the room.

The coven members looked at each other and back to Drake.

"It will take the efforts of every member in this coven to perform it," he said.

"What is it?" an older woman asked.

"Your name please?" Drake asked.

"My lord, I am Ninetta Rossi."

"Ms. Rossi, from what I understand, obscuration spells on massive scales require much power. About as much power as we have in this room. Am I correct?"

Ms. Rossi nodded.

"I know this coven is powerful," Drake said, getting up and examining the old worn scrolls in shadowboxes that adorned the walls. "You will cast an invisibility spell that will obscure Washington state entirely from any and all immortals."

"That will require constant round-the-clock shielding that someone will need to keep up day and night, nonstop," Ms. Rossi said.

Drake crossed his arms and turned around to face the coven members.

"There's eighteen of you. You'll work in shifts."

"Sir, may I ask why you need to hide an entire state?" another gentleman asked.

Drake looked at him inquisitively.

"I am Nicolas Esposito. I am a Magus."

"No, Mr. Esposito, you may not. And remove those sashes—all of you. You have no need for hierarchy here. I am your High Priest now." Drake straightened his suit.

The familiar coven chatter began again as they removed their sashes and tossed them in the middle of the table.

"How long will it take for the spell to work," Drake asked, turning to Lucifer.

"It will be instantaneous, but you understand that I will not be able to see her if you do this."

Drake stared at Lucifer curiously.

"All immortals mean all of us."

Drake's sternness faded to concern.

"What about Celestial Laws? We made a deal. Doesn't that exclude you?"

"It very well could. But bear in mind that even if it did, our deal is done upon your death. The shield is removed. This is not a permanent fix. My brothers will come for her."

"It will buy us time," Drake said, already deep in thought.

Drake turned to the coven members and the pile of sashes in the center of the table. Then he turned back to Lucifer.

"Burn it."

Lucifer extended his arm and pointed a finger. A stream of fire burst from his fingertip to the pile of sashes. A blazing mystical fire took hold and burned the sashes to ash.

MORS VLTIMA LINEA RERVM

CANTICLE SEVENTEEN

"Look into my eyes, you will see who I am. My name is Lucifer, please take my hand." —Black Sabbath

Drucilla rolled a single bead between her fingers, curiously examining the blood droplet contained within the faceted sphere. There used to be fifty-three beads; the beads had dwindled to a mere thirty-seven in total. Drucilla had used sixteen beads throughout the years; all except for four were her own doing. She thought of all the times that this rosary had saved her life. However, it also put her in situations she would not have been in if it were not for her possession of the relic in the first place. Drucilla didn't fully understand the extent of the capabilities contained within this rosary. There had to be more to it. She just didn't know what it was.

Drucilla looked up from her desk just as Dominic entered the gallery with arms full of rolled-up bubble wrap and several plywood planks. She had a few paintings to ship this week, and he had offered to help build the crates.

"You want these in the back?" he asked.

"Yeah, that would be great. Thank you," Drucilla said, getting up to help him.

She grabbed a couple of rolls of bubble wrap from his sizable arms and escorted him to the back office. She set the rolls down against the wall and helped him stack the plywood against the bubble wrap. When she was done, Drucilla sat at her desk chair and looked at Dominic curiously.

"You, okay?" he asked, concerned.

"Yeah, why wouldn't I be?"

"You seem distracted."

"Dom, do you believe in such things as half-human, half-seraphim?"

"You mean Nephilim? Theoretically, they were the first beings to populate the planet. They don't exist anymore," he responded.

"I'm curious. What do you think happened to them?"

"What do I think? I really have no idea. There are lots of different theories. Everything from a massive asteroid, like those that took out the dinosaurs, to mass extinction by *The Cataclysms*. You know, Death, Scourge, Famine, etcetera—the exterminators of worlds. But these are all just stories. I wouldn't put much stock in them. They built rockets and flew off to another planet for all we know." Dominic grinned.

Drucilla nodded at Dominic's explanation.

"Hey, why are you asking me this? Why the interest in religious lore?"

Drucilla shrugged. "I dunno, curiosity. I have this thing, and now I know it's filled with angel's blood. I don't know what I'm asking."

"Ophanim," Dominic said, correcting her and grinning.

"Okay, Ophanim."

"You seem confused. Do you want to talk about it?"

Drucilla shrugged. "I've got a lot going on in my head. I wouldn't know where to start."

"Understandable. Hey, I've been meaning to ask; what's it like? You know to have this kind of ability?" Dominic leaned up against her desk as he crossed his massive arms.

"It really isn't anything. I suppose it's like carrying a handgun. You use it if you need to. I don't really know how to answer the question."

"Yeah, but what does it actually feel like? You know, to crush a bead and just manifest whatever undead being you think of?"

"I've learned that I have to have the bead touching my skin when it breaks. I've tried to break it otherwise, and the beads don't crack open. There's usually this little blue bolt of lightning that shoots up my arm. There's a bit of blood. Until recently, I thought I was breaking my own skin open. But now, I think I'm actually absorbing the blood."

"Wait. You're micro-dosing Ophanim blood?" Dominic asked, taken aback.

"Yeah, I mean, I guess."

"Do you always do that?"

"Well yeah, it probably doesn't work otherwise."

"Dru. You're telling me that you're absorbing Ophanim blood into your body every time?"

"Does that make me a Nephilim?'

"Is that what this is about?"

Drucilla shrugged.

"You have to be born a Nephilim," a voice said, coming from the gallery. Lucifer turned the corner and entered the office. "And no, you are not a Nephilim. What you are is an interesting set of circumstances."

Dominic stood in shock at the beautiful, tall, translucent-skinned being.

Lucifer turned his attention to Dominic.

"Hello. I apologize. I am Lucifer," he said casually, extending a clawed hand to Dominic.

Dominic stood frozen in shock and disbelief.

"He does not talk much, does he?" Lucifer said to Drucilla, squinting at Dominic, leaving his hand out.

"I uh, I've hit him with a lot lately. He just met Adrian. I don't think he was expecting you."

"Okay!" Lucifer said, stuffing his hands into his pants pockets. He changed into a glamor of a blonde-haired, human male.

"Is this more comfortable for you?" Lucifer asked Dominic.

"Dru, Lucifer is standing next to me," Dominic said. He was struggling to get the words out of his mouth. He looked both shocked and terrified.

"Yeah, there's a lot that you should probably know if we're going to be friends. Lucifer isn't even the weirdest thing," Drucilla said regretfully.

Dominic turned back to Lucifer and fixed him in a horrified stare.

"I did not mean to make you nervous. I really am a friend of Drucilla's. Tell him, Drucilla."

"He's okay. Sometimes. Sometimes, he just leaves you hanging out in the middle of Athens like a sheep about ready to be devoured by a wolf," Drucilla said, staring down Lucifer.

He knew what Drucilla was thinking. "Now you're just being dramatic," Lucifer scoffed.

Dominic looked back at Drucilla, confused and uncomfortable about how she was speaking to a King of Hell.

"We have history," Drucilla said, reading his stare.

Lucifer shrugged.

"What can I help you with, Lucifer?" Drucilla asked.

"I thought you might want to know. Your brother is making his final transition."

"Good, I don't care. Drake's been dead to me for ten years. What difference does it make now?"

Dominic's eyes shifted back and forth between Lucifer and Drucilla like a tennis match.

"I feel like I'm missing something here. Final transition?" Dominic asked uncertainly.

"Lucifer made a deal with my brother. Now he's claiming his end of the bargain. I guess."

"Oh. Wait, what?" Dominic said, still unclear. "Is Drake going to die?"

Lucifer flipped his coin in the air and caught it in his hand. He winked at Dominic.

Dominic looked at Lucifer, even more alarmed.

"Dom, remember when we first met, and I told you that Drake's rise to power was a deal with Lucifer, and you thought I was nuts? That's what he's talking about."

"Ok, I didn't actually think you were nuts."

"You totally thought I was nuts."

"Maybe, but only for a minute. After I saw your rosary, I knew you were being truthful."

"Whatever. Can we not talk about my brother?" Drucilla said, becoming increasingly uncomfortable.

"I uh, gotta get back to my shop anyway. I'll call you later, Dru," Dominic said. He got up from leaning against her desk. He kept a sharp eye on Lucifer as he slid past him until he turned the corner.

Lucifer smiled and waved as Dominic left. "He does not trust me at all!" Lucifer said and rocked on his heels.

Drucilla looked down at her beads and started fiddling around with them again. She looked back up at Lucifer. "Why didn't you tell me what these really were?"

"That was for you to discover on your own. That is how the game is played. You find the relic, learn about what it is, and use it to your advantage if you are one of the capable ones. Congratulations, Drucilla. You are the first ever to discover what it truly is."

Drucilla stared at Lucifer for a moment.

"Dominic says I'm absorbing the blood every time I break one. How is that affecting me?"

"I do not know how it affects humans. You are the first, but clearly, you are tolerating it well. Maybe if you took all of them at once, it would be different, but I do not see a reason to break them all at once. They appear to be working as intended. Have you given any thought to what you will do after you run out of beads?"

I never thought of that. It made sense that this foray into necromancy would come to an end, but I never thought there would be a time when I would use all of them. "No, not at all," Drucilla said. She absent-mindedly chewed her bottom lip.

"Well, I can give you a small spoiler. You can still communicate with the dead using the amulet, so do not throw it away after you have gone through them all."

"I assume Calliope will want this relic back at some point. I mean, do I keep it until I die?" Drucilla asked.

"Generally, yes. It is usually buried with the possessor or given away to someone else. It eventually goes back into circulation. It always has. I do not think she cares to have it returned to her. She has no use for it. It is essentially a trophy, a toy. However, she cannot make another one unless she obtains blood from another Throne."

Drucilla looked back down at the beads.

"It has been wonderful meeting your friend, but I must attend to the transition. Many preparations need to be made." Lucifer made a slight bowing gesture to Drucilla as he headed out of the gallery.

"Lucifer?" Drucilla said. She turned her gaze to Lucifer and stood up. She walked over to him and stood in front of him.

"Drucilla?"

"I found the other relic. It's the pen, isn't it? It's Nova's pen."

A slow but intense grin stretched across Lucifer's face.

Drucilla looked at him and exhaled. They held each other's stare for a moment. Lucifer seemed strangely elated that she discovered the relic. As if it was a secret that he was dying to tell her but couldn't. She turned away from Lucifer and walked back to her desk.

"Drucilla?"

Drucilla turned and looked back at him. "What?"

"You might want to check in with your mother. She is going to need her daughter during this time." Lucifer blinked out.

Great. 'Just what I needed right now. A grieving parent and I couldn't tell her why she shouldn't grieve. Hey, don't worry, Mom. He's not really dead— just his earthly body. I'm sure you can see him any time you want to. Take this amulet so you can see him. Yeah, that would go over well, as she's having me put in a room with rubber walls.

Drucilla sat back down at her desk and grabbed a small stack of photos. She began to flip through them but realized she was too distracted to work. She dropped the stack back onto her desk and placed her face in her hands.

What am I going to do when the blood runs out? I can't go back to being like everyone else. Should I stop using them now? Or should I keep using them until they run out and just deal with it? Maybe... maybe I could make more?

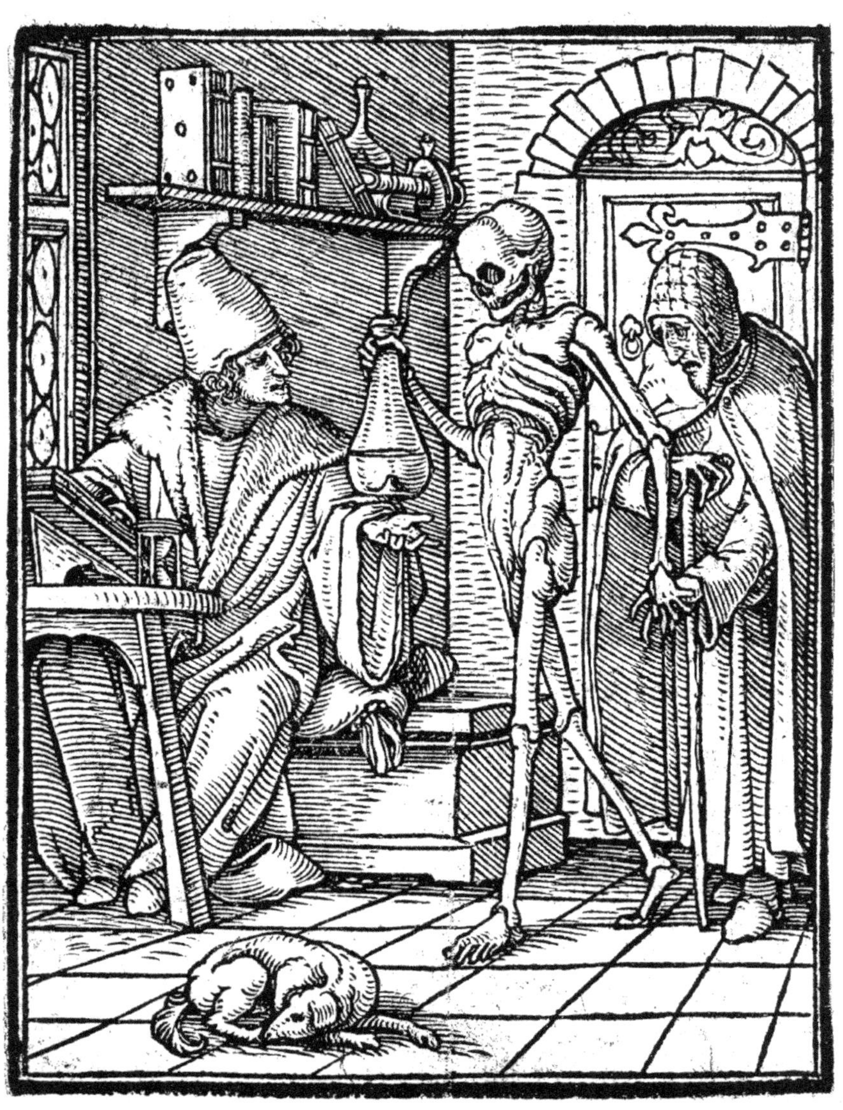

CANTICLE EIGHTEEN

"I don't exist when you don't see me. I don't exist when you're not here." —Andrew Eldritch

Drucilla and Dominic sat at their usual spot in *Siren's Pub*. The TV that was usually tuned to a sports station was peculiarly tuned to a cable news broadcast. All of the TVs were tuned to the same channel.

Governor of California Drake Blackwood is under investigation today for corrupt activity for the past three years, as part of a broader federal investigation by Patrick Deacon, code-named Tarot, which had been going on for two years. To date, eighteen people have been charged in connection with the investigation. Blackwood had long been suspected to be a target of the investigation. U.S. District Judge Collin Evans confirmed that he was the "Public Official A" referred to in the federal indictment...

"Dru, Dru, are you seeing this?" Dominic said with a beer in hand, staring at the TV and smacking Drucilla's arm with his free hand.

"Dude!" Drucilla said, pulling her attention away from her *Archaeology* magazine and watching his hand hitting her arm. Drucilla looked up at the TV and saw Drake heading into a courthouse.

"Apparently, they've got some recorded phone calls or something. They got him on like mail and wire fraud and alleged solicitation of personal benefit in exchange for an appointment to the Senate," Dominic said, still looking at the TV.

"I don't know why this surprises you," Drucilla shrugged nonchalantly.

"I think we can safely say he's not going to be reelected," Dominic said, taking a sip of his beer.

"Oh? Are you not a Drake Blackwood fan anymore?"

Dominic curled his lip at Drucilla. "I never was. I just thought Drake might be doing some good stuff in California. I mean, he's not an idiot."

Drucilla glanced at him.

"I mean, he did his job in California, but… Ok yeah, he's an idiot." Dominic rescinded his statement.

"Whatever, he won't be found guilty anyway."

"What makes you say that?"

"Because Dom, Drake has never failed at anything in his life. He's not about to start now."

"So, if he does, you aren't going to write to him in jail?" Dominic asked, half-joking.

"Send him some anthrax, maybe," Drucilla mumbled. "Besides, we both know that's not where he's really headed." She went back to reading the archaeology article in her magazine.

"Yeah, I suppose we do."

Dominic looked over at her and saw that she was deeply immersed in the archeology article. He put his beer down and crossed his massive arms. "So why did you quit? I mean, really, why did you give it up? You seem to still be interested in it."

"I am still interested in it. I still love it." Drucilla continued to read her magazine.

Dominic stared at her, expecting a different answer to his question. Drucilla didn't say anything.

"Did something bad happen?"

"Something bad always happens." Drucilla ran her fingers over the space where beads used to be on her rosary. "Curiously, whenever I leave Washington state, something bad happens. It's almost like, this place is keeping me safe."

"If you don't want to talk about it, it's ok," Dominic said.

Drucilla folded the corner of the magazine and closed it. She stuffed it back into her bag. The waitress showed up with the check, and they threw their cards on the tray. As she walked away, Drucilla debated to herself, going back-and-forth in her head whether she wanted to talk about her fears or not.

I should probably tell him. It may or may not affect things, but it would give him a little more perspective on how I react to certain situations. Especially ones where Lucifer is concerned.

"It was a couple of years before I moved here. Several incidents happened in one day that changed me in a lot of different ways—"

The waitress returned with the receipts. They paid their bill, got up, and made their way down the stairs of the pub to the street. They began walking in the direction of Drucilla's house.

"It was my last day in Athens. I had been working on a site for about eight weeks. Our team was large. There were about sixty of us at the time including site workers, rather than the usual twenty or thirty. It was an exciting day. Not only were some of us going home the next day, but we were having an opening ceremony of one of the tombs we were excavating near Philopappos' Monument on Mouseion Hill."

She took a breath and glanced at Dominic to reassure herself to keep going. "The tomb was amazing. The walls were intricate Greek mosaic patterns in lapis lazuli, turquoise, and pearls. The sarcophagus lay in the center with statues of Athena, Peplos Kore, and a few smaller ones. Against the wall above the head of the sarcophagus was a large chest. It contained jewels, a crown, necklaces, rings, and clothing that royalty would wear. There was also a smaller chest inside containing about a couple thousand Athenian Owls."

"So, that's where you got those?"

"Yeah," Drucilla responded. They turned a corner and continued to head up the low-grade incline to her house.

"There was a big going away party that evening at one of the clubs in Athens. My now ex-boyfriend, Brandon, decided to end our three-year relationship that day. He left me for a Greek girl named Malva that he literally just met a week before. He brought her with him to the party, as well. That was fantastic." Drucilla said sarcastically. "He also decided not to come back with us and stay in Athens with her."

"That's brutal."

"Whatever. Would you believe that's not the brutal part?"

They continued to walk up the street. "At this point, I've had just about enough of Athens and, well, everyone for that matter. I left the party early with every intention of slamming a bottle of vodka in my hotel room and sleeping until it was time to catch my plane. I left the club, walked about half a block, and found another bar. I decided that locating a liquor store, procuring said liquor, and returning to my room was just far too much of an effort. I opted for the bar to just get my drinking done there. I had just sat down at the bar and ordered a drink when this giant meat-wall of a dude walked in. He was just enormous. When I say enormous, think of someone about one hundred pounds bigger than you. Just massive. I mean, if this guy were a car, he'd be a semi-truck. He looks at me and heads right for me. I have no idea who this guy is. Seeing someone that imposing walk right up to me and sit down next to me—on purpose—was intimidating."

"Who was he?"

"Hades."

"Hades?" he exclaimed, clearly not expecting that answer.

"Yeah, Hades sat down next to me and addressed me by my name. He said: 'Drucilla, you have something that belongs to me.' I'm not even drunk, and I can't believe what's happening. I'm panicking, wondering what the hell I stole from this dude, and apparently, it was pretty serious because he had tracked me down. As he sat next to me, he got close to my face and said, 'Give me the rosary.'" Drucilla started talking faster, "I'm terrified at this point and start wondering if it's worth keeping because he's just going to take it off my dead body. But for some stupid reason, I looked at him and said, 'I'm not going to do that. I won't give it to you.' Granted, I'm about two seconds from having a full-blown anxiety attack. He grabbed my hand gently and looked around the room. To everyone, it appeared that he was flirting, but no." Drucilla paused briefly and then continued, "He wrapped my forearm around his and pulled tightly, threatening to snap my elbow if I didn't give it up. He said: 'Do you know who I am? I'm Hades, a King of Hell, and if you don't offer the rosary to me, I will break your arm and take it.' I know for a fact that he can't use it unless I offered it to him, so his threats really didn't mean anything. I dared him, like an idiot, and I said: 'Do it.'

Dominic let out an audible gasp of disbelief.

"I was a little self-destructive at that point. He stared at me for a moment. Instead of breaking my arm and making a scene in the bar, he started unraveling the rosary from my wrist and wrapped it around his own. He shoved my hand away, got up, and headed out of the bar.

I was livid at this point, so I chased after him. I yelled to him something like, 'That it will never work for you!' He pulled the rosary tightly against his hand and punched a streetlight to break the beads. The ground started shaking for a split second, then it stopped. He glared at me, and he punched the streetlight again. This time nothing. He did it again, and about the fourth time, he got the hint that it was not going to work for him. He was pissed, and he threw it at my feet and demanded that I pick it up and hand it to him.

"Holy crap! What'd you do?"

"As soon as I picked up the rosary, the archaeology crew exited the club and started heading into the one where I was. They all saw me standing in front of this massive dude, and they thought I was with him. They started being friendly, trying to talk to Hades, and Hades is like: 'Why are these people talking to me?' I ducked out during the confusion and headed back into the bar because I figured I was safe being in a place with a lot of people. It would be harder for him to keep his low profile. I ran out of the back door into the alleyway, and I started screaming for Lucifer. Lucifer never showed. It was at that point that I realized I was on my own. No one was coming to help. I quit the University a week later. It was getting to the point that whenever I would go on a dig site, I was putting my life at risk and not from work dangers—just existing with this thing," Drucilla said and stared at the rosary beads in her hand.

"I don't know why, but when I'm here, they tend to stay away from me for some reason. Every Unholy stays away from me except for Lucifer. This is why I'm apprehensive about Lucifer. I thought that I could trust him after Egypt, but clearly, I was wrong for assuming."

"Did you ask him where he was?"

"No. It doesn't matter anymore. I just need to continuously remind myself that he's Lucifer: The Devil."

CANTICLE NINETEEN

*"We must be the first ones in the world to fall off of the
earth." —Chino Moreno*

"Everyone! GET OUT!" Drake angrily yelled at his staff.

The staff hurriedly exited the governor's office in a panic. The last assistant stopped and turned to Drake.

"Sir, uh, just a reminder, you have an 11 a.m. call with…."

"What did I fucking say!" Drake roared, picked up a thick, dense, glass trophy, and threw it at his head. It slammed against the wall with a loud THUNK, right near where his assistant's head would have been if he had not exited the room fast enough. The trophy partially embedded itself into the wall for a moment before dislodging from its own weight and crashing to the ceramic tile floor. The trophy left a decent-sized hole in the deep blue drywall.

Lucifer appeared and sat in the oversized, navy blue, pinstriped armchair in front of Drake's desk. Drake paced the floor of his office, running his hands through his hair. His breathing was deep but rapid, as if he was fighting to calm down and, at the same time was ready to blow. He was a ticking time bomb. Drake noticed Lucifer, stomped back to his desk, and threw himself into his high-backed leather desk chair. He slid his hands down his face, then leaned back and looked at the ceiling. "Fuck," he whispered.

"Everything all right?" Lucifer asked innocently, sitting cross-legged and adjusting the cufflinks on his suit.

"No, everything is not all right," Drake said. He ripped himself out of his chair. He started pacing again with his hand on the back of his neck.

"You know who it is, right? It's that bitch, Bianchi. I should have slit her throat myself!"

Lucifer got up and leaned against Drake's desk.

"This matters not. It is just a minor setback. I do not understand why you are getting so upset," Lucifer commented.

"I am the Governor of California." Drake paused. "I am the High Priest. This, this level of brazen audacity—" Drake stood back behind his desk, livid. "I let her live! I allowed her to keep her life, and this is how she repays me by selling me out. That's it! I want her head! I want her head, now!" Drake yelled. He pulled out his smartphone.

Lucifer got up and put his hand over Drake's phone.

"You need to calm down and think about this. If you kill Bianchi, everyone will know it was retaliation and trace it back to you. We will lose everything, more than we could potentially lose now."

"I don't care," Drake said through gritted teeth. "This has nothing to do with what you want. I will not allow this to go unpunished. I'm making the calls here. Me! Not you!" Drake angrily leaned in, getting in Lucifer's face.

Lucifer's snake-eyes intensified. He slammed the palm of his hand on Drake's desk and wrapped the other around Drake's throat. "You have become entirely too egomaniacal and been nothing but a thorn in my side for the better part of a decade. You must remember your place and how and why you get to enjoy the life I have granted you. I can just as easily take everything from you. You do nothing unless I allow it. Do I make myself clear?"

Lucifers hand began to smolder, burning a hole in the desk. He released Drake from his grasp. A perfectly formed, burned hand impression was left behind in the finish.

Drake stepped back rubbed his neck in shock. He looked in the mirror on the wall behind him to check for damage. He looked down for a moment, then laughed to himself.

"You can't do anything," Drake scoffed. He looked up at Lucifer. "I'm not afraid of you. We have a deal, and you have no other recourse until the deal is done. So, go ahead. Take it all. I'm serious, all of it." Drake leaned in. "If you can—"

"Are you challenging me?" Lucifer grinned malevolently as he studied Drake's face. "Do you really think you can outmaneuver me? Do you forget who I am, child? You are but one of a hundred subjects I have influenced over the centuries, and if you think for a moment that you have any control in this situation, you are gravely mistaken."

Drake leaned his head to the side and grinned. "What are you going to do about it? We have a deal. It's out of your hands."

"Yes. We do have a deal, and unfortunately for you, that does not mean others cannot make deals. You see, there are millions of ambitious young men, just like you, that would trade anything to make a deal with me. Some may even ask to have your life." Lucifer crossed his arms. "Who am I to say, 'No'?"

"You can't do that."

Lucifer sat and crossed his legs.

Drake's smile faded.

"Are you ready to talk, or do you want to see just how far you can push a King of Hell because I promise you, no one has ever won."

Drake sat back down at his desk and folded his hands. He looked down at nothing in particular. He inhaled and looked back up at Lucifer. "Do we pay off the judge? Do we, uh, save a bunch of orphans from a burning building? You know PR stuff?"

"Nothing. We do nothing," Lucifer said flatly.

"What? The election is in two weeks!"

"Drake, you will die in two months. They will not have time to bring anything to trial before then. You will finish your current term. Undoubtedly, you will lose the election, and it will be time for you to take your place in Hell."

"So essentially, I'm done here."

"Think of it as a promotion. You are promoted to King! You will occupy my space, and I can retire for all intents and purposes. Who knows, maybe you can make a deal with another young fellow just as infuriating and pompous as you are."

"You're right. I can probably achieve more in your position anyway—better, too." Drake placed his elbows on his desk and interlaced his fingers while contemplating.

Lucifer sighed at Drake's arrogance.

"What about Drucilla?"

"What about her?" Lucifer shrugged.

"You need to protect her."

"Child, our deal is complete. I have no further obligation to you. You are in no position to make demands."

Drake peered at Lucifer inquisitively.

"I wanna make a new deal," Drake requested.

Lucifer chuckled to himself. "With what? You have no leverage, nothing to offer."

"I still have your coin."

Lucifer again laughed to himself. "No, you do not," Lucifer pulled the Unholy relic from his breast pocket and held it between two clawed fingertips.

Confused, Drake pulled out his keys and unlocked the top drawer of his desk. He started shuffling around, searching for the relic he was supposed to possess.

"Drake. It is over," Lucifer said, stood up, and straightened his suit. "I'll return in sixty days to make the exchange."

Drake slammed the drawer closed in frustration and threw his head back; he put his hands over his eyes. He put his hands back down and looked at Lucifer. "You mean to tell me you could have taken that coin back at any time?"

"Do you forget who I am?"

"You lied to me."

"Did I? Did I not give you everything you asked for? Did I not hold up my end of the bargain? Drake, you will be a King of Hell; what is preventing you from protecting her yourself? Is it because you have no one to do your work for you? I suggest if you want to be a King, you should begin to compose yourself as one."

Emisit eum Dominus Deus de paradi
so voluptatis, ut operaretur terram, de qua
sumptus est.   Gen: 3

CANTICLE TWENTY

"Disappointment is all there is in this life so let me be disappointed with you." —Alex Story

The scissor lift groaned with an awful whine—complaining as though it had been abused from years of lifting heavy caskets as two cemetery workers hopped up on either side. They rode up to the third-highest row in the mausoleum. They pulled off the burgundy velvet curtain as cautiously as possible from that height and slowly let the curtain glide to the floor below, revealing the interment space. The exposed space was hollow, dark, and cold. Drucilla leaned her shoulder against the opposite wall, her phone vibrating against her thigh within her peacoat pocket. Drucilla inhaled sharply and tensed her shoulders. *Not now...* Drucilla groaned to herself and ignored the call.

Drucilla heard footsteps behind her. An opulently dressed older gentleman approached and walked past her. His stark white hair, neatly tied back, streamed below his black hat. The white hair against his black coat offered a sharp contrast in an otherwise bland, marble-beige room with only small pops of muted color from old plastic floral arrangements in tarnished bronze vases. Drucilla wondered who he was; she couldn't tell from the back. *Maybe he's here to visit someone else... Or making his own arrangements?* He didn't look back at her and continued to walk with purpose to the other side of the room and out of the double-frosted glass doors.

The casket was parallel to the gaping hole in the mausoleum wall and aligned perfectly. The casket began its final journey as the workers pushed what remained of Drake Blackwood into the wall vault.

Drucilla didn't go to the funeral; she didn't want to attend. Her cousin emailed her all the particulars a few days before the funeral. Drucilla's aunt and uncle organized the entire event. She didn't have the patience or state of mind to deal with her mother and anticipated that her mother would be a mess. Drucilla didn't know how to tell her that she just didn't care. She hadn't told her mother anything about how she felt.

Drucilla,

Here are the details of Drake's funeral.

Hollywood Forever Cemetery January 21th, 2020 @ 2:30 p.m.

He'll be interred in The Valentino Shrines, 6300 Forest Lawn Dr. in Los Angeles, California.

The wake will be at my parent's house in Woodland Hills. They're still in the same place. Let me know if you need the address.

-Sierra

Drucilla didn't know how her brother died, only that it was part of a Celestial bargain. She also didn't understand why there wouldn't be an elaborate funeral. It was just a quiet one with the family. This whole event seemed out of character for Drake. Then again, they hadn't said a word to each other in over ten years. She recalled the last time she saw him was on TV. He was running for his second term as Governor, which failed miserably, and Drake faded into obscurity after that. She didn't vote for him. Drucilla wasn't a California resident anymore, but she still wouldn't have voted for him even if she was.

The workers stuck long strips of duct tape around the four sides of the metal plate to hold it in place. She didn't want to think about the purpose of the tape. *Clearly, it's another sealing layer for liquid substances.* Drucilla fantasized about what it would be like to be inside the internment. *If I kicked hard enough at the base, could I free myself? Could I kick through the casket and kick that metal plate off and escape?*

The scissor lift lowered, and the two workers loaded the long, flat, marble facade back onto the scissor lift. Unexpectedly the door opened again on the opposite side of the room. The white-haired gentleman emerged from the hall and walked towards Drucilla. This time, he looked at her. Drucilla looked at his face. He was older but unconventionally handsome. She vigorously searched through the memory files in her brain as he approached. *I know I've seen his face before; I just can't recall where.* Her eyes narrowed as she thought harder. He gave Drucilla a slight nod and continued his way past her. She heard the door behind her open, and she presumed he exited the room. She didn't look over her shoulder.

She turned her eyes back to her brother's crypt as the heavy marble facade was inserted into the grooves of the vault space. Large ornate washers and screws were fastened into place. She didn't want to be there, but she couldn't leave, not until she knew he was in there.

Secured. Not coming out. Drucilla stayed a while longer and watched the workers come down the scissor lift, pack up their tools, and push the scissor lift out of the room. The door closed behind them. It was silent: cold and still.

Drucilla lunged forward to pull herself away from the marble wall. Her eyes fixated on the temporary metal plaque on the front of the marble facade. She walked cautiously toward it and leaned back to look up at the mausoleum wall and his tomb inscription.

Drake Victor Blackwood
November 30, 1985–January 6, 2020

"This is you. This is where you are now, I guess," Drucilla said as she tried to think of something significant to say, but nothing was coming to her.

The vibration from Drucilla's phone broke her malaise. She reached into her pocket and looked at the lock screen to see four missed calls and seven text messages. She didn't care to answer them. She knew it was random extended family members wanting to know her whereabouts. Drucilla pushed the side button to stop the alert and placed the phone back into her pocket. She turned her eyes back to the placard.

Maybe his death hasn't hit me; maybe I actually don't care. Regardless, the lack of empathy she felt towards Drake was unnerving. She shook her head. "Enjoy the forever box," she muttered.

She turned her head away, took a deep breath, and faced the door; her body followed. She exhaled slowly as she walked toward the frosted-glass double doors and reached for the brass handle. The door unexpectedly opened from the other side. It was the white-haired gentleman.

Drucilla was about to apologize when he confidently and professionally spoke aloud, "Come with me. We need to talk."

"I'm sorry, who are you?" Drucilla asked with some annoyance.

"Drucilla…" the gentleman said.

"Ok, how do you know me?"

He gave her a ghoulish grin.

"Look, I don't have a lot of time to play this guessing game, so if you have something to tell me, I'd appreciate you saving me the time and just get on with it."

He laughed to himself, "You are just like your brother."

"I don't have time for this." Drucilla snapped.

"Drucilla, I apologize; I didn't mean to scare you or make you nervous."

Drucilla was annoyed at the sheer audacity of thinking he could make her nervous. She stopped walking and turned back to face him. "Sir, you don't scare me. I am limited on time, and I need to catch a plane."

"Headed back to the Pacific Northwest tonight, are you?"

Ok, what... Drucilla peered at him suspiciously for a moment.

"You have two minutes." Drucilla tucked a lock of her long black hair behind her ear and folded her arms. She felt the weighty silver amulet attached to her rosary fall out from beneath the cuff of her coat and tap against her stomach.

He stared at the amulet for a moment before turning his attention back to her face. By his expression, he seemed slightly intrigued.

Drucilla uncrossed her arms and slowly shoved her hands deep into her coat pockets.

He paused to realign himself. "It's a tragedy what happened to your brother."

"Is that what you want to talk to me about? Drake's death?"

"When was the last time you spoke to him?"

"I don't." She paused, "I haven't in a very long time. We aren't on…we weren't on speaking terms." She reminded herself to speak in the past tense. "I'm sorry, can we get back to who you are?"

"E. H. Valiant. I was an associate of your late brother."

"I'm sure he had many of you."

"Your brother had an estate," Valiant said, crossing his arms. "There seems to be a few items missing from it, and I was hoping you could tell me where to find them?"

"How would I know anything about his estate? I told you we—"

"You have not spoken to your brother in quite a while. I understand. But still, there are a few unique items I would like to locate. If, by chance, you happen to know someone in the family who may have them or had given them to someone for safekeeping, I would like to remediate this issue. Should you hear something, please give me a call."

Valiant reached into his inner pocket, flipped out a small white business card, and extended it between his fingers towards Drucilla. The move was super cliché except for the extraordinarily long, thick pointed fingernails fashioned into claws.

Drucilla slid her right hand out of her pocket and slowly reached for the card. She plucked it from his fingers. She held it with her index and thumb as if it were going to bite her.

"I appreciate your attention to this matter." Valiant tipped his hat with a nod. He stepped past her and proceeded down the hallway to the double doors that led to the courtyard.

As she watched him walk away, a flash of lightning streaked across the sky, brightly visible through the glass ceiling in the hall. He opened the doors, and a loud crash of thunder reverberated through the mausoleum, echoing through its marbled halls. The doors shut behind him with a heavy clunk.

Drucilla flipped the card over to view the contact information.

E.H. Valiant, Appraiser
(987)555-5668
Antiques, Fine Art Curator, Collector

Along with the name and number was an embellishment of a gold griffin or strange mythical creature. She ran her thumb over the raised emblem and then remembered how he looked at her rosary. She clutched the amulet inside her pocket, making sure it was still with her. She knew what he wanted. She raised her head and looked at the doors ahead. *And he can pry it from my cold dead hands.*

Valiant walked toward a long black car waiting at the mausoleum entrance. He opened the door to the back seat and climbed inside. Drake turned his attention to Valiant as he took a seat. Drake's snake-eyes reacted to the flash of lightning outside. He sat motionless in his finely tailored black suit. "Did you see her?" Drake asked.

"I did. She stayed long enough to watch your empty casket inserted and sealed within the vault."

"Does she still have the relic?"

"She has it around her wrist, but obviously, she is not willing to part with it. She denies having it. So, we will have to get…creative," Valiant answered ominously.

Drake nodded, and the car proceeded down the road and out of the cemetery.

I
2
Omne quod est in mundo, concupiscentia carnis est,
et concupiscentia oculorum, et superbia vitæ. 1. Ioan. 2
Hieronymus Wierx fecit et excud.
Cum Gratia et Priuilegio
Buschere

CANTICLE TWENTY-ONE

"Ghouls, they keep me company. It's like I'm the wife of Halloween." —Patricia Day

About a week after Drake's funeral, Drucilla was awoken by the sound of her cell phone vibrating on her dresser at the same time that thunder crashed outside. She tried to focus her eyes as she peered out of the bedroom window. It was a strange time of year for a storm. Storms like these usually happen in Spring. Drucilla dragged her sleepy body out of bed and grabbed her phone.

1 new text message

It was from a number Drucilla didn't recognize. Diablo pounced on the bed and beckoned for Drucilla to return.

"No, you just want my body heat," Drucilla protested. Diablo persisted with an insistent *mau*. Drucilla turned her attention back to her phone and read the message.

This is the Law Offices of Osmus and Berg. Please call at your earliest convenience. This is regarding the estate of Drake Blackwood. 213-555-5697

Drake has been dead for weeks. Why are they calling me now? Drucilla put on her robe, pulled Diablo from the bed with another *mau*, and dropped him on the floor.

Groggily, she shuffled down the cool, polished cherry-stained wooden staircase to the kitchen. The thunder loudly cracked again. She propped herself up at the kitchen table and opened her laptop. She searched for the law offices that had just sent the text.

"The Law Offices of Hope L. Berg and Ed A. Osmus," she said aloud.

Drucilla browsed her way through their terrible website, eventually navigating to the *Lawyers* link. There was an image of two distinguished older gentlemen with stark white hair. Both were professionally dressed, and each stood facing each other with a foot on a chair like the pirate pictured on *The Captain's* rum bottle. They looked like identical twins. *Are these guys for real*? Drucilla continued to read their truncated bios.

"Located in sunny Los Angeles. Well, let's see what they want," she said. Drucilla picked up her phone and called the number. Diablo jumped on the kitchen table and demanded her attention.

A cheerful young woman answered, "Osmus and Berg, how may I direct your call?"

"Uh, yeah. Hi, I was sent a text message to call you to discuss my brother's estate?"

"Is this Drucilla?" the woman asked.

"Yes."

"Oh! That was me. I sent the text. Thanks for calling back so quickly. Can you hold?"

"Uh yeah, I gu—" hold music ensued, "—ess." Drucilla tried to answer. Diablo jumped into Drucilla's lap with a loud and demanding purr. Drucilla saw Adrian appear and make his way into the kitchen out of the corner of her eye.

"Do you want breakfast?" Adrian asked while hovering around the kitchen cabinets.

"Drake's lawyer just called me. I'm returning the call."

"That doesn't answer my question."

"Pineapple is fine," Drucilla said, waving him off. She was stuck listening to the dreadful hold music.

"What do they want?"

"I don't know yet. I just got a text to call. I'm returning it," Drucilla repeated, giving Adrian a confused look.

Diablo started to hiss at Adrian angrily and meowed with ferocity.

"Diablo!" Drucilla shouted as she put him down before he clawed the skin off her arms. He meowed loudly and bolted out of the kitchen.

"That cat will never get used to me," Adrian complained.

"Well, Adrian, you're a ghost, and cats are weird about the dead."

Adrian rolled his eyes and went about cutting up a pineapple.

"Ms. Blackwood?" the voice on the other end of the line asked.

"Yes, this is she."

The thunder outside became louder and more aggressive.

"What is with this storm?" Adrian asked quietly, gazing out the window.

"Good morning, my name is Ed Osmus. I am managing your brother's estate. I am responsible for his Last Will, and you are listed as sole beneficiary," he said.

"Me? Why would I be a beneficiary?"

"I am not sure I understand?"

"Well, I've been estranged from my brother for a while—at least fifteen years. I'm just surprised that he would list me as a beneficiary."

"Well, I do not know about any of that, but this Will was written and signed two years ago," Mr. Osmus said.

"Ok—"

"We would like to schedule a reading of the Will. When would be an ideal time for you to attend?"

Another thunder boom happened outside and caught Drucilla off guard. She flinched at the noise and shook it off. "I can be back in Los Angeles anytime this week."

"Would Wednesday at 9:00 a.m. be an appropriate time?" Mr. Osmus asked.

"Yeah, I can do that."

"Wonderful. I will have my secretary send a confirmation notice."

"Yeah, great, thank you."

"You are welcome." Mr. Osmus disconnected.

Drucilla put her phone down and turned to Adrian.

"You were just there," Adrian said. He placed a bowl of freshly chopped pineapple in front of her.

"Yeah, well, people suck at timing," Drucilla said. She shoved a chunk in her mouth.

The room got brighter and brighter as the sun poured into the kitchen. The rays illuminated the crystal on the shelves and reflected on the modern stainless-steel appliances. Adrian and Drucilla both looked out the window quizzically.

"It was just storming," Drucilla said and looked at Adrian in confusion. Adrian returned her confused stare.

"So," Drucilla said, changing the subject. "Ready to go back to LA?"

"Oh! Oh, now you want me to go." Adrian replied. He had an overtly annoyed tone.

Drucilla picked up the small silver urn pendant from the countertop and clasped it around her neck. Adrian looked at her and threw up his arms. "I'm not staying anywhere other than *Chateau Claremont*."

Drucilla shook her head, slid off the stool, and made her way back up the stairs. Adrian followed.

"Do you think I'll see Marylin?" he asked. He clapped his hands together in excitement.

"Adrian, we're not staying at *Chateau Claremont*."

"Oh! John Belushi died there!" he said with giddy excitement. He glided up the staircase behind her.

✝✝✝

"In 1.8 miles, exit the freeway and make a right onto Westwood Boulevard," the female voice from the navigation said. The jolting voice interrupted a *Bauhaus* song.

It was a typical bright warm day in southern California. Traffic was ridiculous, and Drucilla was reminded that she completely forgot to grab coffee with that little achy twinge in her forehead. She hated this place. The air was horrid, the people were insane, and you question whether the state had a budget for road maintenance. Drucilla was pretty sure the trash had been there since the '60s. *Maybe I'm just spoiled by living in Washington state where it's always clean, smells wonderful, and you can drink the tap water.* Drucilla left California a couple of years previous, but it always seemed to demand her presence. She likened it to a bad relationship. *You break up with someone and think it's over but still manage to run into them.* She had been away for five hours, and she was already homesick.

"You're gonna pass it!" a ghostly arm jutted out from behind her head, pointing at the windshield to the turn-off she should have taken and caused her to have a brief but intense panic attack.

"Damn it!" Drucilla yelled. "I didn't let you out! What are you doing?"

"You didn't tighten the lid," Adrian said smugly. "I bet you're glad you didn't. You'd be lost!"

"Believe it or not, Adrian, I made it through thirty years of my life without your assistance. I have navigation."

"Then use it!"

Drucilla reached into her shirt, pulled out the small urn, and tightened the lid. Adrian dissipated. *He's gonna kill me one of these days.*

†††

The Law Offices of Osmus and Berg were located inside of an elaborate stone mansion. The tall, iron gate stood open as Drucilla turned off the street and onto the long, tree-lined driveway. The trees were twisted and old, the branches reaching across to each other in an eerie handshake. The light barely pierced through the leaves. As she got closer to the mansion, clouds began to gather, and the sky grew increasingly dim. Faint rumblings of thunder could be heard in the distance.

Drucilla pulled up to the front of the mansion steps and put the car into park. She noticed two long black cars with tinted windows near the entrance. She reached behind her seat, grabbed her bag, and got out. As she made her way to the stairway, a few rain drops fell. She ran up the stairs to take cover under the portico and pressed the doorbell.

"Osmus and Berg, may I help you?" a woman's voice came over the speaker.

Drucilla looked around for the speaker and button. She looked up and saw a camera. "Hi, yeah, my name is Drucilla and—"

There was an audible door click.

"Please come in and have a seat. We will be with you in a moment," the voice said.

As Drucilla entered the mansion, she noticed the foyer was opulent with ridiculous amounts of carved wood, bronze statues, baroque style paintings, and exquisite Persian rugs. The place didn't smell musty as she expected it to smell, but more like oil and polish. The wallpaper looked like an old pattern from the 1800s, yet still somehow new. Lightning flashed through the windows and illuminated the room with a sudden bright, ghostly white flare. To the right, the large solid oak staircase spiraled up magnificently and dominantly as if to say, *"I'm the reason this house was made…it was built around me."* A large grandfather clock ticked with deep reverberating acoustics in an otherwise silent room.

Drucilla slowly walked through the foyer, examining the paintings on the walls. *Woah, is this really a Caravaggio?*

"Of Saint John the Baptist? Yes," a voice said behind her.

"Is this real?" Drucilla asked in disbelief. She was more taken aback by the priceless painting than the fact that this person heard her thoughts.

"Yes, of course, we have a Rembrandt, as well, over here," the gentleman stated.

Drucilla turned around to see who was speaking to her. The gentleman pointed to another painting on the wall. Drucilla followed him and stood in front of the painting.

"This is Rembrandt's son...," he said.

"...Titus, as a Monk," Drucilla said, finishing his sentence.

He turned to look at her and said, "I see you are familiar with the piece?"

"I run a small art gallery. I'm a bit of an art nerd," Drucilla said. She couldn't take her eyes off the painting. "This is insane. I don't think I've ever seen such a collection outside of a museum."

"The museums display forgeries. All of them."

"Really?" Drucilla asked in disbelief.

"Ask yourself why you would place a priceless painting in an area where just anyone can accidentally destroy it? Private collectors own nearly all original priceless paintings. The museums have reproductions. Some are quite good and require a professional to tell them apart from the originals."

"Wow, well, that kind of hurts," she said in a depressed tone. She turned her gaze to the gentleman.

He smiled at her confidently. "I am Mr. Berg. You may call me Hope." He extended his hand out to Drucilla, and she noticed the same clawed fingernails. She took his hand and shook it slowly and apprehensively.

"Mr. Osmus and I are ready to meet with you and go over the Will when you are ready. If you would like to spend a few moments out here in the foyer and look at the paintings a bit longer, that would be fine."

"Oh, no, that's ok. I'm quite anxious to get this dealt with."

"All right, we will not keep you. Shall we?" the gentleman motioned to the door on the opposite side of the paintings near the staircase. The lightning flashed through the hallway again.

He walked ahead, opened the door for Drucilla, and smiled. He seemed like a pleasant man. As Drucilla entered the office, she noticed that it was an old-fashioned smoking room—a room where gentlemen would gather to have a cigar and brandy. Dueling swords, guns, and books lined the walls. Games like Mahjong, chess, and checkers were laid out on various ornate mahogany tables between two oversized cognac brown leather chairs. An elaborately carved mahogany desk sat at the end of the room, covered in multiple papers and clutter. It appeared to be the desk of someone who was utterly opposed to technology and preferred to do things by hand. Behind the desk, Drucilla assumed, sat Mr. Osmus. He stood up and extended a clawed hand to her.

"Ms. Blackwood," he said, almost yelling.

"Hello," Drucilla said. She reached for his hand.

He shook it firmly. "I am Ed Osmus. You have met Hope."

Hope looked at Drucilla and nodded briefly.

"How are you faring? I take it your journey was pleasant?" Mr. Osmus asked. A loud crash of thunder with a bright flash exploded outside. He sat back down behind his desk.

"Uh, yeah, it was fine."

Drucilla winced at the loudness of the storm outside. She was beginning to get suspicious. *This place, as well as the men themselves, seem a little too staged like this is an elaborate façade. What are they up to?* She clutched the amulet resting in her hand.

"Please, make yourself comfortable," Mr. Osmus said. He motioned to the leather chairs in front of his desk.

Drucilla sat and distractedly looked out the window. The storm was intense.

"Oh, the storm?" Mr. Osmus asked. "I'm sorry about that. I just like the atmosphere, the electricity pulsing outside, the smell..." He closed his eyes and leaned his head back. He sighed deeply.

Drucilla glanced around, uneasy, and fixed her eyes on Hope for a reaction. Hope smiled at her with a devious grin.

"Anyway," Mr. Osmus said. He waved off the sensation. "Yes, I get that it is distracting to some. I apologize. That was rude of me." He sat back upright. He closed his eyes slowly as if to meditate for a brief second. He then slowly opened them again. "There we go!" He turned his gaze to the window.

Drucilla followed his gaze and looked out the window. The storm dissipated quickly, and the clouds cleared away to reveal an azure blue sky.

Drucilla started putting things together in her head and realized their names were anagrams. *I'm dealing with Lucifer's brothers. This was a meager, pathetic attempt to get me to surrender the Queens' relics,* Drucilla thought as she became increasingly livid. *If they want to play this game, I can play, too!* Drucilla was assuming that they were not aware that she had learned what the rosary really was and the power it held.

Drucilla exhaled in annoyance. She hopped out of the leather chair and stood in front of his desk. She threw her hands up, "Let's just cut the shit here. I get that you're trying to intimidate me. Your grotesque display of power doesn't impress me. This kind of intimidation tactic doesn't do anything but bore me to death. Why don't you stop with the stupid games and get to it, or did I come here for nothing?"

Mr. Osmus looked at Drucilla, stunned, then burst into laughter along with Hope. "Your face! You should see your face right now!" He grabbed his stomach and let out a huge belly laugh as if Drucilla was an animal that performed a trick for their amusement.

"Yeah, I bet this is hilarious to you!" she yelled. Drucilla shot a hostile glare as she slammed the palm of her hand down on the desk with a bead from the rosary in her palm. She felt a faint, crushed glass fragment within her hand. Immediately, neon blue veins like branches shot up her arm across half of her face, as her eyes glowed bright blue with anger then faded away to her natural color. She sat back down.

"Heh…heh… *cough*" Mr. Osmus straightened his shirt and adjusted his demeanor. Hope sat silently staring at Drucilla, clearly shocked that she had learned how to unlock the rosary.

"All right, that is fair. Let us proceed." Mr. Osmus replied.

Mr. Osmus handed the Will to Drucilla to review. Drucilla glanced down at it. Abruptly, Hope snatched it back from her hands and ripped it in half in front of her.

"What Will?" Hope said. He smiled ghoulishly again.

Drucilla looked at him in confusion. "What's going on here?"

Mr. Osmus got up from the desk and made his way to the front of the desk, and leaned against it next to Drucilla. "You have something we want. You have a few things to be exact. Surrender the relics, and in exchange, you will have everything."

"What do you mean *everything*?" Drucilla asked.

"This house—This was your brother's, was it not?"

"I don't know. I know literally nothing about Drake. I don't know about any of his assets."

"This house, the house in Prague, the house in Romania, the house in Bali, roughly one billion dollars in cash, his political influence, stocks, luxury cars, boats, jet, and his prized art collection that you were admiring in the hall. All for you in exchange for the relics," Mr. Osmus explained.

Confused, Drucilla stood up and walked around the room. She turned back to him and calmly asked, "What exactly do you think I have?"

Hope stood up in front of Drucilla. "You have Calliope's Sanguis Deus, the Tempest cauldron, and Erato Falx. We just want those old, useless relics and you will live your life in opulence. You will never have to worry about money taxes, and never have responsibilities again. You can just live your life traveling, visiting ancient cities, or you can sit around this beautiful mansion with five-hundred cats. I am offering you a life of whatever you can dream. You will have the means and power to do it."

Sanguis Deus, is that what this is called? What's Tempest? Erato Falx? Drucilla asked in her head and wished she could rewind the conversation.

"We are aware that you possess them and that you have been hidden from us. Your brother had control of a powerful coven. They had been entrusted with protecting you. The Unholy were unable to pursue you due to a grand obscuration spell. All their power, including your brother's, went into keeping you cloaked from The Unholy. When Drake died, the protection spell was broken, and we were able to see you." Hope waved at Drucilla as if he was looking at her through a window. "Hello, I see you."

"So, if I don't comply with what you ask?" Drucilla questioned.

"We would take them and leave you with nothing but a decaying corpse. We would rather not resort to that. We would like to offer an exceedingly generous exchange. There is no need for violence," Mr. Osmus said.

Drucilla threw her head back and laughed at the absurdity. "You're lying! Because if you could kill me, you would have done it by now and saved yourself a lot of trouble. But you know you can't just take them, don't you?"

Mr. Osmus and Hope look at each other blankly.

Drucilla slowly walked over to Mr. Osmus, put her face within inches of his face, and quietly said, "You'll never get those relics." Drucilla looked directly into his eyes slowly leaned her head to the side.

Mr. Osmus quietly snarled like a demon. His eyes reflected an orange glow; his claws dug into the desk as the wood snapped under the pressure.

Drucilla stepped back.

"Do you really think I could be persuaded with stupid, powerless, material objects and money? I mean, really? We both know that you can't do anything as long as I have these relics. You can't take anything from me, and you can't kill me. I know who you are, Asmodeus," Drucilla snapped.

Hope snarled behind her.

Drucilla turned her head quickly and pointed to Hope, "And you too, Belphegor. You tell the rest of your brothers that if they want a fight, bring it. I'll be ready."

Drucilla picked up her handbag and quickly made her way to the door. She looked back over her shoulder as she opened the door. Asmodeus and Belphegor stood angry and silent as she walked out of the room and slammed the door behind her.

Drake looked down from the top of the stairs. His snake eyes fixed on his sister, watching her as if he was calculating his next move. Drucilla was struck with the overwhelming feeling of being watched. She quickly turned her gaze to the top of the stairs. There was no one there. She watched the empty space for a few moments. Finally, she turned her attention to the front door and exited the mansion.

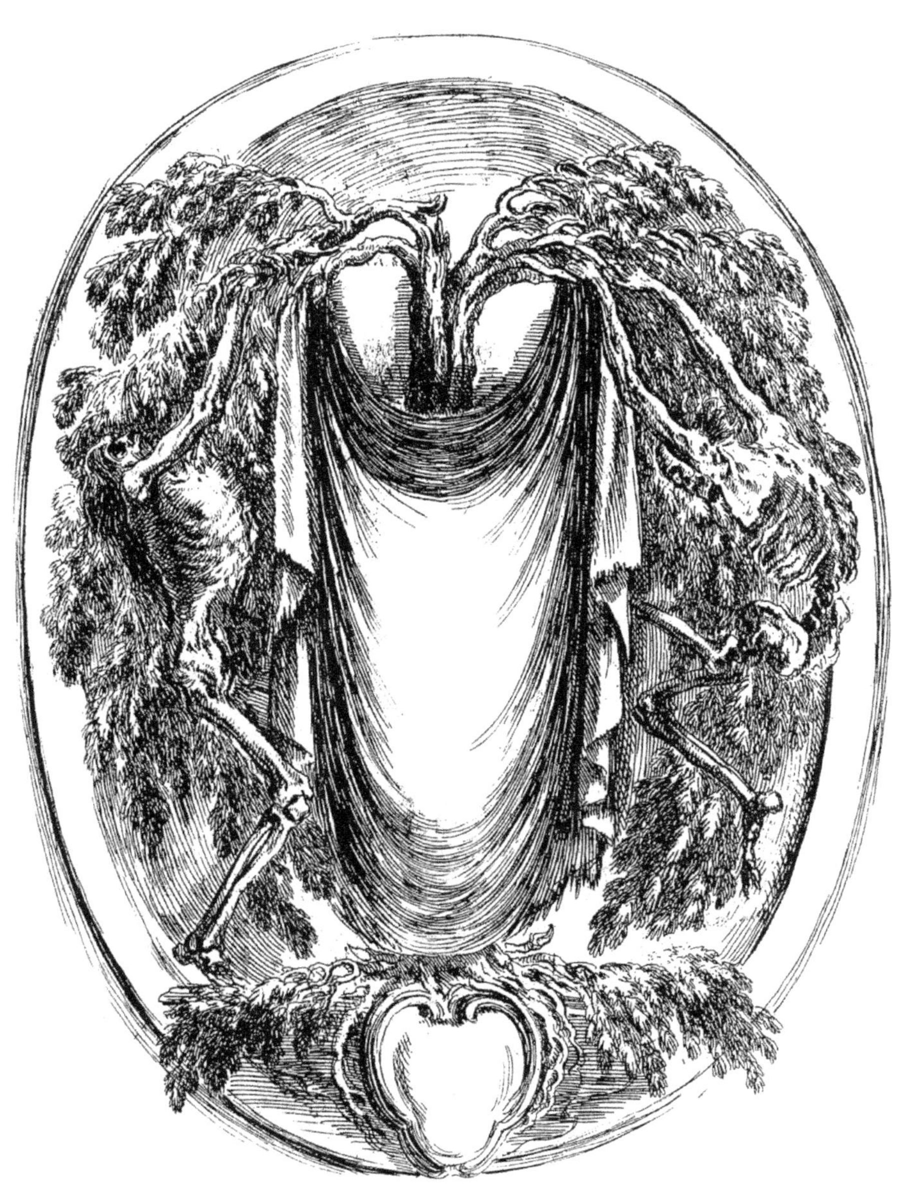

CANTICLE TWENTY-TWO

✝

Adrian and Drucilla arrived at the *Chateau Clairmont* at 5:00 p.m. when other guests were just starting to arrive and check in to the hotel. Drucilla slowly unscrewed the embossed vial of cremated remains around her neck to break the seal.

"Oh my God!" Adrian gasped. "I'm not coming home with you. I am staying here forever. Will you look at this place?"

"Adrian, we used to live in this town, remember?"

"Well, no one ever took me here. I always wanted to come."

Drucilla and Adrian walked up to the front desk and waited their turn. "There are a lot of dead folks here," Drucilla remarked. She noticed the population of ghosts vastly outnumbered the living.

Adrian glanced at her quizzically.

"You couldn't have possibly thought you were the only ghost I could see, right?" Drucilla asked.

"I never thought about it."

"Ever notice how obviously out of place they are? I always expected ghosts to be semi-transparent, glowing people like in movies. But they're like old images frozen in time. You know how you can look at a piece of furniture, and you can tell that it is at least fifty years old?" she asked.

Drucilla inadvertently made eye contact with an apparition of a young woman. "Damn it; she knows I can see her. Now, she's going to come and talk to me." Drucilla quickly looked past her and around the room as if it were a mere coincidence.

"What's wrong with that?" Adrian asked.

"Well, as soon as a spirit figures out that I can see them, then it's: 'Oh can you tell my daughter or tell my husband or tell my mom blah, blah, blah,' and suddenly, I'm a messaging service that's just here to relay their messages from beyond the grave. I mean, I don't dislike them, but they're annoying and entitled to some degree—kind of like living people.

Drucilla took another step forward to the front desk. "By the way, we're out of here at 6:00 a.m.

"That isn't going to work for me. We'll discuss that later," Adrian said. He caught the eye of a tall, dark-haired, handsome gentleman.

"I'm serious; consider me your Fairy Godmother. You will poof like a ballroom gown if I don't see you by morning," Drucilla warned.

Adrian glided away in the gentleman's direction while simultaneously giving Drucilla the middle finger. Drucilla shook her head slowly and stepped up to the check-in counter. She noticed on her left an attractive, well-dressed gentleman sitting in a tall mahogany leather chair as she signed in the desk register. The gentleman leaned his head on his hand. He placed his elbow on the armchair and appeared to be talking on his phone. He was flipping what looked like a gold coin between his fingers. Drucilla briefly stared at him. He made eye contact with her and smiled slightly. Drucilla rolled her eyes, turned her attention to her backpack, and pulled it over her shoulder. She quickly made her way to the elevator. As she waited for the doors to open, she took the opportunity to check her phone. The elevator opened, and she stepped into it. She didn't look up from her phone. After the doors shut, the car filled with a distinct, intoxicating scent of exotic woods, leather, tobacco, and bergamot.

"You are correct. They cannot kill you," the familiar voice said behind her.

Drucilla turned around and saw the beautiful, blond gentlemen as he leaned lazily against the side of the elevator. His black eyes faded out into yellow-hued snake-eyes as he grinned menacingly, which looked more intimidating with his perfectly chiseled cheekbones and chin. His façade faded, and his translucent skin began to show. Drucilla turned back and faced the elevator doors. She watched the floor numbers light up as they moved higher.

"So, how have you been?"

"New look for you? I see you're still partial to the blonde hair," Drucilla said.

"I enjoy updating my appearance from time to time. I am the King of Pride and Vanity."

Drucilla exhaled loudly. "What are you doing here, Lucifer? You can't possibly have anything good to offer." She kept her back to him.

"Now, now…You do not know that."

Drucilla turned to face him and glared. The elevator indicator *dinged*, and they arrived at her floor. Drucilla turned back around and headed down the hallway.

Lucifer followed. "Drucilla, I just want to help."

"You can help by being honest with me for once," Drucilla said. She stopped and looked directly at his face.

"I know you met with my brothers. You've obviously figured out by now that they want your relics."

Drucilla looked at him, dumbstruck by the stupidity of the statement.

"I've really had enough of this garbage for one day, I'm tired, and I want a nap." Drucilla turned to her room and slid the card through the lock. The door clicked, and she walked inside. She closed the door in Lucifer's face and dropped her bag at the door.

"Rude!" Lucifer said. He sat in a chair by the window on the opposite side of the room.

Drucilla threw her hands up, "What is it going to take?"

"Please, hear what I have to say, and I will leave. Fair?"

"I'm not going to make a deal with you. You aren't getting anything from me."

"I do not have any interest in the Queens' relics," he said. "You should know that by now."

Drucilla looked at him and shrugged. "Ok, then why are we having this conversation?"

Lucifer stood up and walked across to the other end of the room. He gazed out of the tenth-story window.

"My brothers, they want to rule Hell. However, they cannot because the Queens stand in their way. They cannot defeat the Queens without the three relics. So, if they were to obtain…."

"If I give up the relics, they can overthrow the Queens and rule Hell," Drucilla said, cutting him off.

"More or less," Lucifer responded.

"Well, good luck finding them," Drucilla said. She threw herself into the chair across from him.

Lucifer laughed to himself. "We know where they are. Do you think we do not know that you keep relics hidden in a subterranean shelter beneath the shed in your backyard?... And Calliope's rosary is right there around your wrist." He pointed to Drucilla's arm. "We know you have them. Everyone in Hell knows you have them. We just cannot take them."

Drucilla stared at Lucifer, trying to understand why Belphegor and Asmodeus insisted that she had the relics.

"They seem to think I have something called Erato Falx and Tempest. My rosary is called Sanguis Deus, apparently. I have no idea what they're talking about."

Lucifer nodded. "Yes, that is the relic's name. Drucilla, I do not want my brothers to get these relics from you. Hell is a delicate balance, and any shift would be catastrophic for both humans and The Divine. I am offering you my assistance, should you need me."

"How exactly would you help me? Again, I'm not making any deals with you."

"I could misdirect them or throw them off your path—I am offering my protection. Think of it as a symbiotic relationship. I'll protect you, and you keep the relics. Hell stays the way it is," Lucifer said. He folded his arms, his serpentine eyes flickered.

"This sounds like a deal."

"No deals. No repercussions. We are just doing a favor for a friend."

"It's not like I was going to give them up anyway."

"My brothers can get creative and force your hand by any means necessary. They can disguise themselves as people you trust. They can create catastrophic situations in which the only way to solve them would be to relinquish the relics. I can ensure that you do not succumb to the pitfalls of their devious acts."

"Won't this make you an enemy of the family?"

"They have done it to themselves. I merely want to keep the peace."

"What do you know about the Tempest cauldron and Erato Falx?" Drucilla asked.

"Should I not be asking you that question?"

"I don't know what this cauldron is. I was accused of having it, and if I do have it, I'd like to be aware of it. As far as I know, I've never seen it before. I mean, I don't even own a cauldron relic. 'Just the bowls in my kitchen cabinets, and I got those from a department store."

Lucifer stood up and paced the room for a moment. "It is not exactly a bowl. More of a cauldron. Perhaps it has not yet come into your possession."

"What about Erato Falx?"

"You don't know what that is?" Lucifer laughed. "It is chiseled on the side of Nova's pen."

"Don't…don't play with me, Seraphim, you know I can't read the symbols." Drucilla took a jab at Lucifer by calling him Seraphim, knowing he hates that word.

He shot Drucilla a hostile glare from his serpentine eyes.

"If we're going to do favors for each other," Drucilla said while making air quotes around the word *favors*. "You're going to have to stop keeping things from me."

"This sounds like a deal, Drucilla." Lucifer used her own words against her.

Drucilla exhaled slowly. "Ok fine, we'll see how it goes. Don't think I've forgotten about Athens."

"Dru, if you will just allow me to explain about that—"

"No, you weren't there. There's nothing that can repair that. I need time to build trust with you. Now, if you'll please leave, I need sleep."

Lucifer nodded in compliance and blinked out.

En Alamodo Heleniam, ditemq; Leuemq; Superbam:
Ossea Iudicicium quod feret ista ſtrues.
D Alamodo Helena Leichtfertig, reich stoltz wie ein Phom,
gedenck an Gottes Gericht behendt, So wirstu han ein gutes endt.

CANTICLE TWENTY-THREE

"Split your lungs with blood and thunder." —Mastodon

✝

"Have you lost your fucking mind?" Dominic was livid as he yelled at Drucilla. Dominic ran his fingers in a panicked fashion through his short, stubbly hair, pulling tightly on his scalp. He turned away from Drucilla in anger and disbelief.

Drucilla didn't look up as the hypodermic needle and syringe pulled the remaining blood from the last crystal bead. Powdered crystal debris and a small jeweler's drill laid beside the pile of broken and spent beads on Dominic's dining room table.

"This will work," Drucilla stated with certainty.

"No! It's suicide! You can't! You can't possibly know that this will work!"

"Dominic, I have to!" Drucilla turned her attention to the blood as she held the syringe at eye-level. She tapped the side to force any air pockets to emerge.

"I refuse to allow you to do this!"

Drucilla carefully put the syringe down and turned to him. "What happens when the blood runs out…When there are no more beads?"

"Then it's over! Or just don't use them anymore... Any number of other possible outcomes, but this! This is insanity! You're killing yourself!" Dominic knelt by Drucilla's side and grabbed her hand. "Drucilla, you are not Divine. You're about to inject divine blood into your body. Please, don't do this."

Drucilla pulled up her sleeve to expose the inside of her arm. She wrapped her hand around her biceps and squeezed while pumping her fist. She felt around for a healthy vein to make its way to the surface. "I was chosen. This rosary was given to me. There must be more," She held the needle to the visible purple vein that had risen to the surface.

Dominic stared into Drucilla's eyes, terrified and in disbelief.

"I mean, I've been micro-dosing, right?"

He doesn't break eye contact.

"If I die, don't play dumb music at my funeral, ok? It's just gonna piss me off." Drucilla pushed the needle into her arm and pushed down on the plunger. The familiar, small neon blue lightning bolt appeared again as it shot up her arm and faded away. Drucilla squeezed Dominic's hand.

He gripped tightly back. They sat quietly, staring at each other. Drucilla felt nothing.

"I don't think it worked," Drucilla said, disappointed.

They stood up. Drucilla grabbed her jacket off the back of the chair and slipped her arms through the sleeves. She looked back at the table with the small drill, crystal dust, and destroyed rosary beads. She picked up the amulet that adorned the bottom of the beads. She handed it to Dominic.

"Here, keep it. If anything, it's a neat trinket for your collection."

"No, you keep it."

"You can still see ghosts with it," Drucilla said. She smiled at Dominic. He nodded at her.

"Wow. I guess it's over." Drucilla seemed remorseful that the blood didn't give her divine power, and now her superpower was gone.

Dominic stood silent. He could feel her disappointment.

Drucilla turned to walk out of the room. Suddenly, she felt fire explode from inside her chest. Like a solar prominence extended from the sun, it touched the center of her body. Everything seemed to be in slow motion as Drucilla fell to the ground. Dominic threw his arms around her waist, screaming her name. Drucilla's chest burst into an intense blue light that bathed the entire room as if lightning had struck inside the house. Drucilla's body was on fire. Every nerve, every vein was exposed and beaming in bright blue light. Drucilla felt every atom in her body explode simultaneously, like a transformer blowing up in a storm. As quickly as it happened, everything went dark, and all she could hear was the distant maniacal laughter coming from somewhere inside her ribcage. Everything fell silent and black.

†††

The sound of a creaky wooded panel being pulled open and slamming against something metal disrupted Drucilla's deep slumber. Bleary-eyed, she reached for her face to rub her eyes, but a warm cuffed hand in a suit with the distinct scent of leather and bergamot grabbed it midway.

"You! You are a damned idiot. Up you go!" the voice said. He pulled Drucilla to an upright position.

Blinking furiously, Drucilla attempted to gain control of her bearings. The fact that she was in a casket slowly came into focus. "What the?"

"Let us go now! Get up. The bearers will be back any minute!" the voice said excitedly.

Drucilla's vision still hadn't cleared, but even with the blurred vision, Drucilla recognized Lucifer.

"You are going to have to assist, Drucilla!" Lucifer tried to pry Drucilla out of the casket, but he had difficulty getting a sturdy grip on her.

"Ok. Um, ok," Drucilla mumbled. She attempted to stand up in the casket as he steadied her balance. Drucilla looked around and noticed that she was in a casket on a bier in a funeral home.

Lucifer jumped down and offered his hand to Drucilla to help her. She stepped out of the casket and jumped down to meet him on the ground level.

"Come, come, let us go!" Lucifer stood behind Drucilla and shoved her towards the doors.

Drucilla looked back over her shoulder to see a beautifully arranged room filled with heliotropes and blue and antique hydrangeas. "What happened?" She tried to process the most recent events that she could manage to recall.

Lucifer quickly ushered her out of the main entrance and down the stairs into the cemetery. "The cemetery workers were coming to button you up in an oblong box and ship you out to your mother. I had but a moment to get you out."

"Am, am I dead?"

Lucifer ignored her question as they briskly walked towards a blacked-out sports car. She was afraid of the answer. Drucilla stopped and looked down at her burial dress.

"Christ, am I actually wearing a periwinkle cocktail dress?" She felt the top of her head and realized her hair was styled in some sort of up-do. A small, glittery gem was incrusted into a lock of her jet-black hair as it swung down onto her face. Drucilla looked at Lucifer, "I don't want to know, do I?"

"Get in," Lucifer commanded.

The doors of a blacked-out sports car popped open at his command. They climbed inside as Lucifer started the engine. "You!" What were you thinking?" Lucifer laughed to himself in disbelief as they drove out of the cemetery gates.

"So, just so I'm clear, I'm not dead, right?"

"No, you are very much alive." Lucifer continued to laugh.

"Ok, stop. Stop the car. I need to process."

Lucifer pulled the car over to the side of the hilly, tree-lined road. Dusk quickly approached, and Drucilla realized that she didn't know how much time had passed.

"I have a lot of questions," Drucilla started. "The blood. I injected the blood."

"Yes, you did! What did you think was going to happen?" Lucifer was still chuckling.

"Can you stop? Please?" Drucilla was becoming irate that Lucifer found this entirely too humorous.

"My apologies. I know this is traumatic for you."

"What happened between the time I injected the blood and five minutes ago"?

"I do not completely know. I was not there when it happened."

"Not like it's the first time you failed to show up." Drucilla crossed her arms.

Lucifer rolled his eyes at her attempted jab. "I did retrieve you. You could be a tad more appreciative," Lucifer said.

"How long was I there?"

"I am still not hearing a *thank you*."

"God damn it, Lucifer, help me!"

"I arrived in time only to find out you had done the stupidest thing imaginable. Dominic was stunned, unable to speak. You were pronounced dead by the coroner. However, there was something inside of you not visible by human technology. Somehow you were being kept outside of death. I am not sure how or why. I figured you probably were not irretrievably dead. I fully intended to fetch you at the morgue, but you know, I was busy, and this was the only time that worked with my schedule."

Drucilla stared at him in disbelief for a moment. "Your what?"

"What? I am extremely busy."

Drucilla blinked rapidly in disbelief and annoyance. "But I did die, right?"

"Oh yes, you were most definitely dead as far as humans can comprehend." Lucifer started to laugh to himself again.

Drucilla glared at him. "How did my mom take it?"

"I am not certain. Undoubtedly, as well as your mother took Drake's death, I would imagine."

"How's Dominic?" Drucilla's frustration turned to concern.

"Dominic will be fine; your mother will be fine. I wouldn't worry about that."

Drucilla stared at Lucifer in confusion.

Lucifer glanced at Drucilla and gave her a slight smirk.

1510

CANTICLE TWENTY-FOUR

*"My heart won't beat forever." —*Cancerslug

†

From what Drucilla gathered, three days had passed. She searched around her doorframe to find her house key and let herself inside. Her phone was nowhere to be found. Diablo sat on the banister of the porch, being exceptionally standoffish.

He didn't miss me.

The house was just as she had left it, cold but quieter than usual. Drucilla could not wait to get out of the awful cocktail dress. She noticed her luggage was still unpacked. Next to her luggage was a large, clear bag from the morgue, resting on the coffee table. Drucilla saw her leather jacket packed inside the plastic. It was what she was wearing when she died. Aggressively and without regard, she dumped the bag's contents on the couch and found her phone and wallet.

Drucilla made her way upstairs to the master bathroom. She stood in front of the bathroom mirror, pulling out what seemed like three-hundred bobby pins. She shook out her hair and pulled off the miserable dress.

"Ugh, this is getting donated," she said to herself.

She turned the knob in the shower and went back to the mirror to inspect her face. In the crook of her arm, the small puncture wound was still visible.

It really happened. I really died, didn't I? She stood in the mirror and inspected her naked body. She looked at her stomach, chest, hands, arms, and shoulders. As she turned her body to the side, something caught her eye.

"What…what is that?" she said aloud. She reached her hand over her shoulder blade and could feel a barely risen, hard lump.

"I must have smashed my shoulder when I fell. They don't hurt, so it can't be that bad," she said, talking to herself. Drucilla turned to the other side and noticed one there as well. "Huh, I must have hit the ground hard…." Drucilla flexed her shoulder blades in the mirror to see if they changed at all.

"Drucilla! My God! Where have you been?" shouted Adrian, startling Drucilla.

A high-pitched shriek escaped Drucilla's throat. "God damn it!" Drucilla yelled at him, "Are you trying to kill me again?"

"Why are you here? You're supposed to be dead!" Adrian yelled, "I had to pick out your dress and floral arrangements, and poor Dominic had no idea how to contact your family; the whole funeral was a disaster!"

Adrian was stressed and paced the floor reliving the past few days in his head.

"Yeah. I know I spent about an hour on the phone with my mother explaining that there was some sort of mix-up at the hospital, and I just had appendicitis," Drucilla explained.

"She bought that?" Adrian asked. He looked at Drucilla with suspicion.

"No, she had no idea what I was talking about, but apparently, no one told her, which made her panic even more," Drucilla said, "It's almost like she didn't know that I died, or she didn't remember."

Adrian appeared confused. Drucilla squinted her eyes as she tried to put things together in her head.

"What?" Adrian asked.

"Adrian, I called Dominic and said that I wasn't dead, and he had no idea what I was talking about. But you remember," Drucilla said, confused as she turned her head to the side and held Adrian's stare.

"What's going on?" Adrian asked.

"I need answers, but first, I need a shower." Drucilla closed the bathroom door. "And how dare you attempt to bury me in this dress!" Drucilla yelled from the other side of the closed door.

†††

Drucilla explained to Adrian all the previous events that she understood from Lucifer.

"So, you're not a zombie?" Adrian asked.

"No."

"Vampire?"

"No," Drucilla rolled her eyes.

"Revenant?" Adrian asked, eliminating possibilities.

Drucilla sighed deeply, "No."

"Ok. So why would you do something so stupid?"

"It just felt like the right thing to do," Drucilla said uneasily, "It was a stupid decision, and I'll own that."

Adrian snapped his fingers when he thought of a new undead being. "Construct!"

"No!" Drucilla yelled. She was even more annoyed. "I would have had to have been created with different parts by a mad scientist and, oh my God, will you stop? I'm not dead! Why do you keep asking me if I'm undead?"

"'Cause honey, you have no heartbeat," Adrian announced.

"What?" Drucilla clutched her chest and placed the palm of her hand against it. Nothing. She started to feel around her neck for a pulse. She felt nothing. "FUCK!"

"Yep, undead."

"I can't be!" Drucilla yelled in a panicked voice, "Lucifer said I was alive."

"Well, that's your first mistake, trusting Lucifer." Adrian clicked his tongue and shook his head in disapproval.

Drucilla paced around her living room in a panic. "Ok, ok…I'm breathing." Drucilla inhaled and exhaled sharply, "So, I have to be pumping blood. Right?"

"Honey, I am no doctor, but I think you're undead."

"Stop! Just stop. I need to find Lucifer. How do I get a hold of Lucifer?" Drucilla paced uncontrollably.

"How do you usually get a hold of him?"

"I don't. Lucifer finds me. Not the other way around…."

†††

Drucilla explained that although she was confident that she had been dead for three days, no one knew about or remembered it other than Adrian. Dominic and Adrian stood shoulder-to-shoulder, studying Drucilla as she sat at the dining room table. She felt like a goldfish in a bowl, and they were just watching. Drucilla shifted in her chair uncomfortably.

"Well?" Drucilla asked.

"Drucilla, you aren't dead. That's clear. You're breathing, and you're warm. What exactly happened to you? Are you sure you died?" Dominic asked.

"I don't know. Yeah, I guess. Maybe?" Drucilla tried to analyze herself and the past three days.

"Well, your body seems to be functioning normally as far as I can tell," Dominic responded.

"My heart isn't working!" she panicked. Drucilla's eyes shifted between Dominic and Adrian.

"It is not that your heart is not working. It is that you do not have one," Lucifer explained as he suddenly and abruptly emerged from out of a dark corner in the room.

"I don't have one?" Drucilla bellowed.

"It has been replaced," Lucifer clarified.

Dominic and Adrian look at each other confused.

"Replaced with what?" Drucilla asked.

"Stand up." Lucifer motioned to her to get out of her chair, "take off your shirt."

Drucilla looked at Lucifer suspiciously.

"Remove the top half of your clothing," Lucifer politely asked, "Please."

Drucilla grabbed the sleeve of her sweater and retracted each arm at a time towards her chest. She lifted the sweater over her head and dropped it to the floor. Lucifer moved to the end of the room and turned off the chandelier that hung over the table.

"There, look…Do you see it?" Lucifer pointed to Drucilla's chest.

Everyone, including Drucilla looked at Drucilla's chest where her heart should be. There was a faint violet-blue glow emerging from her ribcage. Drucilla looked down and ran her fingers over her sternum. She then looked up at Lucifer, whom she could barely make out from the moonlight that beamed through the window.

"What does this mean?" Drucilla desperately tried to remain calm.

"I am not sure how to explain this, but you have a living being inside your body," Lucifer said.

"An entity?" Drucilla asked, confused.

"It's from the micro-dosing, isn't it?" Dominic glanced at Lucifer suspiciously.

Lucifer leaned back and flipped on the light switch. He walked back over to Drucilla, bent down to pick up her sweater, and handed it to her. Drucilla poked her hands back through the sleeves, and just as she was about to pull it over her head, Lucifer grabbed her arm and put it down.

"Turn around," Lucifer commanded.

Drucilla slowly turned her back to Lucifer. He reached out and slid his hand down over her shoulder blade.

"Curious. I did not think that was possible," Lucifer whispered to himself.

Dominic and Adrian moved over behind Drucilla to see what Lucifer was referring to.

"What? What's going on?" Drucilla tried to look over her shoulder.

"Is that…?" Dominic started.

"Yes, I believe so," Lucifer confirmed his assumption.

"What?" Drucilla jerked away from Lucifer and tried to view her backside. She wanted to see what everyone was so interested in. "What are you seeing?" Drucilla asked, devoid of patience.

Dominic turned his head to the side and studied Drucilla's body. Lucifer crossed his arms, fascinated. Nothing about the situation made Drucilla less paranoid.

"Drucilla, how does your back feel?" Lucifer asked.

"Fine, I mean, I have these lumps from when I hit the floor…."

"About that..." Lucifer glanced at Dominic. "Those are, I guess, what we could call buds."

"Buds?" Drucilla repeated, startled.

"Yes. Like rosebuds. They grow and bloom into big, beautiful roses. But in your case, wings," Lucifer responded.

"ARE YOU KIDDING ME?"

"No, I am not," Lucifer flatly responded.

"Dru, the blood you absorbed into your body was divine. An entity, an angel…." Dominic explained.

"So, you're saying I'm becoming an angel?" Drucilla asked in disbelief as she pulled her sweater down over her body.

"Dominic, you are partially right, but that is not just angel's blood. That is the blood of an Ophanim: the order of the Thrones. The highest celestial order, the most divine in all existence. They are the creators of the universe. They would be what you would consider being a God here on earth."

"Is that even possible?" Dominic asked Lucifer in disbelief.

"I do not know. Drucilla is the first human to have ever taken divine blood."

"Will a Throne pop out of my body at some point? Am I a host, or will it take over when it's, uh gestated?" Drucilla was running a million scenarios through her head.

Lucifer studied Drucilla's face for a moment. "Come with me, Drucilla, please." Lucifer extended his clawed hand as he asked for hers, "Let's go for a walk, shall we?"

Lucifer and Drucilla walked down the heavily tree-lined street. The full moon was glowing above with opalescent rings and filtered through the leafless branches. It was a cool winter evening. Lucifer seemed cautiously optimistic about how he addressed Drucilla. He didn't want to appear overly confident and remained reserved with his speech. His approach seemed like a doctor's when they had to deliver bad news to a patient but were still optimistic about a treatment plan.

"A host? No, not exactly. Theoretically, you and the entity are becoming one being," Lucifer explained. "You and the entity have entered a symbiotic relationship. The entity is dependent on you to survive and vice versa. This is the only way for you to exist."

"Ok, so how does this fit into my mortality? Am I omnipotent like a god?"

"I do not know. As I said, you are the first," he responded.

"Second question," Drucilla stopped walking and turned to face him, "How do I get rid of it?"

Lucifer looked puzzled at Drucilla's question. He studied her face before replying. "I do not believe you can. When you took the divine blood into your body, you started a reaction—your body has forever changed. This is not a splinter that you can remove," Lucifer said.

Drucilla turned away from Lucifer and continued to walk along the road.

"You are afraid," he observed.

Drucilla didn't say anything.

Lucifer stopped and grabbed Drucilla's hand. "What you did was incredibly senseless and shortsighted. I have no idea what compelled you to go and try such a thing, but this right here is the best outcome for which you could have ever hoped. You are alive when you should not be. This stunt should have killed you. It did kill you, but somehow you defied the odds, and you continue to draw breath. Now, you want to get rid of it. This is even more irresponsible than your initial stunt," Lucifer said with no small amount of disappointment.

Drucilla just stared into his serpentine eyes. "I don't know what's going to happen to me, Lucifer. I just want to stop it from doing any more damage."

"That is understandable. But you are alive now; does that not matter to you?"

"About that, why doesn't anyone remember that I died? It's like everyone forgot, except for Adrian."

"Yes, that is curious."

Drucilla glared at Lucifer; she expected more of an answer.

"Why did you mix the blood with your own, Drucilla?" Lucifer asked, changing the subject.

Drucilla turned away from him and looked at the ground. She shoved her hands deep into the front pockets of her black jeans. "I don't know. I just thought, I guess I was afraid there would be a time when I ran out of beads. How would I get more? I guess I thought if I could make an endless supply using my own blood, it would never run out. I thought this was something I could control. I don't even know how I got here. Everything just happened so fast. I mean, now I'm standing here in the middle of the night on a dark street talking to the Devil as if he was my friend."

"Drucilla, I do not like your kind. My involvement with humans has always been nefarious. I play with you humans like puppets for my own amusement. I have for a millennium and will continue until the stars burn out, but I see a bit of myself in you. I suppose it is why I have an affinity for you. You remind me of someone I once was—curious, ambitious, and fearless."

"Affinity?"

"I do not have the capability to feel love for you humans, but I will say that because of our *simpatico*, I will look out for your well-being."

Drucilla smirked slightly, but the momentary amusement faded to paranoia. "Thank you," Drucilla said quietly, "I now know you're trying to help me even though I've made a massive disaster of things. I still don't entirely trust you, and I still think you're going to sell me out to your brothers one of these days, but I really appreciate you giving me a head start."

"I am going to help you, Drucilla. I assure you."

Drucilla shook her head. "I want to trust you. I do, and I want to believe you, but..." Drucilla motioned wildly at his entire presence.

"Fair," Lucifer shrugged.

Drucilla and Lucifer continued to walk down the road in silence, while in their minds they imagined scenarios both optimistic and catastrophic. Still, at that moment, everything was ok...for now.

...GREDIMVR CVNCTI DIVES CVM P... VPERE MIXTVS

CANTICLE TWENTY-FIVE

"Cuz, I'm bad news, everywhere I go." —Johnny Cash

✝

Winter, in its last gasps, was losing its grip to spring. The days were becoming longer and the evenings warmer. Drucilla walked around Port Townsend and took in the sun and mild temperature. It was St. Patricks' Day, and the townsfolk walked around in green clothing and green plastic hats. Many people were day drunk on green beer, and others were happy that the gloom had begun to recede.

Life had pretty much returned to normal—Drucilla's version of normal. Adrian would decorate and update the house while she was away, he would make dinner in the evenings, and Drucilla would read whatever divine books she could acquire. She regularly borrowed books from Dominic and his extensive collection. Drucilla's version of normal was living with a gay ghost and a useless cat. Her best friends were an occult-obsessed Russian antique dealer and the Devil himself.

Drucilla rummaged through the refrigerator and stuffed a handful of olives in her mouth. Adrian yammered in the background about bathroom textiles. Drucilla was an artist but couldn't care less about interior design, so she usually just agreed to whatever Adrian wanted.

"So, you're not going to go out tonight?" Adrian asked.

"No, not really into the whole Saint Paddy's thing."

"You really should try and go out sometime. What about the girl that sold the house next door? The real estate agent. Didn't she give you her phone number?"

"She wants to sell my house. I doubt she's interested in hanging out," Drucilla glared, tearing off a piece of a firm baguette.

"Someone's here," Adrian said. He promptly faded out.

Puzzled, Drucilla left the kitchen and walked into the foyer. She stopped short of the front door and didn't hear anyone outside. She then opened the curtain and peeked out into the front yard. She didn't see anyone or anything. "What is he talking about?" Drucilla mumbled to herself. Behind her, she heard the clanking of barware. Startled, she turned around to see Lucifer pouring himself a drink.

"You know, it's generally considered good manners to knock on the door, right?" Drucilla said to Lucifer in an annoyed tone.

He smirked to himself and tossed back a shot of scotch.

"Okay, what brings you here," Drucilla said, looking down at her watch on her wrist, "at nine o'clock at night?"

He walked over to Drucilla and sat in the oversized Queen Anne chair in front of the fireplace, and placed his glass on the edge of the chair arm. "I bring news," he said with a grin.

Drucilla sat across from him in the other chair and looked intently at him, "Go on…."

He pulled on his cuff and straightened out his sleeves. He then smoothed out his suit with his hands. He looked up at Drucilla and said, "She wants to see you."

"She, who?" Drucilla asked, furrowing her brow.

"She, the Queen."

Drucilla paused for a moment and turned her head to the side. Lucifer stared at her intensely as if he was telling her something telepathically, and she couldn't hear him. However, Drucilla didn't need telepathy to understand that he meant Calliope. Drucilla took a deep breath and exhaled slowly. "Why?" Drucilla said in monotone.

"I do not know. I was not privy to that information. Calliope requested that I bring you to her as soon as possible."

"What if I say no?"

"This is not something in which you have a choice. You are not being asked." Lucifer leaned back in the chair and placed his interwoven fingers on his lap. He looked austere.

"What are you not telling me?" Drucilla asked in the same suspicious monotone voice, becoming increasingly annoyed.

Lucifer silently stared at her, unflinching.

"Fine. When does she want to see me?"

Lucifer flicked his wrist out of his suit sleeve and looked at his watch, "Twenty minutes," he said, getting up from his seat.

"So," Drucilla looked around nervously, "Do I have to go to Hell for this meeting?"

Lucifer chuckled, "No. Do you want to?"

"Not particularly…."

"She will meet us shortly. Come, let us get coffee," he offered Drucilla his bent arm.

Drucilla slowly reached and grabbed onto his elbow. Within a blink of an eye, they were standing on the sidewalk in front of Lenny's coffeehouse. Drucilla and Lucifer entered the café and sat in a quiet corner away from the entrance.

"Sugar-free vanilla latte with oat milk and a splash of cinnamon, correct?" Lucifer asked.

"How did you know that?"

He grinned and pointed to his head as if he could read her mind and walked away.

Well, that's frightening, she thought. Drucilla was paranoid. She had no idea what was going to happen. *I'm actually going to meet a Queen of Hell.* Drucilla fumbled around with the effigy that previously adorned the end of the rosary beads. She kept it in her pocket. Drucilla didn't know why, but in addition to seeing Adrian, it gave her a strange sense of comfort.

The day drinkers turned into evening drunks as they got progressively louder and more obstinate as the evening wore on into the night. People were stumbling in for a coffee to sober themselves before returning home to their significant others or maybe parents. Lucifer returned with Drucilla's coffee and sat across from her at the small round dining table. He set her drink before her, then leaned back and crossed his arms.

"Nervous?" he asked.

Drucilla just looked at him; she didn't know how to answer.

"You look nervous," he says, smiling.

Drucilla leaned in from across the table and said in a quiet tone, "Is this fun for you? Are you enjoying my freak-out here?"

"Well, yes, a little," he said and smiled to himself.

Drucilla was not at all amused.

"Ah, there she is, twenty minutes on the dot, impeccable timing," he said. Lucifer stood up to greet her.

Calliope looked nothing like Drucilla imagined she would look. She was older, early 70's, she assumed. She had long silver hair that she pulled back into a low ponytail. She was wearing a velvet tracksuit with comfortable walking shoes. Calliope seemed like one of those mature fitness ladies who liked to power-walk ten miles a day. She appeared very human except for her mannerisms. She was very much a queen. She extended a hand to Lucifer as he guided her to their table. She looked unimpressed with the shop, like it was beneath her to be in such a human place. She glided when she walked but walked extremely confidently and carried herself like a woman with infinite power. Drucilla stood up and extended her hand to shake Calliope's hand.

"I'm Drucilla."

Calliope looked at Drucilla, looked down at her hand, then back up to Drucilla's face. Calliope slowly turned her gaze to Lucifer. *I guess she doesn't want to touch me,* Drucilla thought as she put down her hand while slowly sitting back down on her chair.

Lucifer and Calliope sat next to each other, "Drucilla, Calliope has a proposition for you."

Calliope slowly turned to Lucifer and looked at him as if she wasn't pleased with speaking for her. "Drucilla," she finally spoke. Her voice was deep, slow, and powerful. Her tone was intense, as if one word from her could wipe out all of existence but still human.

"I'm sorry, I don't know how to address you. Are you, My Queen? Do I use your first name? I've never met anyone, um, like you before," Drucilla said, fumbling with her words.

"Drucilla, I have very little time. These human bodies do not last long."

"Calliope has taken a human host to meet with you. This isn't her true form," Lucifer piped in.

I guess I kind of knew that…She didn't look like a Queen from Hell, Drucilla thought and nodded at Lucifer.

"Drucilla, you have taken in divine blood into your body. No human has ever done that before, until now. Because you have taken it upon yourself to mix your blood with the blood of the divine, you are becoming divine," Calliope said. She grabbed Drucilla's wrist and waved her hand over Drucilla's bare arm. The veins in her arm began to surface. Blue lightning veins began to branch out and glow beneath the surface of her skin.

"The blood of Thoth courses through your veins," Calliope said.

Drucilla watched the supernatural blood flow through her capillaries.

"He betrayed me. I had slain him eons ago," Calliope said without remorse. She glanced at Lucifer. "Drucilla, you have two options." Calliope's eyes began to glow bright orange, becoming more intense by the second.

"This body isn't holding," Lucifer said, concerned.

She gazed at Lucifer unappreciatively and said, "It will hold." Calliope turned her attention back to Drucilla.

"Okay, what are you saying?" Drucilla asked, not wanting to know the answer.

"You cannot stay here, you are becoming Divine, and after your transformation is complete, you will die," she warned.

"WHAT?" Drucilla said, snatching her hand from Calliope's grip.

Calliope looked offended that Drucilla would pull away from her. Her eyes met Drucilla's with an intense orange glow. "This, I cannot prevent. Your form was not meant for such transformations," Calliope said.

"What are my options?" Drucilla asked, trying to look for a way out of the situation.

Calliope turned her gaze to Lucifer and held out her hand as if he was supposed to give her something on cue. Lucifer handed Calliope what appeared to be a small, elaborate perfume bottle adorned with gold fillagree and rubies. It looked ancient. The cuts in the gems were crude, and the texture worn. She slowly placed the vial in front of Drucilla and retracted her hand.

Drucilla stared at the vial for a moment, then slowly picked it up.

"Your first option is to consume the contents of that vial, and you will die peacefully and without pain. This I can assure you," she explained.

Drucilla stared momentarily at the bottle. That didn't seem acceptable to her. "What's the second option?"

"You die an agonizing death after the transformation is complete and Thoth is reborn," she stated plainly.

"What? No! Why?" Drucilla demanded.

"You took divine blood into yourself; you cannot stay. You must die. The universe cannot afford your existence. You could potentially drive Eorthe into chaos if Thoth were to reemerge. You could solely be responsible for billions of lives. We cannot allow Thoth to be reborn. I had slain Thoth to save Eorthe once to save your kind from certain destruction by the rogue Throne. You must drink the elixir. You must stop this transformation. You must save yourselves," Calliope explained.

"Drucilla, listen to me. Your body will not hold. You are mortal, and your body will break." Lucifer said. He motioned to Calliope, whose own skin was starting to burn from the inside. "Look at her, Drucilla, this is what will happen to you."

Calliope's skin began to smoke. She was starting to draw attention from the people in the café around them.

"Mrs. Palmer!" the barista yelled out, "Mrs. Palmer!" The barista ran to Calliope with towels as if to smother a fire. "Someone! Call an ambulance!" The barista yelled to the patrons.

Calliope's host body began to deteriorate before their eyes. Calliope grabbed Drucilla's hand and looked into her eyes. "Drink the elixir. Do not let Thoth return," Calliope demanded. With that, she collapsed to the floor. The patrons rushed around her and tried to revive her as the smoke died down and her host body smoldered.

Lucifer pulled Drucilla out of her chair by her elbow. He dragged her out of the café and out onto the sidewalk. People noticed the commotion and started peering into the windows.

"What happened to Calliope?" Drucilla asked Lucifer sternly.

"She's gone. She left a moment before the host collapsed," Lucifer said, dragging Drucilla down the sidewalk.

"Damn it, Lucifer, STOP!" Drucilla yelled as she yanked her arm from his grasp.

Lucifer, lacking patience, grabbed Drucilla's arm again, and with a blink, they were outside Drucilla's house on the cold, dark street. Drucilla pulled herself away from Lucifer.

"What the hell was that about?" Drucilla continued to yell.

Annoyed and impatient, Lucifer started pacing and looking around the street for something.

"Lucifer, I need answers! Why did I need a visit from the Queen of Hell to tell me to kill myself? Why doesn't she just possess another body and kill me herself?"

"BECAUSE!" Lucifer yelled.

"WHY?"

His eyes finally fixated upon a long piece of rebar. He pulled it out of the ground in front of the newly constructed house across the street from Drucilla's home. He walked furiously over to Drucilla, and with a twirl and a flourish as if he was handling a rapier, he impaled the rebar directly into Drucilla's chest with a dreadful crunch. He gave it another thrust deeper into her chest until it popped out of her back.

Stunned, Drucilla looked into his snake eyes, unable to breathe, unable to think. He held her stare, and with the same force, he ripped the rebar back out of Drucilla's chest and dropped it to the ground. It bounced with a *KLANG*.

Drucilla gasped for air and slowly touched the gaping wound in her chest. She looked down at the blood and the wound site. Drucilla felt dizzy.

"Because Drucilla," he started pacing again and ran his hand over his bald head, "you cannot die from mortal weapons, maybe not even divine. I do not know to what you are impervious, but the elixir is a chosen death that cannot be stopped. It is the only way. Remember when you asked me how you could remove the Throne? This is how."

Surprisingly, Drucilla realized she was not in pain and still breathing. She unbuttoned her shirt to expose her bare chest. To her surprise, her chest was covered in blood, but there was no wound. Drucilla looked back at Lucifer, unable to speak.

"You are transforming. You are a lot further through the process than I had realized," Lucifer said with some remorse.

Drucilla tried to gather her thoughts. She breathed deeply and looked up at Lucifer. "That's not the only thing," Drucilla said calmly.

Drucilla unbuttoned her blouse the rest of the way and dropped it to the ground. Drucilla, naked from the waist up, gathered her hair on top of her head and turned her back to Lucifer to show him the miniature, rudimentary wings she could independently move.

"Oh, Drucilla," Lucifer said. He covered his mouth with his hand in concern.

PERCVTIAM PASTOREM & DISPERGENTVR
OVES.
. XXVI . MAR . XIIII .

302

CANTICLE TWENTY-SIX

"For the Angel of Death spread his wings on the blast, And breathed in the face of the foe as he passed; And the eyes of the sleepers waxed deadly and chill, And their hearts but once heaved and forever grew still!" —Lord Byron

✝

Drucilla slept horribly that night, maybe about ten minutes of sleep altogether. Diablo decided that Drucilla had tossed and turned enough, and it was time for her to get out of bed and feed him. Drucilla donned her bathrobe and stumbled down the stairs towards the kitchen.

"You look lovely," Adrian said sarcastically.

Drucilla could only offer him her middle finger, and Diablo hissed at Adrian as usual.

"He's never going to get used to me," Adrian shook his head.

"No, probably not," Drucilla mumbled.

Adrian was going on about his design ideas for the dining room. Adrian mentioned something about a pass-through; Drucilla was only half paying attention. She couldn't hear him over her own thoughts. *What am I supposed to say to Adrian? Hey, we'll have one more thing in common soon. Why did I even do this to myself?* Drucilla's brain was actively trying to figure a way out of the whole situation, but it was too far out of her league. *I really have no choice but to see this out to the end because I don't think I can take the elixir. I don't think I have the strength.*

The day seemed to fly by, and Drucilla hadn't engaged in life at all that day. It was closing time, and she walked around the gallery, straightening pillows and frames. She wandered around into various small rooms to make sure everyone had cleared out for the evening before she started shutting off the lights. Drucilla fished around her bag for her keys and then tossed her bag over her shoulder. She made her way to the front door. She was about to shut off the last light switch.

"They are lying to you, Drucilla," a masculine voice said behind her.

Drucilla turned around quickly and dropped her bag to the floor.

A well-dressed man in a black suit with slicked black hair and a thick black scarf around his neck lifted his head slowly to face Drucilla. His eyes were black, like *Black #3* black. Drucilla couldn't be sure he even had eyes if it wasn't for the shadowy rings around them. His pale skin in the dim lighting created chiseled contrasting shadows across his thin face. He looked human, but at the same time, he didn't. He stood silently, statuesque, studying Drucilla's facial expressions.

"Who's lying to me?" Drucilla asked, confused, "And who are you? Do I know you?"

"No, most likely not. But you will if you drink that elixir that you keep in your satchel," he responded, gesturing to Drucilla's purse.

Drucilla stared at him for a moment.

"Death," Drucilla said under her breath, realizing that this was whose eye-sockets of endless darkness were staring back at her.

"Azrael, my name's Azrael," he said, introducing himself properly. "I'm actually a Seraph. I go by many names: The Grim Reaper, Santa Muerte, Psychopomp, if you will." He adjusted his heavy looped scarf and looked back at Drucilla. Drucilla's eyes were wide and fixated on Azrael's eye sockets. "And I'm speaking of Queen Calliope and her imp, Lucifer," Azrael responded.

"I don't understand. Why would Lucifer and Calliope lie to me?"

"You tell me, Drucilla. Why would a Queen such as Calliope be afraid of you?" Azrael asked. He hoped Drucilla would think about the question. He slowly approached her. Drucilla slowly stepped back the closer he got. He stopped and looked at Drucilla, amused. "I'm not here to take you away with me," Azrael reassured Drucilla.

Drucilla looked at his face, but she couldn't read him.

"You don't know?" he asked. He interlaced his fingers. His hands were white, thin, with spindly fingers, and a black onyx mourning ring on his smallest finger. He didn't carry a scythe or even wear a hood as one would think. He looked like an average New Wave subculture cliché from 1982: waifish and incredibly tall; about eight feet tall. Drucilla half expected him to pull out a pack of cloves and start smoking them at any moment.

"You're becoming divine; more and more every day and she can't have that," he explained.

"It's going to kill me, so why does it matter?" Drucilla responded in a defeated tone.

"If anything were to kill you, I'd certainly know about it," he assured her.

"What are you saying, Azrael?"

"Drucilla, why do you think you're dying? Because she told you that you were?" he started pacing around the gallery. "Calliope wants you to drink the elixir because she doesn't want you to become who you are becoming. Do you remember when you found the rosary fifteen years ago? Doesn't it seem too random, too perfect of a set of circumstances for you to come into possession of her rosary?"

Drucilla stared at Azrael for a moment before responding. "But she put it in my path. How could she not know what would happen? Wasn't this planned?"

"Did she, though? Are you certain it was she who put it in your path?"

Drucilla's eyes shifted around the room nervously. She seemed to have more questions each passing moment.

Azrael walked over to one of the oil paintings on the gallery wall and ran his fingers over the thick and sharp features of an ocean wave; he seemed fascinated by the slick, raised texture of the art piece. "If it were Calliope who placed that rosary in your path, it seems like a mistake on her behalf if she didn't know that you would figure out what it truly was. Thrones are omniscient, no?" he asked, tracing the waves up the length of the painting with his hollow eyes.

Drucilla furrowed her brow.

"Why would she give something powerful like the essence of an Ophanim to you, knowing that you would take it into yourself?" Azrael asked.

"I don't know. Why?"

He turned his attention back to Drucilla. "I honestly have no idea what is so special about you, but you were the one who was chosen. It's clear to me that this was not Calliope's doing. This was deliberate by another. This is what has her so agitated. Someone broke the order, cheated at the game, if you will, and gave it to you. Granted, you are not the first person to own it. However, you are the first human to discover what it truly was."

"So, all divine knew what this relic was?" Drucilla looked to his face for confirmation.

"Oh, yes. Most definitely. It's a one-of-a-kind celestial object made with Ophanim blood. Every Divine knows what it is," he said while moving on to another painting. "Well, what it was…."

"Why didn't she anticipate that I would take the blood internally, I mean if she's all-knowing?" Drucilla asked.

"Now, you are asking the appropriate question," Azrael said with relief in his voice. "I don't think she had that foreknowledge. However, you should not have lived through it," he said, looking away from the painting back to Drucilla. "You did die, but you came back, and now, she knows you're Divine. You were an unanticipated, unmitigated accident. No one, Divine or Unholy, could have known that you would come back into being. Bottom line, you are not supposed to be here, Drucilla. We don't know why you are. Your death was an intervention by someone, and there are very few who can breathe life back into death without consequence. Only Thrones can create life. Whoever did this defied Celestial Law."

"Can Lucifer do it?"

"No, he can't. No Seraphim can; Not even I."

Drucilla picked up her bag and pulled out the vial to examine it.

"God?" Drucilla asked, looking back up at Azrael.

"God is an idea, a concept; God doesn't exist. God is the agglomeration of the Divine and the Unholy. It also helps you, humans, wrap your heads around otherworldly occurrences by putting a face on it."

Drucilla raised an eyebrow.

"Why should I believe you?" Drucilla asked.

"I have nothing to gain from your existence or your death. It doesn't make a difference to me or my position, but Queen Calliope does. Drucilla, you have the potential to become the most divine being that's existed since the time of the Thrones, which is causing anxiety with Calliope. She doesn't want you to live and will stop at nothing to end your life if you continue to defy her. She needs you to drink the elixir. If you don't, it puts her existence in jeopardy. Do you understand? You have free will. You are free to drink the elixir if you like, and I can take you away or you can throw it away and be whom you are meant to become; it's your decision."

"Calliope said she had slain Thoth once before. Are you telling me she can't do it again?"

"Drucilla, you are something completely different. Something that we have not ever encountered. You are neither human nor Ophanim; you are neither alive nor dead. You exist in a space between the Divine and the Unholy. You are neither; however, you are both. If I had to hazard a guess, you might even frighten Calliope. No one in the universe has any idea who or what you are."

"What about you?" Drucilla asked.

"I don't know what you are either."

"No, I mean, whose side are you on, the Divine or the Unholy?" Drucilla folded her arms.

"I don't take sides. I exist outside of the hierarchy. I am constant. I reap human beings, I reap the Divine, and I reap the Unholy. I will continue to reap everything that exists until existence stops, and then," he looks around, "I suppose I can rest."

"But you're an angel, aren't you?"

"Seraph. Angel sounds simple and juvenile. However, it depends on whom you ask," he said nonchalantly. "No, Drucilla, I am something else entirely. I am a Cataclysm, one of four. We exist as a third dominion. Humans refer to it as purgatory, limbo, or judgment. It's called Malakut. Although it is no place for humans nor has it ever been. We are not beholden to either side."

Drucilla stared at Azrael for a moment and attempted to read his face. He seemed to look quizzically at Drucilla, through his hollow eyes. Drucilla looked down at her hand and studied the vial again for a moment. She shook her head as she tried to make sense of everything.

"So, if I don't take this, I'm supposed to believe that the transformation will kill me. You are telling me that the transformation won't kill me. However, Calliope wants me to think that it will, and if I don't, she will try and kill me. Is that about the gist of it?"

"That is correct. Yes, she will try."

Drucilla looked at Azrael's deep voids masquerading as eye sockets. She looked back at the vial once more. "You're telling me the truth, aren't you?"

Azrael nodded slowly.

"I believe you." Drucilla didn't know why, but she trusted him, and with her decision made, she rushed past him to the back of the gallery. She unlocked the back door to the deck and ran to the end up against the railing. Drucilla raised her arm, held the vial, and flung it as far and hard as possible to the ocean below. Drucilla turned around to look at Azrael. "If she wants me to die, she's going to have to take me out, herself," she said firmly. Drucilla's eyes flickered with a blue glow.

In the midst of Life Death doth us pursue,
Let each therefore with Speed for Mercy sue.

Jn.º Lightbody delin et Sculp.

312

CANTICLE TWENTY-SEVEN

"Will you tell us why you are not at rest?"
—The Changeling

A few months had passed, and Drucilla was attempting to navigate her new life as a celestial being and a human. Dominic was becoming increasingly fascinated by Drucilla's supernatural abilities and wanted to explore all of them. She sat on a tall, oak swivel stool in Dominic's library. She slowly spun herself counterclockwise as she tapped on the seat between her legs, waiting for Dominic to find something in a book through which he had been perusing. "Bah!" he groaned as he tossed the book on the table, picked up another, and was speed-reading through random pages. They looked like spiritual books, at least in the sense that they were about contacting spirits or entities.

"Oh, I got it!" he exclaimed as he left an antique book titled, *A Guide to Mediumship and Mastery* by Herman Fitzgerald spread open to the page he was trying to find. He ran his index finger over a couple of sentences and nodded. "Hang on, I'll be right back!" he said excitedly. He ran through his kitchen down his basement stairs with heavy steps. From downstairs, Drucilla heard a loud crash. It sounded like he dropped about five metal bowls. "I'm okay!" he yelled to Drucilla from afar.

"Okay," Drucilla yelled back, scrunching her nose, and shaking her head slowly.

With quick heavy stomps, Drucilla heard him as he ran back upstairs. "I got it!" he said, rushing back to the dining room table. Then, with one big swoop, he shoved back a couple of stacks of books and placed what appeared to be a huge, two-foot-high metal funnel in the middle of the table. He sat the wide end down; the narrow end pointed upwards. He held his hands out, palms up, at the funnel as if to present it. "Eh?! Eh!?" he said. He grinned from ear-to-ear at Drucilla, clearly excited about the object.

Drucilla glanced at him curiously. "What? Are we making juice or something?"

"No, no!" he said, looking at Drucilla as if she should know what he was referencing. He continued to point to the funnel with his hands.

"I…I don't know what this is," Drucilla said as she hopped off the stool, extended her index finger, and nudged it.

"Really, you don't know?" he said, clearly amused at Drucilla's ignorance.

Drucilla glanced up at him and back at the funnel.

"It's a Spirit Trumpet! Isn't it cool?" he announced as he grinned and stuffed his hands into his jeans. I got it from the estate of Madame Marie DuPont," he said with a thick French accent, "Pretty cool, huh?"

"Dom, why is there a Spirit Trumpet on the table?"

"I'm glad you asked. We're gonna do Parlor Tricks! Here, sit down," he said. Dominic pulled the chair out at the head of the table and had Drucilla sit in front of it. "We're going to conjure spirits! We're going to speak to the other side." Dominic's eyes were wild and excited.

This is apparently Dominic's version of Christmas, Drucilla thought and giggled to herself.

Dominic picked up Drucilla's hands by her wrists and placed them on either side of the funnel. He took a seat on her right and said, "Ready?"

"I'm not quite sure what we're doing." Drucilla felt like a cat wearing pants.

"Since you have a direct line to the dead, I figured we'd have a séance, but you're an actual medium in this case," he responded.

"But I'm not," Drucilla corrected him.

"Well, we don't know exactly everything you can do, so let's give it a shot, ok?" he said more enthusiastically than he had any right to be.

Drucilla shook her head. There had been a lot of crazy in her life, but this was edging its way up the list. "Okay, how does this work?"

"You'll attempt to contact the dead, and then the spirits will make the trumpet float, and it will stop in front of the person it wants to talk to. The trumpet also amplifies the spirit's voice," Dominic explained.

Drucilla just blinked at him in disbelief. "Can we play light-as-a-feather-and-stiff-as-a-board afterward?"

Dominic's eyes lit up; he smiled a broad, open-mouthed smile as if to say, *Can we!?*

"No, Dom, I'm kidding, just… Please continue." Drucilla shook her head.

Dominic closed his eyes and drew in a deep breath. Drucilla followed his lead and did the same.

"So? Who are we contacting?" Drucilla asked, a little joyful. She was starting to get into it a little bit.

"Well, uh," he pulled the book back in front of him, read for a second, then slid the book back, placed his hands palms down on the table, and connected pinky fingers with Drucilla. "Let's just do this like we're searching for radio stations on a dial; just ask if anyone wants to speak to us and see who answers," he said with a huge grin.

Drucilla nodded and closed her eyes. Then, Drucilla said aloud, "Spirits! Hear me! Is there anyone who wishes to speak to Dominic or me?" Drucilla opened one eye and peeked at Dominic. Dominic was concentrating, eyes closed. Drucilla closed her eye again.

"Do it again," he whispered.

"SPIRITS!" Drucilla shouted, "HEAR ME! I COMMAND YOU TO MAKE YOUR PRESENCE KNOWN! SHOW YOURSELVES TO US!"

The room quickly got warmer by a few degrees, and the distinct smell of sulfur began to fill the air. Dominic and Drucilla both popped open their eyes and looked at each other. Drucilla stripped off her jacket, Dominic pulled his hoodie off over his head.

"What's going on?" Drucilla asked, concerned.

"I think we made contact; keep going," he gestured for Drucilla to continue.

Drucilla's eyes darted around the room nervously. "Someone's here," she said quietly.

Suddenly, the Spirit Trumpet started rocking violently, slowly lifted off the table and began to levitate. They watched in awe as the Spirit Trumpet raised high above their heads in a rotating motion.

"What do I do!?" Drucilla said, panicking.

Dominic was utterly paralyzed with curiosity and fascination and wasn't answering Drucilla. He just stared. "Holy shit!" he yelled and started laughing.

"Drucilla," a disembodied voice that didn't sound human but also sounded male and somewhat familiar, called Drucilla's name.

"Hello?" Drucilla shouted.

"Drucilla, help me! Help me!" the voice, garbled and fleeting, seemed to come from ten different directions, but Drucilla could barely hear it.

Dominic looked at Drucilla; his eyes were the size of dinner plates.

Then it dawned on Drucilla. "Drake!" Drucilla yelled as she darted straight up.

The Spirit Trumpet crashed to the table with a loud clatter, smashing part of the rim. The chandelier above the table started shaking wildly, and the paintings clattered against the wall. Pages flew out of the open books, and candles instantaneously melted within their candelabras.

"Dru! Control it!" Dominic yelled.

"Drake! How can I help you?" Drucilla yelled out.

The chandelier broke free from the ceiling and crashed to the table. Drucilla fell backward to the floor, and Dominic rushed to pick her up.

"Dru, you have to control it!" Dominic yelled again, this time with the edge of authority like he was giving an order.

Drucilla looked down at her hands and saw the blue lightning branches as they shot up her wrists and forearms. The ceiling had cracked, and the windows started to crack into long-ranging spiderweb shapes across the glass. Evil laughter could be heard echoing throughout the house. Black smoke began to rise from the floor in an unnatural swirling motion as if something was attempting to manifest.

"I don't think it's Drake," Dominic said, becoming increasingly concerned.

Drucilla didn't know what possessed her to do it, but she yelled out "PROHIBERE" in one loud shriek. The sound reverberated through the room, and in an instant, everything stopped.

The house fell silent.

Dominic straightened himself, brushed off the dust from his arms with his hands, and looked around the room.

"Dom, your house," Drucilla said sadly.

"Are you okay?" he asked.

"I think so?" Drucilla looked back down at her arms. They were normal again.

Dominic slapped the top of his head and slid his hand down to the back of his neck. He threw his head back and looked up at the ceiling with a deep exhale.

"Dom, I'm so sorry." Drucilla started trying to pick up the pieces of his chandelier. He looked at her for a second and paused. A smile slowly began to form across his face, followed by a burst of laughter.

"That was so cool!" he beamed. He laughed with his hands in his face. "Oh my God, you spoke Latin!" he said, amused and shocked.

"Y… yeah?" Drucilla bit the inside of her lip.

"Woooo!" he laughed and threw himself down into his chair.

"Well, mediumship is something we'll definitely have to practice," he said.

"Maybe outside next time?" Drucilla added.

✝✝✝

It was a chilly late autumn afternoon. Dominic and Drucilla were in the middle of a clearing in the forest about a mile hike east from Dominic's house. The sun was setting, and Dominic was dragging his feet through the fallen leaves as he attempted to clear an area on the ground. He held a crooked petrified wooden staff in his hand and used it to balance himself while he cleared the path.

"What are we doing out here?" Drucilla asked Dominic.

"Here, stand over where I am, face North," Dominic instructed.

Drucilla walked over to Dominic. He grabbed her shoulders and pointed her in the direction he wanted her to stand, facing the clearing. "Hold this." Dominic handed Drucilla a ceremonial dagger of some sort. Drucilla examined the worn bronze hilt adorned with intricately carved snakes with emeralds for eyes.

"What's this?" Drucilla asked. She continued to examine the dagger, "Mesopotamian ceremonial dagger?"

"Yeah, Mesopotamian. About 1500 BC. But I'm sure you already figured that out," he responded. After he was satisfied with the cleared area, he drew symbols on the ground about half a meter from each other in a half-circle around Drucilla.

"Stay on that side of the symbols," he commanded.

Drucilla shrugged.

"No, Dru, it's important that you stay on that side of the symbols, okay?" Dominic warned.

"Okay yeah, fine." Drucilla rolled her eyes.

"I'm serious, don't move from that side," he said sternly.

"I got it!" Drucilla threw her arms up in frustration.

He tapped the dirt from the bottom of the staff against his hiking boot.

"So, what are we doing out here?" Drucilla asked.

He raised his eyes to her, in that same wild stare, "Reanimation!"

Drucilla blinked quickly. "What? How? Where are the books?" Drucilla looked around on the ground.

"We don't need them for this. You're powerful. I don't think they can teach us what we need to know in those books."

"So, what are we reanimating?' Drucilla asked warily.

"We're going to raise an undead army."

"A what?" Drucilla started giggling uncontrollably at the ridiculousness of it.

Dominic walked over to Drucilla and stood at her side. He raised his arm and pointed straight ahead. "The old civil war cemetery is just over there."

Drucilla squinted her eyes and tried to see what he was looking at, but in the distance about 200-feet away, Drucilla could barely make out the obscured tombstones standing behind a short, weathered, wooden fence line. "You know, to anyone else, this would seem insane. Like, put-you-in-the-paddy-wagon-wearing-the-little-white-jacket-with-the-sleeves-in-the-back kind of insane, right?"

Dominic paused for a moment to think about what Drucilla had said. "Yeah, I suppose you're right," he shrugged, "But straitjackets haven't been used in mental facilities since, like, the 70s or 80s. I'd probably be okay."

It would have been difficult for you to miss the point harder. Drucilla thought.

"Anyway, remember, don't move," he reminded Drucilla again.

"Why do I have this dagger? To throw at the skeletons in case they get out of hand?" Drucilla smirked.

Dominic pulled a folded piece of paper from the inside pocket of his jacket and handed it to Drucilla between his fingers. Drucilla grasped the paper and unfolded it. "What's this?" Drucilla asked, studying the words. Quickly she dropped her hands stiffly. "Oh God, Latin, again?"

Dominic gave her a smug look. "You should think about learning the language. All the antiquated Catholic books are written in Latin. Since you are, you know, you, it might be a benefit."

"I still don't see how the dagger fits into this." Drucilla flipped the dagger back and forth.

"When you're ready, chant the words on the paper."

Drucilla shrugged, inhaled, and exhaled deeply. Dominic moved to stand behind her as Drucilla held the paper at eye level and read the words aloud, "Idcirco praecipio tibi ut resurgemus!" Drucilla looked ahead and saw nothing. "I don't think it's working." Drucilla kept her eyes on the cemetery in front of her.

"I need you to trust me on this part, okay?" Dominic asked politely.

"Okay?"

"Cut your hand with the dagger and throw your blood onto the symbols on the ground."

"What? Why do we need my blood?"

"Because Dru, you must give something to get something. In this case, you give life to create life. Blood is life. It's Necromancy 101."

"I don't know about this, Dom…" Drucilla raised an eyebrow. "Besides Dominic, you know this won't work. The blade won't cut me." Drucilla looked over her shoulder at him.

He just looked at her and nodded to proceed.

Drucilla dropped the paper to the ground and opened her left hand. She placed the dagger's blade into her palm and closed her hand around the edge. She quickly ripped the dagger out of her hand. Drucilla opened her hand, and her palm began to well up with blood. "How?" Drucilla whispered.

"Throw the blood!" Dominic commanded.

Drucilla glanced over her shoulder again and threw the blood onto the symbols. The blood splattered to the ground in small splashes that flared with a bright blue glow.

"Stay behind the symbols," he repeated for what seemed like the tenth time.

Heavy crashing and rumbling were coming from somewhere in the distance. Their eyes searched for some indication of what was happening. Visibility had decreased quite a bit, as the sun had set into the blue hour and the light slipped away into the evening sky. The smell of rotting flesh, moldy flowers, rusted iron, and dirt permeated the air. It was a sickening smell, sweet but grotesque. A grinding sound and clanking of wood and metal could be heard as it emerged closer. Dominic struggled to light the lanterns he had sitting on the ground behind him. The sound was getting closer. Drucilla could make out multiple figures as they lumbered through the darkness toward the semi-circle. Drucilla's hands began to luminate. She could see the blue branches of light beneath the skin of her hands come to the surface and become brighter. Drucilla pulled off her leather jacket to expose the doomy, neon blue nerves, and veins in her arms, illuminating her body. One by one, the skeletons emerged into the light. Two became three; three became six, suddenly there were at least fifty lumbering towards her in tattered, rotted Civil War uniforms, dragging their rusted weapons, and coming to a halt in front of the symbols on the ground.

"Oh, thank God!" Dominic clutched his chest in relief.

Drucilla turned and looked at him in confusion.

"I wasn't certain the symbols would stop them, but it worked." Relieved, he gave Drucilla a thumbs-up.

"What do I do now?" Drucilla turned her attention back to the undead. The skeletons were standing in front of her waiting for a command.

"They're yours. You decide what they do," Dominic responded.

"Um, do you have some Latin for this or something?"

Dominic looked nervously at Drucilla, shrugged, and shook his head. "I didn't know we would get this far."

Drucilla stood before the army like a conductor at a symphony. Drucilla's arms glowed, casting an ethereal blue light across their dead, expressionless skeletal faces.

Suddenly, a voice crashed out of nowhere like glass smashing against a rock. "What do you think you are doing?"

Dominic and Drucilla turned toward the direction of the voice. Azrael emerged from the forest. He looked confused and annoyed. "I said, what are you doing, Drucilla?" Azrael stepped closer to Drucilla and Dominic. Then, he turned to the undead army, waved his hand over the crowd, and they collapsed with a massive clatter of dry bones hitting the ground. 'Necromancy?" He pointed to the piles of bones and looked at Drucilla out of the corner of his eye. "Necromancy is forbidden!"

Dominic stood at Drucilla's side as if he was ready to protect her if it came to blows.

"Azrael, this is Dominic."

"I know who he is," Azrael nodded in greeting to Dominic. Dominic did a slight nod back, confused.

"Wait, you're the Angel of Death?" Dominic asked wide-eyed and taken aback by Azrael.

Azrael stared down Dominic, confused as to why he would ask a blatantly obvious question.

"Drucilla, you know Death as well?" Dominic asked in disbelief.

"Well, sort of. We just met not too long ago, but yeah, I guess."

"I need a drink!" Dominic exhaled and ran his hand over his head.

Azrael looked to the ground at the symbols that Dominic drew. "Angelic script." Azrael looked at the ground. "Clever, but Drucilla's blood is divine. Drucilla's blood alone would protect her. The symbolism is redundant."

"Yeah, we're new to this," Dominic commented sheepishly.

"But necromancy… acts of necromancy is not a tool of the Divine. It is a device of The Unholy; of irreverence," Azrael scolded. Azrael grabbed Drucilla's hand to expose her wound. Drucilla noticed she was not healing. Azrael grabbed a handkerchief from his chest pocket and wrapped it around Drucilla's hand. He saw the bronze dagger dripping with blood in Drucilla's other hand. He snatched the blade from her, and sniffed the dagger. "The enchantment is very old. I am surprised it worked." He handed it back to Drucilla. "The wound will heal slowly, I'm afraid."

"Why are you here?" Drucilla asked Azrael.

"You aren't taking one of us, are you?" Dominic asked slowly, afraid of the answer.

Azrael sighed unamused at Dominic. "You raised the dead."

"Okay?" Drucilla asked.

"I am the Reaper," he said, gesturing vaguely to himself.

"Oh! I get it," Dominic said. "The dead bodies…."

Azrael raised his head to the sky and exhaled. It was apparent he was unamused by the shenanigans. He lowered his chin and looked back at Dominic. "Generally, when I reap humans, they stay dead." Azrael folded his arms and shot Drucilla the same unamused look. "I do hope you can think of other activities to fill your days and not interrupt mine."

Dominic and Drucilla both looked at each other.

Azrael placed his hand over his face and rubbed his forehead as if Drucilla were giving him a headache. "Just, just go home and stay out of trouble," Azrael groaned. He waved Drucilla and Dominic off, turned, and walked out of the clearing.

"' Think he's mad?" Drucilla asked Dominic with a smirk.

Dominic rolled his eyes and shook his head. "That guy's a dick."

Fui non sum etenim quid hucusque?
Vanitas uanitatum et omnia uanitas. Eccl. 1.
Joannes Bernardinus S. inuentor
Joannis Eillardi formis
Egberte de P. sculpsit.

CANTICLE TWENTY-EIGHT

"E'en hell hath its peculiar laws." —Johann Wolfgang
von Goethe *Faust*

✝

"Ugh, this is stupid," Drucilla groaned as she sat up straight and stretched out her back in the dining room chair of Dominic's library. Drucilla placed her hands up, threw her head back, and looked up at the hideously grotesque ancient paintings that lined the walls. Strange depictions of demons, snakes, and seraphim decorated Dominic's former dining room-turned-library. The paintings seemed to be ancient Catholic artwork.

"' Just humor me, Dru. Let's try again," Dominic pleaded.

Drucilla exhaled and cleared her mind. She lowered her head back down.

Dominic shuffled the Zener cards and drew the top one from the deck. He then held the card up to his face with the back of the card facing Drucilla and locked eyes with her.

Drucilla paused for a moment to concentrate. "Circle," Drucilla said with confidence.

Dominic looked at the card and then looked back at Drucilla. He dropped the stack of cards and put his face in his hands, groaned, and shook his head. "You know Dru…statistically, non-psychic people get between three and seven, correct."

"How many did I get?"

"One. Just one. The square," Dominic responded, disappointed as he looked at the one card pile of which he hoped to be multiple positive hits.

"Nuh-uh, I got that other one right."

"That's because I accidentally showed you the wrong side of the card."

"I told you. I'm not a psychic."

"Clearly." Dominic got up from the table and headed to his bookshelf to find another book. "How about..." Dominic took two steps up the ladder to reach the higher bookshelf tier. He ran his index finger along the binds of the books. "Ah, here we go." Dominic grabbed a book and jumped off the ladder. He dropped the book on the table in front of Drucilla.

Drucilla leaned her head to the side to read the book "Astral Projection Techniques " by Margot Thorne. I'm going to astral project?"

"Hopefully!"

"Dom?" Drucilla looked at him curiously.

"Hmmm?" Dominic looked at his book with his thumb pressed against his lip as he slowly turned the pages of the astral projection book with his other hand. He seemed deep in thought.

"So..." Drucilla leaned back in her chair inquisitively, "hypothetically, what would happen if someone were to break a deal with the Devil?"

Dom looked up at Drucilla and raised a thick brow. "What do you mean, like what?" He curiously looked at Drucilla.

"Well, say that I decided to sell my soul for a cupcake. But when I received the cupcake, it was chocolate, not strawberry, so I didn't want it. In turn, I decide to break the deal and not give him my soul. What would happen?"

"Do you want cupcakes, Dru? Are you hungry?" Dominic squinted at Drucilla as he attempted to read deeper into her question.

Drucilla sighed and got up from her chair to walk over to his side of the table. Still contemplating, Drucilla leaned against it and crossed her arms. "I mean, what will happen if I decide to renege on my deal?".

"Well, you can't."

"Why not?"

"Because once you make a deal, the deal is a binding contract. Unless, of course, both parties agree to redefine the terms."

"How can it be a binding contract? It's not like there's any divine lawyers or something, right?"

"There's no legal recourse here. These are Celestial Laws. There's no refusing to pay. You don't get a choice."

Drucilla narrowed her eyes.

"Ok, look, celestial binding contracts between mortals and the Unholy are essentially out of control from both parties after they are bound. These contracts change the mortal's fate and rewrite their destiny. Their current course is halted, and a new path forward is created."

"Who creates these paths?"

"Well, the Norns."

"You aren't talking about Nordic fates, are you?"

"Yes, exactly. Some believe the Norns are female beings who rule the destiny of men. They roughly correspond to other controllers of humans' destiny, such as the Fates." Dominic paused for a moment. "Urdu the Norn of the past, Verdandi the Norn of the present, and Skuld the Norn of the future," he counted a fate on each finger. "The readjusted destiny creates a new path forward."

Drucilla blinked in disbelief. "They exist?"

"After everything you've seen from Lucifer to Death, you think that's out of the ordinary?" Dominic gave Drucilla a confused look. "Each culture has their own names for these Fates, but essentially, they're all the same thing," he explained as he returned to his book.

"' Just so that we're clear…I make a deal, my life changes, and it can't be undone because of celestial laws," Drucilla reaffirmed.

"Yeah, that's right."

"Can the Divine make a new deal that overwrites the old deal that someone makes with the Unholy?"

"Contracts aren't dominion specific. Any Divine or Unholy can create them. The Norns just process the request, so to speak. It would require the immortal and the mortal to create a new deal to change the path forward, unless…."

"Unless?"

"Every mortal has an expiration date. That can't be changed. When your time is up, that's it."

Drucilla glanced around processing.

"There's only so much sand in an hourglass, only so much wool in a spindle. You can't put the toothpaste back in the tube. After it's gone, it's gone."

"Still not following—"

Dominic sighed and set down his book. He picked up his pen and drew a straight line on a notepad with dots on either end of the line. "This timeline represents your life. This is when you are born, and this is when you die." Dominic pointed to each dot on either end of the line. "Anything on this line can be changed, manipulated, etcetera." Dominic drew branches off the timeline. "When your destiny is changed, there are new timelines. However, it doesn't extend your line, you just finish in a different place, but it always has an end."

"What if the Divine or the Unholy gave the Norns more sand, so to speak, would it extend the life of the mortal?"

"Ah, now you're talking sacrifice." Dominic sat in front of Drucilla.

Drucilla sat in the dining chair beside him as she waited for him to continue.

"That's the caveat. A mortal can give their life to another mortal to extend their timeline," he stated.

"Everyone has a set amount of sand, but to obtain more sand, you would have to get it from another, but it has to be given freely."

There was a long silence.

"What about me?" Drucilla asked.

Dominic sat in silence and thought for a moment.

"Theoretically, you don't have one, a timeline, I mean," he said, unsure of himself, "I suppose you, like the immortals, exist outside of the timeline."

"But immortals can die," Drucilla added.

"Sure, but in theory, immortals are only defeated by other immortals, and that's by pure chance. It isn't destiny; only humans have a destiny."

"In theory."

"In theory," he nodded.

Drucilla sat silent and processed the new information.

Dominic retrieved his book and continued to read. He moved his lips occasionally and nodded his head when something made sense to him. Finally, Dominic stood up and placed both hands on the table. He studied Drucilla's face for a moment as she looked up at him. "Are you ready?"

"Should we be keeping track of these experiments by number?"

Dominic grinned, picked up his phone, pressed voice record, and spoke into it. "The date is the 20th of October 2020. The time is 19:35, 0735 Zulu. Experiment number four: Astral Projection. The subject, Drucilla

Keket Blackwood, has consented to this experiment as a willing participant."

"You are a complete nerd." Drucilla shook her head.

Dominic raised his arm to direct Drucilla to the living room. They entered the living room, and he pointed to a beautifully elaborate, antique-looking green and gold Persian rug that he recently unrolled on the hardwood floor. The edges of the carpet maintained their curled ends. "Sit down, make yourself comfortable. I'll be right back," Dominic said.

Drucilla sat cross-legged on the rug, placed her elbows on the insides of her knees, and her hands under her chin as she awaited further instructions.

Dominic returned with his arms full of white pillar candles and a book of matches clenched between his teeth. He knelt outside the rug and randomly placed the pillar candles about two feet from each other. "You know where I got this rug?" he asked while placing the candles.

"Tell me?"

"There is a story of a flying carpet." He lit the match and placed the flame near the first candlewick. "Prince Husain traveled to Bisnagar in India to purchase a carpet. The carpet was described as 'Whoever sitteth here on this carpet and willeth in thought to be taken up and set down upon another site will, in the twinkling of an eye, be borne tither, be that place nearhand or distant in a day's journey and difficult to reach.'"

Drucilla sat, stunned at his words. "Is, is this real? Is this really that carpet? Drucilla's eyes widened to the size of saucers.

Dominic finished lighting the last pillar candle, shook the flame out on the matchstick, and sat beside Drucilla. "No, I got this online from a place called HandmadeMarketplace.com," he said as he killed the suspense. "But it's cool, no? The girl I bought it from loomed it herself."

Drucilla exhaled and gave him an unamused look.

"Ok, I need you to lie back and try and make yourself as limp as possible. Just relax every muscle in your body," Dominic advised.

Drucilla followed his instructions and tried to make herself as relaxed as possible. She placed her arms to her side and adjusted herself to an optimal position.

"I want you to count backward from ten, taking slow deep breaths and growing increasingly relaxed as you do so. After you feel totally relaxed, imagine where you want to be, it can be anywhere; it doesn't matter—a place where you feel the safest and secure. Soon, I will name some objects, and when I say them, I want you to feel them in your hand using only your mind. One after the other, ok?"

"Yeah," she said quietly. Drucilla began counting in her head and imagined herself at a waterfall.

"A peach. Feel its weight, the fur, the softness of it," Dominic began. "The peach becomes a rose, feel the petals, smell the fragrance, the stem is prickly, you feel pain when you press your finger against the thorn. The rose becomes a snake. Feel the weight of him, the smoothness of his scales as he slithers through your hands. What you're currently doing is exercising your ability to detect spiritual sensation. The snake is now a rope; it's a strong thick nylon rope. I want you to wrap the rope around your waist tightly; it will hold you and keep you secure. I will be holding onto the other end. I want you to go ahead and detach yourself from your body; the rope is still tied tightly to you as you feel yourself leave. Call out to me if you need me to pull you back," he said.

...and with that, silence.

Drucilla opened her eyes, and she was in what appeared to be a cavern. Stalagmites and stalactites growing from every direction. Drucilla didn't recognize the place. She had never been there. Drucilla tried to recall if this was from an archaeology trip she had forgotten about. The cave was deep, there wasn't much light, but she could see that she was only a few feet inside. Drucilla wanted to move forward, but it was too dark. She couldn't see any further than about 50-feet in front of her, but she could tell that it angled downward. The cavern was high; the ceiling was about a hundred-or-so-feet above her head. It was cold, but not freezing. There used to be water there at one time; she could tell by the soft gravel beneath her feet that caused her to sink in slightly as she moved. Drucilla looked at the geology of the cave and the colors.

"I'm in a large cavern of some type. I think I'm somewhere in Central America," Drucilla said with her eyes closed, in a quiet sleepy tone, "maybe southern Mexico."

"What else do you see?"

With a massive, thunderous boom, the back of the cavern exploded into a fiery opening. Drucilla heard the rush of fire, screams, and debris as it flew out at incredible speeds. "Something's happening…" Drucilla said in a panicked tone.

Instinctively, Drucilla tried to cover herself, but the rocks and small boulders seemed to pass right through her. She was completely unharmed from the explosion. Drucilla turned her head and put her hands over her face as she tried to shield her eyes from the blinding, fiery light. "There was an explosion and a bright light. I can't see anything..." Drucilla said, trying to put her hands up over her face. She heard thunderous steps as if a giant was moving at a quick pace toward the cavern's entrance from the newly created hole the blast created. Drucilla tried to see what had burst through with such force. In front of Drucilla was what she could only assume was a huge metallic blue-glowing orb, about 50-feet in diameter with giant blazing bright blue coronas emitting from and seeming to encircle it. "There's a fiery blue orb; it's huge. It looks like…the sun…."

The heavy steps were getting closer, and the earthquakes became more intense. An enormous, hundred-foot humanoid being of light, draped in fire and swirling sashes of molten silica, stepped up to the orb with a sonic scream. "There's another being. She's made of fire. She's gigantic. And, she has a sword..."

"Calliope?" Dominic asked with concern and excitement.

The enormous being swung a fiery broadsword over her head and impaled the orbital light with a thunderous wave of force. She drove the sword through its center and into the earth below it. A fountain of blood and fire exploded from the entry point as the fiery orb dimmed and the fire died.

"She killed it!" Drucilla shouted.

The monstrous light humanoid drew the sword back out, swung it over her shoulder, and turned and walked back into the entrance from where it came, causing the earth to quake with every step until the earthquakes reduced to tremors. After the light being was gone, Drucilla came out from hiding behind the stalactites. She wanted to get a closer look at the slain orb. Her arms and legs began to glow with intense blue light. The light was starting to tear through her flesh. Drucilla felt intense, crippling pain in her chest that caused her to hit the ground.

"DOMINIC!" Drucilla screamed. Then, Drucilla felt herself being ripped out of whatever dimension she was in and pulled back to reality. Drucilla jumped to her feet on the rug in Dominic's living room. Her skin was smoking, but her veins' blue light began to fade. Her breathing was rapid; her pulse was well out of normal range. Drucilla struggled to catch her breath. "I saw it!" Drucilla carefully made her way to Dominic's couch and sat. She gripped the end of the couch arm and dug in her nails. Even with a death grip on the couch arm, her hands would not stop shaking.

Dominic rushed to the kitchen and returned with a glass of water. "Tell me," Dominic said, kneeling at Drucilla's side handing her the glass.

"I saw Calliope kill the Throne, Thoth. I saw it. I saw it happen in real-time!" Drucilla said, trying to catch her breath.

Dominic's eyes grew wild in excitement. "Retrocognition!" he yelled out.

"Wha, what?"

Dominic began to bounce excitedly, "You saw an event that happened in the past: retrocognition!"

Drucilla shook her head. "I'm going home. I need sleep." Drucilla groaned, got to her feet, and headed for his front door.

"This is great!" he said, entirely too excited and grinning wildly, "Wow!"

"Great, you can tick that box." Drucilla pulled her bag up over her shoulder, opened the front door, and closed it behind her.

CANTICLE TWENTY-NINE

"For a timepiece never changes pace." —Cocteau Twins

Drucilla stood in the middle of what appeared to be some sort of town square. The street was paved with square stones, and the masonry encircled a giant obelisk in rings like pond ripples. The street was empty. The sky was a dreaded orange with burnt sienna clouds blotting out any light source. The only exception being intermittent flashes of heat lightning flickering randomly throughout the sky. At the end of this square stood a cathedral. The cathedral was impressive in its size. It was adorned with six spires of random height and large rosette windows.

Everything on the street was quiet. It almost reminded Drucilla of Vatican City with its layout, but it looked completely different from its building and structures. Drucilla quickly walked down the stone street to the cathedral doors. The black double doors met in an arch. They loomed over her and looked incredibly heavy. The door handles looked almost too small to push or pull the weight of the doors. The stairs were cracked and broken, and some of the stairs had eroded away completely. It was clear that no one had been there for possibly centuries. The left door was ajar. Even so, Drucilla had to put quite a bit of effort into it to shoving it enough for her to squeeze through the opening. The grand space was dim and dusty. Tall, tapered candles were the only light, illuminating a path to the altar at the end of the vast room. The walls were lined in towering, stained-glass windows between columns. They featured depictions of beings Drucilla had never seen before: strange creatures, some with wings, others with claws and fur, several with canine features, a few with scales, and some with two and even three heads.

What kind of a church is this? Drucilla reached the altar, and it was empty. There were no pews in this cathedral—just an open hall. There appeared to be a wooden door directly behind the altar. This was the only internal door in this cathedral that Drucilla could see. The other doorways to the left and the right presumably led back outside. Drucilla walked over to the wooden door and opened it to find a corridor stretching out in front of her. Multiple wooden doors line either side with large iron hinges and prominent round door pulls. There were lit torches placed on the sides of the walls for the length of the corridor. At the end was another set of wooden doorsThere was another set of wooden doors at the end, just like the others. Drucilla made her way to the end and pulled the doors open. She looked inside. Below she was a stone staircase leading downward, a landing, and then down another flight. There was no light inside, so Drucilla grabbed one of the torches and headed down the stone staircase. The staircase went down for four flights and terminated to a long, stone, arched hallway.

The hallway was dark and cavernous; even with the torch, Drucilla couldn't see anything with much detail.

Drucilla walked carefully to make sure she didn't trip on the broken and loose stone floor. Immediately it dawned on her. This looked exactly like the newly discovered Catacomb area she saw when she was seventeen years old. Everything from the pillars to the broken floor was identical, except there were alcoves instead of cubby holes that lined the walls. Inside the alcoves were squarish, stone, elaborately carved caskets resembling sarcophagi. However, with Drucilla's archaeological background, she could not determine from which period they were. They potentially exceeded even the oldest sarcophagi she had seen in her career.

In the darkness, something swiped at Drucilla's hair on the back of her head. Drucilla turned around quickly to see what it was, but there was nothing or no one there. She glanced around in confusion and shook her head. She thought she imagined it and continued to walk down the hall. The hallway smelled musty, but at the same time, there was a sickly sort of sweetness in the air. As if the fruit was left to rot among the caskets at some point. Drucilla had no idea how far the hallway went, but she felt like she had walked a couple of hundred feet, at least.

"Drucilla," a quiet but broken, disembodied voice with shifting pitch called to her from low to high. Almost like a warped record.

Drucilla halted. "Who's here?" She looked around and shone her torch in the direction the sound. Drucilla felt the blood in her veins beginning to burn. The bright blue veins in her hand holding the torch began to rise to the surface and increase in intensity. The light from her body intensified and overtook the light from the torch. Drucilla dropped the torch to the ground and navigated down the hall using the illumination emitted from her body.

"Drucilla. Stop," the voice said again.

"Stop what?" Drucilla called out as she looked around swiftly.

"Go back," the voice responded.

"Why do you want me to go back?" Drucilla continued to look for the source of the sound. She turned around to face the direction she was headed and came face-to-face with a translucent veiled head floating in front of her. Terrified, Drucilla fell backward to the ground. The face glided down to her.

"Drucilla, you should not be here," the face said with its broken, disembodied voice.

"Why? Who are you?" Drucilla got to her feet. The face glided up to meet hers.

"I am the Guardian. You are about to enter Perdition. Your kind cannot enter. You do not belong here."

"My kind?"

"Go back, Ophanim. Go back before they find you."

Drucilla heard heavy footsteps from the end of the dark hall ahead, but she couldn't see who or what it was.

Whatever it was, it was coming towards her. She heard a low, guttural, inhuman growl.

"Drucilla, now!" The apparition swiftly turned to the end of the hall and subsequently vanished.

The steps, snorts, and growls were getting closer. Drucilla panicked as her body burned brighter and brighter. Drucilla heeded the warning, turned, and ran back down the hall the way she came. Drucilla felt the heat from the breath of the beasts directly behind her. She didn't dare turn around. Whatever it was, it was big and terrifying. Drucilla placed her hands on her head and let out a blood-curdling scream as Diablo hissed violently and jumped off the dining room table with a growl.

"What the shit?" Adrian yelled and came darting into the dining room to see Drucilla as she gripped onto the back of the chair. She tried to catch her breath as her body started to dim.

"What's happening? Are you ok?" Adrian rubbed Drucilla's hand to calm her down.

"Yeah, I think so," Drucilla said as she tried to regulate her breath. "Did I fall asleep?"

"I don't know. I went upstairs after I made you dinner."

"How long ago?"

"Maybe forty minutes?" he shrugged, "Are you sure you're, ok?"

"Yeah, yeah," Drucilla tried to shake it off. "I'm uh. I'm going to head over to Dominic's house for a bit," she said, rubbing her forehead trying to make sense of what just happened.

†††

Drucilla sat on her usual swivel stool in Dominic's study. She slowly twisted back and forth as she laid out the details of her experience in what she assumed was Hell. Dominic leaned against his desk, ankles crossed and thumb on his bottom lip. *That's how you know he's deep in thought. He always holds his lips closed with his thumb,* Drucilla thought to herself as she watched his reactions. "I wasn't trying to astral project," Drucilla assured Dominic. "Seriously, I was just sitting down to eat dinner, and bam! I'm in Hell."

Dominic looked up at Drucilla and shoved his hands in his front pockets.

"You actually didn't astral project," Dominic started. "For instance, you wouldn't have had to manipulate doors to go through them if you had. You would have just passed through them or any other solid object. No, this was different. Did Adrian notice you were missing?"

"Adrian said he didn't know. He went upstairs after he made dinner. He just heard me scream and rushed down."

"And how long do you think you were away?"

"Adrian said probably about forty minutes, but it could have been longer."

"This is straight-up old-fashioned teleportation. Which I would assume would be something you could do. Considering Lucifer does it, why wouldn't you be able to?"

Drucilla shrugged.

Dominic sat in his desk chair next to Drucilla and crossed his massive arms.

"So, this floating face that you spoke to, did it say it was 'A guardian' or 'The Guardian?'" he asked pointedly as he leaned over to his laptop and opened a browser window. He started to type into a search engine.

"Um, 'The Guardian,'" Drucilla responded.

"Mmm-hmmm," Dominic mumbled as he read his screen.

"Ok? Who is it?"

"So, from Greco-Roman lore, The Guardian to the portal to Hell is a Roman soldier named Curtius," he read aloud.

"That doesn't make sense." Drucilla crinkled her nose. "The veiled face was a woman. Not a man."

"What?" Dominic said, looking at Drucilla.

Drucilla nodded.

"Wait, what did she look like? Just give me any detail you can remember."

Drucilla got up and started to pace around his study. "Well, her voice was feminine but disconnected, like a warped record. She would speak, and her voice would trail off and change pitch, like if you had randomly slowed down an audio recording. She had feminine features. I couldn't see her eyes, but her nose was small, and her lips were full. She was shrouded in a long thin veil."

Dominic looked like he was putting things together in his head as he nodded.

"What color was she? Did you notice a smell?" he asked, leaning towards Drucilla.

"Purple? I don't know, my body was glowing, and she appeared purplish. It also smelled like rotten fruit down there," Drucilla said with a snarled lip as if she was disgusted at the thought.

Dominic hopped up from his chair and walked over to one of his massive bookshelves. He pulled down another one of his old books. This time it was a Greek mythology book. He dropped it down in front of them and flipped open to a photograph of a baroque era painting of a woman. He turned the image to face Drucilla. The painting depicted a beautiful woman draped in a red toga and a red veil holding a skull in one hand and a pomegranate in the other.

"Is that her?" he asked.

Drucilla leaned her head to the side to study her face. "Not exactly, but it's close,"

Dominic nodded. "A lot of these paintings are drawn from descriptions. Most of the time, the artist had never seen the subjects."

"Who is she?"

"That..." Dominic began as he sat back down in his chair, "is Persephone. The rotten fruit you were smelling was pomegranate. The fruit of the underworld."

"No shit," Drucilla said, amused.

"What about the beasts that were chasing me? Who were they?"

"Honestly? Most likely Hell Hounds, Cerberus, they have lots of different names. They also guard the entrance to Hell. But that's just mythos. Could have been anything, really," Dominic explained. "Dru, do you know what caused you to teleport?"

"It wasn't anything. I was sitting at my table. Diablo was next to me. Adrian had just made an amazing rosemary lemon chicken linguine, and the next thing I know, I'm standing in the middle of that Vatican-type village square."

"You weren't thinking about anything in particular?"

Drucilla looked down and tried to recall what she was thinking at the time. "Ok, yeah, I remember. I was thinking that I hadn't seen Lucifer since our meeting with Calliope and I wondered where he was," Drucilla stopped and looked up at Dominic in surprise.

"And there it is," Dominic said, leaning back.

Drucilla's eyes widened.

"I honestly didn't think you could do that at your stage. I figured this is something that would happen to you after you've progressed further in your transformation," Dominic said.

"Wait, I've never been to Hell. Wouldn't I have to have been there before to teleport there again? Can a Divine just blindly teleport?" Drucilla asked.

"Drucilla, there is a lot we have yet to unlock about you. Where were you for three days when you died? Are you possibly recalling Thoth's memories? Unfortunately, I don't have an answer for you right now." Dominic picked up a pen and twirled it between his fingers.

"So, what does this mean?"

"It means our experiments will start involving control, rather than whether you can do them or not. We're going to assume that you have all the abilities of an Ophanim. We need to figure out how to use them."

"I think this is going to require more than just books. We're going to need to consult an expert," Drucilla said.

"Heh, yeah. 'You know one?" Dominic smirked as he flipped through the mythology book.

"As a matter of fact, I do," Drucilla grinned mischievously.

✝✝✝

Dominic and Drucilla stood side-by-side in the cold winter evening in the middle of Laurel Grove cemetery in front of Charles Eisenbeis' obelisk.

"Ready?" Drucilla looked at Dominic.

"Yeah," he said reluctantly.

Drucilla stepped up to the half-sunken crypt entrance. Dominic stepped back.

"You know, what exactly is wrong with researching? I like researching," Dominic complained.

"What are you scared of?"

"I'm not scared. I just don't like *him*." Dominic handed Drucilla the old bronze dagger with some trepidation.

"It'll be fine," Drucilla said calmly.

Dominic grumbled something inaudible to himself as he moved further behind Drucilla.

Drucilla cut her hand and said the chant in Latin again. She tossed her glowing blue Ophanim blood directly on the grave, on top of the frozen grass in front of the obelisk. A slight tremor shook the ground. A decomposed skeletal hand punched an arm through the cinderblock-covered, half-sunken mausoleum opening and into the cold night air. With another punch, the skeleton pulled itself from the hole it created. It lumbered toward Dominic and Drucilla and stopped within feet of Drucilla as he waited for instructions.

Drucilla turned around and looked at Dominic. Dominic stepped up to her side and held up his lantern to the rickety, rigid, skeletal remains of Charles Eisenbeis.

"You think maybe we shouldn't have chosen a beloved icon of the town to raise from the dead?" he asked.

"Why not?"

"Kind of in poor taste, isn't it?"

"It's just a skeleton," Drucilla shrugged.

"Yeah, but he's kind of a celebrity, you know. Maybe we should have just, I dunno, picked someone at random, not the first mayor of Port Townsend?"

"Yeah, but they wouldn't garner as much attention as Eisenbeis," Drucilla explained her logic, "and besides…."

"Oh, bloody Hell! You two again?" Azrael threw his hands up in the air.

"Azrael!" Drucilla chirped.

Dominic shifted his eyes upwards under his brows.

"Do you not understand that it interrupts my schedule every time you raise the dead? A woman who has cancer must keep suffering while I deal with your shenanigans before I can take her," Azrael scolds.

"Oh. No, I didn't realize that."

"No, you did not. This is extremely selfish of you," Azrael continued to berate them.

Dominic rolled his eyes and pushed his hands deeper into his peacoat pockets to keep warm.

"What is it this time? You wanted to see if you could raise one instead of fifty?" Azrael rubbed his forehead in frustration.

"I actually need your help. I have questions," Drucilla announced.

Azrael put his hand down and looked at Dominic, then back at Drucilla. "Tell me, Drucilla, how can I help you?" He clasped his hands together and rocked back and forth on his heels. He was clearly unhappy with her request.

Drucilla looked at Dominic before she spoke. "I teleported this evening. I don't know how, but I did it."

"Yes, that is something that our kind does," he nodded and gestured for Drucilla to move it along and waited for her to get to the point.

"How does it work?" Drucilla asked.

Azrael creased his brow for a moment in confusion. His hollow eyes seemed to be glaring. "You want to know how to teleport after you have already teleported?"

"I don't know how I teleported," Drucilla said, "How do Seraphim do it?"

"Normally, I just think of where I need to be and here I am."

"That's it?"

"More or less, yes," Azrael answered.

"What else can I do?"

"What else can the Divine do? Or you?"

"Both, I guess."

Azrael thought for a moment. "Drucilla, as I said before, you exist in a different space than the Divine. You may or may not have the same abilities. Like the Unholy, you may or may not have the same abilities they do," Azrael explained.

"She can raise the dead, and the Divine can't," Dominic said, interrupting.

"Yes, although she should not." Azrael peered down at Drucilla in disappointment.

Drucilla shifted her eyes away from Azrael sheepishly. "Presumably, you can take life from one and give to another," Azrael added.

"Wait, what?" Drucilla interrupted him, "I can transfer sand?"

"Sand? What?" Azrael asked.

"It's a metaphor for extending a lifespan. You know sacrificing your life to give to another…there's only so much sand in an hourglass and etcetera," Dominic explained.

"I suppose if that makes sense to you…." Azrael looked at Dominic, puzzled. Azrael turned his attention back to Drucilla.

"But only if someone willingly sacrifices their life to give more life to another person, right?" Drucilla reaffirmed.

"No, not all of us," Azrael answered.

"No?" Dominic and Drucilla both exclaimed simultaneously.

"The Unholy usually just take life willingly or not. They do not need consent, unlike the Divine. As for the Cataclysms, we are unable to make Celestial Deals. We do not have the ability," Azrael explained. He started to pace around the top of Eisenbeis' submerged crypt. "That is the biggest difference between the factions. The Divine is bound by Celestial Law; the Unholy technically are not. However, both may suffer the consequences of their actions. That is universal, so they both are bound for all intents and purposes."

Drucilla looked at Dominic for a moment before she turned her attention back to Azrael. "What else?"

"As I said, I am not entirely certain of you specifically, but for the divine energies, we essentially have infinite strength. You can lift that obelisk over there if you feel compelled to do so."

Drucilla's eyes lit up.

"We can tell facts about a human by touching an object in their possession," Azrael said as he thought about his abilities.

"Psychometry," Dominic muttered.

"We can acquire information about a distant or non-local place, person, or event using our mind," Azrael continued.

"Remote viewing," Dominic nodded.

Azrael seemed to glare at Dominic.

"We can transmit information from one person to another without using any known human sensory channels or physical interaction."

"Telepathy," Dominic simplified.

"Do you want to explain this, or shall I?" Azrael snapped at Dominic.

Dominic threw up his hands and backed away.

"Oh, levitation and flight, but that depends entirely on your wings," Azrael added.

"What about my wings?"

"You're in your infancy. You'll grow into them and use them eventually."

Drucilla looked at Dominic and then over her shoulder.

"Now, if there's nothing else, I must attend to my duties," Azrael said, looking impatient.

"What if I need you again?"

"Well, there's always prayer," Azrael quipped.

Dominic laughed.

Azrael shot Dominic a disapproving look.

"Oh, and keep your necromancy to a minimum. It is better for everyone that way," Azrael scolded Drucilla as he glanced at the skeletal remains of the former Eisenbeis in front of Drucilla. Azrael waved his hand over the skeleton, and it collapsed to a pile of bones. Azrael disappeared in a blink.

"Did I mention that I think that guy is a dick?"

"You might have once or twice," Drucilla said, glancing at Dominic.

"Can we go? It's cold as balls out here." Dominic bounced to keep warm.

"Gimme a sec." Drucilla stepped up to the obelisk of Charles Eisenbeis. It was taller than she realized as she stood beside it. Drucilla slowly placed both hands on the side of the obelisk.

"Dru, maybe you shouldn't…."

"If it falls, I can just pick it up, right?"

Dominic raised his finger and opened his mouth but decided to remain quiet and put his hands back in his pocket.

Drucilla got her hands into a comfortable position and planted her feet. Drucilla inhaled and exhaled in quick breaths. She pushed with every ounce of strength in her arms, but the obelisk didn't budge. Drucilla, confused, stopped and looked at the obelisk. She braced herself again and shoved once more. Still, it didn't move.

"Damn it," Drucilla groaned.

"Dru, let's go!"

"One more time," Drucilla shouted.

Drucilla shook out her arms and concentrated on Drake. The thought of her brother abandoning her made her angry all over again. Her arms began to glow, and she braced herself one more time. She shoved with everything she had, and with a loud explosion, Drucilla obliterated the obelisk. Rocks and debris rained down around Drucilla and Dominic, inside of an enormous dust cloud.

"Shit!" Drucilla yelled.

"Shit, shit, shit, shit!" Dominic yelled as he ran out of the cemetery.

Drucilla jumped down off the crypt and ran to catch up to Dominic.

"Get away from me, Dru, I'm not going down for you!" Dominic yelled over his shoulder as he ran.

"Bullshit! You're complicit!" Drucilla yelled as she ran behind him.

Drucilla and Dominic ran out through the iron gates and down the street at top speed.

MEMENTO MORI.
1626. H. inventor et sculpsit. Cum privill.
1

CANTICLE THIRTY

"It's not our fault if the Reaper holds our hearts." —His
Infernal Majesty

Drucilla stepped out of the shower into the steamy bathroom. She twisted up her hair into a toweled turban. She used the other towel to wipe down the mirror. She examined her face and neck in the mirror. Slowly, she turned to the side. Drucilla arched her shoulders back slightly and flexed her trapezes muscles, and pushed out her developing wings.

What the…? Her eyes widened. She was startled by what she saw.

††††

Drucilla pulled her Jeep up to Dominic's house and parked on the street. She headed up the worn, white, wooden steps to his front door and looked around the outside of Dominic's home. Dominic lived in a modest, medium-sized, white, and maroon-colored, three-bedroom Craftsman with a second story. It was about a mile from her place, up a hill. His yard was surrounded by a white picket fence and short shrubbery, which Dominic meticulously maintained. The gate was never closed due to a broken antique latch. Dominic would only replace it with the exact one if he ever found it. The house wasn't as old as Drucilla's grandmother's house, but maybe thirty or so years younger. Drucilla could hear the rhythmic thumping of bass coming from the inside as she approached the front door. Drucilla opened the door and was blasted in the face with Journey's *Separate Ways*, probably turned up to ten.

"Dom?" Drucilla yelled, knowing he probably couldn't hear her with the music cranked up that loud.

Drucilla moved through his living room and into his formal dining-room-turned-library. He worked out of the dining area because it was the largest room in the house. The ceilings were high enough to use the tall space for his book collection and antiquated Catholic artwork. There was a ladder attached to the curved cornered bookshelves that he could roll around the entire room. The window and chandelier were replaced, but she could still see a couple of cracks in the wall.

Drucilla peered into the kitchen and saw Dominic, in jeans, no shirt, no shoes, and mixing protein powder into a plastic container. He apparently just finished lifting weights, which she surmised by the sweat beads on his forehead and between the short hairs on the top of his head. Tattoos covered his upper body in several motifs. Symbols and imagery representing various aspects of religion, the occult, and demonology were all well-represented. He had a tattoo of a snake that hung around his neck, tattooed plate armor pauldrons on his shoulders, and a Russian nesting doll inside his left forearm. Drucilla realized she had never before seen his bare arms. Dominic always wore long-sleeved tee shirts or jackets. She was impressed by his chiseled physique, which undoubtedly took decades to develop. He stood at the counter, bouncing and singing at the top of his lungs.

Caught between confusion and pain, pain, pain
Distant eyes
Promises we made were in vain, in vaaaaaaaaaain, in vaaaaaaaaaaain

When he sang that last line, he threw his head and arms back and belted it out as loud and as forcefully as possible. He put the lid on his container and shook it vigorously. He turned to Drucilla on his way out of the kitchen.

"HOLY SHIT!" he yelled as he noticed Drucilla. His knees buckled as he grabbed his bare chest. He looked up at Drucilla and looked back at his bare chest, realizing that he wasn't wearing a shirt. He dashed past her and grabbed a black hoodie from the dining room chair. He pulled it over his head as quickly as he could. Drucilla smiled. She was amused at his whole Victorian demeanor and fear of looking inappropriate.

He picked up his phone off the table and stopped the music. "Dru. Uh, what's uh, going on?" he said, popping the top open on his protein shake and taking a drink, moderately embarrassed.

"I'm sorry I didn't mean to interrupt you, but I called a couple of times, and you didn't answer, so I came over. I yelled for you when I got here, but I guess you couldn't hear me."

"It's cool. Um, you didn't just see me, uh..."

"Pulling a Steve Perry? Oh yes," Drucilla grinned and nodded.

Dominic turned multiple shades of red.

"I can't say I'm impressed with nor approve of your musical taste, but you aren't a bad singer." Drucilla smiled.

He took a huge gulp of his shake that made his cheeks bulge out a little while he looked at Drucilla out of the corner of his eye.

Drucilla walked over to his shelves and looked upward.

"I think we have a problem," Drucilla started.

"What's going on?" he asked, taking a seat at his desk and crossing his ankle over his knee. He leaned back and intently looked at Drucilla. It amused her that he knew how to take a seat when he was about to get important news.

"Where is your angelic book section?" Drucilla said, looking around the bookshelf.

"What kind of angelic book?"

"The ones about the Thrones."

He reached over on top of his desk and placed an old Christian angelology book in front of her. "You'll want to look at the chapters about the First Spheres: Seraphim, Cherubim, and Thrones."

"You just have this book handy?"

"You're not the only one concerned about this transformation, Dru,"

"Fair enough," Drucilla said, scanning through the book for pictures.

"So, what's going on?"

"I wanted to see the book's depictions of Thrones. I want to see what I'm turning into," Drucilla said, not looking up from the book.

"But you've actually witnessed the slaying of Thoth. What can my books tell you that you don't already know?"

Drucilla exhaled and crossed her arms. "I don't. I don't know. It's just… it's probably better that I just show you." Drucilla grabbed the bottom of her sweater and pulled the back of it up to her neck. She flexed her trapezes muscles.

Dominic rubbed his chin as if he didn't understand what he was seeing. Drucilla looked over her shoulder at him. He raised his hand to touch the rudimentary wings.

"Yeah," Drucilla said, answering him before he could ask, "No, that's not your imagination. There really are four wings." Drucilla pulled her shirt back down and sat in front of Dominic. "I think Calliope is right. I think I'm transforming into an actual Ophanim," Drucilla said nervously.

"Azrael wouldn't lie to you, Dru. He doesn't need to." Dominic tried to reassure her.

"I'm also unique. Literally the first case. Azrael has nothing to base his assumption on, so how would he know for sure?"

"That…that is a valid question," Dominic said. He put his thumb to his lip.

"You know what we have to do, right? We need to contact Azrael," Drucilla explained.

"Dru, if you contact him again, he'll probably take us with him this time. We can't just force him to show up by reanimating corpses. He was really pissed about the necromancy," Dominic said, rebuffing her suggestion.

"Well, why don't we go to him?"

Dominic sat and thought about her suggestion for a moment. "What are you thinking? 'Just hang around a hospital or a nursing home until he shows up?" Dominic asked

"Unless you have a better idea?"

"Well, we could be waiting a while. We would need to figure out a way to know exactly when and where someone is dying and be there at just the right time," Dominic said. He stood up and paced around the table.

Drucilla slowly looked up at Dominic and stared at him for a moment. He could see the gears turning in her head.

"What?"

"Can…can I do that? I mean, do I have that ability?"

"To locate the dying?" Dominic looked at Drucilla with curiosity. "Maybe," he said. Dominic paced and mulled it over in his head. He glanced up to his bookshelf at a pile of rolled-up maps. "But I have an idea…" he mused while biting the inside of his lip.

Dominic pulled the ladder over to the bookshelf with the maps stacked on top. He climbed up, pulled down an armful of them, and placed them on the table. He looked at the edges of each rolled map and read the titles. Finally, Dominic located a map of Port Townsend and the outlying areas from Sequim down to Kingston. Essentially, the top right corner of the Washington peninsula. He laid the map out flat and placed books on the corners to keep the ends from curling.

"Ok, this will probably not work, but let's give it a shot." He picked up the old bronze dagger from the cabinet behind Drucilla and handed it to her.

Drucilla took the dagger and looked at him.

"Just prick your finger and flick the blood onto the map," Dominic suggested.

"What if I end up raising the dead of the entire peninsula?" Drucilla questioned his method.

"This is a map, Dru, not a cemetery," Dominic said firmly, "If I'm right, your blood should serve as a locating beacon."

Drucilla shrugged and jabbed the end of the dagger into her index finger. She squeezed her finger with her other hand to work the blood up to the surface. She pressed her fingernail into her thumb and flicked the blood onto the map. The blood hit the map with tiny sparks of blue light then died down. Drucilla and Dominic both leaned over the map inquisitively to see if anything would happen. They looked at each other and back at the map.

"Nothing's happening," Drucilla commented.

"Nah, doesn't appear to be," Dominic said disappointedly and flopped down into the chair.

They were just about to give up when Drucilla closed her eyes and held her hand over the map. She opened her eyes slowly, and suddenly a tiny point of light started to pulse.

"Dominic, look!".

Dominic stood back up and looked at the pulse of light.

"I honestly didn't think that would work," Dominic said, surprised.

"I wanted it to—I willed it!"

Dominic shrugged and looked down at the map. "This looks like the Olympic Medical Center in Sequim."

"I'll drive." Drucilla placed the dagger back on the table and headed for the front door.

†††

The drive was about forty minutes or so outside of Port Townsend. As they arrived at the hospital, they pulled into the parking lot. Drucilla turned off the Jeep.

"How do we know where to be?" Drucilla asked.

"I think maybe we should start relying on your intuition from this point."

Drucilla shrugged.

"Where do you think we should go?" Dominic stared at the building.

Drucilla looked at the doors to the emergency room entrance, "ICU?" she shrugged.

Dominic shrugged back.

They entered through the emergency room entrance. To the right was a waiting room and admitting desk. In front of Dominic and Drucilla were double doors that led into a long hallway. Drucilla pushed open the doors and headed down the hall. They carefully looked at the modest signs attached to the walls near the doors.

"Do you feel anything in particular?" Dominic asked.

"No, nothing."

"Well, maybe it's not the emergency or the ICU," he commented. "Should we go up to the rooms?"

Drucilla nodded in agreement. The pair found the elevators and pressed the button to open the doors. After they were inside, Drucilla looked at the lighted number pad with the departments listed. The doors closed.

"Pick a floor, I guess," Dominic said.

Drucilla saw one of the lights on the buttons flicker ever so slightly. Curious, she moved her finger closer to the button. The button reacted to her and glowed an eerie orange glow.

"I think I know where we're going." Drucilla pressed the button to the Cardiology floor.

The elevator stopped, and the doors slid open. As they exited the elevator, Drucilla noticed the lighting in the corridor was an orangish hue on one end, and there was no coloration on the other end of the corridor.

"This way," Drucilla told Dominic as they headed towards the orange illumination.

Dominic followed.

They quickly walked down the hall and came upon a particular patient's room, *Theodore Roberts*. The room door cast a brighter orange hue.

"In here," Drucilla whispered. Dominic and Drucilla both looked around the hall to see if anyone spotted them. Drucilla cracked open the door and quickly pushed her way through with Dominic close behind her.

They saw an older gentleman in a bed, hooked up to a cardiogram in the room. The slow beeping was signaling that these were the last few beats of this man's life. Dominic and Drucilla stood over the stranger.

"This feels wrong, Dru," Dominic said reluctantly.

"It's either this or grave desecration. Besides, we have nothing to do with this man's life. We're just here at the right time."

The slow beeps finally faded into one long, drawn-out beep. Drucilla reached over to turn down the volume. Dominic and Drucilla leaned against the large window ledge and waited.

Just as they had hoped, Azrael suddenly blinked into existence and placed his hand on the man's forehead. Feeling their presence in the room, he stood up without looking at Dominic or Drucilla and let out a heavy sigh. He rubbed his forehead again in annoyance. He put his hand down and slowly looked over to them, giving them an irritated look.

"Drucilla, Dominic," he said, unamused.

"Hey! At least I didn't disturb any bodies this time," Drucilla said with a bit of positivity in her voice.

"What is it now?" he said calmly and clearly annoyed. He crossed his long spindly arms.

Drucilla lurched off the wall from her leaning position, walked over, and stood in front of Azrael.

"I have four wings," she announced. "Why do I have four wings?"

"Because you're part Ophanim. Why does it matter?" Azrael asked, shaking his head.

"Is that all? Is that the extent, or is my body going to be torn to shreds when I'm fully transformed? Am I going to turn into flaming wheels with an enormous eye like an Ophanim? I mean, I've seen a Throne in real life. I know what they look like!" Drucilla said with a bit of paranoia and fear creeping into her voice.

"No, you will not," Azrael said.

"Yeah, but how do you know? I'm the first human to transform. You have nothing off of which to base your assumption! You can't possibly know what's going to happen to a human hybrid. You aren't all-knowing. You aren't a Throne!" Drucilla's voice escalated and got louder. "Are you lying, and you really know, but you just won't tell me? What aren't you telling me?" As Drucilla became increasingly irate, she was vaguely aware that her hands and face were beginning to glow.

"Drucilla…" Azrael leaned in towards her, bent down to her level, and gritted his teeth. "I told you that you will not die. You will not be torn to shreds. You will transform, but you are also human, and the entity resides within your human body, not the other way around. Thoth cannot live outside of your body and therefore is dependent on your form to stay alive. That would be the equivalent of a fish pulling itself out of water for no other reason than to die. I have no reason to lie to you. Am I making myself clear?" Azrael's eyes glowed bright red but quickly died back down to black hollow wells.

"But I'm a new thing. This has never happened before. How do you know for certain?" Drucilla asked again without yielding.

"Because I've already seen it!" Azrael snaped back at Drucilla.

"Precognition," Dominic said softly as if to himself.

Azrael squinted at Dominic, shook his head slightly, and turned his attention to Drucilla. "Now, if you two are done with this little ambush, I have business to which to attend."

Drucilla just looked at him. She was still not completely satisfied.

Azrael blinked out of existence.

Dominic looked at Drucilla, and Drucilla stared at the vacant space that Azrael had left.

"Azrael is kind of a dick, but I do think he is being truthful with you," Dominic said, breaking the silence.

"For someone who doesn't like him, you sure stick up for him an awful lot."

"Dru, he's not Lucifer. Think about it. He has nothing to gain from dishonesty. He isn't an Unholy or a Divine. He doesn't even play those stupid relic games. I mean, what could he possibly gain from lying? I think you can trust him. I do."

Drucilla looked at Dominic, she wanted to thwart his logic, but she knew deep down that he was right.

"Look, I know you're scared. I'm scared for you. The unknown is terrifying, but if I had to put my money on someone, it would be Azrael," Dominic added.

nihel

HGoltzius excud.

QVIS EVADET?

H.G.

Momento breuis hæc, certeq obnoxia morti
Vita, quasi fumus, bullula, flosq perit.
Cur ergo teneris (pròh stulti) fidimus añis!
Cur non sponte mori discimus ante diem!

Excussa blandæ carnis, dum vita superstes,
Compede, post mortem liberiore gradu
Spiritus astra petet, iam sedem vbi fixerat ante
Ciuemq agnoscet cælica turba suum.

CANTICLE THIRTY-ONE

"You should reach the limits of virtue before you cross the border of death." —Tyrtaeus

Dominic sat next to Drucilla on the couch. Drucilla was silent for a moment before shifting herself to face him. He looked confused by her demeanor.

"What's up, Dru?" he asked, concerned.

Drucilla looked him in the eyes for a moment and exhaled. She opened the end table drawer and pulled out the small black oblong box that contained the pen. She held it on her lap for a moment. Drucilla ran her hand over the box before looking back up at Dominic's face. He looked deeply concerned while Drucilla slowly handed him the box. He looked down at it and back up to her face as he took the box.

Drucilla laced her fingers together tightly. "Dominic, there is no other human, demon, angel, or otherwise that I trust more than I trust you."

"Uh-huh," he said, still looking confused.

"I spoke to Lucifer. He had confirmed, more or less, that we were right. It's the pen of Nova. I mean, as much as he could confirm. It actually has a name. Its Erato Falx."

"Erato Falx?"

"Do you know what it means?"

"Well, Falx means any sort of slashing weapon in Latin, and Erato is the name of one of the nine muses in Greek mythology."

Dominic, I want you to keep it."

"What? Dru no, I can't take this," Dominic protested, attempting to hand it back.

"Dom, I need you to keep it. Please," Drucilla said, getting up from the couch and pacing around in front of him. She rubbed her hands nervously.

"I don't understand." Dominic held the box out slightly like he wanted Drucilla to take it back.

Drucilla stopped as she knelt in front of Dominic. "Look, Dom, I think I have it for the sole purpose of giving it to you. I can't explain it. Maybe it's the divine blood inside of me, but this is right. I don't know whether you believe in destiny or fate or any of it, but the pen was undoubtedly meant to be yours. You need to be its guardian, and I need you to learn how to use it."

"Are you sure? I don't know what to say," Dominic removed the relic from the box.

"Absolutely. I've never been surer about anything since this whole thing started. So, is that a, yes?"

Adrian walked into the room as he heard the last thing Drucilla said. He looked at Dominic sitting on the couch and Drucilla kneeling in front of him. It looked like a marriage proposal.

"Y'all," Adrian said, putting his hands on his face like he just witnessed something personal.

Alarmed, Drucilla and Dominic turned their attention to Adrian. Drucilla stood up quickly.

"I mean, Dom, I always thought you were asexual, but I mean, I demand to plan the wedding," Adrian started.

Dominic rubbed his forehead.

Drucilla groaned and rolled her eyes. "Adrian, no, that's not what's happening here…."

"I mean, you could do worse, Dru," Adrian commented.

Drucilla waved him off and turned her attention back to Dominic.

"Of course, yes, I'll guard it with my life." Dominic nodded at Drucilla.

"There's just one thing, I ask in return. 'Just a promise," Drucilla looked at Dominic with intensity.

Dominic looked at Drucilla and nodded for her to continue.

"If I, you know…become that being, the Ophanim? Promise me that you'll open a portal to Hell and throw me in there because I am going to go berserk and straight-up fucking murder every single Unholy being that I can find. I will annihilate Hell like I did that obelisk in the cemetery. Because I am the LAST human, they will ever toy with. There will not be another. I promise you that!"

"Dru…" he got up and stood in front of Drucilla, "if that day comes, I'll be right beside you. We're going Hell to together, and we're going to fuck shit up."

Drucilla grinned mischievously.

"Let's just hope it doesn't come to that." He picked up the box containing the relic, and he opened the lid to inspect it. Dominic pulled the relic out of the box and held it. The pen had transformed from the simple lathed wooden pen back into the black iron stylus now that it was in his possession.

CANTICLE THIRTY-TWO

"If the devil is the ultimate deceiver, then words must be the very devil." —Marty Rubin

"You look well!" Lucifer said. He turned his head to the side, leaned back, and crossed his arms in an overly designed, turquoise, crushed velvet chair in Drucilla's art gallery.

On Drucilla's way to lock the front door, she stopped and side-eyed at him.

Lucifer got up and walked toward her.

"What are you doing here?" Drucilla said, annoyed.

"I just came to check in with you to see how you are doing."

"You know how I'm doing. As if you haven't been watching me every second of my life for the past fifteen years," Drucilla said with hostility as she crossed her arms. "Why are you really here?"

Lucifer ignored her and walked over to a table with a few delicately carved yet intricate and complex floral patterned ceramic vases. He held a hand against his chin as he examined the carved pieces. "Too bad they did not have the stylus. Could have made these pieces so much better," Lucifer said with a grin.

Drucilla just stood and stared at him.

"I see your large friend has a new toy," Lucifer said and turned his head to see Drucilla's expression. Then turned back and continued to examine the artwork. "You should see what he can do with it. It is most impressive. He is a smart gentleman, you know…for being a hick," Lucifer smiled.

Drucilla rolled her eyes and walked over to a support beam in the center of the gallery. She leaned against it and glared. "You lied to me."

"No, that does not sound like me at all," he said, still not looking up at Drucilla. Almost like he refused to make eye contact with her. Whatever game he was playing, he didn't want her to call his bluff. Instead, he leaned further over the ceramics, "I rather like this red one. I want to purchase this. This would look lovely in my new lair."

"I'm serious, Lucifer."

"So am I. Wrap this up for me, please?"

Drucilla forcefully exhaled and walked over to the cabinet behind her counter. As Lucifer waited, Drucilla pulled out a sturdy, black cardboard box as well as a small roll of bubble wrap and tape and placed it on the desk. Lucifer extended the vase out to Drucilla as she walked up to him and took it. Drucilla gave him dagger eyes as she walked back to the counter with it.

"Seven hundred, is it?" He reached into his chest pocket.

"Yes." Drucilla wrapped up the vase.

Lucifer laid a wad of cash on the desk in front of her. The tension between them was palpable. "I do not know what you want me to say, Drucilla." Lucifer attempted to end the stand-off.

Drucilla stopped packing and looked up at him. "How about saying something about how you conspired with Calliope to get me to kill myself? And then follow that with saying something about how you're standing here and acting like you don't know that?"

Lucifer paused and stared at Drucilla for a moment. He seemed to be looking for the right words. "I know that if you did die, it would be the best outcome for our kind."

"Of course. Why wouldn't it be all about you, Lucifer?"

"I have loyalties to my kind. Part of me wanted you to die, but part of me needed you to live."

Drucilla scowled as she sealed the box. "Forgive me if it's hard for me to believe you have loyalties to anyone but yourself. Do you even want to know how I found out?"

"Let me guess, black-winged fellow, deep-set eyes. He looks like something out of the early 80s New Wave scene. Speaks like it too, with his slang and contractions—so very crude." Lucifer picked up the box.

"That doesn't seem to surprise you."

"Azrael? Nothing he does surprises me. He actively avoids the Unholy and has no love for Calliope or me. We have a bit of history, but that is unimportant. Drucilla, I swear, I do have your best interests in mind."

"It doesn't matter," Drucilla said, rubbing the bridge of her nose. Moving away from the desk, she walked over to the turquoise chairs and sat.

"Drucilla…" Lucifer sat next to her and then grabbed and held her hand.

Drucilla glanced at his hand on hers. His hand was warm and soft.

"I'm on your side. You have to believe me," Lucifer said softly, his snake-eyes intensified. "Who pulled you out of that coffin? Who has kept you hidden from my brothers?"

Drucilla stared at Lucifer. At that moment, he was the most beautiful being she had ever seen. She trusted him completely. Suddenly like a kick to the head, she snapped out of it. She snatched her hand back and crossed her arms. "Oh my God, are you seriously trying to manipulate me right now? Your manipulation power isn't going to work on me. You have to know that!"

Lucifer raised his eyebrows and looked away from Drucilla. "You are definitely further along than I anticipated," he mumbled.

"Yeah, you snatched me from the clutches of death, but you also tried to put me right back by shoving a three-foot chunk of rebar through my chest!" Drucilla yelled as she stood up.

"Because I knew it would not kill you!"

"You could have just told me I was invincible instead of proving it!"

"Drucilla, I brought you back. I was not going to allow you just die. You still cannot trust me?"

Drucilla walked around fuming, then looked back at Lucifer. "You conspired with Calliope to get me to kill myself! And now you're sitting here telling me that you're protecting me? How could I possibly trust you?"

Lucifer stared at her for a moment before speaking. "I had to…I had to make Calliope think I was on the side of the Unholy. If she knew that I was protecting you, I would have never known what she was planning to do."

"So, you're playing both sides?"

"More or less." Lucifer shrugged, "but it is truly on your side that I am. Drucilla, look at me. I cannot manipulate you—that is a fact. You tell me. Am I telling you the truth?"

Drucilla stood in front of Lucifer and stared into his serpentine eyes. She looked away and ran her hand through her hair to push it out of her face. "I want you to know something, Lucifer. When this is over, when the transformation is complete, and I become whom I'm supposed to be," Drucilla started pacing again around the room and then stopped in front of Lucifer. "I'm going to kill Calliope and anyone else that stands in my way." She looked pointedly into his reptilian pupils.

Lucifer watched her and didn't say a word.

"You, out of all people, know I am perfectly capable of doing it. I know Calliope tried to get me to kill myself because she knows what's happening to me, and she knows, in the end, I'm going to be more powerful than she is. I'm going to come for her. She also knows there's nothing she can do to stop the transformation."

"I know you will," Lucifer said, "and a big part of me wants you to...but you have to understand what I would be losing, too." Lucifer got up and stood directly in front of Drucilla. "Drucilla, do you know how you came back from the dead?"

Drucilla pressed her lips together and looked at Lucifer.

"You did die. You died most horrifically—You with your limp, lifeless body and a cavernous, burned-out hole in your chest. Every artery, every vessel was burned. Your eyes and even your hair had disintegrated. You were nothing but a husk, drenched in divine blood. When I shoved life back into your body, the blood accelerated your healing process. Essentially, you are still healing, transforming, in a manner of speaking."

Drucilla's mouth dropped open a bit. "How did you put life back into me. Azrael said that Seraphim can't do that?" She suddenly remembered Lucifer insisting he wasn't a Seraph.

Lucifer stared at her for a moment. "That is," he paused, "that is a conversation for another time."

"Why did you bring me back. I mean, what was the real reason? What are you not telling me?"

"Mostly to fulfill a bargain with your brother."

Drucilla stared at him. She wasn't buying it.

"And also, why I no longer reside in Hell. We have been through one great war. I do not want to go through another," he admitted.

"What was the bargain, Lucifer?" Drucilla asked.

Lucifer stopped and listened to something Drucilla couldn't hear. "The large fellow is here," Lucifer said.

"Lucifer, what bargain?"

Heavy steps started to build from the back entrance to the front. Dominic looked surprised to see Lucifer in the gallery. "Lucifer," Dominic said, pointing with his chin.

Lucifer nodded back.

"Dom! What's up?" Drucilla tried to calm herself.

"It's uh, Friday," he started. "You know, burgers and beer next door?" he said, slightly motioning to outside.

"Well, I should be going. Lovely vase. Please give my compliments to the artist," Lucifer said with the box in his hand. Lucifer blinked out and vanished.

"I feel like I interrupted something,' Dominic said, looking concerned.

Drucilla chewed the inside of her cheek and stared at the empty space Lucifer had occupied.

†††

Dominic and Drucilla sat at their usual table as they scarfed down fries and talked about their week.

"So, what did Lucifer want?" Dominic finally got around to asking as he shoved his burger in his mouth.

387

"Dom?" Drucilla said, taking a sip of her beer then putting the bottle down in front of her, "I have a weird question."

"You don't have any other kind," he said with this mouth full in between chews.

Drucilla shrugged and nodded as if to agree. "The day I died. What do you remember?" Drucilla leaned back in the booth.

Dominic thought for a moment before swallowing. "I remember yelling at you." His eyes shifted up and to the left like he was accessing information in his brain.

"And?"

He lowered his voice so no one could hear him except Drucilla. "I remember that after you injected yourself, we thought it didn't work."

"What else?"

He leaned his head to the side and glanced around at nothing, trying to recall the event. "Huh, I can't remember." He wrinkled his nose, and randomly looked around.

"You don't remember the blood ripping a gaping hole in my chest?"

He scrunched his face for a moment and recoiled from the thought. "No! That sounds horrible! No, nothing like that. I just remember thinking it didn't work. Then apparently, you said you died, which I have zero recollection of. Then I saw you the next day, and you suddenly didn't have a heart. Is that weird that I can't remember anything else?"

"No, I'm pretty sure that was intentional. Dominic, no one knew I had died. It's as if everyone's memory was wiped."

"You think Lucifer wiped my memory or something?"

"Yeah...Or even that maybe those days were removed from the time altogether," Drucilla replied.

"Huh. You mean like a reset?" Dominic pondered and took a sip of his beer.

"No, I mean, time had passed, but it didn't…no one remembered anything. Anyway, from what I understand…my chest exploded. And apparently, all the veins in my body were burnt, and you somehow called Lucifer? You got him to show up, somehow. Then, I guess he managed to bring me back," Drucilla explained.

"Nope, definitely don't remember any of that. He can keep those memories. I don't want to remember my best friend like that," he said, looking up at the TV above the bar and taking another sip.

Drucilla smiled at the sweetness of the comment. "He mentioned a bargain," Drucilla admitted.

"What kind of bargain?"

"He framed it in a way that makes me believe that he had to bring me back to fulfill an agreement."

Dominic looked perplexed, "With whom?"

"Drake."

"Your brother?" Dominic asked.

"Also, Lucifer told me he left Hell."

Dominic winced for a moment, still watching the TV. "Why would he do that?" Dominic turned his attention back to Drucilla.

Drucilla paused then said, "Because he knows what's coming. If he knows, she does too."

Dominic stared at Drucilla, trying to process what she had said.

"Dominic, if you want out, I understand." Drucilla raised her eyes to his face.

Dominic gave Drucilla a disgusted look like she had just punched his grandmother in the face. "Dru, there are very few people I'd walk through Hell for. You're at the top of the list," he said, pointing at her with his beer bottle.

Ipse morietur, quia non habuit disci-
plinam, & in multitudine stultitiæ suæ
decipietur.   Proverb. —

CANTICLE THIRTY-THREE

"I am the pick in the ice. Do not cry out or hit the alarm. You know we're friends till we die." —Thom York, Radiohead.

It was a late Monday evening. Drucilla returned home from the gallery and threw herself down on the couch. She stared up at the ceiling and exhaled. She struggled to maintain the balance of her gallery and the rapid yet exhausting transformation of her body. But now, all she wanted was a moment of peace. She slowly lowered her eyelids as her chin slid down to her chest. Her cathartic moment was abruptly interrupted by the tune of her ringtone.

Drucilla retrieved her phone from her pocket and hit the answer button. "Dom?"

"Dru, I uh, I need you to come over," Dominic said.

"Now?"

"Yeah, now. I need you to see something."

"Okay, give me twenty minutes."

It was a warm late spring evening, and she decided to walk to Dominic's place, which was only about a mile away from her house. Drucilla pulled out her earbuds and placed them in her ears. She demanded a meditative moment to herself. As she strolled down the road, she felt the sensation that she was being watched. She had the nagging feeling that someone was perched on the short brick wall to her left.

"You know, this could be considered stalking," she said aloud. Drucilla heard the drop of someone jump down onto the road. "What do you want now, Lucifer?" Drucilla slowly turned her head to face him.

Lucifer grinned wildly as he walked over to her.

"Well?" Drucilla shrugged, waiting for an answer.

"I want to see your face when you see it," Lucifer said with his ridiculous, wild grin.

"See what?"

Lucifer grabbed her elbow, and they popped up onto Dominic's front porch.

"I kind of wanted to walk, but okay, I guess we'll do the things you want to do." Drucilla rolled her eyes. She stuffed her phone and earbuds back into her black jeans.

Lucifer maintained his unsettling grin as he reached for the door handle latch. He pushed the door open and directed Drucilla to go ahead of him.

"Dru!" Dominic shouted when he saw her, "And…Lucifer," he pressed his lips together and nodded.

"What is going on, guys?" Drucilla asked, looking at Lucifer and back at Dominic.

"Well, I don't know what Lucifer wants, but check this out." Dominic headed to the library with Lucifer and Drucilla in tow.

Drucilla sat on her usual stool, and Lucifer stood beside her.

"The stylus." Dominic faced Lucifer and Drucilla as he held up the weighty iron object at eye-level with one hand, then turned the stylus horizontal and clutched it inside his fist. He punched forward in a quick thrust, and both ends of the stylus instantly shot out in opposite directions to a double-ended, pointed, razor-sharp rod, about six feet in length.

"What the..." Drucilla said with her jaw open.

"It's a javelin!" Dominic said, visibly excited that he was holding ancient weaponry.

Drucilla got up and walked over to the javelin that he was holding steady. "That's pure iron, I mean; that has to be ridiculously heavy."

"Have you seen him, Drucilla?" Lucifer shrugged and pointed to Dominic's physique sarcastically.

Drucilla looked at one of the sharpened ends. She held her finger up to one of the points and pressed it into the razor-pointed end. The javelin pierced her skin. She peered at her finger curiously and rubbed the blood between her thumb and index finger. She looked back at Dominic.

"Step back, Dru," Dominic said. With the same quick forward thrust, the javelin transformed back into a stylus. Dominic turned his hand upright and balanced the stylus on the center of his open palm.

"That's insane," Drucilla said, shaking her head.

"That was a brilliant and calculating move you made by gifting the pen to him, Drucilla," Lucifer turned to face Dominic. "The stylus conforms to the wielder, and so do its abilities. Dominic is a powerful fighter, so the stylus gives him a warrior's weapon."

"What else does it do?" Drucilla asked.

"To be completely honest, I have not seen this object used in this manner for nearly two thousand years, not since Spartacus. But I do recall a couple of things. For instance, Dominic, when you thrust your hand forward, when the javelin forms, try squeezing the center tightly." Lucifer walked around Dominic.

Dominic shrugged and thrust his hand forward as the javelin instantaneously slid outward. Dominic looked at Lucifer then squeezed the javelins' center. On either side of the weapon sprung two orange-hued blades side-by-side on each end, as it became a vicious, double-bladed polearm. Dominic grabbed the polearm with both hands and turned it on its end to examine the razor-sharp blades. Dominic looked at Lucifer in amazement.

Lucifer placed his hand to his mouth in thought. "Mm-hmm," Lucifer nodded as he circled Dominic.

Dominic transformed the polearm back to a stylus and looked at Lucifer. "How do I open portals?" Dominic asked.

Lucifer was taken aback by the question. "How do you know about that?"

"It's uh, mentioned in one of my books," Dominic said hesitantly, lifting his chin as he motioned to his bookshelves.

Lucifer sat at Dominic's desk. He picked up a pencil and spun around in the chair to face Drucilla and

Dominic. He started rolling it between his fingers. "You must understand the dominions. There are many entrances into Heaven and Hell. However, all are protected and guarded, so you can never enter without it being known. You are either invited or accompanied; no one just walks into the dominion. Unholy can never enter Heaven, and conversely, Divine can never enter Hell," Lucifer stated as he got up and walked over to Dominic.

"The portal allows you to move between the dominions undetected. Essentially, you are ripping a hole in a wall and walking through it. This spell is very dangerous in the wrong hands. For instance, an entire Unholy army could just walk right into Heaven and lay waste to thousands of the Divine without anyone knowing when or from where they came," Lucifer explained.

"Show me," Dominic said.

Lucifer exhaled and stood shoulder-to-shoulder with Dominic. "Place the stylus in your fist, and hold it up like a hammer," Lucifer bent his elbow and raised his forearm and balled fist.

Dominic mimicked his motion with the stylus.

"Imagine where you want to enter in Hell: the caves, the desert, the forest, it does not matter, whichever you choose," Lucifer directed.

Dominic put down his arm and looked at Lucifer, "Lucifer, I've never been to Hell; I wouldn't know."

Lucifer paused and rested his hand on his chin. "Ah, that is right; I suppose that could prove to be a problem."

"Books!" Dominic said, "What about *The Vision* or *The Divine Comedy* of Dante Alighieri? Could I use one of those images?"

"You have got to be joking." Lucifer rolled his eyes.

Drucilla put her hand up and piped in, "I've been to Hell."

"Drucilla, you showed up on the front porch and were chased off the property by the dog. You have not been in Hell," Lucifer informed her.

Lucifer thought for a moment. Then turned to Dominic.

"Dominic, I am going to place some images in your mind, and I want you to choose one. They may be difficult to comprehend, so prepare yourself," Lucifer instructed.

Dominic looked at Drucilla, then looked back at Lucifer. He nodded.

"When you're ready, close your eyes," Lucifer said.

Dominic nodded and closed his eyes.

Lucifer placed his hands over Dominic's temples. He held his head in his hands for about five seconds before Dominic shoved his hands off him. "I got it. All right, I got it." Dominic said, clearly upset and shaken.

Lucifer nodded in understanding at what he knew Dominic saw. Lucifer hoped he wouldn't mention it to Drucilla.

"—Dru?" Dominic looked back at Drucilla. He held her stare for a moment as if he saw something upsetting but didn't know how to tell her.

Drucilla turned her head in confusion at his peculiar gaze.

"I do not have much time," Lucifer said to Dominic to divert his attention to the matter at hand. "When you are ready, and you have it in your mind, you are going to stab straight forward and rip down like you are tearing an opening in a curtain."

Dominic blinked rapidly and shook it off as he turned to face the empty space in front of him. He stabbed the stylus forward and ripped down as a bright orange light filtered through in swirls of smoke around the frayed edges like a tear in the universe.

They all leaned over as they attempted to look through the rip in the fabric of reality. A rocky forest with red terrain was visible through the tear. There were sparse tree-like silver structures, and the sky was twisting, deep orange with black swirls.

"Is that Hell?" Drucilla questioned.

Before Lucifer could answer, Dominic, asked, "How do I close it?"

"You have to walk through and create a new portal to return. The portals will close behind you. Dominic, listen to me. Entering either dominion could be catastrophic. Use it in life-or-death situations only," Lucifer warned.

Lucifer ducked into the tear, and the hole closed behind him. He abruptly blinked back into the other end of the library. He straightened his suit and walked back over to Dominic and Drucilla. "I mean it, do not use it," Lucifer warned again.

✝✝✝

Lucifer and Drucilla walked silently from Dominic's house. Neither of them wanted to discuss what they knew the other was thinking. Drucilla stopped in front of the walkway to her front door before turning to look at Lucifer. Lucifer shoved his hands deep into his front pants pockets and looked down at the ground. He kicked out a small stone with the tip of his shoe from under his foot before he looked up at Drucilla.

"I have an artist coming by early tomorrow." Drucilla looked at her front door.

"How are the… you know, coming along?" he made flapping wing motions with his hands.

"Big." Drucilla nodded as she tried to remain calm about her burgeoning appendages. "Um there uh, there are four. Which was unexpected," she said, blinking and looking at nothing.

Lucifer looked amused for a moment and then nodded. "You know," Lucifer said, changing the subject, "You and your brother have many similarities," Lucifer paused to look at Drucilla's face for a response.

"We're twins, so, that's a fact," Drucilla said with snark.

Lucifer ignored the comment. "You are both extremely passionate, very determined. Seeing things to the very end no matter the outcome."

Drucilla looked at him curiously.

Lucifer took Drucilla's hand in his and covered it with his other. His translucent skin against hers was warm, bordering on hot. "I have grown quite fond of both you and Drake. Drake was essentially the greatest protegee I have ever had the pleasure working with, and quite honestly also the worst," Lucifer commented.

Drucilla looked down at her hand in his, then back to his face.

"Drucilla, I am afraid I have not been entirely honest with you."

"Here we go…" Drucilla exhaled as she took her hand back. She crossed her arms and leaned her head to the side. She looked directly into his amber snake eyes.

"You used to ask me if Drake ever asked about you. The truth is..." Lucifer paused and looked downward. He seemed almost ashamed of what he was about to say. "He did. It was usually one of, if not the first, thing he would ask whenever I would see him.

Drucilla's eyes widened with disbelief.

"He did love you, Drucilla. I need you to understand the reason you were kept away from each other was to protect you and, to some extent, him."

Angrily, Drucilla pulled her glowing blue fist back and punched Lucifer as hard as she could in the jaw. Lucifer fell on his back and slid on the sidewalk for a few feet. Shaken, he sat up, grabbed his face, wiggled, and rubbed his jaw. He looked shocked that she could strike him that hard.

"You are Goddamned lucky you didn't explode!" Drucilla shrieked.

"No, you are right; I deserved that." He climbed to his feet, still rubbing his jaw.

"Do you realize I went years? Years, Lucifer! Thinking that he hated me?" Drucilla yelled furiously.

"You are right, Drucilla, but you must understand this was at his request. He did not want you involved in any of this. I was merely honoring the deal."

Drucilla paced back and forth like a caged lion, her body glowing blue through her clothes. Drucilla finally stopped and looked at Lucifer. "What would you tell him?"

Still stunned from the blow to the face, Lucifer wiped his jaw and looked at his hand. "Well, he knew everything from your high school and college graduation. He knew about your adventures in The Valley of the Kings, Athens, Denmark, and so forth. He knew that you bought your grandmother's house, all about your gallery, and your large friend. He was very happy for you, Drucilla. He always expressed his concern for your well-being and was ultimately always proud of your accomplishments."

"Wait, why are you telling me this now?" Drucilla asked, still visibly upset.

"There is more." Lucifer stepped towards Drucilla.

Drucilla sat on the first step of her porch and looked up at him as she tried to calm herself. "Go ahead," she shrugged, "I can't possibly be more pissed off at you than I am now."

Lucifer nodded and continued. "You asked me a few days ago about the bargain. At the time, I had avoided your question, not because I did not want to answer, but because it was not the right time to answer it. I realize there is no right time, so, here it goes...." He sat next to Drucilla. "Do you remember years ago when your mother told you she had a brain tumor, and you were so angry because she never told you about it?"

"You healed her, didn't you?" Drucilla asked.

"No. I did not. The tumor is still there, it is obscured, and she feels no effects from it. It is essentially dormant," Lucifer explains.

"I don't understand. What was the point if the tumor is still there?"

"Insurance policy if you will, but that is irrelevant now that the deal is complete. But do you remember the conversation you had with Dominic about sacrifice, adding more sand to the hourglass?"

Drucilla nodded, a little creeped out that he overheard that conversation.

"How sand cannot be made out of nothing, but you can give your own to another?"

"Yeah, I remember."

"The sand came from your brother."

Drucilla covered her mouth as her eyes widened. "Why didn't you ask me? Why take it from my brother?"

"You found the vestiges of the Queens. He found my coin. He offered the exchange."

"Her life for the remainder of his," Drucilla said, staring off into the night.

Lucifer stood up to face Drucilla. "Her life, my personal protection of you, in exchange for running my cabal. He also received other benefits like money, assets, women, anything any earthly thing he desired. Essentially, when Drake died, our agreement was complete," Lucifer explained.

"Okay, okay, this is a lot. First question: Why would I need to be protected?" Drucilla stood up.

"Drucilla, has it not ever crossed your mind why Belphegor and Asmodeus had not come for you until Drake's passing?"

Drucilla's eyes darted around as she thought about that fact.

"You were protected by the coven's obscuration spell that hid you from any immortals while he was alive and as long as you remained in Washington. But after you stepped out of the state, you were fair game. However, because of my pact with Drake, I was immune to the effects of the spell," Lucifer explained.

"So that's what they were talking about," Drucilla recalled the last meeting with the kings at Drake's house. "They did come for me after Drake died. Now that I'm thinking about it, they haven't since I died." Confused, she looked at Lucifer.

"That is to your advantage. They must think you are still dead, and I have done nothing to make them think otherwise."

Drucilla paused for a moment. "Why are you still here? I mean, if the deal is finished, and your brothers think I'm dead, why do you hang around?"

"As I told you, I do not reside in Hell anymore."

"That doesn't explain why you're still watching me."

"You need me, Drucilla. Regardless of how under control you think you have things, you do not."

"You're just helping me out of the kindness of your heart? That's laughable," Drucilla snarked.

"Drucilla." He paused to collect his thoughts. "When the reckoning comes, I want to be on the right side this time."

"And there it is…" Drucilla looked into Lucifer's eyes. She could tell he wasn't lying. Drucilla walked up the porch steps and opened her front door. She paused for a moment before turning back to him. "You know the outcome, don't you?"

Lucifer studied her face for a moment. "There are many potential outcomes, Drucilla. It changes daily, but I need to believe you will prevail."

Drucilla rested her hand on the inside door handle and looked at it for a moment before looking back at him. "I accept your help, Lucifer. I don't think we could do this without it," Drucilla admitted.

"You will have it." Lucifer bowed his head slightly.

Closing the door behind her, she kicked off her shoes and walked to the kitchen. She stopped for a moment to grab a piece of fruit as she mulled over what Lucifer said. Drucilla climbed up to the breakfast bar and sat, tearing at the husk of her orange. *The right side? Is he attempting to get back into Heaven?* So many questions flooded her mind. *He thinks I stand a chance at defeating Calliope.* She reached into her pocket, pulled out the amulet that used to adorn the end of the rosary and ran her fingers over its worn edges.

"For what it's worth, Drucilla. You have more allies than you know," a familiar voice said.

Drucilla lifted her head and turned to the voice behind her. Azrael stood in the doorway. He walked into the kitchen and leaned his back against the refrigerator, and looked at her.

"You?" Drucilla asked with a level of surprise in her voice.

"Drucilla, you and Dominic make my job extremely difficult. You're both infinitely tedious and frustrating, and I don't know why you think you deserve my assistance on a whim. But know that as much as I disagree with your choice of company," he motioned his head and eyes towards Drucilla's front yard in reference to Lucifer, "he isn't wrong. There is going to be a reckoning, and I do hope for your triumph. You may consider me an ally."

"I thought you didn't take sides, that you exist outside of the whole dominion thing?"

"Drucilla, I answer to no one. I am the Seraph of Death. Eventually, everyone is reaped by me. It also makes me a sovereign, autonomous if you will."

"I see…"

"From this point on, feel free to call upon me. I'll hear you."

Drucilla nodded.

Azrael blinked out and disappeared.

"Me too," Adrian said, appearing next to Drucilla, "But I think that's a given."

Drucilla turned to him and smiled. "It's still good to hear."

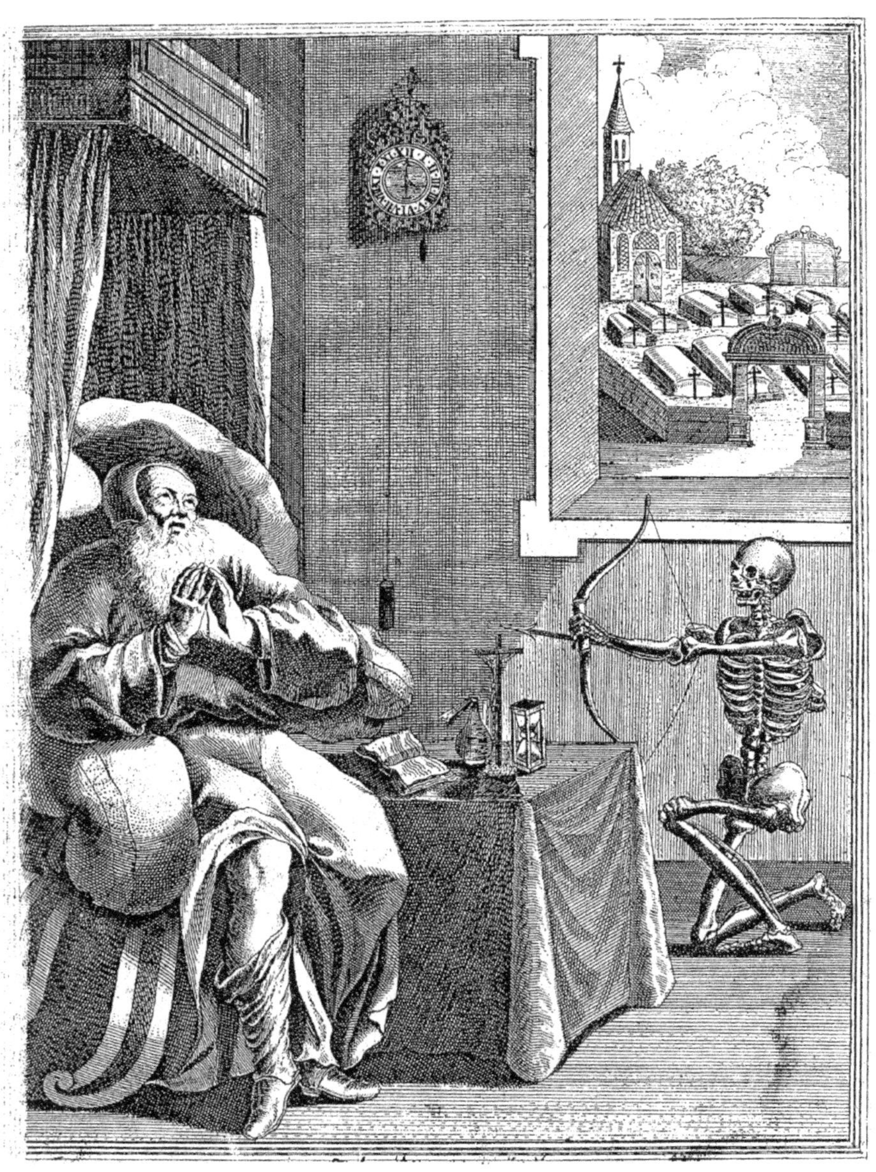

CANTICLE THIRTY-FOUR

"If a girl walks in and carves her name in my heart, I'll turn and run away." —Real Life

Lucifer sat halfway on the dining room table with one foot on the floor facing Dominic. Dominic leaned leisurely back in a desk chair with his hands folded on his stomach. He clenched a plastic mechanical pencil between his back teeth while Adrian stood in front of Drucilla with his arms crossed in concern.

"Guys..." Drucilla started.

They stopped what they were doing and turned to give Drucilla their attention.

"You're probably wondering why I wanted you all here. Other than the fact that I don't like to repeat myself, there's something that I need to tell you. I don't want you to be alarmed or feel that you need to do something. I've got it under control. I'm good. Okay?" Drucilla reassured.

Dominic glanced at Adrian curiously. Adrian glided over to Dominic's side.

Drucilla stood in front of everyone as she stripped off her jacket and threw it onto one of Dominic's chairs. She wore a white racerback tank top, black jeans, and Adrian's small urn pendant. On a different chain, the old rosary amulet hung around her neck down to her belly button, tapping her belt buckle. "Wait," Drucilla said, changing her mind at the last minute. "Azrael!" Drucilla shouted out to the ceiling in the room.

Lucifer scoffed. Dominic glanced at him.

Azrael appeared in front of Drucilla. He looked at her with his black, deep-set eye sockets, less irritated this time. He placed his hands inside his black overcoat; his heavy black looped scarf obscured his chest. The way Azrael dressed in cold-weather layers, you could never judge how big or small his body was. The only noticeable thing was that he was much taller than Lucifer and Dominic. He always had that smell of wet, freshly turned earth. It was beautiful but also sorrowful at the same time. It made Drucilla wonder if he had to pull bodies out of the ground at times. She cringed at the thought.

"I want you here for this too," Drucilla told him. Azrael walked over and stood near Lucifer and Dominic.

"Tobit," Lucifer said, heavily enunciating the T's. Lucifer nodded in greeting. He didn't turn to face Azrael.

"Beast," Azrael hissed at the word slowly in an irritated tone, regretfully acknowledging Lucifer.

"That is original. Prithee, where did you dig up that corpse." Lucifer quipped.

"Oh, Lightbringer, always such a blessing to be in your company."

"If you guys are done with your overly-affectionate greetings..." Drucilla said. Drucilla was having none of their nonsense.

They turned their attention to Drucilla.

"Okay," Drucilla said, shaking out her arms and throwing her head back. Drucilla put her chin down, clenched her fists as tightly, and like a bodybuilder, flexed her biceps and pushed her trapezius muscles out with as much force as possible. The blue veins began to intensify within her hands and forearms. Suddenly, two sets of fully developed greyish-blue-hued wings burst from her back. One stacked on top of the other—each wing approximately five-feet in width.

Dominic stood up slowly in shock and dropped the pencil from his mouth. He slowly approached Drucilla from across the room.

"There's more," Drucilla said, looking at Dominic. Dominic stopped in his tracks.

Drucilla closed her eyes, then opened them again slowly, along with the many other eyes that lined the heavy ridge on the tops of each wing. Forty eyes, ranging from large near the base, becoming progressively smaller as they open down the spine towards the tip of the wings. Each eye was blinking in random order.

"Can you..." Dominic pauses for a moment, "see out of those eyes?"

Drucilla gave him an uncomfortable look and a nod. "I can and, it's definitely um, it's an experience," Drucilla said. She was still alarmed at the fact.

Azrael forced his hands into his pockets deeper, causing him to stand more rigid as he walked around to Drucilla's backside. Drucilla followed him with her eyes shifting from her prominent eyes on her face to the eyes on her wings. He stopped and stood behind her. Drucilla then used her prominent eyes to look over her shoulder as he slowly extended his white hand and touched the ridge of one of her wings.

"What do you see?" he asked.

"I see all of you, but so many perspectives give me an intense, almost panoramic view of the room if that makes sense?"

"They're functioning as they should." Azrael nodded while he examined Drucilla. "Ophanim have so many eyes because it allows them to watch all directions simultaneously. Not only were they able to see everything holistically, but they were also able to see the past and the future. They saw everything that ever was or ever will be. They knew all the secrets of the universe. Thoth even more so than the others."

"You say were, are there no Thrones left?" Drucilla asked Azrael.

"Most Thrones haven't existed in an eon. Thoth was one of the last living Thrones that I knew of, aside from the Queens. Thoth died over many millennia ago if I recall correctly. If the others do exist, they've hidden so well that even I can't see them."

Dominic stood in front of Drucilla, scanned her entire body with his eyes, and slowly encircled her.

"Been flying, have we?" Azrael asked her pointedly.

"What?" Drucilla asked in confusion.

"Can you fly?" Azrael asked.

"I don't know. I don't know how." Drucilla thought about that for a moment. She never thought about flying until now. "How do I do it?" Drucilla looked at Lucifer.

"Don't ask me. Raphael threw me off the Golden Citadel when we were new Seraphim. We learned by falling," Lucifer said, only half-joking.

"Dominic, do you mind if we use your roof?" Azrael asked.

Azrael and Drucilla sat in a perched position on top of one of two gables on Dominic's roof. Perching offered the best position for balance when wings are extended. The wings weighed easily as much as Drucilla's body. Drucilla kept looking around, terrified that someone was going to see them. She hoped the evening sky was dark enough that no one would look upward. Drucilla could feel her blood start to get hot within her skin.

"What do I do?" Drucilla asked nervously.

Azrael instructed, "Use your wings as resistance; try and glide. When you get close to hitting the ground, I want you to start pushing yourself upwards as hard as possible."

Drucilla stood up and peered over the edge. She inhaled and exhaled deeply, stepped back, and looked at Azrael dubiously. He motioned for her to jump. Drucilla stepped forward to the edge again and saw Dominic and Lucifer on the ground below her.

"Maybe she is flightless?" Lucifer looked up, arms crossed, resting his thumb and index finger on his chin.

"I CAN HEAR YOU!" Drucilla yelled.

"If she were, it would be like shoving a penguin off the roof," Dominic said, hands on his hips, looking up as well. He started to chuckle.

"Maybe an ostrich," Lucifer added, chuckling.

"Emu," Dominic laughed.

"Kiwi," Adrian added.

"HEY, CAN YOU GUYS SHUT THE HELL UP?"

Lucifer, Adrian, and Dominic continued to giggle at Drucilla's expense.

"I can't." Drucilla retreated to the chimney.

"You can, Drucilla. You're stronger than you realize," Azrael encouraged her.

Drucilla exhaled again and walked to the edge of the gable. She looked back at Azrael. He nodded at her to proceed. She looked down again. It seemed a lot higher being on the roof than when she was on the ground looking upward. Anxiety took over, and Drucilla's body started to glow.

"Drucilla, you need to control your emotions. No matter what, you'll be fine," Azrael assured her.

Drucilla took a deep breath. She glanced back at Azrael one last time before turning her attention back to the ground. Drucilla lunged forward and jumped off the gable. She didn't float. She didn't hover, fly, or even glide. She essentially did a superhero jump. She hit the ground with a thunderous explosion that created a fifteen-foot-wide, five-foot-deep crater and obliterated Dominic's backyard.

Drucilla opened her eyes as dirt, dust, and rocks settled around her. Her body dimmed as she got to her feet. Lucifer, Dominic, and Adrian gathered to the crater's edge and looked down at Drucilla. A lawn chair fell into the hole behind her.

Azrael looked over the edge of the roof, opened his mouth like he was about to say something but decided not to say a word. Dominic looked around his yard in disbelief as Lucifer ran his hand over his bald head and started to laugh. Adrian clicked his tongue and shook his head slowly.

"Can someone help me get out of here?" Drucilla asked, looking around the hole she had made.

Melior est Mors quam Vita.   Eccles. 30.

CANTICLE THIRTY-FIVE

"But someday I'm gonna change my mind.
Sometimes I'd rather kill." —Agent Orange

✝

Drucilla sat on the broad, flat railing of her wrap-around porch with her legs dangling off the edge as she looked out onto the street at the row of houses that lined the road. Lucifer crossed his ankles as he leaned against the porch column facing the house. He watched Dominic and Adrian poke through Drucilla's new wave album collection from the large living room window. Above, the moon was waxing, just past the first quarter. It was one of those unusually clear spring nights, still chilly, but tolerable.

Lucifer and Drucilla sat in silence for what seemed like forever. Drucilla assumed neither of them knew how to start a conversation when it wasn't imperative. The sound of a multitude of crickets chirping created a low hum. It was a comforting, familiar kind of white noise.

Drucilla finally decided to break the silence. "Lucifer..."

He slowly turned to Drucilla as he kept his head against the column. He glanced at her under his brow.

"If you're having second thoughts," Drucilla said, as she attempted to read his silence, "If you want to back out..."

"Did I say I wanted to back out?"

"You're not really saying anything. Are you worried?" Drucilla swung her legs back over to the inside of the porch.

"No. Not at all." He pulled himself away from the column and stood in front of Drucilla. "You are powerful, Drucilla, and I do not want you to think for a moment that I do not think you are capable."

"But?"

"But Calliope is a Queen. She is of the highest order. She is among the first celestial beings. She created and has dominion over death, whereas Azrael is just a glorified groundskeeper."

"But Thoth was her equal. I'm essentially Thoth."

"You are a shade of Thoth. You are he as far as his divinity and abilities go, but you are not he. You do not have his consciousness, his memories, or even knowledge. He just inhabits your body like a parasite."

"That is not exactly the way I would look at it. So, why don't you tell me about him?" Drucilla stood up and walked over to the window.

"There was a time that we knew each other. Thoth was arrogant, selfish, condescending, with an overly inflated ego. Unapproachable. Everything and everyone, beneath him. He knew everything. He saw everything. He was part of everything. He was the universe and everything within it. He was infinite knowledge and wisdom. I suppose that is why Calliope wanted him as her right hand. They ruled together with her sisters for eons. Hell was a much different place than it is now,"

Lucifer said, fidgeting with one of his rings, "A monarchy: Queens, Kings, Princes…We all had a common goal: to rule the Celestial Empyrion, which you call Heaven, the Infernal Sphere, Hell, and this universe in which you presently live."

"So pretty much everything," Drucilla shrugged.

"That is what is so amusing about humans. Your inability to see past what you already think you know. You think that all your finite stars, galaxies, and planets are all that exist. There is so much more that you could not even comprehend," he responded with a chuckle.

Drucilla rolled her eyes at Lucifer's blatant arrogance.

"Calliope is not a demon, nor is she Seraphim. She is as old as existence. She is not like you and me, any of us really. In the most simplistic of comparisons, if we are all ants, she is the ant farm. Do you understand?"

"But she can still die," Drucilla reminded him.

"Yes, but death for her means something else. Killing her means killing what she is."

A heavy thud was heard at the other end of the porch, interrupting them. Lucifer and Drucilla both turn their attention to the sound. Azrael walked over to them, crossed his arms, and peered at them with intensity.

"There's an issue…" He jerked his head to the side, motioning for Drucilla and Lucifer to go into the house with Adrian and Dominic.

"We're going to finish our conversation later," Drucilla said to Lucifer.

Lucifer nodded.

They entered Drucilla's living room to see Dominic on his stomach with a few of her records on the floor. He had a record jacket for New Order *Low-life* spread open in his hands. Adrian was lying down next to him and commented how great it was when they used to print lyrics on the insides of the album covers. You didn't get that kind of attention with digital media these days. Azrael walked past them and cleared his throat at Adrian and Dominic to get their attention. Dominic noticed Azrael as he stood in front of him impatiently, got to his feet. Azrael turned to face everyone.

"Good, I'm glad you're all here. This will save some time. There's been a recent development that you should all know," Azrael started to pace in a small area in the living room. Dominic sat slowly in an oversized chair, not breaking eye contact with Azrael. Drucilla sat on his armrest.

"Calliope has started to organize. She knows you've made the decision not to heed her command. She has made the decision to end your life herself. She will not allow Thoth to reemerge."

"Organize? End my life?" Drucilla said, irked.

"Drucilla…" Azrael walked over to her and sat on the edge of an ottoman to be at her level. He looked directly into her eyes. "You need to start making some decisions."

"I've already made my decision. If Calliope comes for me, I'm gonna stab the bitch in the heart!"

"There are consequences," Azrael said sternly, "and I need you to think about your actions. I mean, I need you to take some time and really think about this."

"Why?" Drucilla said slowly as she studied Azrael's face suspiciously.

Azrael glanced at Lucifer. Lucifer looked at Azrael and nodded slowly as if they were having a non-verbal conversation.

"I think now would be a good time to tell her. It may help her decision-making," Azrael said, looking at Lucifer.

Dominic and Drucilla looked at each other.

Drucilla had become short on patience with this non-verbal communication. "Tell me what?" Drucilla gave Azrael and Lucifer a concerned look.

Nervously, Lucifer took a deep breath. He sat across from Drucilla on the edge of the chair. He placed his elbows on his knees and covered his face for a moment. Azrael glanced at Drucilla.

"Is someone going to tell me?" Drucilla asked sternly, becoming angrier.

Lucifer looks up at Drucilla empathetically. Drucilla shook her head.

"Lucifer, if you tell me that you haven't been entirely honest with me one more time, I swear to everything Divine and Unholy I will punch you through that wall into the street!" Drucilla growled through gritted teeth; her eyes started to glow.

"Drucilla!" Lucifer stood up and yelled, "not everything is about you!"

Drucilla stood up angrily and took a menacing step towards Lucifer.

Dominic grabbed her hand. Drucilla turned to look at him with her glowing eyes. He shook his head at her.

"Dru, c'mon. Let's just hear what he has to say," he nodded as he attempted to calm Drucilla down.

Drucilla jerked her hand out of Dominic's grip and sat back down with a scowl.

Lucifer straightened his suit.

"Drucilla," Azrael starts. "The fight with Calliope has become more complicated with her new ally."

Drucilla turned her head to the side to make sense of Azrael's words.

"Your brother rules Hell in my stead," Lucifer admitted, looking at Drucilla unflinching; he crossed his arms.

"What does that mean?" Drucilla asked as calmly as possible.

"I think it means that Drake is the new Lucifer?" Dominic said, looking at Lucifer for confirmation. "I mean, that is what you're saying, right?"

Lucifer looked at Dominic and nodded.

"He fights for her now," Azrael said.

Drucilla took a deep breath. Her eyes darted around the room, processing.

"How is that even possible?" she asked.

Lucifer remained silent when it suddenly clicked in Drucilla's head. "The bargain, it was the bargain, wasn't it?" Drucilla asked, her eyes flared as she looked at Lucifer.

Lucifer nodded as he held Drucilla's stare.

Adrian looked at Drucilla in surprise, "She's taking it a lot better than I thought she would. I would not be taking it this well."

Drucilla slowly got to her feet. She looked up at Lucifer. Drucilla's eyes now glowing as bright as dense dwarf stars. Her body intensified with light until she became a radiant blue being of light. Her wings tore out of her jacket and unfurled until fully expanded. She raised her arms and shoved Lucifer's chest with the force of a freight train as he flew backward through the living room, out through the plate glass window. Glass exploded along with part of the wall. Lucifer landed on his back on the front lawn. Drucilla held out her hand again, and the front door blasted off its hinges. Seething with anger, she stepped out onto the porch and slowly headed to Lucifer. Her feet seared the wood floorboards leaving scorch marks as she made her way down the stairs to the front yard.

An enraged Lucifer got to his feet. His translucent skin turned a bright shade of orange-red, his snake-eyes lit up like a flame. His claws turned black and elongated, extending far beyond his fingertips. His body began to welt up in unhuman muscle formations as he ripped off his shirt. He doubled, then tripled in size. Black, slick horns slid out of his temples.

"Come on, Drucilla! This has been a long time coming!" Lucifer said, his voice is deep, demonic, echoing as he got into a fighting stance.

"Oh Lord, they're gonna kill each other," Adrian lamented, shaking his head in disbelief.

Drucilla stepped closer and closer to Lucifer as her hands became brighter. Drucilla held out her hands and formed huge, swirling balls of blue flames in her upright palms. She raised her arm, preparing to throw the fiery, divine wrath at him. Lucifer brought his clawed hands back, ready to strike Drucilla. His demon tail cracked like a whip. He snarled and exposed his elongated incisors on his bottom and top jaw like a demonic panther.

Drucilla and Lucifer got within feet of each other; they were locked in each other's hostile gaze.

Azrael appeared between them and touched their foreheads at the same time. Drucilla and Lucifer collapsed into an instant slumber. Drucilla's body morphed back and returned to a smoldering, human form. Lucifer's wings covered his body like a blanket.

Dominic and Adrian ran out to the front yard as they saw Lucifer and Drucilla's lifeless bodies.

"No, they aren't dead. But they're going to sleep it off for a bit," Azrael said, answering the question before they could ask it. He was disappointed with how this strategy session had ended.

"Should we just leave them here?" Dominic asked.

Azrael looked down at Lucifer and Drucilla's unconscious bodies, shrugged, and nodded. "Yes, I think so. The cold air might help the situation," Azrael advised.

Dominic sat on the front porch, noticing the burned footprints that Drucilla had created. "So, what is this about Drake being in Hell? Is he an immortal?" Dominic asked Azrael.

"Lucifer made a deal with Drake years ago to take his place. So essentially, yes. Once he died, he was reborn as an Unholy. Drake is well-suited for the position if I'm being frank. He has control of a demonic army and runs several cabals here on earth. He's rapidly becoming the strongest, most intelligent, and tactical ally that Hell has ever known. He's fast becoming a favorite pet of Calliope." Azrael sat next to Dominic.

Dominic looked out over Lucifer and Drucilla's bodies as the steam swirled about in the cold air. "I've always known she's had a complicated relationship with her brother. But this, I just didn't realize how bad it really was," Dominic said with concern.

"Drucilla is in a terrible space. She both loves and loathes her brother with equal passion. I'm afraid that what you just saw will be but a hiccup in comparison to when she comes face-to-face with her brother. There's a lot of resentment and abandonment where he is concerned," Azrael explained.

"Right, but didn't Lucifer admit to Dru that Drake had been protecting her?" Dominic asked.

"Drucilla doesn't see it that way. She's sees everything that Drake did, or more didn't do, as a conscious decision he alone made. He chose to abandon her. She isn't wrong in that assumption." Azrael stood up and prepared to depart.

Dominic also stood up and rubbed his hands together to warm them. "Wait, I get the impression that this wasn't the only thing you wanted us to know."

Azrael turned to Dominic and adjusted his large, looped scarf. "You need to understand, and maybe you can convince her that if you kill Calliope, death essentially ends," Azrael said plainly.

"Death ends? You mean, no one dies anymore?" Dominic asked for clarification.

"That's exactly what I'm saying. The transition to death no longer exists."

"Okay, so people live forever. How is that any different from the Divine or the Unholy?"

Azrael crossed his arms and thought to himself for a moment about how best to explain the issue. "Imagine living in a world where there's disease, violence, starvation, wars, and so forth just like this one, but no one dies. For instance, imagine being in so much pain from disease your only release is death, but you can't die. You see, you will all go on in your weak, deteriorating human bodies, but you won't die. Your mother in her ossuary isn't dead. No one in the cemetery is dead. They're trapped inside their decomposing corpse."

Dominic, wide-eyed, stood in disbelief. Azrael turned away to leave.

"Wait!" Dominic said again. Azrael turned back to him. "You know this isn't going to change her mind," Dominic said.

"For your sake and your mother's, I hope it does." Azrael disappeared.

CANTICLE THIRTY-SIX

"You're a creature of destruction, Yeah, you know. Into the night, Into the night to fight." —45 Grave

The blaring daystar rudely awoke Drucilla. The sun had drenched her room in bright white light. Solar rays collided mercilessly into her woefully unprepared eyes. Drucilla reached to grab a blanket to throw it over her eyes when she realized she was on top of her covers, and she was still wearing the clothes from the night before. Drucilla looked around the room and noticed that Dominic was slumped over in a chair at her footboard. His socked feet were propped up on the end of her bed. *He must have stayed here all night to keep an eye on me.* Drucilla sat up and rubbed her face, trying to remember what happened.

Dominic woke up and put his feet down.

"Hey," Drucilla said with a groggy look.

He rubbed his face and looked around the room. "I must have passed out," Dominic yawned.

"How did I get here?"

"I carried you up here. I mean, I'm pretty sure your neighbors hate you anyway, so, I didn't want to give them a reason to call the cops," he explained.

"What happened? One minute I was..." Drucilla tried to recall the evening.

"You remember fighting with Lucifer?"

"Kind of," she said. Drucilla paused for a moment as she tried to piece the events together. "Did I win?"

Dominic scrunched his face at her like she had said the most nonsensical thing in the world. "No one wins, Dru," he said unamused. "If we have any chance of taking out Calliope, you've got to get your anger under control."

"Me? What about Lucifer?" Drucilla stood up. Annoyed, she attempted to straighten her tee-shirt and then noticed the back was torn.

"Lucifer needs to stop playing whatever stupid game he's been playing and start being upfront about things if he wants to work together as a team. If we can't trust each other, we have nothing," Dominic exhaled, shaking his head.

"Thank you! I couldn't agree more," Drucilla said, feeling justified.

"Dru, this doesn't mean it's not your fault, too. You need to start thinking rationally and maybe try talking to him instead of trying to murder him all the time. You are extremely over-reactive whenever something comes out. You get violent instead of trying to figure out why he isn't telling you. You need to realize that what he had going on with Drake had nothing to do with you."

"Whose side are you on?" Drucilla asked, squinting her eyes.

"We're all on one side. That's what you need to understand. There isn't your side or Lucifer's side. We're all working together now. From this point on, we are one team," Dominic insisted.

"Do you trust him?" Drucilla asked, sitting on her bed facing Dominic. "I mean, really trust him?"

Dominic grabbed his shoes from the foot of Drucilla's bed. He bent down and started putting them on. "That's a complicated question. It's, uh…situational, I guess," he replied.

"Like what?"

"Are you asking me if I trust Lucifer to pick out an appropriate gift for my father or set me up on a blind date? No, not at all. If you're asking me if I could depend on Lucifer to save my life? Absolutely. Without question. He's proven himself in that aspect to you most of all, many times."

"Yeah, right. Always there to help," Drucilla groaned.

"You gotta let that Athens thing go," Dominic said, standing up as he headed for Drucilla's bedroom door.

"He wasn't there, Dominic. Hades could have killed me, and he didn't even bother to show up. Hell, he didn't even apologize or even offer an explanation," Drucilla complained.

"Maybe this is something you can talk to him about. You know, as I said, try talking to him?" Dominic reiterated.

Drucilla exhaled sharply in annoyance and looked down at her lap.

"I've got to go open my shop. I'll see you later."

Drucilla listened as his heavy footsteps rushed down the stairs. She heard the back door open and then closed behind him.

Drucilla grabbed a fresh set of clothes from her dresser drawer and carried them into the bathroom. As soon as she stepped out into the hallway, Adrian stood in front of her looking extremely angry.

"What the hell's wrong with you?" Drucilla snapped.

"What the hell is wrong with me? What the hell is wrong with you!?" Adrian snapped back.

"What?" Drucilla said sharply.

"Have you seen what your little temper tantrum did to my living room?" he asked, angrier.

"What? Oh…OH. Oh, God." Drucilla started to recall what happened.

"You're going to get your ass on that phone and get the insurance company out here or something!" Adrian demanded.

"I'll see what I can do," Drucilla said, waving him off as she walked into the bathroom.

Drucilla took a shower and threw on fresh clothes. She didn't know whether it made her feel better or not but picking out dead leaves, twigs, and grass out of her hair and wings was not a project on which she had planned. She headed down the stairs and into the living room to inspect the damage. The five-foot plate-glass window and some smaller decorative windows that had surrounded it were destroyed. Chunks of the windowsill and the bottom part of the wall were also demolished. It looked like someone drove a car through the window from the inside of the house. Drucilla assessed the damage while she stepped gingerly around the bits of broken glass. Oddly, most of the damage was thrown outside of the house. Part of the railing on her porch was taken out, as well. Drucilla exhaled slowly and placed her hands on her face.

Adrian stood beside her with his arms crossed.

"I'm sorry, I lost it. Dominic is right. I need to learn to control myself. I'm sorry, Adrian," Drucilla said remorsefully.

"Just fix it." He glided away from her.

"Christ. Is everyone mad at me?" Drucilla threw her hands in the air. She gathered her keys and bag and turned to head out of the front door. That was when she noticed the door lying on the porch. *I need coffee.*

Drucilla's regular coffee spot on Water St. was usually pretty packed this time of day, but as luck would have it, not today. *I guess things aren't that bad after all; she* smiled to herself. Drucilla ordered her usual sugar-free vanilla latte with oat milk and a splash of cinnamon. She called the insurance adjuster to file a claim as she waited. After a few moments, the barista called her name, and she grabbed her cup. As Drucilla turned to head out of the shop, she glanced out the window onto the street, just as two familiar gentlemen in black suits, black hats, and white hair walked past. One of them noticed Drucilla through the window, gave a slight nod, and kept walking. Stunned, Drucilla dropped her coffee.

The coffee splashed into a large puddle on the floor. Drucilla didn't take her eyes off the window.

"You've got to be kidding me," she said under her breath. Drucilla bolted out of the coffee house to chase them. She got to the sidewalk and looked in the direction they had walked. Drucilla ran to the corner, thinking they had turned, but they were nowhere to be seen. Drucilla ran three blocks down Water St. to Dominic's shop.

Drucilla grabbed the door handle and flung the door open so hard that the inertia from the door slammed into the frame and caused the plate glass window to vibrate furiously. The tiny tinkling bell dislodged and flew off the door frame. It barely missed Dominic's head from behind the counter. The bell smashed to the wall behind him. Dominic instinctively ducked.

"Jesus, Dru!" Dominic yelled as he looked at the slight indentation in the wall behind him.

Drucilla was too agitated to apologize at the moment. "They're here!" Drucilla yelled as she ran into Dominic's back office.

Confused, Dominic walked over to his shop entrance, turned his sign over to *Closed*, and locked the door. He joined Drucilla in the back office.

Drucilla paced the floor like a caged animal as she tried to sort out her thoughts. Her mind was racing. Dominic closed the door behind him and grabbed her arms to hold her still.

"Dru, what's going on?" Dominic looked paranoid

"Belphegor and Asmodeus. They're here in Port Townsend. I, I just saw them."

"Are you certain? Where?"

"I was just leaving the coffee shop when I saw them through the window."

"Are you positive it was them?"

"Yes, Dominic. Belphegor looked me in the eyes and nodded at me as he walked past." Drucilla sat on the couch and put her face in her hands. "Why are they here? What could they possibly want?"

"I assume they're scouting. I mean, they've got to be, right? Why else would they come here? They're looking for you."

"They're hoping I'm vulnerable," Drucilla responded. "Someone must have told them I'm alive."

The conversation came to a halt when they heard the tinkling of the front door bell as if someone had entered the shop. Dominic and Drucilla exchanged wide-eyed glances.

"That bell..." Dominic started.

"… isn't on the door anymore," Drucilla said, finishing his sentence.

Dominic pulled the stylus from his pocket and flipped it in his hand. Drucilla nodded to him. He nodded back and opened the office door to the store. Drucilla slowly exited the room with Dominic behind her. Belphegor and Asmodeus stood side-by-side, looking like ghoulish twin grandfathers with their dark suits and black bowler hats. Their long-clawed fingernails both gripping a similar cane in front of them.

"Drucilla," Belphegor said.

Drucilla's eyes flickered blue as her luminous veins rose to the surface of her hands. She slowly walked towards them.

"Who is your new friend?" Asmodeus asked. He examined Dominic.

Dominic gripped the stylus. The javelin elongated and slid out from each end. He held it at the ready.

"We are not here to fight," Belphegor said calmly.

"What do you want?" Dominic asked sternly.

"Calliope merely asks that you return to her what is hers, and we can end this now," Asmodeus explained, looking at Drucilla.

"The Rosary? I don't have it anymore," Drucilla shrugged.

"We know. You've absorbed the cosmic essence of Thoth. You need to surrender Thoth's essence to Calliope. It does not belong to you. In fact, you should not even be alive at all," Belphegor said.

"You want Drucilla to give her life to you? Not gonna happen, bro," Dominic said, ready to impale anyone that approached.

"I didn't want this in the first place. Calliope is the one that started this. She's the one that put it in my path," Drucilla retorted.

"Did she now? Interesting. Well, if you refuse the Queen's demand, this will result in a war. I can tell you that the Infernal Sphere, nor Eorthe needs a war of this magnitude in its realm," Asmodeus said.

"Did you really come here to threaten me?" Drucilla felt her blood getting hotter.

"If you continue to defy Calliope's wishes, we will have no other choice than to defend ourselves," Belphegor explained.

Dominic squeezed the javelin. The blades slung out on either end. He glared at Belphegor to intimidate him.

"You tell Calliope that if she wants it, she better come and take it herself," Drucilla warned as her eyes began to glow with brighter intensity and blue veins branched across her cheek.

Asmodeus and Belphegor glanced at each other and then back at Drucilla.

"It seems we are at an impasse. Very well, we will relay your intentions," Belphegor said in a professional tone. Asmodeus tipped his hat.

They both turned and filed out of the store. Drucilla watched them walk away down the street before she let her blood cool. Dominic collapsed his javelin and placed it back in his pocket. He stood beside Drucilla as they stared out of the plate glass window.

"Dominic," Drucilla said, breaking the silence, "I need to know what they're planning."

"How do you suppose we're going to do that?"

"I need passage into Hell." Drucilla walked over to the counter.

"Dru, you tried teleportation. You couldn't even get past the guard dog," Dominic said, heading back behind the counter.

"I don't need to teleport to get in," Drucilla said, staring at him intently.

"Ok then, how?" Dominic inquired. He paused and stared at Drucilla for a moment. Suddenly his eyes widened as it clicked in his head.

"No! Absolutely not!" he said firmly.

"How else am I going to get in?" Drucilla tried to reason.

"Dru, are you serious? No!" he said sternly.

Drucilla crossed her arms and pressed her lips together.

"Lucifer said never to use the portal."

"Yeah, but this is kind of an emergency. Those are ok, right?"

"I have never met anyone so intent on killing themselves as much as you. Why do you have such a death wish?" Dominic said, throwing up his hands, "No. There has to be another way."

Frustrated, Drucilla paced the floor, then stopped.

"We haven't tried remote viewing. I mean, that is a thing I can do, right?" Drucilla asked.

"Remote viewing into hell?"

"Unless you have a better idea? Do you even have any books that teach that?"

"Do I have any books that will teach that? Please," Dominic scoffed at the absurdity of the question.

Drucilla motioned with her hand as if to say, "Well?"

"Yeah, I got something. Meet me at my place tonight," Dominic responded.

VE
ACH
VE

CANTICLE THIRTY-SEVEN

"I want to watch your world burn down around you as you're suffering." —Alex Story

Dominic put his finger on his lip as he looked up and perused his vast library. He gazed at the highest shelf and started to read his way down the shelves. He slightly muttered to himself. Drucilla wasn't sure how he knew what half of the books were because many of the bindings were blank. Clearly, Dominic had some sort of filing system. He finally found a few promising books, judging by how he quickly ascended the ladder to a shelf, second from the top.

"Dru, come grab these," he commanded, holding out a book while not looking at her.

Drucilla took the book and watched him pick another and then another. He handed them to her one by one.

"*US Sponsored Psychic Spying*?" Drucilla inquired as she leaned her head to the side, turned the book upright, and then placed it down on the table. She read the title of another, "*Project Stargate*," Drucilla scoffed at the title. "You know Dom; you're a weirdo."

Dominic glanced at her. "Hey pot, you're black," he said and kept handing books to Drucilla.

"*The Lesser Key of Solomon*?" Drucilla asked, raising her eyebrow at the title.

"Just put it on the table, Dru," he said, unwilling to discuss anything at the moment.

Drucilla shrugged and waited for him to hand over more books.

"You know, this would probably go a lot faster if we could get Lucifer over here," Dominic said with his eyes still fixed on his bookshelf.

"Psssh," Drucilla scoffed.

"Dru now isn't the time to hold grudges. Especially when we need him as an ally."

Drucilla didn't respond.

Dominic climbed down off the ladder and stood in front of the table. He leaned over and grabbed one of the books, and cracked it open. Feeling Drucilla's palpable anxiety, he stopped and looked up at her. "Do you want to talk about it?"

Drucilla flopped down into one of the dining chairs and ignored the question. She leaned over and grabbed one of his books, and threw herself into a slouch. She opened the book and started flipping through pages.

Dominic stared at Drucilla for a moment, then set down his book. "Dru, I think there's something you should know."

"If you're going to go on about your crush on Lucifer, we can skip it," Drucilla said, flipping through the pages and not looking at Dominic.

"I think we should consider giving Calliope what she wants."

You could almost hear a record needle scratch at that moment.

"What?" Drucilla said in shock. She sat upright. She couldn't believe what she was hearing.

"I think we should really think about this," Dominic said.

"What's there to think about? I have to die to give her what she wants! How could you even consider?! I mean, what the actual fuck Dominic?!" Drucilla yelled as she stood up.

"Dru, listen to me! If we kill Calliope, death dies with her!" Dominic blurted.

"What do you mean, there's no death? So what? That's a good thing, right?" Drucilla asked.

"Well, no. Not the way Azrael explained it."

"Drucilla, no one will ever die. Instead, they will rot inside their bodies until they are nothing but bones and dust," Azrael said. He abruptly appeared out of nowhere. Azrael slowly emerged into the light of the dining room and stood beside Drucilla.

"Dru, my mother died about twenty years ago. I can't even fathom what it would be like for her to wake up inside of a casket, her brittle bones contained within a sealed vault, in the middle of the catacombs," Dominic cringed.

Dominic's description made Drucilla queasy. "This sounds like you're asking me to sacrifice myself." She slowly glanced at Azrael and Dominic.

"Dru, there has to be another way. We just need to figure it out," Dominic assured her.

Drucilla looked at Azrael for confirmation. Azrael gave a slight shrug in agreement. "Ok, like what?"

"Well, there has to be like, I don't know, maybe an exorcism. Some way to remove the Throne," Dominic said.

"No, and exorcism won't work. She's Divine for all intents and purposes, and the only way to remove the entity would require the help of another Throne," Azrael explained.

"But you said they don't exist anymore, and why are we even discussing this? I'm not giving up Thoth. I can't!" Drucilla exclaimed.

"We don't know, Dru. However, I think there may be at least a few Thrones left. Life continues to flourish, so we can assume that Gaia must still exist. Somewhere," Azrael responded.

Suddenly, there was a slight vibration that started to grow and grow into an intense rumble. The table began to shimmy, the chandelier above the table began to jiggle violently. Books began to fall off the bookshelves, barely missing them.

"It's an earthquake!" Dominic yelled.

Dominic and Drucilla dove under the table, and each of them latched on to the table leg. A thunderous explosion was heard in the distance as if a skyscraper had fallen in the forest.

The shaking stopped. Dominic and Drucilla looked at each other in disbelief.

"What the hell?"! Drucilla yelled as she jumped out from underneath the table.

"Dru! Are you ok?.

"Yeah, I'm ok. Where is Azrael?" Drucilla asked, looking around the room. He was nowhere in to be seen.

"He probably popped out when the shaking started," Dominic said.

Dominic and Drucilla both turned at the same time and looked out of his large dining room window that faced the forest. A bright reddish-orange glow came from above the tree lines a few hundred feet away.]They look at each other in disbelief.

"Is that a fire?" Dominic asked.

"That's not any fire I've ever seen," Drucilla replied.

Dominic and Drucilla grabbed their coats and dashed through the kitchen and out of the back door. They raced across Dominic's backyard into the forest. The glow from the tree line was becoming more intense. They didn't say a word to each other. They focused on the horizon in front of them. Drucilla wondered if it was possibly a plane crash or maybe a meteor. Whatever it was, it was big. Really big.

Dominic and Drucilla made their way through the obstacle of dense pine, evergreen, and cedar trees. It was bright enough that they could see a clear direction, and it was getting brighter. They came upon a rocky ridge ahead that neither of them had ever seen before, a freshly erected barrier. The area's temperature increased about twenty degrees, and the distinct scent of brimstone and sulfur permeated the air. They stepped up onto the rocky ridge and looked down into the crater. Dominic and Drucilla stood in awe at what they saw.

"You gotta be kidding me," Dominic said with a level of resignation and numbness in his voice. Drucilla couldn't tell whether it was fear, or he was just that calm right now.

Drucilla was terrified. *I'm not ready for this. I wasn't expecting this to happen so soon. I need more time to prepare.* Drucilla frantically tried to develop a strategy in her head but was unable to form a single thought—just anxiety.

Dominic and Drucilla looked at each other briefly before looking back down to the enormous fiery crater where the ground exploded. Roughly two hundred feet down, the Infernal Sphere had burst through the ground and had given birth to a fiery Hellscape. In its wake were blown down trees, dislocated boulders, and burning foliage. The hole in the center looked like the surface of the sun. They couldn't look directly into it without shielding their eyes. Rumbling and chaotic noises coule be heard coming from the center, as deafening as a storm. The storm got louder and more intense until a swarm of demons emerged and crawled out of the fiery pit. They just kept coming, hundreds of them.

The demons skittered towards Dominic and Drucilla as they scrambled over debris and leaped over crevices.

According to what Drucilla could remember from Dom's books, they were lesser demons. They had long legs like arachnids and large heads with ram's horns and massive eyes. Their long jaws held rows of sharp, serrated teeth. They howled and hissed as they sped towards Dominic and Drucilla. Two giant, identical demons, Drucilla assumed to be Asmodeus and Belphegor, emerged from the hole as if they were commanding the demons. They were both spindly and rigid with natural scale-like skin. They look like the lesser demons, but much more significant and their faces were twisted and grotesque versions of their human disguises. They screeched in a similar cadence that made Drucilla think they were shouting commands to their horde in a demonic language.

In unison, the demons looked up to Dominic and Drucilla on the ridge of the hellscape. Asmodeus raised his hand pointed his long-clawed finger at Drucilla. He screeched again.

"Hey, remember the thought exercise about how many waves of third-graders you could beat up with a sixth-grade boss in-between?" Dominic asked, "This is kinda like that." Dominic's voice seemed confidant and sure.

Drucilla didn't know whether it was Thoth or her, but suddenly, like a light switch, her fear was replaced by adrenaline. Her skin slowly began to glow as the welcomed Divine blood started to pulse through Drucilla's veins. She could feel her body become hotter.

Drucilla looked at Dominic and grinned maniacally.

Drucilla ripped off her jacket and unfurled her large expansive wings. Her skin cranked up the wattage as she began to beam with intense blue light. Dominic pulled out his stylus and transformed it into a polearm. They took a final look at each other before they descended from the ridge as it gradually sloped to the battlefield.

When they reached the bottom, the demons began to swarm Dominic and Drucilla. Drucilla instinctively wrapped her wings around her body like a cocoon as they attempted to bite and claw at her wing shield. Dominic swung his polearm and sliced through them like they were made of paper. The demonic army was flayed, dismembered, and sliced in half, littering the ground with their appendages.

Drucilla thrust her wings outward as the clinging demons flew off and dashed their bodies against nearby boulders. Drucilla opened the palms of her hands to create balls of energy when suddenly the demons started dropping dead.

Scores of them dropped lifelessly to the ground. It was almost as if their batteries had run out. They didn't scream or fight; they simply collapsed where they stood. Asmodeus and Belphegor appear stunned by this turn of events as the demonic army now laid lifeless, scattered around the battlefield. Drucilla looked to her left. She saw Azrael upon the ridge. He held out his arm, pointing his long white slender finger to the field of recently deceased demons. He looked at Drucilla, looked at the corpses, and then looked at Drucilla again like he was waiting for something.

"Raise them, Dru!" Dominic yells as he kicked the last remaining demon corpse off his polearm.

Drucilla's eyes widened at Azrael. She ripped out a feather from her wing and pierced the palm of her hand. She tossed divine blood onto the ground. She held her hands over the field, "Idcirco praecipio tibi ut resurgence!" Drucilla screamed.

The corpses of the dead demons slowly began to reanimate and get to their spindly legs just as quickly as they had dropped dead. Asmodeus and Belphegor's expression changed from confidence to fear.

"Impetus!" Drucilla screamed again and thrust her hand forward to shove them back at Asmodeus and Belphegor.

The demons followed Drucilla's command and scurried back over the boulders and crevices. They swarmed Asmodeus and Belphegor like insects and started tearing and biting at their demon flesh. Asmodeus and Belphegor screeched orders at them in a language Drucilla didn't understand, but the demons ignored their pleas and remained attached to their former masters. They shredded and ripped their bodies until they were nothing but tattered clothing, drenched in Unholy blood.

The center of the pit erupted again, belching forth fire and magma. Something massive was emerging. Dominic stood at Drucilla's side.

"I didn't think it was going to be that easy. 'Glad to see I wasn't disappointed," Drucilla snarked.

Dominic smirked.

Drucilla stood in awe as a towering, dark demon began to climb out of the pit. He was massive. He looked to be easily 100-feet tall and 60-feet wide at his bare, inhuman, muscular chest. You could see every protruding muscle fiber in his body, giving him an almost black but skinless look. His eyes blazed even brighter than the Hellmouth from which he emerged. Massive, black spikes protruded from his elbows and shoulders, with a set of curled ram's horns on his head. Its hands and claws were easily the size of a car. As this massive demon stepped up and out of the fiery pit, Dominic and Drucilla stared, speechless. The earth shook with each step. Azrael unfurled his wings and shot upwards into the black sky. The demon let out a horrifying, deep, demonic roar that caused the ground to vibrate.

"Drucilla," it said her name in a low guttural, vibrating bass tone. It shook the earth around them once again. The lesser demons were biting and clawing their way up to his massive frame. He tore them off and pulled them apart like toys. He stepped out of the pit. The ground reverberated with each terrible step, crushing boulders and snapping tree trunks like mere twigs.

"Hades," Drucilla said to herself. Dominic looked at Drucilla wide-eyed.

"You skipped the part about him being that big," he commented.

"We can take him," Drucilla reassured him.

Dominic and Drucilla readied themselves to rush the beast. Immediately, they heard trees snapping and cracking like giant matchsticks behind them on the ridge. Something big was approaching Dominic and Drucilla from the opposite direction. They quickly turned around to see what was coming from behind them. Fortunately, they were quick enough to see it and move out of the way.

Lucifer burst forth from the forest and jumped onto the field in front of the pit. Lucifer was massive in height, nearly as tall as Hades, but lither in his build. His body was red and luminous, with a long tail serrated like a barbed whip. His sleek black horns were long, pointed, and sharp. Spikes lined his body, down his arms and legs, resembling some sort of a dragon. He pulled back his clawed hand and took a deep swipe into Hades' chest. Hades howled as the undead lesser demons continued to swarm him, rushing in to widen the wounds left by Lucifer. He continued to pull the undead off his body, prying them off and tossing them aside. He grabbed Lucifer by the throat with a lunge and picked him up off the ground. Hades threw him into the fiery pit. Dominic and Drucilla looked at each other in disbelief that Lucifer was quickly subdued. Hades turned around to face Dominic and Drucilla and resumed his advance towards them as the earth trembled again.

Hades raised his demonic arm and pointed to Drucilla as he let out another low, bellowing growl. He charged at Dominic and Drucilla.

Drucilla lunged backward as hard and as fast as she could up into the air as Dominic sprinted to the left to get out of the way. Drucilla's wings caught her and stabilized her in a hover 30-feet off the ground, giving her a better vantage point to attack the massive Hades. Drucilla smashed her hands together and slowly pulled them apart, forming a miniature sun of azure fire.

Drucilla launched the fiery orb at Hades, aiming center mass. Even if the charging colossus wanted to dodge it, he could not have. The intense energy blast from the sphere threw Hades back to the pit entrance. He dug his toe-claws into the ground and skidded to a halt, preventing Drucilla from knocking him back into the pit of Hell. Drucilla readied another energy orb in her hands. The sheer intensity of it seemed to have almost a gravity of its own.

Suddenly, in a crimson blur, Lucifer jumped back out of the pit. He latched on to Hades back, grasped Hades by his horns, and wrenched his ebony head back. Lucifer's massive, serrated tail whipped and glided effortlessly across Hades' neck like a hot knife through butter. Lucifer released his hold on the black horns, and Hades' head rolled off his shoulders to the ground. His body fell after it. Lucifer kicked his decapitated head back into the pit while the undead lesser demons tore at the headless corpse.

Drucilla glided back down to the ground. Dominic and Drucilla moved closer to the pit. It was blazing. It was like standing in front of an oven. Lucifer morphed into a smaller size but still far beyond a human. He looked at Drucilla affectionately with his snake eyes as if to remind her that he was here to help. Drucilla looked up at him and nodded. It looked like he finally showed up to protect her from Hades. *Better late than never,* she thought.

The pit dimed as the fire began to recede.

A sudden shrill was heard coming from the pit. It sounded like someone was speaking a language in a high-pitched tone that Drucilla could barely discern. The sound was an assault on her eardrums.

"She is here," Lucifer said, looking back at the pit in his low demonic voice.

"Calliope," Drucilla said under her breath as she gritted her teeth.

Dominic, Lucifer, and Drucilla ran backward, trying to put distance between them and the pit. They climbed back up the boulders up to the edge of the ridge and looked down. The pit erupted into a column of Hellfire. A massive, glowing, orange female figure emerged from the flames. It looked like a giantess clad in a bodysuit made of pure, molten steel. She was towering, much like Hades was. Bright, orange flames circled and danced around her. Drucilla could see the multiple eyes embedded in the rotating flames, each looking like a white dwarf star. Calliope walked out slowly, dragging a bright fiery, golden sword behind her. She looked at Drucilla and held out her hand. The amulet Drucilla wore around her neck, the Thoth effigy, gravitated towards Calliope and snapped off Drucilla's neck. The amulet flew to Calliope's hand, and it melted in her fiery palm. She dropped the molten object to the ground. The demonic undead fell to the ground all around them, lifeless. Drucilla lost the ability to control the dead.

Calliope pointed to Drucilla, and she felt herself as she began to hover above the ground, against her will.

"Resist her, Drucilla!" Lucifer yelled. "You're stronger than she is!"

As Drucilla struggled, she looked down at Lucifer and Dominic below her. Ahead she saw Azrael in the shadows, staring at her. Azrael nodded to her and telepathically reminded her that she was stronger than she realized. Then, in a moment of clarity, she released her apprehension. She stopped trying to control her power and let the blood of Thoth ignite her with pure wrath. Thoth knew who this was, who they were up against. Drucilla's body started to glow brighter and brighter, and the surface of her skin started to tear. The blood of the Throne restructured her body, growing into a massive entity of blinding blue light; blue flames encircled her like orbiting rings.

The eyes along her wings opened and began to glow white. Drucilla became pure energy, a conduit for celestial fury. Drucilla pulled away from her grip and created another small sun of blue fire. As she threw it at her, she could see reality-bending and warped around it with the sheer intensity of the power it contained. It impacted Calliope and dissipated. She looked no more damaged than if Drucilla had thrown a basketball at her. Calliope rushed towards Drucilla up the steep ridge. When she got to Drucilla, she screamed and kicked Drucilla with inconceivable force as Drucilla's body flew back into a pile of fallen trees. Calliope moved toward her with predatory intent as the earth vibrated beneath her feet.

This is a repeat of how she had slain Thoth in the cavern eons ago. It was happening all over again. Drucilla saw a flash of herself as Thoth lay there among the stalagmites. *No! This time, I refuse to let her win.*

Calliope stood over Drucilla and brought her sword above her head, ready to impale Thoth once again.

Dominic rushed in from behind Drucilla. He swung the polearm up over his head and sliced into Calliope's knee, severing the lower half of her leg. She let out an unnatural, piercing scream. Calliope hit the ground in agony, dropping her sword. She looked at Dominic and threw him with an immense blast of energy into a large boulder, the crunch of his ribs and spine was audible. Drucilla's wrath ignited again, and she jumped onto Calliope, knocking her backward. Calliope tried to sit up, but Drucilla stomped her back down with her foot on her chest. Drucilla looked at Dominic's broken body and screamed. In a mindless rage, Drucilla pummeled her body. Blows that could collapse buildings rained down on Calliope. Molten blood spattered around the growing crater.

Shrieking an unearthly wail, Drucilla wrapped her glowing hands around Calliope's head and picked her up as if holding a play doll. Drucilla remembered when Azrael told her about Divine strength, and she recalled exploding the obelisk in the cemetery. Drucilla gripped on to Calliope's head, ready to crush it to atoms. Suddenly, Calliope's fiery sword violently protruded from the center of her chest, narrowly missing Drucilla by mere inches. Calliope was impaled through her back.

Drucilla looked at the sword that was inches from her stomach. The blade suddenly jerked upward through the top of Calliope's chest cavity, through her neck, between Drucilla's hands, and up through Calliope's head. Stunned, Drucilla fell backward to the ground. Drucilla watched as the top half of Calliope's body split in half and dropped lifeless to the ground. Drucilla looked up slowly, expecting to see Lucifer standing there with the sword.

It wasn't Lucifer. It was Drake.

Drake stood before Drucilla in gold-plated armor. He looked like a King. Locks of his black hair are being held down by a weighty, gaudy, golden crown. He was expressionless and impassive as he looked down over Drucilla, holding Calliope's sword as it dripped molten light.

Drucilla scrambled to get to her feet. "Drake?" Drucilla asked, looking for confirmation.

He didn't say a word. His eyes serpentine, much like Lucifer's, stared at Drucilla. It was eerie. It was like he didn't know who Drucilla was.

"Drake, it's me. It's Drucilla," she said, almost pleading with him. Drucilla's glowing body started to dim down, and her eyes returned to normal.

He held his hand out over Calliope's body as the radiant energy from her body started to grow into tendrils of orange light that swirled and rolled around like smoke towards Drake. The energy slammed into Drake's chest as he absorbed Calliope and everything that she was.

Drucilla started stepping back slowly.

Lucifer, who was back in his typical humanoid shape, searched for Dominic and saw him clinging to life as his broken body lay against a boulder. He dashed over to Dominic.

"Dominic, I need you to trust me," Lucifer said.

Dominic grunted and slowly looked up to Lucifer, holding his body together with his arms.

"Dominic, please offer me the stylus," Lucifer said, looking at the energy swirling around Drake with fear in his eyes.

Dominic looked at Drake as he walked towards Drucilla and looked back at Lucifer. He nodded and held out the stylus to Lucifer.

"Take it," Dominic whispered weakly.

Lucifer nodded and took the stylus from Dominic. Drucilla looked over at them, and Lucifer caught Drucilla's eyes and jerked his head towards Drake.

Drucilla looked back at Drake. Just as Drake began to swing the sword back to strike Drucilla, Lucifer blinked behind him and tore a hole in reality. A new portal to another place in the Infernal Sphere.

"Drucilla!" Lucifer yelled, standing in front of the portal.

Drucilla gathered all of her energy and shoved a fiery blue ball out of her hands, launching Drake forcefully into the open portal. The portal sealed behind him.

A loud cacophony of large flapping wings could be heard overhead. Lucifer grabbed Drucilla and dragged her further into the trees out of the way. They looked up and saw a host of Seraphim. They tossed dozens of massive boulders into the fiery pit below, sealing the entrance. Drucilla's body started to cool down to her normal state. Lucifer, noticing her bare human body, offered Drucilla his blazer. She took it from him and slipped quickly into it.

"Dominic!" Drucilla suddenly remembered. She rushed back down the ridge to Dominic's body.

He was dead.

"No, no, no!" Drucilla screamed as bright blue branches reached across her face. Her eyes started to glow and well up with tears.

Azrael stood beside Drucilla and put his hand on her shoulder as he looked down at her. Drucilla looked up at him as Azrael reached out to Dominic to touch his head. Drucilla shoved away his hand.

"No! You can't take him, Azrael!" Drucilla yelled. She continued to shove him back away from Dominic.

"Drucilla, we can't leave him in there!" Azrael shouted as he tried to reason with Drucilla.

"No! Lucifer can bring him back!"

"No, Drucilla, he can't. He does not have that ability," Azrael tried to explain to her.

"Yes, he does!" Drucilla looked at Lucifer.

Azrael looked at Lucifer curiously.

"I have not been entirely honest with you, Azrael," Lucifer said.

Azrael dropped his jaw slightly and looked taken aback by Lucifer's comment. Lucifer knelt and placed his hands onto Dominic's chest. A small bright light formed in Lucifer's hands and sunk down into Dominic's chest. Dominic started to wake up slowly, looked around, and sat upright. He looked around at everyone in confusion for a moment. Drucilla threw her arms around him and buried her face in his neck.

"Dru," he said, grunting and tapping her arm. "Dru, ease up. I can't breathe like this."

"It's ok," Drucilla said muffled, "Lucifer will bring you back."

Dominic jerked his head up to look at Lucifer, surprised. Drucilla released Dominic and helped him to his feet. They all stood together and watched the Seraphim standing around where the pit used to be. They appeared to be casting a spell because the boulders were glowing with intertwining lines of blue angelic script. Azrael turned his attention to the ridge on the opposite side. Three dark figures were standing still.

"Who's that?" Drucilla asked.

"Those are the Cataclysms," Azrael said, looking at them.

"What do they want?"

"To observe. They are here to observe. Generally, extermination is our job."

Dominic and Drucilla exchanged glances.

One of the Seraphim glided down in front of them. He folded his wings and walked over to the group.

"Drucilla, Dominic," he said with a slight bow. "I wanted to introduce myself. I am Sariel. I am the General of the Virtues."

"Well, Sariel, you're a little late to the party," Drucilla commented sarcastically.

"We try not to interfere when it is not necessary," Sariel said. He looked over the newly placed stones with the angelic script. "The barrier is only a temporary solution. We have warded the surface. The Infernal Sphere is still present, but they are essentially sealed within the pit."

"So, they can't get out?" Drucilla asked.

"For now, yes, they are imprisoned, but this seal will not hold forever. They can and will find a way out. We have bought us a bit of time," Sariel responded.

"Us?" Lucifer pointed out.

"This war is ours now, too, Lucifer," Sariel said. He then turned his attention towards Dominic and Drucilla.

"We are the guardians of Eorthe, which you call Earth. Eorthe belongs to us, the Divine. This is an act of war, and we must defend the realm," Sariel explained. "Drucilla, we want to offer you a place among us in the Celestial Empyrion. You are Ophanim. You are of the highest order and the only Divine Throne in existence. We would be honored to have you join us."

Drucilla paused for a moment before responding.

"See, I'm not a very good Throne. I know I'm supposed to be this all-knowing entity with vast universal knowledge, but there are some days when I can't even remember my PIN," Drucilla explained.

"Drucilla, you have it within you. You just do not know how to unlock it, how to access it. We can help you," Sariel replied.

"Thanks, but I don't think I'm ready for that yet. I'm still trying to figure out who and what I am. I mean, I am still human, I think, maybe," Drucilla said. She looked back at Dominic, Azrael, and Lucifer.

"Well should you change your mind." Sariel nodded.

"Lucifer. You have more than proved yourself this night. Should you wish to return, the Celestial Empyrion is open to you," Sariel said.

"What do you need, Sariel?" Lucifer asked. He knew there was a catch.

Sariel stared at Lucifer for a moment. Lucifer stared back at him as if he was reading his mind.

"Fair enough. Yes, we would like your guidance on preparing for the next battle. You have extensive knowledge of the Infernal Sphere. Our tactical advantages are few, and we must use whatever we can in defending Eorthe," Sariel conceded.

Lucifer looked at Drucilla. She smiled and shrugged slightly. "It's your call," Drucilla said.

Lucifer pondered the offer for a moment.

"I accept," Lucifer said.

"Good!" Sariel said, satisfied.

"Dominic," Sariel studied Dominic and peered at him with confusion and surprise, "Your heart is authentic and unsullied. That is extremely rare to find in a human. I have never seen that until now. What is your parentage?"

"My what?" Dominic asked, confused.

"Your parentage, your linage," Sariel pressed Dominic further.

"Uh, I'm uh, Russian?" Dominic said, looking around, not entirely sure how to answer the question.

Sariel seemed unsatisfied with the answer. He felt there was something more to Dominic but could not figure out what it was. "When it is your time to leave this place, you will undoubtedly be placed among our ranks," Sariel said.

Dominic nodded and gave a confused thumbs-up.

Sariel continued to stare at Dominic like he was something new and novel as if he was unsure of what to make of him. Sariel's wings unfurled. He nodded to Azrael and shot upwards into the dark sky.

Azrael looked at Dominic and Drucilla. "You two are still tedious," Azrael slightly smirked as he turned and walked away out of the rubble and blinked out of existence.

Lucifer, Drucilla, and Dominic started to make their way back to Dominic's house through the treefall and scorched forest. Drucilla glanced at the place where Calliope died. There was nothing there but a pile of smoldering lava rocks.

Justus ut palma
Florebit in
Domo Dñi
Mulier formosa superne ossa sub ornata fœtida sola latent
Ne te decipiat
Venetijs Lucæ Bertelli for. 1573

CANTICLE THIRTY-EIGHT

"Dance with me the gallow dance. As long as we're... as long as we're not hanging." —Lebanon Hanover

When Dominic, Drucilla, and Lucifer arrived back at Dominic's house, it was a disaster: books and relics littered the floor. Drucilla bent down, picked up a handful of books, and placed them on top of the table.

"Dominic," Lucifer said, getting his attention.

Dominic turned to Lucifer.

"I believe this is yours," Lucifer handed Dominic a well-worn, gilded, silver fountain pen. It looked like an antique from the Edwardian era.

Dominic looked at it curiously and squinted his eyes. He nodded, took the pen, and shoved it back in his pocket. Exhausted, he made his way to the couch. He bent over to take off his bloody shoes but fell to the side and promptly went to sleep. Drucilla stuffed a throw pillow under his head. Lucifer and Drucilla watched him sleep for a moment.

Drucilla grinned at Dominic before she turned away and headed for the front door. Lucifer followed her out of the house. Drucilla stood on the porch for a moment as she looked out onto the street.

Lucifer turned to Drucilla curiously, "Are you all right?"

"There's a lot I need to sort out. I think the most rattling thing was seeing Drake. It was like he didn't even know me," Drucilla said with an alarmed tone.

"He is not who he once was. Drake is not Drake. He is something else entirely," Lucifer said as he pondered his own words.

Drucilla looked at Lucifer and nodded. They continued to walk down the pathway to the sidewalk. They walked in silence for a moment. Drucilla finally stopped and looked at Lucifer.

"You knew, didn't you? I mean, that's why you left Hell. You knew what was going to happen?" Drucilla asked him

"I did not know, actually. I was too fearful of what would happen if we did not make it out alive, so I let it play out."

"Afraid? You?"

"I care for you deeply, Drucilla. If something happened to you, I would be distraught."

"Wow, distraught," Drucilla said with a level of sarcasm.

Lucifer ignored the comment.

As they walked down the dimly lit street, the sky slowly turned a lighter shade of deep blue as dawn was approaching.

"Did you notice how Sariel looked at Dominic?" Drucilla asked, changing the subject again.

"Well, Dominic is a decent man. I am sure they do not run across many of those."

"Maybe, but it was more than that. Do you think..." Drucilla said but stopped herself mid-thought. "No, that's stupid." she shook her head.

"That Dominic is Divine in some way?" Lucifer asked. He seemed to be reading Drucilla's thoughts.

Drucilla shrugged and nodded.

"I have sensed something like that in him—possibly an ancestor. Human DNA is strange. Some switches that lay dormant for centuries suddenly activate. Some call it a feature; I call it a flaw," Lucifer commented sarcastically. "He is unusually resilient, powerful, and intelligent. I would not be surprised."

"Yeah. Unnaturally powerful, and he's like massive."

"I agree."

A few minutes later, Lucifer and Drucilla arrived in front of Drucilla's house. Lucifer stopped and looked at her.

"You've impressed me. You understand your capabilities and used them effectively," he said smiling—his snake-eyes reflected the streetlight's glow.

Drucilla slowly smiled at him.

"I'll get this blazer cleaned and get it back to you. Thanks for letting me borrow it," Drucilla said, looking down at the only article of clothing she was wearing.

"Goodnight, Drucilla," Lucifer said. Lucifer smiled as he blinked out of existence.

Drucilla walked up the walkway to her house. She lost her phone somewhere that evening, so she could not unlock her door from her phone. *It probably vaporized at some point*, she thought.

She felt around the top of the door frame for her house key and let herself inside the house. She flipped on the light switch.

"Adrian?" Drucilla called out to him. It was silent.

"Adrian!" Drucilla yelled out again. She raised her eyebrow suspiciously.

Still, she heard nothing. Drucilla bit the inside of her cheek and tried to grab the amulet around her neck. She was suddenly struck with the realization that it had been destroyed. Drucilla felt her heart sink from her chest into her stomach.

Drucilla and her allies will return in book two.

The Hallowed Blood Bonds of the Eternal

Coming October 2023

ACKNOWLEDGEMENTS

References and acknowledgments

- Reddit "Ask Reddit" community:
  reddit.com/r/AskReddit/comments/dzlur0/whats
  _the_most_horrible_way_to_die_that_youve
- Stock photos obtained from unsplash.com,
  commons.wikimedia.org
- Cover photo of Impasse Saint-Eustache, Paris,
  France by John Towner via Unsplash.
- Additional artwork was designed and illustrated
  by Michelle C. Stewart
- Reedsyblog: blog.reedsy.com
- Niccolò Machiavelli "The Prince"
  gutenberg.org/files/1232/1232-h/1232-h.htm
- A Dictionary of Angels by Gustav Davidson
- Book of Enoch by R.H. Charles
- Vault Editions (woodcut art)

MUSIC

*Songs I was listening to during various
canticles in the book.*

Drucilla explores the crypt: *Holiday on the moon* by Love and Rockets

Belynn's party: *Kennedy* by Kill Hannah

Drucilla fights the Grigori: *Closer (Ash Code Remix)* by Antipole, Eirene, Ash Code

The music playing in the club in Egypt: *Love Hurt Bleed* by Gary Numan

Drucilla runs from the thieves in Egypt: *The Unseen* by Funker Vogt

Drake takes control of the Cabal: *Never Coming Back* by A Place of Bury Strangers

Dominic and Drucilla raise the dead: *On the Run* by Timecop1983

Drucilla explores Hell: *Depraved* by Mammals

Drucilla and Lucifers big fight: *Bloodstains* by Agent Orange

Drucilla and Dominic arrive at the hellscape: *The Beginning of the End* by Crosses (originally by Cause and Effect)

Battle scene: *Die on the Battlefield* by Cancerslug

Last chapter: *Initiation* by Crosses

Tons of Danzig, New Order, Type O Negative, Joy Division, Christian Death, and of course Cancerslug.

OUTTAKES

"This part didn't make it into the book, but I put it here for the laughs. Also, I don't know why this is a quote but just roll with it." —Michelle Morningstar

Dominic put his arm down and looked at Lucifer, "Lucifer, I've never been to Hell; I wouldn't know."

Lucifer paused and rested his hand on his chin. "Ah, that is right; I suppose that could prove to be a problem."

"Books!" Dominic said. "What about *The Vision*, or *The Divine Comedy* of Dante Alighieri? Could I use one of those images?"

"You have got to be joking!" Lucifer scoffed and shook his head, muttering something to himself. Dominic and Drucilla exchanged a confused glance.

Dominic looked at Lucifer, puzzled.

"It is just such a STUPID piece of writing!" Lucifer seethed as Dominic's confusion turned to surprised wide eyes.

"It is…it is just some Florentine dickhead writing the 14th century equivalent of a…of a teenage diary!" Lucifer yelled, grasping for a metaphor.

Drucilla gave Dominic a questioning look. Neither Dominic nor Drucilla had heard Lucifer curse so casually before.

Dominic answered her look with a frown, shrug, and a slight nod.

This is Dominic's nonverbal shorthand for "Probably." Clearly, this is a sore spot for Lucifer. Time to poke the bruise. "Well, stupid or not, it was one of the most important literary works of the middle-ages," Drucilla said, paraphrasing the encyclopedia article, she looked upon her phone, *but he didn't need to know that.*

"Important? WHY? So unwashed Italian peasants can go on a fantasy cruise through a nine-layer cake made of absurdity?!..."Fine…FINE!" Lucifer began angrily pacing around the room. "Emo-boy gets exiled, boo-hoo, and suddenly he is in a dark wood, and who shows up to help him out? Virgil! A poet that he idolized! That is convenient that he is so extraordinarily special that his fantasy mentor just pops out to say 'Hello!' Then he goes on a tour of Hell, and whom does he keep running into down there? Oh! It is all the people that were mean to him! How remarkable is that? They are all getting stabbed or wandering in rings filled with excrement or any other childish revenge fantasies. But hey, no problem, Dante just merrily strolls past SATAN---" Lucifer punctuates this by jerking a thumb angrily at himself. His reptile eyes are starting to illuminate slightly. "—and Satan is just too busy gnawing on sinners with his three horrific heads to stop him, so he just zips on up to Purgatory."

Dominic raised his hand as if to ask a question, but Drucilla caught his eye and shook her head.

Lucifer continued to pace and chew angrily on the talon on his thumb.

"First of all, there is no purgatory. If there were, it would be right here!" Lucifer spreads his arms wide, making a vague gesture to indicate the whole world. "But it is not. It does not exist. But that is fine, whatever, let us continue on Dante's logic, shall we? Virgil continues to guide him through the most exceedingly boring of these three books, where Dante manages to ace all the tests that these famous people have allegedly spent centuries failing miserably at and keeps ascending towards heaven. But wait! Virgil died before Jesus, and he is not magnificent enough to keep guiding Dante into heaven." Lucifer claps his hands over his mouth in mock horror. "But luckily, someone else is ready to take the fucking reigns."

"Who?" Drucilla asked.

Dominic drew his eyebrows together as he glanced at Drucilla,

Drucilla had no idea. She never thought about any of the parts after the Inferno. Lucifer was making her want to go back and read the books.

"Who else but Beatrice!?" Lucifer continues mockingly. "Beatrice, the lady that 'friend-zoned' Dante and then went off and died. That's who's waiting up there to give him a tour of Heaven and tell him how brilliant he is. That is some childish fantasy-fulfillment incel trash." Lucifer is now grasping his hands together tightly and his suit seems to be smoldering slightly. His eyes have a malevolent glow, like embers in a campfire. Dominic and Drucilla exchange an uncomfortable look.

An awkward silence hangs in the room as everyone considers Lucifer's outburst.

Dominic decided to break the silence first. "So—"

Lucifer cuts him off. "So, No. We will not be using any of the fantasy illustrations of the nonexistent places in Hell. We will not be going to the Forest of Suicides, we will not be visiting the virtuous pagans in Limbo, we will not be visiting the flaming tombs of the heretics, and we will not be visiting a frozen lake where I hang out munching on...JUDAS!" Lucifer paused and looked around, suddenly aware of how animated he had become. He noticed the smoke rise up from his suit and seemed to slowly come back to himself.

He looked at Dominic and Drucilla and cleared his throat. "I apologize."

He stood and straightened his suit. For a moment, he looked almost vulnerable and embarrassed as he looked down. But it only lasted a moment before his bravado returned. Lucifer clapped his hands together. "Enough with the literature lesson. We still have a bit of a quandary on our hands. Dominic cannot open a portal to Hell without knowing what it looks like..'

www.ingramcontent.com/pod-product-compliance
Lightning Source LLC
Chambersburg PA
CBHW060812120726
47909CB00006B/1889

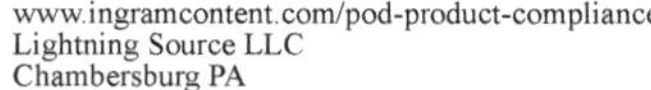